RECKLESS
ENDANGERMENT

Also by the author

Irresistible Impulse
Falsely Accused
Corruption of Blood
Justice Denied
Material Witness
Reversible Error
Immoral Certainty
Depraved Indifference
The Piano Teacher
No Lesser Plea
Badge of the Assassin

ROBERT K. TANENBAUM

RECKLESS ENDANGERMENT

A DUTTON BOOK

DUTTON
Published by the Penguin Group
Penguin Putnam Inc., 375 Hudson Street, New York, New York 10014, U.S.A.
Penguin Books Ltd, 27 Wrights Lane, London W8 5TZ, England
Penguin Books Australia Ltd, Ringwood, Victoria, Australia
Penguin Books Canada Ltd, 10 Alcorn Avenue, Toronto, Ontario, Canada M4V 3B2
Penguin Books (N.Z.) Ltd, 182–190 Wairau Road, Auckland 10, New Zealand

Penguin Books Ltd, Registered Offices:
Harmondsworth, Middlesex, England

First published by Dutton, an imprint of Dutton NAL, a member of Penguin Putnam Inc.

First Printing, June, 1998
10 9 8 7 6 5 4 3 2 1

 REGISTERED TRADEMARK—MARCA REGISTRADA

LIBRARY OF CONGRESS CATALOGING-IN-PUBLICATION DATA:

Tanenbaum, Robert.
    Reckless endangerment / Robert K. Tanenbaum.
        p.   cm.
    ISBN 0-525-94347-1 (acid-free paper)
    I. Title.
    PS3570.A52R43   1998
    813'.54—DC21   98-4902
                                                                          CIP

Printed in the United States of America
Set in MPlantin
Designed by Leonard Telesca

PUBLISHER'S NOTE
This is a work of fiction. Names, characters, places, and incidents either are the product of the author's imagination or are used fictitiously, and any resemblance to actual persons, living or dead, events, or locales is entirely coincidental.

To the ones I love,
Patti, Rachael, Roger, and Billy

ACKNOWLEDGMENTS

Again, and yet again, all praise belongs to Michael Gruber whose genius and scholarship flows throughout and who is primarily and solely responsible for the excellence of this manuscript and whose contribution cannot be overstated.

A special thanks to Bob Diforio for his outstanding representation and guidance.

ONE

He thought he would get more pleasure from killing the Jews, not that he was actually *doing* it for pleasure, no, it was a necessary act, a political act, he knew that, still . . . he had expected to feel something more. It had been too much like killing chickens in the street outside the shanty in Gaza. Mahmoud seemed much more excited, dancing around the little establishment on the tips of his toes and waving his knife, although he hadn't used it all that much when the Jews were alive. Ali had not come into the shop at all, which was correct, because his post was to stand lookout in the doorway.

"We should write a slogan," said Mahmoud. "*You* should write one. Death to the Jews! Write it in the blood!"

"It is difficult to write in blood," said Yussuf chidingly, "and also incorrect." (He used the Arabic phrase *alil el adab*, which means shockingly indecent.) "Only sex criminals write in blood. I will write in marker."

He drew a large green Magic Marker out of the side pocket of his field jacket, and wrote the graceful Arabic letters on the mirror that ran the length of the shop, right above the corpses. Then he looked down at them. The woman was lying across her husband's chest, facedown. The back of her tan raincoat was dark, brown-red with blood, as was her hair, which had been white and done up in a neat bun. The man's face was covered with blood too, whether his own or his wife's Yussuf was not sure. The man's thick gold-rimmed spectacles were jammed askew up on his forehead, as if he had paused in reading to rub his eyes.

"What have you written?" asked Mahmoud. Of the three of them, Yussuf was the only one who could write more than a few simple words and his name. This was why he had been chosen leader.

"I wrote, 'Death to Israel,' here, and 'Free Palestine' here, and I signed with the initials of the movement here. Now we must leave."

They moved toward the door, avoiding the spreading pool of blood and the tumble of bagels that had spilled out of the two large paper bags the man had been carrying when they struck. As they passed the cash register at the front of the shop, Mahmoud leaned over and rang the drawer open. The bell seemed unnaturally loud, and Yussuf started.

"What are you doing?"

"It is empty," said Mahmoud. "Where is their money?"

"Idiot! They have not yet opened for business. They keep the money in a little bag. They do not leave it overnight."

Mahmoud looked over at the still bodies. "Why don't we search for it, then?"

"*Ya salem!* Because we are not thieves. We are soldiers."

"But it is permitted to take from the enemy what we need," Mahmoud objected. "Look! Cigarettes! I will take the Jew's cigarettes." He reached over the counter to the vertical cigarette racks and began to stuff packages of Salems and Marlboros into the flap pockets of his field jacket.

Yussuf grabbed his arm roughly and yanked him away. Packs of cigarettes spilled from the rack and scattered on the floor. He pointed at his new wristwatch and said angrily, "We must be on our train in three minutes. Do you want us to be caught at the very beginning of our campaign?"

With that, Yussuf left the store. The hulking Ali followed him, and after a moment so did Mahmoud. It was just past seven a.m. on a Sunday, and Fourteenth Street was nearly deserted. They walked swiftly, not running, but at a good pace eastward, where they entered the Canarsie line BMT subway and took the train back to Brooklyn.

Seven minutes later, a blue-and-white radio-patrol car of the NYPD pulled up in front of the murder scene, Abe's Elite Appetizing. Two officers, a man and woman, climbed out and confronted the two frightened NYU students who, in search of an early morning toasted bagel with cream cheese, had discovered the blood-covered bodies within. The female officer, a stocky blonde named Sherry Koota, pulled out her pad and took down the students' personal data and what they had to say about the crime, which was not much. They had come in, seen it, and immediately called 911 from the pay phone in the shop. Koota's partner, Patrolman Edwin Roscoe, had meanwhile entered the shop, gun in hand. He gave the bodies a wide berth and checked behind the glass-fronted cooler display and the short serving counter, and then went through a narrow hallway, checking the storage closet, the toilet, and the rear entrance, which was locked from the inside with a heavy bar, and alarmed. Then he went back to the shop proper, holstering his pistol as he went.

By this time Koota was kneeling over the two victims, peering at the woman's head.

"Don't touch nothing, Koota," said Roscoe, who, with three years on the force, was the senior of the two, and had been made painfully aware that the only duty of the so-called "first officer" at a murder scene was to take the names of witnesses and secure the area from any disturbance, especially from those far too common disturbances caused by first officers.

"I'm not," said Koota, "but look at this."

Roscoe knelt too, being careful not to tread in the congealing pool of blood.

"You see that strand of her hair, over the ear, the bloody one?" Koota asked, pointing. "Just watch it for a second."

Roscoe did. He said, "It's moving! Holy shit, she's alive!"

"She's dead," said Koota confidently. "The guy under her, *he's* alive."

Detective Sergeant James L. Raney, working homicide out of Midtown South, carefully copied the squiggles on the mirror in Abe's Elite Appetizing into his notebook. The crime-scene unit people had taken any number of photographs of the interior of the shop and the bodies (now departed, one to the morgue and the other to nearby Beth Israel Hospital) and the bloodstains, but Raney was a careful detective and liked to have the relevant material on his actual person during the course of a case.

He put the notebook away and regarded himself frankly in the dusty brown-speckled glass. Raney was in his mid-thirties, young for a detective sergeant, with a map-o'-Ireland face, blue-eyed model. The eyes were cop eyes, although he had managed to avoid the cop gut. A good dresser too, Raney. His blue suit came from Hickey-Freeman; his shoes, which were highly polished, were Florsheim Imperials. He didn't take bribes, but he didn't, like many cops, have a string of ex-wives and kids to support, either. Beau James was one of his three departmental nicknames. The second, which adverted to an incident some years previously, in which he had killed four armed robbers in fifteen seconds by shooting them each through the head, was Pistol Jim, although not to his face.

Raney wandered over to where the head of the crime-scene unit was gathering up his equipment.

"Do any good?" he asked.

"Oh, yeah," said the man. "We got an actual bloody thumb print on the cash drawer there. Some sneaker prints in the blood. You're looking for a pair, by the way. Two different prints. You catch these fuckers, they're gonna go down for it." He looked around the little shop and frowned. "Fuckin' shame, right? Looked like a couple of decent people. The guy gonna make it?"

Raney shrugged. "White's over at Beth Israel finding out. Maybe he'll come to and say something. Funny thing about that thumb print—the money was in a zip bag in the vic's pocket, the woman. They couldn't have got away with anything but some smokes."

The CSU man grunted, no longer surprised by any funny things to do with murders.

After that Raney went outside and chatted with Roscoe and Koota and their sergeant, spread some compliments around, and arranged for a local canvass, to see if anyone knew why someone would want to murder Abe and Reva Shilkes, aside from the obvious thing, a robbery gone sour. There was a daughter too; he would have to talk to her as well. He went back into the shop and used the pay phone for twenty minutes and then came out to the sidewalk, paced for a while, and scrounged a *Post* from the front seat of the CSU van. The sports pages were of little interest. Raney followed only baseball and basketball. It was now the baseball season and, a month in, it was perfectly apparent that neither the Yankees nor the Mets had the remotest chance of a pennant in 1981. Raney had been born in 1949, and for the first twenty years of his life the Yanks had won the pennant fourteen times. This had shaped his consciousness of the way things ought to be and, like many a New Yorker, he regarded the recent trend as a prime symbol of the city's decline. Much of the news section was devoted to the aftermath of the assassination attempt on President Reagan. There, at least, they had the guy. He snorted, folded the paper, and tossed it back on the van's seat.

Raney hated this case already. It was, first of all, a mystery, which is what NYPD detectives call a murder when the murderer is not readily apparent, in contrast to a grounder, when they find the guy weeping in the front room and the wife and the ball bat and the blood are to be found in the bedroom. It was not that he feared that they would fail to find the murderers. The crime scene had convinced him that they were not dealing here with Dr. Moriarty, the Napoleon of Crime, but with a couple of assholes, and by and large, assholes were easy to find and catch. It was the other stuff that irritated him: the victims were Jewish, and while Raney was no linguist, the scrawls on the mirror looked like Arabic writing to him. That stank. The only thing worse than a mystery was a mystery with ethnic politics smeared over it.

A dark brown Plymouth Fury drove up to the curb, and Detective Second Grade Alonso White got out. This person, whose skin was the color of damp coffee grounds, was about a third larger than Raney and not nearly as well dressed. He was wearing a leather hip-length car coat, which he had purchased, along with the rest of his clothes (gray slacks, black rubber-soled shoes, a black-checked shirt and a knitted tie, with the wrong end sliding over his belt buckle) in one of the cheap men's shops to be found on Sixth Avenue in the Forties. He had two ex-wives and three children. Raney like him well enough, for, although he had a mild case of the racism nearly universal among his caste and class, he also held that carrying the tin made you, on the job at least, an honorary Irishman. He also sort of liked the man's habit of extending a hand that looked like a bouquet of knockwursts, grinning gaudily, and saying, "Hi, I'm White."

To Raney's inquiring look White responded, "It looks like he's going to make it. Took a couple of holes in the gut and one to the neck. Lucky." He laughed. "Not exactly the right word, considering."

"Did you talk to him?"

"Uh-uh. He's recovering from the surgery. I'll go by later. What's up?"

"CSU says it's at least a couple of mopes. No money taken, but they helped themselves to the cigarettes—packs scattered all over."

"Guys had a nicotine fit," said White. "They plead temporary insanity and walk. What about that shit on the mirror?"

"I set up a meet with a professor at Columbia, we'll get it translated. Meanwhile, assuming we're dealing with Arabs, we need to touch base with Brooklyn, the Eight-Four." White nodded. Atlantic Avenue, Brooklyn, where the Arabs lived.

Dr. Philip Adouri was younger than he had sounded to Raney over the phone, and proved to be a gentle-faced Lebanese in his early thirties with a slight accent and a careful manner of speech. He looked at the eight-by-ten photographs of the mirror graffiti for so long that Raney thought he had dozed off.

"Um, is there some problem with the translation, sir?" Raney asked.

"Oh, no, no, it is quite clear as to the meaning. It is just that . . . who did you say wrote these?"

Raney and White shared a look. "That's what we're trying find out, sir. It's an investigation."

"Oh, yes, of course—how stupid! Well, then, as to the meaning. This line, here, is *mot lil yehudeen*, 'death to the Jews,' and this below is *huriyah li falastin*, 'freedom for Palestine.' This," he said, pointing a slim finger at three large single letters at the bottom of the screed, "this means nothing, unless it is the initials of some organization; in English the closest equivalent would be D.D.H."

"You have any idea of what it means, Doctor?" Raney asked, writing the translations neatly into his notebook. "Any organizations you're familiar with . . ."

The professor smiled and made a dismissive gesture. "Oh, Arabs are always making organizations. They come and go like the clouds. This could be three people, four people in a back room, or it could even be the initials of a person. But, you know, the orthography is interesting. The person who wrote it . . . I should tell you that while written Arabic is the same all over the world, spoken Arabic is quite different from nation to nation, region to region. A Mahgrebi, from Morocco, say, can hardly understand a Lebanese. There are also differences, slight differences, in the way the letters are formed in different places, just as you would notice, for example, a German's writing is different from an American's, even in English. So . . . this person—educated to a degree, but certainly not a university graduate or student. Perhaps the equivalent of high school? In any case, an unpracticed writer. There are errors—here he has used the medial rather than the final form, there, the wrong letter. Not a Mahgrebi. Not Iraqi. Egyptian perhaps, but more likely Eastern Mediterranean—Palestine, Lebanon, Jordan. Notice here how he writes this letter, the long ee sound, slanting over to the left., and here—"

Raney's beeper sounded, and he was saved from learning more about Arabic calligraphy than he wanted to know. He asked to use a phone and called Lieutenant Meagher, his watch commander, who ordered him to return to the precinct house *forthwith*, which is a word that NYPD officials use when they want you to do something so immediately and so urgently that it is not worthwhile thinking of excuses not to.

Raney and White thus left the professor with brief thanks and headed south from Columbia on Broadway. On the way Raney called the desk sergeant at the Midtown South Precinct and asked what was going on; Meagher had been excessively terse.

"Oh, we got a lovely situation here, Raney," said the desk sergeant. "Wait'll you see this!"

"What?"

"Jews, Raney. We got black hats, we got the TV, the radio, we got suits from downtown, we got the Tacticals coming. Oh, it's rare . . . what? Raney, I got to go now."

There were some odd sounds over the receiver and then silence. White frowned and stomped harder on the pedal. Raney slapped the red flasher on the roof, and they sped south.

The Midtown South homicide squad is responsible for homicides in the fat band across the island of Manhattan that runs from Central Park down to the north side of Thirteenth Street. It is housed in the Manhattan South Precinct at 357 West Thirty-fifth Street. As it happens, this location is in an area even more bountifully supplied with Jews than the rest of the city. The garment district, the theatrical district, and the diamond district are all within an easy hike, and in fact, there is a synagogue right across the street. When Raney and White arrived, they discovered that what looked like a large proportion of all these people had converged in front of Midtown South.

They had to leave their car at the corner of Ninth and Thirty-fifth. The street was impassable: besides the mob itself were TV vans, the buses from Tactical, and a number of large, shiny vehicles in which police brass traveled through the City. The crowd was composed largely of black-hatted, bearded men, although there was also a good number of men in contemporary business and working garb, and a sprinkling of women. They filled the street from wall to wall, and their angry attention was directed at the front steps of Midtown South, where, behind a wall of tall, broad Tactical cops in helmets and body armor, stood a group of worried-looking police officials.

White used his bulk to cleave through the crowd, holding his gold shield before him like the bowsprit of a clipper, Raney followed in his wake. The Tacticals parted to let them through, and Raney was immediately spotted and hustled through the door by his lieutenant.

"What the fuck *is* this, Loo?"

"This is your case, Jim, the Shilkes killing. The natives are restless, son. That asshole on the car's been pumping them up for the last twenty minutes."

Raney looked out through the door and saw a man wearing a black hat and suit and a short black beard standing on the hood of a car haranguing the crowd through a bullhorn. Raney could not make out the exact words, but he seemed to be displeased with the NYPD.

"Who is he?"

"Rabbi Lowenstein," said Meagher, an expression of profound distaste forming on his broad, pink Irish face.

Raney nodded. Lowenstein was semi-famous in the city as the leader of a paramilitary group he called the Guardians of Israel; his relationship with the NYPD was not good, that organization taking a dim view of groups with vigilante pretensions.

Meagher seemed to recall something and turned to Raney, scowling. "Why the hell didn't you keep a watch on Shilkes? That's how this whole mess started."

"Loo, the guy was out cold. I'm trying to solve a case here. What did he have to do with it?"

"Out cold? Well, he woke up, and he talked to his daughter, and she got in touch with the good rabbi there, and here we are. The story is, the guys who killed his wife came in shouting Arab slogans, Allah, Allah, whatever, and so now we got it blown into a gang of Arab terrorists is starting a campaign of assassination against Jews in New York. Lowenstein is demanding protection— ha!—and also, and especially, that we grab the mutts who did it, preferably yesterday. So—what do you have?"

"Have? For crying out loud, Loo, I been on the case three hours. The guy up at Columbia says the killers wrote 'kill the Jews' and 'free Palestine' on the wall and the writer was probably a Palestinian who couldn't spell real good. That narrows it down."

Meagher kept glancing over at the group of suits and brass standing in a small group behind their guards. Huge fake-fur-covered mikes on poles thrust up at them like a hostile phalanx. Below, the press was baying questions. One of the suits gave Meagher the eye, and the lieutenant hurried over. They conversed briefly, and the suit spoke to another suit, who moved forward and addressed the cameras. To his dismay, Raney heard the words "already several suspects" and "arrest imminent," and the suit went on to mention a $25,000 reward for information leading to, put up by the United Jewish Philanthropies of New York.

White, who had skulked in the background while Raney dealt with Meagher, came up and said disgustedly, "Oh, great! Now every hard-on in town is gonna be on us with his cousin Charley did it. What'd the Loo say?"

"Shilkes is conscious again. Get over to Beth Israel and take his statement. Go now! Before the riot starts."

White left and the riot did start, as more Tacticals de-bussed at Ninth Avenue and started to clear the street, moving in a line with helmet shields down and batons swinging. A thrown bottle shattered against the door frame. The suits all hunched momentarily and then, some glancing about to see if anyone had noticed, strode boldly to their cars and departed.

As he watched, bemused, the dispersal of the Jews, Raney felt a hand on his arm. "Whatever you need, Jim, just ask!" said Lieutenant Meagher. "And forget everything else you got on the board. But wrap this one up fast, wrap it up good! Make it disappear!"

Napoleon, they say, when presented with an officer to be promoted to the rank of general, always asked, "Is he lucky?" Raney was a good, bright, conscientious detective, like many another on the force, but he was also lucky. This was apparent, since he had, after all, gone into that darkened bakery after four robbers armed with shotguns and automatic weapons and had killed them all without suffering a scratch himself. Lucky Jim was his third nickname.

"So, Lucky Jim," said White later that day, as he drove them across the Williamsburg Bridge to Brooklyn, "is our ass in a sling now or what?"

"Partially," admitted Raney. "On the up side, I don't think we're dealing with a big international mastermind here. Carlos the Jackal is probably not a player."

"They were sloppy, you mean? The tracks, the cigarettes . . ."

"Yeah. On the other hand, they didn't just walk down Fourteenth and go, 'Hey, look, Jews, let's waste them.' "

"Why not?"

"Because the thing was cased. The Shilkeses opened the store at seven every Sunday carrying fresh bagels, like clockwork. The perps knew that and they were waiting. Then they disappear. How? I doubt they just strolled away. They either had to have a car, or they took the subway, and if they took the subway, they had to know what the train schedule was going to be early on Sunday, because they sure as shit didn't want to be hanging around on a platform with maybe blood on their clothes for twenty minutes. So, planning."

White thought about that for a while, and it did not amuse him. "What do you think? Is Brooklyn going to do us any good?"

"Oh, I don't know," said Raney, leaning back and watching the gray tenements of Williamsburg rush by. "It could be we'll catch a break."

Their first stop was the Eighty-fourth Precinct, on Gold Street, in the shadow of the Manhattan Bridge. The Eighty-fourth is a squat little precinct that has the misfortune to include both the gentrified brownstones of Brooklyn Heights and the ungentrified brownstones of South Brooklyn, a once decent working-class neighborhood ruined by freeway construction, gone slummy, and full of people wishing to prey on the conveniently nearby gentry. It logs a lot of robbery, a lot of burglary, and somewhat under a hundred killings a year, all of which argued against the cops there having much time to spare for accumulating deep knowledge of Arab fringe organizations.

The detective squad room there was a near duplicate of the many in which Raney had spent the past decade, the banged-up furniture, the green paint, the brown tile underfoot, the pervasive reek of to-bacco, the continual din of ringing phones. Two cops were at desks, one phoning, one typing slowly. A thin brown man, obviously a skell from the tank downstairs, was pushing a broom desultorily across the floor for cigarette money.

"Arabs, huh?" said McIlvey, the day-shift detective sergeant. "Yeah, we got Arabs up the ying-yang, but they don't usually give us much trouble. Peaceful bastards, and a lot of them are illegals; they don't want to see us much." He creaked back in his chair, to demonstrate peacefulness. McIlvey was a white-haired, heavyset Irishman of the booze-blossom-nosed type, nearing retirement and not apt to get exercised over a Manhattan case, no matter what the bosses said.

They showed him the pictures of the graffiti from the crime scene.

"We think those initials down at the bottom are an organiza-tion," said Raney. "You recall seeing anything like that sprayed on walls or on tattoos?"

"Nah. But I don't get out as much as I did. What I'll do for you is post it in the squad room, maybe somebody saw something. Like I say, we got 'em, but we don't got 'em. Not like the spics, you know?"

They knew, and if White had not been there it would have been the niggers too. Raney sensed his partner's intense desire to get away from this useless man. He was just thinking that they would have to come back and talk to the night-shift people, maybe get a live one, when McIlvey said, "You know, it's funny, we had one of them in here last night. Yo, Harris," he called to the man at the typewriter, "what was the name of that crazy fucker last night?"

"The fuck I know, Sarge," answered Harris, and went tap. Tap. "Ask his roomie there." Tap.

"Oh, yeah," said McIlvey, and turned to the broom. "Skeeter, what was your pal's name there, that AY-rab?"

"Not my pal, Sarge."

"Well, fuck it, anyway. Fuckin' thing too," said McIlvey. "Cou-ple of our guys brought him in last night, late in the graveyard. Driving like a bat out of hell down Fulton Street in a fuckin' bak-ery truck, no taillights, so our guys, Pendergrass and Newton . . . hey, Harris, it *was* Pendergrass, wasn't it?"

"Yeah, right," said Harris. Tap.

"Yeah, so they give chase, like they say, going seventy, eighty down Fulton Street, got a couple more RPCs in on it, and they finally got the mutt in a box and he gave it up. Guy had a knife on him as long as your arm. Didn't have a license, no registration. Insurance? Lots of luck! I don't know, the fuckin' people this country lets in nowadays. . . ."

Raney had been looking for a graceful way to pull away, but the mention of the knife sparked a flicker of interest. "You say they picked this guy up late last night?"

"Morning, actually. Maybe four."

"So he was in custody at like around seven this morning?"

"Oh, yeah. He must have gone out with the van to central booking at eight or around there. But like I say, that's unusual. Most of 'em are pretty peaceful. Although, now that I think of it, a couple months ago we had a guy beat up his wife pretty bad, an Arab—"

"Yeah, well, look, Sarge, we got to get going right now—" Raney began, and then the broom said, "He was gonna kill him some Jews, that boy. Boy had a motherfuckin' *thing* about the Jews. Him and his friends. Said he had some damn organization. Damn sumbitch didn't have no more sense than a chicken. I said to him, hey, man—"

"Say, Skeeter?" Raney interrupted, vibrating now, feeling the luck flow and the sweat pop up on his scalp. "This kid say exactly which Jews he was planning to kill?"

"Nah. He just running his mouth, you know? Like, he said his organization was gonna do one this morning, and he was real pissed he wasn't gonna be there, on account of his ass being in jail, you know? He was hot to go. He kept asking me, when we get out, when we get out? Like I the fuckin *judge*, you know?" The man laughed, a phlegmy, unpleasant rattle that turned into a cough.

Raney said, "Sarge, I think we're gonna need to borrow Skeeter for a while." McIlvey grunted and looked at the floor, and for an instant Raney actually thought he was going to refuse until Skeeter finished a sweep and a damp-mop.

The Arab misdemeanant, whose name was Walid Daoud, had a job and a father who owned a business, and so had been released on his own recognizance by the time they got to the Brooklyn jail. They drove the short hop to Atlantic Avenue, where the bakery was at which Daoud supposedly worked. Raney looked around him with greater interest. This neighborhood had expanded a good deal in the last decade. Once a relatively small community of Syrian and other Mideastern Christians, it had burgeoned down Atlantic Avenue east of its former boundary at Court Street and become more exotic, more Muslim. Women with shawls and shapeless dresses whose hems touched their shoes pulled shopping carts and hand-held strings of olive-skinned children down the street and in and out of small shops. There were even some women wearing the full traditional robes, with veil, and there were old bearded men wearing checkered headdresses. Sunday was clearly a big shopping day among the Brooklyn Arabs. There were a lot of kids. The day had turned warm, a herald of spring, and the storekeepers had moved the merchandise out on the sidewalk on homemade flats, and the clothing merchants had hung garments up on poles, giving the street the air of a *souk*, as did also the odors, burnt coffee, baking bread, and something spicy that Raney did not recognize, but which, he thought, was probably as familiar to these people as . . . what was a typical Irish fragrance? Cabbage? Whiskey? This had been an Irish neighborhood once, eighty years back, then Italian, now Arab.

Raney reflected on this transition to White, who was unimpressed. "Mutts are mutts, it don't matter a fuck where they come from."

"No? You don't think there's a difference? A Jew mutt and a black mutt?"

"What, you think the Jew mutt is smarter?"

"No, I didn't mean that. Just . . . different people put a different curve on the ball. It changes, but it's always the same. Twenty-five years the houses and stores'll still be here, but the cops'll be Arabs and the people, the mutts'll be, I don't know, Eskimos, Tibetans, whatever."

The interested tone in Raney's voice did not spark any enthusiasm in White, who was a sports-and pussy rather than a sociological-speculation kind of guy, nor in Skeeter, who was snoring liquidly in the backseat. They drove in relative silence therefore until Gallatin Street, where White said, "There it is. Want me to go around the back?"

"No, I don't think so. This guy's not going to run."

Nor did he. Walid Daoud was summoned from the back of the shop by the pretty, sullen teenage girl minding the counter and came out trailing his father and clouds of white dust. The detectives made the usual explanation about wanting to ask a few more questions, the father berated the boy strenuously in Arabic, swatted him on the head a few, and they left without resistance. If Walid was surprised to see Skeeter in the car, he made no show of it, riding in silence during the twenty-five-minute trip to Midtown South.

They got Walid in the little room, and White, of course, was the bad cop. Raney thought he did a good job, no rough stuff, but a lot of shouting, and banging of chairs and throwing of telephone books, and impugning the manhood of the interviewee. You and your friends planned this, and then you chickened out, didn't you? You little coward! What are you, some kind of faggot, you don't have the guts to knife an old Jew? And so on, which got the expected rise out of Walid and an excuse—I was going, I was hurrying, I got arrested. What were their names? Your friends? Silence. Rage from White, threats, a final chair kicking, and then Raney stopped it and hustled White out of the room.

Offer of coffee, offer of cigarettes, apologies for White, a little racist remark, just to solidify the bond, we're white men, you and I, he's . . . well, you know what *they*'re like. Then the schtick.

"Look, Walid, you know, if it was a political crime, that's one thing, we respect that. I mean, a man's got to stand up for his rights, am I right?"

Walid nodded at this. A good-looking kid, Raney thought: big eyes, clear skin, good little body. Those eyelashes—little shit probably gets more pussy than Warren Beatty.

"We are fighters for free Palestine, *fedayin*," said Walid with feeling.

"I appreciate that, Walid, but I got to say, you're in a lot of trouble over this. I don't like to see that, a kid your age."

"But . . . I was not there!"

"Yeah, we know that. But you're what we call an accessory. You helped your friends plan this crime. You can be charged with conspiracy. You could go to jail for a long time."

"I do not care!" said Walid. "The Zionists put hundreds in jail, hundreds, hundreds, so I join them. I do not care."

"Right, I see that, but Walid, for you it wouldn't be like that. You see . . . I'm not supposed to tell you this, but . . ." Raney looked over his shoulder and leaned forward conspiratorially. "The thing is, your friends robbed the people they attacked. They took the money from the store, so this won't be treated as a political crime at all. It's just gonna go down as another store robbery and murder. It's not gonna help your cause one little bit."

Walid stared, his mouth slightly open.

"Yeah, see, they screwed up, and the shame of it is, you're gonna have to take the fall, for nothing." He let that sink in for a moment and then resumed. "Now, this place where you planned the thing, the attack, that's your organization headquarters, right?"

"Yes. Duhd el Dar al-Harb. This is us."

"Uh-huh. What does that mean exactly?"

"It means, Against the House of War. It is the struggle. The Dar ul-Islam fights against the Zionists, the imperialists. These we call the Dar al-Harb, the House of War." He banged his fists together violently to mime the intensity of the thing.

"I see. Now in this headquarters you probably have posters, pamphlets, all about what you're doing, political stuff, right?"

"Yes, of course. We have this. And cassettes, from Palestine."

"Well, that's great, Walid. So, if we went there and found that stuff, see, it *would* be political then. You'd be in a whole different situation. You'd be a hero."

Walid frowned. "You want . . . just the place, the garage. Not the names. I don't give the names."

"Hey, right, just the place. You're a stand-up guy, Walid. We respect that. No, just the address. So we can get the political stuff."

Raney left the room elated, with an address. An hour later, armed with a search warrant and backed up by a dozen heavily armed and flak-jacketed uniforms from the Eighty-fourth, Raney and White burst through the back door of a garage on Adams Street, Brooklyn, where they found posters of Yassir Arafat, pamphlets justifying the destruction of Israel, cassettes urging the same, a pair of field jackets spotted with a reddish-brown substance, one with a big green magic marker (similarly stained) in a pocket, and the other with eight packs of Salems in a pocket, two eight-inch hunting knives, stained with a reddish-brown substance, and two surprised young men. The young men did not speak much English, but sometime later they were identified (with the aid of a Syrian-American patrolman from the Eighty-fourth) as Yussuf Naijer and Mahmoud Hamshari, both late of Gaza, in the occupied territories of Palestine, and illegally in the United States. They were both taken to Midtown South, where they were put into a lineup and videotaped, which tape was then brought to Beth Israel, where it was shown to

Mr. Shilkes. He had no trouble picking Naijer and Hamshari out as the men who had killed his wife. Raney went back to Midtown South and booked the two men for murder and Walid for conspiracy to commit murder.

As he sat down at his desk to complete the paperwork, he looked at his watch. It was a little over twelve hours since the crime. The suits would be pleased.

Ali al-Qabbani watched the police take away his two comrades and seal the room behind the garage. He doubted that Abdel, the garage's owner, would wish to re-employ him after this, which meant that he had no money, no job, no clothes or possessions other than what he stood in now, and no place to sleep. He had, however, one place to go, and so he went there.

It was a long walk in the waning light, up Atlantic Avenue and south down Sixth Avenue into the more genteel, tree-shaded precincts of Park Slope. There he walked through a wrought-iron gate up to a nicely groomed brownstone and rang the bell. The man who answered it was well-fleshed and short, with a beautiful head of dark hair swept back from his forehead. He was wearing red leather slippers, blue jeans, and a white shirt buttoned at the collar. And he was sleek in the way that some men were where Ali came from, the men with the big cars and the bodyguards. You went to men like that when you were in trouble, and they helped you or they did not. The expression on this man's face when he saw Ali standing there did not promise well.

"What are you doing here, you idiot?" he said in Arabic. "You were told never, ever to come here."

Ali looked down from his height and said, "Please, Khalid-effendi, the police have been to Abdel's. I have no place to go and no money."

Chouza Khalid's angry look was replaced by one of calculation and then one of beneficence, which, had Ali any brains at all, would have made him flee as from wild dogs. Instead, he followed the man's gesturing arm into the tiled entranceway and then through another door into a carpeted hallway lit with sconces and furnished with a gold-framed mirror, a shining wooden table holding a vase of flowers, and a carved red velvet chair. There Khalid bade him wait and he did, standing, of course, because it would never have occurred to him to take the liberty of sitting in the velvet chair.

Khalid left the hallway and went through a large, modern kitchen to a door, which he unlocked, and then descended to the basement. He then unlocked another door and entered a small darkened room, where a man sat on a couch, smoking and watching television. The man had a short gray-black beard, deeply socketed dark eyes, visible now only as pits lit by the flickering TV, and long, tapering, elegant fingers. He was wearing a white *djelaba* and a white, knitted skullcap. He did not take his eyes from the TV as Khalid spoke.

"It is Ali."

"Inevitably," said the bearded man. "The poor lad has nowhere else to go. Tell me, he is our only contact?"

"Yes. I ordered him not to tell, and he is an obedient boy. Dull like the rest, but reliable. I don't think he would have spoken of it to Naijer or Mahmoud. He didn't like them. He was most friendly with Walid, but, of course, Walid did not participate, and will not be much bothered by the police, if God wills. So . . . a long journey?"

"Yes, by water," said the bearded man. For the first time he looked up at Khalid. "And the other enterprise?"

"They arrive tomorrow, men and supplies. It is all arranged. If God wills, it will all go as we have planned."

"If God wills," echoed the bearded man and then returned his full attention to the screen, where a drama depicting the lives of the police was in progress. Apparently the American police spent much of their time seducing women, which was interesting if true. The bearded man watched television almost all the time. He felt it was the best way for him to understand this truly amazing nation.

Dismissed, Chouza Khalid went up the stairs, locking both doors behind him.

TWO

The office of the District Attorney for the County of New York (that is, the island of Manhattan) has for years, and with some reason, considered itself the best prosecutorial organization in the nation. Within this office the Homicide Bureau is the elite corps. The chief of this unit, therefore has every right to consider himself at the very top of his profession, and the current chief had no trouble doing so. He had worked hard for the job, and he felt he deserved it. His name was Roland Hrcany, and he did deserve it. He was an excellent homicide prosecutor, tough-minded, skilled in the law and its stratagems, on excellent terms with the NYPD, and possessed of both a bullish determination and a keen political sense. As for his vices, he was, in the office, perhaps too fond of throwing his weight around, too quick to judgment, too slow to admit error, and in the personal sphere too fond of women way too young for him (he was thirty-seven), of whom he had a prodigious skein.

Had Roland been at all capable of self-examination, he might have found an explanation for both virtues and vices in his own sad history. Aged eleven, he had walked out of the Hungarian forests across the Austrian border, holding his father's hand. His mother had fallen to one of the innumerable bullets fired during the confused days of the 1956 rebellion. Settled at last in New York, the elder Hrcany (once a high school teacher) had found work as a superintendent of a building in the rough Brooklyn neighborhood known as East New York, also moonlighting as a truck driver. Roland, then a spindly, nervous kid, had been sent to public school, where his fate was what might be expected for a smallish boy speaking broken English, with a funny name and studious to boot, among what was then a rough Irish and Italian crowd. He was tortured, with no one to tell about it. His father was working like an ox in the good old immigrant way, and Roland could not bear to bother him. Instead, inspired by an ad in the subway, and without telling anyone, Roland joined the Boys' Club, where there was a weight room. By the time he was fourteen, Roland, though still short, had a seventeen-inch neck and could bench 220. Nobody bothered him in school anymore. He also joined the Police Athletic League, where he began his lifelong love affair with the NYPD, and also excelled at football.

Meanwhile, his father had taken to capitalism as one too long deprived of its healing magic. Saving every conceivable penny from both his jobs, he managed to buy the building he worked in, and then immediately used his equity in this as collateral to buy a shabby brownstone in Brooklyn Heights. Working nights, with Roland at his side, he renovated it, sold it, bought another. He had a good eye for gentrifying neighborhoods, in an era when it was hard to lose money in New York real estate. By 1968 he was a millionaire, and when the stock market went sour that year, he bought everything he could at distress prices. Now he was a multimillionaire, semi-retired, living in a duplex penthouse on Sutton Place with his third wife, who was three years older than his son.

In whom he was disappointed. He could not understand why a boy so bright would want to labor for a pittance in the bureaucracy, like the despised *apparatchiki* of the Soviets, when there was so much money to be made in America. Nevertheless, the old man was generous. Roland lived rent-free in the first floor of one of his father's buildings, a brownstone in the east Seventies, had substantial trust income, and could use his pittance salary for fun.

An odd history, then, and Roland cultivated an appearance to match. He looked like a professional wrestler, or what professional wrestlers would look like if they wore beautiful hand-tailored, European-cut suits. He wore his white-blond hair swept back and long enough to reach his collar, and kept his face tan and his body rippling with layers of stony muscle.

In contrast, the man sitting across from him this morning, two weeks or so after the Shilkes killing, was a native of the City, and had been reasonably well off since birth, although he was not ordinary in appearance either. He had been the previous incumbent of the position Roland now held, before being kicked upstairs to a vague and (Roland believed) meaningless sinecure: Deputy District Attorney for Special Projects. His name was Roger Karp, answering still to the name "Butch," although this was a faintly absurd name for an enormous, serious man in his late thirties, which he well knew, but still, he stubbornly kept it. In fact, he was the same age as Hrcany and had started at the D.A. in the same week, back in sixty-eight. Since they were the two standouts in their class, they had maintained a friendly rivalry during the intervening years, sometimes not so friendly. Roland, it must be said, had difficulty being friends with men whom he could not dominate at some level, and he could not do this with Karp. First, the physical thing: Roland was five-eight, and although he could now bench nearly four hundred pounds, this did not compensate for Karp being nine inches taller. Roland had been a varsity football player at Penn State, making up in sheer strength and will what he lacked in height, but Karp had been an all-state basketball star, and an all-conference player at Berkeley, *and* had played part of one season in the NBA. Second, at work too Karp had been always half a step ahead, his win record not *much* better than Roland's, but undeniably better. He had lost but one murder case in his career, a politicized monster that was what had gotten him kicked upstairs, leaving the job to Roland. This rankled, but what rankled most of all was that Karp did not, by word or action, recognize, nor had he ever recognized, that any competition was going on at all.

They were talking now, sports and light shop talk, Roland waiting with growing irritation for Karp to spit out what it was he had come down from the D.A.'s office to learn or tell. Yet another rankle: Karp should have been castrated by his promotion-demotion. In the D.A., trying and winning cases was the way you weighed the testicles, especially in Homicide, and Karp did not try or supervise the trying of cases anymore. He was really just an overpaid office boy for Jack Keegan, the D.A. He should have been diminished. He was not. He seemed, on the contrary, more relaxed and happy than he had in the past. Roland yearned for Karp to tell him to do something he didn't want to do, so that Roland could get angry and rush upstairs to Keegan and get Karp reversed, thus demonstrating the difference between an essential bureau chief and an exiguous staff drone. But Karp never did.

Roland now reached for the needle. "So, Butch, keeping busy? All those important meetings? Saving office supplies? Who gets their place painted first? Affirmative action?"

Karp smiled. "Oh, yeah, there are a lot of meetings."

"You better watch it, you don't become a lard-ass. A lard-ass your size would be a terrible thing. They'd have to upgrade the elevators."

Karp kept the smile. "You know, Roland, now that you bring it up, Jack asked me to mention affirmative action to you."

"You have to be kidding."

"Nope. You have one black man and two women as attorneys here. Felony has six and twelve. There are rumblings."

"Fuck the rumblings!" snapped Roland, his face starting to flush. "Not to mention who I inherited this staff from."

"Good point," said Karp equably. "You can profit from my mistakes. But the point is, it's your staff now and you need to make an effort."

"Okay, fine! Give me the fucking quotas and I'll go down the hall and hire the first ones I spot. Do I get to use two-fers?"

"Just make an effort, Roland. Build a record. Interview from the entire spangled rainbow that is our great city. Keep records. I'm sure you can do it." This was said in an even, almost tired tone. Roland realized that Karp was treating him like just another recalcitrant bureaucrat. He found himself grinding his jaw.

"Oh, and another thing . . ." Karp continued. "Jack wants to know who's going to handle the Shilkes trial. I said you'd probably go with Ray Guma or Tony Harris."

"No," said Roland instantly, off the top of his head. "I'm going to do it myself."

A pause. Karp said, "Uh-huh."

"What's *that* supposed to mean?"

"It doesn't mean anything, Roland," Karp replied. " 'Uh-huh' is an acknowledgment that I've understood your statement and have no opinion about it. Why are you, by the way?"

"Taking the case? Why not?" He rolled his shoulders and flexed his biceps, a habit of his when under tension; the cloth in the arms of his shirt made a small but audible creak. "What, you don't think I can win it?" Roland said this with a challenging scowl.

"Not at all. It seems like a straightforward case." Karp answered the scowl with a benign look. "Anything else doing? How are the Mexican brothers?"

"Ah, the Mexican brothers! Jesus and José are fine, Butch. I'll tell them you asked after them. It'll brighten their day."

Karp's smile grew a little strained, as it does when we spend time among people for whom sarcasm is the natural mode of discourse. "I assume they're still denying."

"You assume right. Somebody else killed that cop. Somebody else fired the shot that killed the cop from José's gun and dropped the gun in their apartment. And ripped them off. The usual horseshit, we din do nothin'. They'll go down for the murder one." Then, suspicious again, "Why? Jack doesn't think I can handle this either?"

"I didn't even imply that, Roland," said Karp, starting to lose patience. "A cop killing's always on the top of his to-do list until the trial's over. There's no chance they're telling the truth, then?"

"None." He grinned. "You want to hear the cherry on top? They tried to bribe me."

"Yeah? How much?"

"A hundred K. They call me over to Rikers, me and Frank Czermak, I figure, great! Finally they're going to give it up, so I get there and Jesus says, okay, you get us out, fifty K, cash. I look at Czermak, like I can't believe I'm hearing this, and they whisper for a minute, and then the offer goes up to a hundred. I tell them it's a crime to bribe a public official, and they kind of smile, like, oh, yeah, right. I mean, these guys think they're still in Mexico. A cop gets in your way, bang, bang, and then you fix it with the judge, with the prosecutor, and it's back to business."

"That's quite a story. It's just my luck to get canned from the job before the real money starts getting passed around. I'd feel a lot better, though, if we had a witness, or some evidence besides the gun. Also, I noticed the forensic report on the gun says there are nice prints on the bullets that don't belong to either of the two Obregon boys."

Roland was surprised that Karp knew this; it meant that Karp was following the case details at least as closely as Roland himself was. Roland didn't like this at all. He put on a cajoling expression and said, "So they used a gun loaded by persons unknown. Who gives a shit? It's the gun that killed Morilla, and José's prints are all over it."

Karp gave Roland a long, uncomfortably searching look. "So that's still the case, a gun and zip else?"

"Come on, Butch! They're dope dealers. They got a Mexican sheet as long as your arm. They come up here with a suitcase of brown smack, they try to sell it to Morilla, they find out he's a cop somehow, and they waste him."

"So where's the smack, Roland?"

"The fuck I know!" replied Roland, flushing again. "They moved it. Shit, maybe they shot it up. It's not germane to the case, and anyway . . ."

Roland was about to get seriously angry, because Karp had put his finger on the flaw in the Mexican brothers case, which Roland knew all too well, and on which every cop that could be spared in Manhattan was working: who were these scumbags, how did they get connected with Morilla, who was working undercover on something entirely different, where was the dope that Morilla was supposedly going to buy from them, where was the marked money that Morilla had for the buy? Roland changed the subject to one where he felt an undoubted superiority to Karp, which was sex. Karp was chained to a wife and three kids, the wife seriously over the hill now, must be thirty-five, and one-eyed, and with a screw loose.

"So, how's the family?" he asked, slyly smiling. "How's Marlene?"

"All fine," said Karp. "Marlene's doing okay. Business is booming."

"So to speak. She hasn't shot anybody else recently?"

"Not that I know of," said Karp uncomfortably, after which Roland regaled him with a detailed accounting of his own recent date with a model whose image, clad only in designer undies, was plastered over nearly every vertical surface in the City. Having gotten back on top, as he imagined, Roland made a show of checking his watch, a Le Coultre made from a twenty-dollar gold piece, and said, "Well, Butch, I'd love to chat, but unless you have any more little messages from upstairs, I got a bureau to run. Don't you have another meeting?"

Karp rose. "Always a pleasure, Roland," he said, and left.

He nodded to some of his former bureau colleagues as he left the office. They seemed not to miss him very much, he observed; not one of them clutched his knees and tearfully pleaded for him to return. Karp had to admit that Roland, despite being a male chauvinist, demi-racist son of a bitch, was much more popular around the bureau and the D.A.'s generally than Karp was. Roland was extremely charming when he wanted to be, a quality Karp lacked. He flirted with the secretaries and clerks, and was lavish in his distributions of birthday flowers and candy and purchases of pastries for the coffee room. The cops and the younger assistant D.A.'s seemed to prefer Roland's hearty obscenity to Karp's graver demeanor, and his histrionic rages to Karp's icy contempt. A cold fish, was the book on Karp.

These thoughts did not much engage Karp as he ascended on the elevator to the D.A.'s suite on the eighth floor of the Criminal Courts Building. His life had moved into a quiet harbor after a decade and a half of the most extreme combat his society offered for professionals not actually carrying firearms, and he was content to let the weed and barnacles accumulate on his hull. He liked his boss well enough, and the job itself, though tedious, was, as his wife often remarked, indoor work with no heavy lifting.

He gestured inquiringly at Marcie O'Malley, Keegan's iron-faced, iron-haired guard dog, who looked up from her typing and waved in the direction of the door. Karp knocked perfunctorily and went in.

The district attorney was on the phone. Karp sat on a leather couch, selected a *Sports Illustrated* from among the publications lying on the coffee table in front of him, and leafed through it until the call was over.

"That was John Haddad," said the D.A. He rose from his desk and walked over to sit in a club chair near the couch. Keegan was a big man with white hair and a broad pink Irish face. He still moved, at sixty, like the fullback he had once been at Fordham.

"You know who he is?" Keegan asked. Karp did not. "He's a city councilman from Brooklyn. A leader of our fine Arab community. He doesn't want a lynching. I assured him that the suspects in Shilkes would be treated precisely according to law, and that I would encourage the judge in the case to be tyrannical with the press, and that absolutely, positively we would not attempt to denigrate the Arabs during our presentation, and that there would be no damaging leaks to the press from this office. The usual. What did Roland have to say?"

"What he always says. Everything's okay, the case is a lock, and would I not bother him. He's taking it himself, by the way."

This last was received as Karp knew it would be: reddening face, flashing of blue eye-sparks, muttering of curses. "Why in *hell* is he going to do that?" Keegan demanded.

"Oh, I think that's pretty clear. Last year I took a big political case, which I shouldn't have as bureau chief, and lost it. He's going to take a big political case, which he shouldn't as bureau chief, and win it. It's important to Roland to show me up."

"Of all the *asinine* things . . ."

"Hey, boss, that's part of the package with Roland. God bless him, he's a hell of a prosecutor, but he does carry a ruler along when he goes to the john, make sure he's still got the longest dick."

Keegan grumbled some more, but Karp understood that he would make no changes in Roland's plan. One of Keegan's great virtues as a boss was his policy of giving his subordinates complete autonomy and demanding absolute accountability if they screwed up. It worked too. Karp did not think that Roland would screw this one up, and he reflected sourly, that Roland's case—where the culprits were a suspect minority with literal blood on their hands—compared hardly at all to his own signal failure, which was a complex insanity plea labyrinth with the greatest defense lawyer in the galaxy on the other side.

As if reading his thoughts, Keegan said, "Well, it'd be hard for him to lose this one, all the physical evidence we've got. Meanwhile, I also heard today from representatives of our fine Jewish community, Rabbi Lowenstein foremost among them. I told him you were representing the office for all matters connected with the Shilkes case. I told the same to Haddad."

"This is now a special project?"

Keegan smiled. This was something of a joke between them. Karp's absurd title meant that the D.A. could dump upon him anything the D.A. did not want to handle for any of a variety of reasons. Things, for example, that had to be done but which were not politically expedient for the D.A. to do himself—distasteful things, like firing old crocks whom Keegan knew personally, or things for which the D.A. had to maintain a modicum of deniability. Karp did not object to this, particularly. He was learning a good deal about how politics worked in the big city, and while he understood that he would never make a politician himself—he lacked that essential agreeableness necessary to the political life—he made (somewhat to his own surprise) an excellent politician's assistant. He had an infallible memory for detail. He had, unlike most staffers, an exhaustive knowledge of the actual workings of a prosecutorial organization. He was devoid of sympathy for the incompetent. He was dead loyal and as close-mouthed as an elderly Mafioso. And he could unholster, when required, a terrifying presence.

"Right," said Keegan. "So you'll see Haddad. And Lowenstein. You should get on well with the rabbi."

Karp brought out a leather-bound notebook and made a note. "Yeah, we can compare circumcisions. Haddad won't object to dealing with the *yiddim* on this?"

"Fuck 'im if he does. This is New York. Now, what about Morilla, my other hemorrhoid?"

"Well. Roland's confident on it. Frank Czermak's the lead."

"Roland's always confident. I don't like your face. What do *you* think?"

"They have the murder weapon with José Obregon's prints on it in the brothers' apartment, and he's got a heavy sheet for drugs and violence in Mexico. They're clean here, though. That's about it. Something else still could turn up. . . ."

"That's pretty thin. The cops really like these guys, huh?"

"They love them, as does Roland. I'd guess it's a strong probable for conviction on the top count at trial."

"Not good enough. A cop killing—what I don't need is the police commissioner, bless his heart, in my office playing 'Flowers of the Forest' on his bagpipes. Look, sniff around this, would you? Make sure they're aren't any nasty surprises."

Karp was surprised. "What, in Roland's face? He'll go ballistic."

"No. I mean privately. Don't mess with Czermak or anything, but keep me up to speed." He stood up abruptly and walked to the closet where he kept his suit jacket. "I got a banquet to go to. Anything else?"

There was not. Karp went to his own office, next door, and started to make calls.

In the mess hall at one of the ten jails of Rikers Island, Jesus Obregon, called Jodón, wrinkled his nose in disgust and pushed away his plastic tray. "I can't eat this garbage," he said to his brother José. José looked up at his brother from his own tray, where he had been concentrating on shoveling the watery stew, potatoes, and canned corn into his mouth, and said in tones indicating surprise, "It's good, Jodón. It's much better than the food in Zaca." José had spent four years in the maximum-security wing at Zacapoaxtla, the legendary penitentiary where the federal government of Mexico keeps its incorrigible criminals. Jesus Obregon, in contrast, had never spent a day in jail until this recent fiasco.

"Yes, for you," Jodón said, "for you it is fine, but you know I have always had delicate health, a sensitive stomach." He looked around the noisy, cavernous hall. "This place is going to kill me, José. I will die here, far from home."

José looked down at his brother, wiped the grease from his chin, and said, "If we increased the *mordida* for the Ape . . . ? "The Ape" was their uncharitable epithet for Roland Hrcany. "Or it might be that one of the guards could become reasonable."

Jodón shot a disapproving look at the other man. It disturbed him when José tried to generate ideas, or, in fact, when his little brother did anything at all without first being told to do so. He was trying to construct in his mind some way of blaming José for this disaster, but could find none, which made him even more disconsolate. Coming to New York had, after all, been his idea. He had left his profitable business as one of the links in one tributary of the vast braided river of heroin routes that led from the south to the great drug markets of North America. He could have spent his life running product from the western ports of Mexico or from rural airstrips, up from Hermosillo to Nogales and the border, and grown rich and respected. But the thought of being forever a medium-sized fish in a small pond irked him. He felt capable of larger things. So, as he sat in his comfortable house with the new refrigerator and color TV and stereo system, with the shiny Buick in the dusty street outside, he considered his career choices. The first step was to take over the Escondido organization in Nogales. To do that he needed money, huge quantities of money, money to bribe the people Escondido had protecting him on both sides of the law (and this would be particularly expensive because, naturally the local and federal police were already extracting from the regnant cartel all that they thought the traffic would bear) and when bribery was not possible money to pay *chuteros* for the requisite murders. Where to get the money? Going into business on his own, locally or in California, Arizona, or Texas, would be simple suicide. Not Denver or Chicago either: the Mexican gangs were well established there. But New York . . . that was different, a virgin field. Jodón had seen all three parts of *The Godfather* several times each, and so he was reasonably familiar with how things were done in that great city. If the Mob was fat and arthritic, as seemed the case, then the only other competition would come from *los negros* and *los puertorriqueños*, which Jodón considered no competition at all.

So the plan was put into action. Slowly, so as not to arouse suspicion, Jodón started buying heroin on his own. In six months he had accumulated two hundred kilograms of the pale brown powder, which he kept secreted in the walls of his bedroom. Six weeks ago he had packed the thick plastic bags containing the drug into the rocker panels of the Buick and rewelded them. Or rather José did. José was also the one who drove the loaded car across the border, while Jodón waited in the Ramada Inn in Tucson. This was the way they divided the work of their enterprise: Jodón made the plans, and José took the risks and performed the necessary actions, which was only fair considering their respective physical endowments. The brothers were the result of a mating between a small, elegant pimp from Nogales and a very large Hermosillo prostitute. Jodón had taken after his father, José after his mother. People in their Hermosillo barrio looking at the boys standing beside each other were reminded of a rooster keeping company with an ox; these were their earliest nicknames, and provided a source of local amusement until Jodón decided he didn't like it and told his brother to make it stop. Which he did. Still, people had to call him something besides Jesus, a name many Latino youths bear, and which, out of respect, is always converted into a nickname for daily use, usually Chucho or Chui, but in this case the choice was Jodón, which means ruthless, opportunistic, deceptive. Jodón did not mind this.

The brothers had driven together in the Buick from Arizona to New York, obtained an apartment on Avenue C, and, somewhat later, a woman for Jodón, a Dominican-American named Connie Erbes. José did not want a woman, as he was married with five children. He used whores instead. Business, once they put samples on the street, was not slow in arriving, because their merchandise was very pure. Jodón expected word to filter up the lines of dealers until it reached someone who could move weight, and so it did.

The man was extremely plausible, although, since they had no business contacts in New York and naturally could not ask their own *cartelistas* for advice, they had to make him as right with only their own instincts. He called himself Lucky. He had the sharp clothes, the large white car with the smoked windows, the retinue of sullen dark men that marked a legit big-timer dealer. But Jodón was careful. He sniffed around. He found that yes, Lucky was a dealer on a substantial scale. He bought large and sold large. Jodón set up a moderate buy: five kilos of ninety percent pure product, two hundred grand. The deal went off like clockwork. Lucky was friendly, delighted to have found so good, so economical, a supplier. Immediately after the deal the Obregons moved out of their apartment to a place in Washington Heights, taking Connie, their money, and the bulk of their dope. There they lay low and waited. José ventured out and made a few buys in various parts of the City. Sure enough, their dope was moving through the usual channels, chopped to bits but still recognizable. The usual bulk suppliers were malignantly interested in the new source. Lucky was moving the dope on the street, ergo was definitely not a cop.

Jodón set up another deal, a much bigger deal: fifty kilos, two million dollars. He rented an apartment in East Harlem for the transaction. He hired a half dozen guards for the transport. He had a local man watch the meeting site for a week beforehand, to make sure no one was casing the venue. On the day of, Jodón was trembling with nerves. He snapped meaningless and contradictory orders to José in the driver's seat, snarled at Connie as she tried to calm him.

Right on schedule, however, there came Lucky, with two men, one hauling a large blue Samsonite case. Handshakes all around. The case opened, the neatly wrapped hundreds in stacks of $10,000, two hundred of them, in lovely green rows. The two tin trunks unlocked, the bags sampled, tested, smiles all around.

Then chaos. The door smashing inward, the room full of uniformed men and detectives. Lucky and his guards beaten down, handcuffed, A gun in Jodón's face, cuffs on his wrists, dragged down the stairs. Where were his guards? Fled, the bitches! Then the ride in the van with José and Connie, his mind frozen, refusing to believe the disaster, the beautiful money gone, his merchandise gone and then . . . nothing. The van stopped. They heard laughter, slamming doors, cars pulling away.

They waited in silence, then escaped from their cuffs, which is easy if there are at least two of you and no one is watching. They emerged from the van to find themselves in a waste area, strewn with trash, under an expressway.

Back in the Washington Heights apartment, Jodón got drunk and beat Connie until his hands ached, but neither action relieved his profound depression. Because he was drunk, he did not respond when José emerged from his room, a bemused expression on his moon face and expressed puzzlement that the pistol he had brought to the meeting, and which he had thought confiscated by the police, was back in his room, and, by the smell, had been fired recently. Then the real cops showed up.

Jodón had to admit, although only to himself, that he had been greedy and stupid. He should have made a few small deals and gone away. Made a few small deals and gone away again, moving slowly, spreading the risk among a number of buyers. He should have arranged the buy at an out-of-town site, in the open, at a place with many roads. That was how it was done among the big men. *Poco á poco se va lejos.* Next time he would do it that way, little by little. But first he had to get out of the present situation.

Obviously, a bribe was not going to work. He still felt embarrassment when he thought of how the Blond Ape had spurned his offer. He recalled the gold watch on the man's wrist—he had never seen anything so marvelous, a watch made out of a gold coin! And his suit, his shoes! He should have realized that a man who collected the sort of bribes available to a prosecutor in New York City would have been insulted with his petty hundred thousand, although that sum would have easily purchased a brace of federal judges in Mexico.

Another way, then, one that would combine revenge with escape. *"Hijo de la chingada madre!"* he said between his teeth. José, standing next to him in the exercise yard, started and said, "Who?"

"Who do you think? That one who cheated us, who set us up with the police. I tell you what we have to do, my brother. We must have him found, this Lucky, the *pato!* We must have him go to the police with the evidence necessary to expose what he did, how he killed the policeman Morilla and blamed it on us. He must be in jail, where I am now. Only then will I have his throat cut."

José nodded appreciatively. It was an excellent plan. José did not mind jail as much as Jodón, but he would have preferred to be elsewhere. Slowly, as he considered it, a small flaw in the plan dripped through his muddy brain to the centers of comprehension.

"But, Jodón—why would he do that? He is safe and we are in here, no?"

Jodón rolled his eyes and rapped his brother sharply on the crown of his head, as he had done for as long as either of them could remember. "*Pendejo!* We will have to call someone, who will find him and convince him to do this."

José started to laugh. He had a hearty, bubbling laugh, and he gave it full play as he thought of some person trying to convince Lucky to confess to a murder of a policeman in order to free the Obregons. "Who . . . who . . . who, could do that, Jodón?" he sputtered. "God Almighty? The Virgin Mary? The Devil?"

"No," said his brother, maintaining his dignity. "I will send for El Chivato, from Nogales."

José stopped laughing. "Oh, El Chivato," he said, "yes, then of course. If he will come."

After speaking on the phone with John Haddad and Rabbi Lowenstein, Karp called his wife at her office, and got instead her receptionist and general factotum, Sym McCabe. Sym was one of the waifs Mrs. Karp used to staff her complex life.

"Whom shall I say is calling?" said Sym.

"Sym, you only ask that if you don't know who it is," explained Karp. "You know who I am. Where's Marlene?"

"Ms. Ciampi is with a client."

Karp bit back a sharp comment. The kid was bright and trying hard, but for reasons Karp could never quite grasp, she always gave him a hard time. "Could you buzz her, please?" he asked. "I need to talk to her."

The line went dead, and for a moment Karp thought the girl had accidentally-on-purpose cut him off. Then Marlene's voice came on the line.

"Sorry," he said, "you're with a client."

"I'm with Tran. What's up?"

"I have to do something later this evening, and I was supposed to pick Lucy up at Chinese school."

"Oh? What do you have to do?"

"I have to go to Williamsburg and get yelled at by Rabbi Lowenstein. He won't come to the office because the streets are teeming with Arab terrorists and his life would be in danger. Will there be a problem with Lucy?"

"No, Tran can do it, but you owe me one. Are you going in your deputy D.A. capacity or your Jewish capacity?"

"Both, I think," said Karp after a moment's thought. "Although by the rabbi I'm probably not much of a Jew."

"He should talk to my grandmother. Are you going to tell him you're married to a shiksa?"

"If it comes up," Karp replied.

After he got off the phone, he had forty minutes before his appointment with John Haddad. He reviewed a copy of the Shilkes case file, gleaning nothing that he did not already know. Two half-educated illegal Palestinians had killed a Jewish shopkeeper to make a point about the international Zionist conspiracy. The organization they claimed to represent seemed to be nothing more than a figment of their imaginations. The evidence was damning, and Karp reckoned that for the next quarter of a century they would fight Zionism from behind the walls of Attica.

Haddad, who showed at the appointed time, proved to be a small, well-dressed, fussy-looking man with round spectacles and a head the color and approximate shape of a brown egg. After the usual pleasantries, Haddad cleared his throat and said, "Mr. Karp, my major concern is with the impact that this trial may have on the Arab-American community in New York. In terms of defamation, I mean."

"Yes, the D.A. told me you were concerned that we would somehow use whatever prejudice against Arabs that exists locally to inflame the jury against the defendants. Mr. Keegan wanted me to reiterate his position that this is absolutely not going to happen. On the other hand, one of the counts on the indictment is conspiracy, so it's going to be necessary to show that the defendants were part of an organization dedicated to harming Israeli interests and Jews in general. That's not going to add to their popularity, not in New York."

"No," said Haddad grimly. "The Jewish dominance of the local media is quite complete." There did not seem to be much Karp could add to this sentiment, so he waited, and Haddad added, "What I'm concerned about is that there's going to be open season on Arab organizations. Every neighborhood club is going to be suspect. Our kids are already getting harassed in school. And the damned thing is, there *is* no organization."

"Isn't there?"

"No! What you have here is three undereducated Palestinian kids who decide that they're going to play guerrillas in the big city, and they get plenty of encouragement from maniacs. It's pathetic, really. The Hamshari boy is only eighteen."

"Right, but they're old enough to have butchered an old lady and half killed her husband."

"The Shilkes family has my every sympathy," Haddad responded quickly. "It was a horrendous act. That the Israelis do worse than that every day in the occupied territories still doesn't excuse it."

"Right. But to move back to the point you were raising, Mr. Haddad, the prosecution in this case is not going to rest on the ethnicity of the defendants, but on the evidence, which is overwhelming. We don't need anti-Arab diatribes in the courtroom."

"What about outside the courtroom? What about this continual inflammatory rhetoric about a terrorist conspiracy?"

"Well, there's not much we can do about that, Mr. Haddad," said Karp. "People can say what they like in this country."

"What about this?" the man asked, and from his briefcase he brought out a sheaf of clippings and tossed them on the table. Some of them were columns from the down-market local dailies, but the bulk were from *The Guardian*, the Williamsburg sheet that Mendel Lowenstein put out. Karp glanced through them as Haddad railed on. Karp was content to listen passively and make occasional sympathetic noises. He had found, over time, that a good deal of the anger that citizens wished to express against the D.A.'s office could be dissipated through nothing more than courteous listening. He had spent many years listening to the complaints of the relatives of murder victims, and this was nothing in comparison with that. But something was tugging at his mind, something Haddad had said. When the man had run down somewhat, Karp asked, "You said there were three men involved. But there're only two defendants. Who was the third man? Or do you mean the Daoud boy?"

"No, my information is that there were four boys involved, Daoud, the two defendants, and one named Ali al-Qabbani, who served as a lookout. That's another thing, Mr. Karp. Ali al-Qabbani hasn't been seen since the morning of the alleged crime."

"Aren't the police looking for him?" asked Karp, carefully avoiding the question of how Haddad knew so much about the conspirators.

"No. They don't believe he exists. They think the other two are making him up so they can put off the blame on him. Ali planned it, we didn't know what we were getting into, and so on. And Ali was an illegal. No records, few possessions—he lived in a corner of the room where they met, he did odd jobs, spoke hardly any English. Where could he run to? But he's vanished."

"Maybe he's back in Palestine. Maybe the terrorist network got him out."

"Oh, please! I told you, there *is* no network. This organization—Against the House of War—it doesn't exist. It's a fantasy that's shared by those idiot boys and Lowenstein. I certainly hope that the D.A.'s office doesn't buy into it."

"Well, personally, I have no opinion either way, and I doubt Mr. Keegan does either. As I say, it'll only touch on the prosecution as it affects the conspiracy case. What do *you* think happened to this Ali?"

"Isn't it obvious? The Jews got him. Lowenstein and his gang of thugs. But you know very well that the police will never follow up on *that* angle."

"I wouldn't be too sure of that, Mr. Haddad. Unlike our mayor, the district attorney doesn't run his own foreign policy. We have a deal with the secretary of state—we don't negotiate with foreign nations and he doesn't prosecute murders. I promise I'll look into it and get back to you. As a matter of fact, I'm meeting with Rabbi Lowenstein later this evening. I'll ask him about it."

Haddad snorted. "What do you expect him to do, admit it?"

"No, but his denial will be informative. Thanks for coming by, sir. We'll stay in touch."

At Battery Park, the Statue of Liberty ferry was pulling out for its last run of the day. Aboard were a group of seventh-graders from Hyattsville, Maryland, on their class trip. A cluster of boys were at the stern, laughing under a teacher's watchful eye as they tossed bits of snack food into the air for the miraculously hovering gulls.

"Hey, look," shouted one, above the wind and the engines, "there's a guy swimming!" They all clustered at the rail and looked.

"Jeez!" said another, "he's buck naked! You can see his ass!"

More laughter, shoving to look. The teacher frowned and moved toward them. Then the bow wave of the ferry tossed the man and he rolled slowly over, and they saw that he was not swimming at all.

THREE

Karp had not been to Williamsburg in a long time. As a child he had been taken there at long intervals to visit an aunt of his mother's, Aunt Reva, an elderly widow who lived alone in a small apartment crowded with massive dark furniture and dense with crocheted doilies and old-people smells—Vick's, frying chicken fat, scorched feathers. Aunt Reva had pinched his cheeks painfully and given him macaroons and tea rich in lemon and sugar in a thick-sided tumbler. He had played on the floor with a menagerie of glass animals while his mother and her aunt had gabbled in Yiddish. The last time in Williamsburg had been when he was twelve. The glass animals had lost their charm. Karp resented the time spent away from basketball. His older brothers no longer had to endure the visits, but Karp, the last baby, still had to go. On this occasion the sulking Karp had deliberately snapped the legs off a glass deer and his mother had smacked him, the last (nearly the first) occasion of violence between them. He had run out of the suffocating apartment, down the stairs to the street, a street not a hundred yards from the street by which he now traveled.

Karp was not a particularly reflective man. His recollection of that day at Aunt Reva's had been neatly plastered over, along with the repugnance he felt at the odd, un-Americanness of Williamsburg's self-ghettoized Jews, along with the usual tag ends of guilt and remorse. Karp was a believer in the sacred American right of re-invention. The Williamsburg of his youth had seemed to him an antique remnant of a doomed way of life. Jews were like anyone else. They played basketball and lived in houses with lawns, and if they were religious they went on Saturday morning to modernistic buildings indistinguishable from Baptist churches (except for the lack of a pinnacle cross) and ate what everyone else ate.

The idea that people might *choose* to live like Aunt Reva, that people with education, people his age, might volunteer to live in the tenements and brownstones their grandparents had occupied and pursue a life of piety and ritual, was something his imagination could not grasp. He probably had (something he would be reluctant to admit) more real sympathy with that bunch of black kids hanging out on the stoop of one of the battered brownstones on Union Avenue than he did with his putative co-religionists. The kids at least played basketball.

The Jewish part of Williamsburg is a small trapezoid lodged uncomfortably amid substantial districts inhabited by American and West Indian blacks, Puerto Ricans, and (this zone a more recent one) immigrants from various parts of Central and South America. The line is as sharp as any in Beirut or Belfast. On one block the stores cashed checks and sold liquor, Latino or reggae records, and cheap furniture. Every sixth storefront was a barbershop, a hair parlor, a nail joint, or a Pentecostal church. The people were variously brown.

On the next block the stores sold kosher meats, dairy foods, cheap clothing, and slightly better furniture. There were neither barbershops nor liquor stores, and every sixth storefront was a *shul* or a ritual bathhouse. The people were white, pale white, the men in black clothes, hatted and bearded, the women scarf-headed and accompanied by clusters of children, each little boy with his knitted yarmulke and dangling side locks.

"This is it," said Karp to his driver, a black detective named Morris. They were on Boerum Street, in front of a substantial pink sandstone building, formerly a private home, that had been converted into a synagogue-cum-headquarters for the Ostropoler Hasidim. The house was set back from the street, and an iron paling surrounded what had once been a small garden. This had been paved over in the fashion of the Orthodox, who begrudged the time that gardening would steal from their duty to God. Karp had a vague awareness that an ancient named Reb Moise Koppelman was the leader of this small community. Reb Mendel Lowenstein, the man he had come to see, was the rebbe's son-in-law and heir presumptive.

The street in front of the building was thronged with men, dressed either in black suits, with fedoras, or in the traditional long gabardines with round hats trimmed with red fox fur. They shot hostile looks at the car and its driver. A man came up and told Morris he couldn't park there. Morris put a cardboard POLICE sign on the dashboard. Another couple of men came up and started arguing with Morris. Karp got out of the car. "You'll be okay?" he asked Morris.

"I got a radio and a gun," said the driver. "How long will you be?"

"As short as I can make it," said Karp. He had to push through the crowd on the sidewalk and the stoop, the men yielding to him reluctantly. At the door, a burly youth wearing a brassard marked with a star of David and a lion looked Karp over, frowning. Karp told him he was here to see Reb Lowenstein, and the youth handed him a yarmulke and waited until he had placed it on his head. Then he led the way through dim and crowded hallways to a small chamber fitted out as a waiting room, told Karp to wait, and left. There were a dozen or so men waiting with him, talking softly or reading. The room was warm and stuffy; from time to time men would be called to the door at one end of the room and exit, but the room did not seem to grow less crowded. No one spoke to Karp.

After fifteen minutes of this, a thin young man with a sparse reddish beard emerged and beckoned to Karp and then led him through the door. On the other side was a small, windowless, cluttered office within which, behind a desk piled with papers, sat Mendel Lowenstein. There were several other men in the room, engaged in some business around an adding machine, which clicked and buzzed as they talked. Lowenstein looked up as Karp walked in and gestured to a straight chair in front of his desk.

Karp had been in drug dens, in wretched apartments where people had been murdered, places with blood on the walls, and he had been much in the company (almost always without rancor) of some of the worst people produced by his society, but he had not often been as angry or as uncomfortable as he was at this moment. He really didn't like these people, and although he kept his face neutral, he sensed that Lowenstein knew it. The rabbi was a stocky, brush-bearded man with a high, domed forehead and the large, liquid, intense eyes of a fanatic or a saint, assuming there is a difference.

These examined Karp for a long, uncomfortable moment before the man spoke.

"So, Mr. Karp, here you are. What have you got to tell me? Are you going to stop this pogrom?"

Clearly no pleasantries were going to be exchanged, which was fine with Karp. He said, "I'm not sure what you mean, Rabbi. I thought a pogrom was an anti-Semitic mob organized by the government."

Contempt blossomed on the rabbi's face. "Bah! What, you didn't see the police beating our boys with clubs? We get slaughtered and the police beat *us*? What do you call it, then?"

"I would call it controlling a riot, sir. Objects were thrown at the police station, and several police were injured."

Lowenstein pointed a stubby finger at Karp, "See! This is how it starts. This is what happened before the Nazis took over. You, a Jew, sit here in the house of God, may his name be blessed, and defend the beating of Jews. It's a *shandah*! A *shandah*!"

At this word the clicking of the adding machine ceased, and all the men in the room stared at Karp. Their faces indicated that they had accepted their leader's verdict. It was indeed shameful.

Karp felt his face heat, and he allowed himself a calming breath. The rabbi was not finished, however. "You think because you act like the goyim, and eat like the goyim, when the time comes the goyim are going to protect you? Like they protected the six million?" And more of the same for some time. Karp let the man run out his spiel. He was more than adequately familiar with the Holocaust. Karp's mother had been a fierce Zionist and something of a connoisseur of Holocaust details, and had imbued Karp from an early age with the necessity for Jews to be ever vigilant in an implacably hostile world. The lesson had not taken deep root in Karp's soul, however, although he had considerable experience with practical anti-Semitism. On the streets of Brooklyn, where he had been raised, it was given that a group of Irish or Italian kids would beat up any Jewish kid they found, and Karp's own little gang of Jews was not loath to return the favor. That they used fists, sticks, and rocks rather than the semi-automatics that later became fashionable in settling youthful disputes did not detract from the sincerity of their violence, and this experience had, perhaps regrettably, tempered his sympathy for the six million. He simply could not imagine walking meekly with his children into a cattle car, not while he had breath to fight.

Besides that, as an athlete Karp was a convinced meritocrat. Could you make the shot, could you scuffle successfully under the boards—these were to him the cosmic questions. And he had found early that he had absolutely no religious interest whatever. When he thought about it at all, which was rarely, he considered it to be a kind of talent. He himself could fling a ten-inch ball unerringly through the air into a slightly larger hoop from distances up to twenty-five feet, and he could convict people of homicide. Others could talk to God and get comfort from it. His wife, for example, or his daughter, both Catholics.

"Go outside!" Lowenstein was saying. "Go three blocks from here in any direction, and what do you find? Jamaica! Egypt! El Salvador! We are closed in by hostile goyim. Every day our people are robbed, beaten up, raped. And what do your precious authorities do? *Nothing* is what they do. They write up papers, and they forget. No one is ever arrested. You can see them, the cops, thinking, oh, the Jews, they got plenty, who cares! And I'm warning you, we will not tolerate it. Cursed be those who despoil Israel! And now they have started to kill us—"

"Yeah, right, Rabbi," Karp interrupted, "things are tough all over. It's the city, it's a high-crime precinct you're in here." He noted, with some satisfaction, that the rabbi's eyes had widened. His mouth was still slightly open, showing yellow, uneven teeth. He was not used to being interrupted, especially when he was in full spate about the travails of the Jews.

"Meanwhile," Karp went on, "the reason I came over here was that Mr. Keegan asked me to report to you on the progress of the Shilkes investigation, as a courtesy. As you know by now, we have two suspects in custody, and we will charge them with murder and assault. We have substantial evidence against them, but only with respect to the crime itself. At present there's no substantive evidence of a wider conspiracy, much less plans for a campaign against Jews generally."

"You believe this?" Lowenstein snapped. "You think these stupid savages thought this up themselves, that they were not brought to it by some evil intelligence?" The rabbi had a habit of leaning forward in his chair and drumming his fists on his desk in rhythm with his words. Karp hesitated momentarily. The same thought had occurred to him, but he was not about to share it with Lowenstein.

"There's no evidence for it," said Karp a little lamely.

Lowenstein swiveled his chair abruptly away from Karp and said something in Yiddish to several of the other men. They responded with sour laughter, and Karp realized that this was the first laugh he had heard since alighting from the unmarked—not, in his experience, the usual state of affairs among Jews. The rabbi swung his chair around like a tank turret and directed the muzzle of his glare toward Karp. Again the finger.

"Listen to me—while you're gathering this evidence, which you could trip over walking down the street if you had eyes, while you are looking, we will take care of ourselves. We are not pacifists, Mr. Karp. We have ample authority in the Talmud to protect ourselves against those who mean to harm us. Do I make myself clear?"

"Oh, yeah, Rabbi. I should point out, however, that we're operating under the Constitution and the statutes of the state of New York here, which may have a different interpretation of self-defense than your version of Talmudic law. We would not tolerate any attempt to take the law into your own hands, for example, by pursuing people you thought might be involved in the Shilkes murder, Arab boys, for example."

Karp was watching Lowenstein carefully as he said this, but the man gave no obvious sign of guilt or nervousness. The clicking of the adding machine stopped, though, and the elderly man using it was staring at Karp with an expression of . . . what? Doubt? Anger? Concern? It was hard for Karp to read these bearded, grave faces.

Meanwhile, the rabbi sniffed, rolled his eyes, sighed, and made a small dismissing gesture with the tips of his fingers, as if shooing away a small, bothersome creature. Karp might have felt diminished had he not been vaccinated against just this guilt-making ritual by his maternal grandmother, who had used almost the same mannerisms.

"Go away, Mr. Karp," said Lowenstein in a weary voice. "Go back to the goyim, live out your little make-believe. Someday, you decide you want to be a real Jew, we'll still be here, we'll welcome you with open arms."

In the car, Morris said, "How'd it go?"

"It went shitty, Morris," said Karp, settling back in the seat and rubbing his face. "The rabbi decided I wasn't enough of a Jew to understand their situation there. You ever get that, when you were uptown?"

Morris glanced at him. "What, that I wasn't enough of a Jew? Hardly ever. Why?"

Karp laughed out loud, probably for longer than the remark warranted. "No, from the Muslims, from the Panthers, whatever," he explained. "Like you were letting the team down."

"Oh, that. Yeah, some." He shrugged. "The Uncle Tom business. You let shit like that get to you, you might as well hang it up."

While Karp drove back to Manhattan, his wife was doing something that she was as bad at as her husband was at mollifying militant Hasidim, which was teaching women to shoot pistols. She was now in the basement firing range of the West Side Gun Club, on Tenth and Forty-eighth Street, standing behind and to the left of an insurance company office manager named Joan Savitch, who was blazing away with a Smith & Wesson .22 revolver at a silhouette target twenty-five yards down-range. She was getting some good hits, but her pattern was lousy, and although Marlene knew enough about shooting to know that tight pattern was the key, she did not know enough to tell Savitch what she was doing wrong.

The woman expended her final bullet and clicked the traveler switch to bring the target home. They both looked at it. "Am I getting any better?" Savitch asked doubtfully. Like most New Yorkers, she had never fired a pistol before. She was a short woman, somewhat overweight by the standards of the fashion magazines, with a pleasant, intelligent, forty-ish face. Her blond-streaked light brown hair was arranged in a stylish flip cut. She was wearing a maroon jersey over the skirt to her gray suit. An ordinary New York woman of the moderately successful professional classes, two young sons in an apartment in Peter Cooper, formerly married to a guy who turned out to be a maniac. It happened, more often than people supposed.

"You're doing fine," said Marlene, although in truth she did not think there had been much improvement over the last half box of rounds. One of Marlene's people, Lonnie Dane, usually took this duty. Dane (now, unfortunately, running a touchy assignment) was a gun nut who really thought that being able to put five holes through a playing-card-sized area at twenty-five yards was as important as the ability to tie up one's sneakers, and he was a good, patient teacher, and a man, which Marlene, to her dismay (she being a good enough feminist) found that most of her clients (all female) really preferred. The remarkable things about Marlene and guns were (in ascending order of improbability): she thought they were necessary to her work; she hated them; she was a crack shot. This last had come as a considerable surprise—that she shot like an expert the first time she had ever picked up a pistol. Dane had assured her that, while rare, such things were not unknown in gun circles. Marlene had already used this skill to kill three men, and more than practically anything else in this world, she wished never to have to do so again.

This was, in fact, a prime reason for the training. Four years previously, on leaving the D.A.'s office, Marlene had started a private security agency for the express purpose of protecting women from the deadly attentions of men. Ninety percent of this work was paper shuffling and phone calls—arranging for protective orders, urging the police to enforce same, riding herd on the prosecution of villains, or a kind of social work—encouraging women to get out of violent situations. When this did not work, in perhaps nine percent of her cases, Marlene moved bodies, supplying women and their children with new homes, in apartments if they could afford it, or shelters if they could not, and new identities when required. Marlene was also not averse to engaging in heart-to-heart talks with the men involved, explaining in some detail what would happen to them if they did not lay off. Often this worked.

It was the remaining one percent that caused Marlene the most trouble. This small fraction consisted of men who would not be dissuaded by the law or by Marlene's threats. Some odd derangement of their brains had conflated love with absolute possession, so that if they could not have access to their chosen one on their terms, they would eventually kill her, any children that happened to be convenient, and, ordinarily, themselves afterward. Marlene preferred that they die before rather than afterward, and since she could not afford to mount a perpetual watch on the women in question (for the proportion, while small, represented in a city the size of New York a considerable number), she had started the gun classes.

Strictly speaking, this was illegal. New York does not approve of its citizens carrying concealed weapons, and Marlene tended to agree. New York makes an exception for retired cops working private, security guards, and storekeepers, but not usually for women in fear of their lives. Marlene's scam was to "hire" Joan Savitch and her other clients in similar straits as "trainees." They paid Marlene a fee, and she trained them as bodyguards, each of whose sole client was herself. Thus they could carry guns under Marlene's ticket, just like Wackenhut's square-badge legions.

"Let's forget about the .22 now," said Marlene to her trainee. "The statistics tell you that most people who get shot get it from a range of seven feet or less. The main thing here is not to turn you into Annie Oakley, but to get you used to firing a serious pistol."

Savitch pointed at the .22. "This isn't a serious pistol?"

"No." Marlene opened an aluminum suitcase lined with foam fingers and brought out a Smith & Wesson Airweight Model 49 and a box of .38 Special + P hollow-points. "This is a serious pistol. A .38, two-inch barrel, weighs a pound and a half loaded, got a shrouded hammer so it doesn't catch on anything. Load it up and try it."

Savitch took the thing, grimacing as she felt the solid weight of it, and filled the cylinder. Marlene clipped a new target to the traveler and sent it down-range, but only for about ten feet. Savitch took aim and fired a round and yelped.

"Yeah, it's a lot louder. You have to get used to it. You're going to have to shoot a couple of loads with the earmuffs off too."

The woman shot off the rest of the cylinder, in two-round bursts as she had been taught, nicely chewing up the chest area of the man-shape. Still a crummy pattern, but Marlene was mainly interested in her pupil's ability to get off large-caliber rounds without flinching. She had the woman reload and fire again.

"How do you like it?" asked Marlene.

"I love it," Savitch said with an edge in her voice. "Do you have it in beige?"

"Yeah, right," said Marlene. "This is what we do instead of Tupperware. Want to try some more?"

"No, I think I'm all shot out today." She placed the pistol—thud—on the shooting stand and turned away from the target.

"That's your gun, Joan," Marlene said gently. "You have to take it with you. No," she added as Savitch started to put it in her purse, "you have to load it. It don't work without the bullets."

Savitch started her cry then, during which Marlene held her and tried to say all the right things, thinking it was better she got this over with now, and also that she, Marlene, was perhaps the only woman in the city who regularly left for work with a supply of both bullets and Kleenex.

"I can't do this, Marlene," she said, snuffling. "I really . . . I just *can't*!"

"Uh-huh. Well, maybe you can't. I can't make you do it, and in fact, even advising you *to* do it is probably illegal. All I can do is make it possible for you to protect yourself, and advise you as to your rights of self-protection."

Marlene disliked the sound of her own voice, too dull, too law-yerly, as she generated these necessary and familiar words. "You know that your ex is getting out of prison on Tuesday, after serving five and a half for first-degree assault. On you. Before that he served an eighteen-month sentence for second-degree assault. On you also. After that first stretch he went directly to where you were living and committed the crime for which he did the second stretch. Okay, so what do you think he's going to do the minute he gets off the bus at the Port Authority?"

The woman seemed to ignore the question. "I can't do it," she wept. "I . . . just . . . can't."

"Yeah, that's a possibility. Some people can't," Marlene agreed.

Savitch glared wetly at her. "It doesn't seem to bother *you*."

"What? Wait, you think I *like* this? You think this is *fun* for me? I *hate* this. The only thing I hate worse is when the guy kills the woman and the kids *before* he shoots himself."

Renewed crying. Marlene led the woman to a metal folding chair and sat her down in it. She knelt beside her and held her hand. "There's something wrong with his brain, Joan. I wish there was something we could do for him besides what we've been talk-ing about, but I don't know of anything. The law kind of stalls out on stuff like this. It frowns on locking people up for things they're probably going to do. But the law allows you to protect yourself with deadly force under a particular set of conditions. If you're ac-costed on the street, unless you're in imminent fear of your life or of grievous bodily harm, you have to retreat. You can't just spot the guy across the way and shoot. If he approaches with a weapon, then you are in immediate fear, et cetera, and you *can* use deadly force. In your home or place of work, you're under no obligation to retreat. If he refuses to leave, you can shoot him. And, Joan? This is very important. If you draw a gun, you *must* be prepared to use it.

It's not the movies, where you have a conversation while you're pointing. Draw bang bang, just like we've been practicing. Do you understand?"

Marlene wasn't sure if this was penetrating at all.

"Joan? Do you understand what I'm telling you? This is a *legal* alternative to imminent death or serious injury to you or someone else. Like your kids."

"I could leave. I could hide someplace."

Marlene kept her tone neutral. "Right. And there's a woman I know who helps people in your situation do just that. I'll put you in touch with her if you want. I don't want to sell you on something you're not completely comfortable with."

"Why don't you?" asked the woman, reaching for some theme that would distract her from her predicament.

"Do get-aways? Because I have a moral objection to asking an innocent person to live in terror for the rest of her life. You have a life here, your job, your kids' school, your friends and relatives. You could give it all up and trade it for the chance he won't find you out in Tucson or wherever, but I personally think that's wrong. My thought is, you defend your life, you make your stand, with deadly force in the last extremity, if and when deadly force is being used against you."

Savitch nodded woefully, and after another fifteen minutes of quiet talk, Marlene got her together enough to face the street. She had scheduled another two sessions, after which Joan Savitch would be on her own. Marlene hoped she would do the unpleasant thing and put enough bullets into her ex-husband to make him dead, but she also knew that, oddly enough, women involved with men like Gerald Savitch often declined to defend themselves, even in the face of imminent death. She was a good deal less optimistic about her work now than when she had started, and also about the possibility of any simple resolution of the politics of sex.

After bundling her client into a cab, Marlene went back into the range and set up a fresh silhouette target, and sent it twenty-five yards down the lane. She composed herself and took a few deep breaths. Then she pulled her own pistol out of a cross-draw holster on her hip and shot the target twice. She replaced the pistol and did it again. And again. Marlene used a Colt Mustang .380 Pocketlite, which at twelve and a half ounces—about the heft of a set of pliers—was the smallest serious weapon she had been able to buy.

She punched the traveler switch and brought the target back. Its upper arms were decorated with neat pairs of holes, very close together. This was another part of Marlene's plan for not killing anyone anymore. Combat shooters are taught to fire at the center of mass, and that is what Marlene taught her clients to do as well. But Marlene was interested in reliably shattering the bones and nerves of the upper arms. which was a lot safer for the target, if also a lot riskier for the target's target. Marlene did not care; let the women do the killing, was her thought.

She shot off the rest of her box in this way, then packed up and left. Marlene crossed Tenth, walking in the quick, aggressive manner of the born New Yorker, swinging her aluminum case. She was wearing jeans, a black turtleneck jersey, a navy pea coat, and black Converse high-tops. Now in her early thirties, Marlene remained a semi-beauty; although the startling bloom of her youth was gone, she still had the bones, the oval, strong-featured face beloved of Baroque sculptors. She still wore her hair as a tumble of thick black, neck-length curls, skillfully cut so as to draw attention from the left side of her face, where the eye was glass. Marlene had a wiry, muscular body, not quite that of a flyweight in training but close; she worked out with boxing bags and ropes every day, as she had since childhood.

Marlene's car, a venerable VW square-back in yellow, was parked illegally as usual, and as usual the old D.A. placard had kept the meter maids away. In the luggage space in the rear of the car lay a Neapolitan mastiff, coal black, red-eyed, and of prodigious size and excellent training. It responded to commands in Sicilian and answered to the ridiculous name of Sweetie.

Marlene entered her car and drove off to the south. She turned the radio on and then snapped it off again. Instead, she sang to herself. She had a decent, soft contralto. She sang a verse from the old Billie Holiday song: "If I don't call no copper, when I get beat up by my poppa, ain't nobody's business but my own." Yes, indeed.

Lucy Karp waited outside the old building on Mott Street that housed the Chinese Consolidated Benevolent Association and its famous Chinese school. It irked her that she had to wait to be picked up, as she was less than a quarter of a mile from home, but she understood that her mother had enemies who might try to hurt her. Lucy was the only Caucasian person in her class at the Chinese school, which had been founded to transmit Chinese culture and language to the children of immigrants. Why the authorities had allowed her entry was something of a mystery, although Lucy thought that it had to do with the net of favors both her father and her mother had bestowed in the past and might bestow in the future to various residents of Chinatown. Besides this, the elders of the association had allowed themselves to be charmed by the idea of a *gwailo* child who spoke their language so well, rather as they might have been charmed by a performing dog, and Chinese-American parents were wont to use her example as a rod to inspire their less willing offspring to excel in their studies.

The accomplishment had not been anticipated, although Lucy had been playing with Chinese children since before kindergarten, picking up Cantonese. It had turned out, much to her own and her parents' surprise, that Lucy had something of a genius for languages. Besides Cantonese (in which she was perfectly bilingual and now affected a slangy Hong Kong accent) she had learned Mandarin in school, spoke enough Sicilian to impress the few remaining speakers of that tongue in Little Italy and delight her aged great-grandmother, and was working successfully on several other tongues.

She slouched against the wall, swinging her book bag, chatting casually with other students and people she knew. Chinatown is a tight community, and Lucy was mildly famous in it; people would actually seek her out to converse in Chinese with the prodigy. But, of course, Lucy was not actually Chinese, not bound by the loving, merciless bonds of family and clan, and her demeanor was not all that could be wished from a young girl, the lowest and most useless of the ten thousand things, not sufficiently deferent at all, which was why, when the young people said her name in Cantonese they slightly lifted the tone of the first syllable so that it came out almost as *lóuhsai*, which in that language is a less-than-respectful word for boss.

Lucy felt a hand on her shoulder and started, and then relaxed and smiled when she saw who it was, a reedy oriental man in his early fifties, dressed in a cheap plastic raincoat over a navy blue suit and a white shirt, tie-less, buttoned to the collar. He looked at first glance like a clerk in one of the many trading firms of the neighborhood, but closer inspection would have made that assessment unlikely. For one thing, his face was curiously scarred, in particular by an indentation in the skull behind his right eye, as if someone had battered it in with a pipe. The hand he laid on the girl was scarred too, its nails malformed and yellow. And he did not move like a clerk.

"*Cháo ông,* Tran," said Lucy.

"*Cháo cô,* Lucy," said Tran Vinh, and he continued in Vietnamese. "How was your day in school? Did you study hard?"

"I studied sufficiently," said Lucy in the same language, sliding past the question. School was a bore, and she studied just enough to keep out of trouble. Learning Chinese or other languages was no work at all, so she preferred to devote her energy to that. Unfortunately, this is often a consequence of special genius. "Can we go for *goûter,* Uncle Tran?" she said, switching to French. He had taught her French in four weeks, much to her mother's annoyance, since she no longer had a private tongue for discussions with Tran. Tran worked for Marlene in various capacities, some of which required a good deal of privacy.

"Of course, my dear," said Tran. "Noodles or cake?"

They continued down the street, holding hands, chatting in a mixture of French and Vietnamese, she asking for translations of things seen and thought of, he answering, making small jokes. He was happy, more than he could recall being for a long time. The girl was about the age his daughter had been when she was killed, along with his wife, by American bombs. After that the war and hope for victory had kept him alive, and after the victory, when the northerners had purged the people who had led the war in the south, especially those like Tran who came from old bourgeois families, nothing had kept him alive, except his apparently indestructible body and a mild desire to see what the next day might add to an already incomprehensible life. That he now found himself amanuensis to a remarkable woman and bodyguard to various other women and to this little girl was a situation no stranger than the rest of his life, which he had begun with the desire to teach French literature in a Saigon *lycée* and raise a family. Now he no longer thought of making plans beyond the day, beyond sharing a little meal with this child and walking her home.

Lucy, for her part, was as fond of Tran as she was of any adult besides her parents. He taught her things, he was amusing in three languages, and he did not treat her like a baby, which her father, for all his many virtues, still did. At ten, Lucy had entered that period when the interior life is first discovered, the period to which many intelligent women look back across the bleeding battlefield of sex as to a golden age. She had always been a somewhat secretive child, but now she fully inhabited a world separate from that of her parents, and resented their intrusions into it, especially those of her mother. Lucy loved her mother dearly and admired her to the high heavens, but would have preferred a mom who was not, by profession, a detective. Thus she cherished her outings with Tran, a man at home with secrets, a man from a world utterly outside the conventional tedium of home and school, a man with the air of those mysterious characters that appeared in the fantasy novels she had recently discovered and now devoured in stacks. She knew, of course, that Tran was a . . . no, not an assassin, but someone who could efficiently and calmly kill. She had the previous summer observed this with her own eyes. She accepted this as she accepted, in the reasonable manner of children, the presence of violence and danger in her own life, as a child living near a pulp mill accepts the stench or the daughter of coal miners will come to ignore the omnipresence of black grit. On a similar level of subconsciousness she understood that Tran loved her and would do, within very broad limits, what she asked, and would not necessarily tell her mother about it. This knowledge contributed in no small way to her already remarkable self-confidence, similar to that exhibited by children in fairy tales who come into possession of a genie.

"Uncle Tran," she said around a mouthful of chocolate eclair at Ferrara's, "will you take me shooting this weekend?"

"I will," said Tran, "providing you have done your lessons properly and if your mother permits. You know we must borrow the little revolver."

"I don't want to shoot the little revolver. I want to shoot your pistol, the Tokarev."

Tran's face did not show it, but he was surprised. He was not aware that Lucy knew he owned a Tokarev TT 7.62mm pistol. Of course, he lived in a room behind Marlene's office, and Lucy had the run of the place. He wondered what else she had discovered. He became conscious of the hard lump the pistol made in the small of his back. He had owned the thing for nearly thirty years, ever since it had been sent from the Soviet Union with a load of other military junk as a gesture of fraternal socialist solidarity with the Viet Minh in their anti-colonial struggle, had hidden it when he was arrested, and it had been nearly the only thing he had taken with him when he fled his country. It had gallons of blood on it and even Tran, who was the last thing from squeamish, did not care to see it in Lucy's little white hand.

"That would not be wise," he said. "It is too large for you, and your mother would never allow it."

"It is not too large," said Lucy, shifting from French to Cantonese, where she had the advantage of fluency. "My mother let me shoot a nine once, which is larger. Also, suppose a kidnapper came in here and shot you. I would have to take your weapon and defend us both. How could I do that, never having shot it before?" She affected her most fetching sulk. "Besides, it is because I am only a girl. If I were a boy, you would never object."

After a considerate pause, Tran replied, in French, "It is certainly true that you are a girl—more to the point, one who does not know her place. Your attempts to manipulate me are shameless indeed. Were it up to me, I would have you drowned."

Lucy giggled. "But, truly, *Bác* Tran, will you?"

"Truly, it is up to your mother," said Tran. "Myself, I wash my hands."

On the passenger manifest of the Delta flight from Tucson to O'Hare and that of the connecting flight from O'Hare to La Guardia he was listed as Fernando Zedillo. His mother, whom he worshiped, called him Paco, as did his four sisters. Had he any friends, they might have called him Paco too, but he was not the friendly sort. In the company of men, there would be drinking, and someone who did not know him, or was drunk enough to forget who he was, would say something impugning the virtue of his mother, or comment on Paco's physical appearance, after which Paco would be obliged to commit one of his frequent murders. This inevitably came as a surprise to the company, since Paco had the face of an angel: his eyes were large with long, thick lashes, the bones of his face were delicate and sharply etched, his neck was narrow, long, and graceful, his mouth a pouting, dusky rose. He wore his thick black hair long, with long sideburns.

Paco was, as might be expected, a terror among the women, and had been getting it regularly from the age of twelve, which was two years after he had committed his first assassination, number one of, at last count, thirty-two. He was at this time twenty-three years of age. His actual success with women made any accusations of effeminacy particularly hard to take, and he did not take any, not ever.

Subsequent to his first few killings in the environs of Nogales, Arizona, one of his uncles had sent him down to the ancestral home in Hermosillo, in Sonora state, to make himself useful to another uncle. Paco's family had been gangsters of one sort or another for several generations, and while *chuteros* were easy to find, one who both looked as if he had just come from his mother's breast *and* who shot with such utter calm was rare indeed. Besides this, he had no problem doing women and children, which was not usual in those circles, but sometimes desirable. His reputation grew in the underworld of Sonora, until the mere rumor that he had been retained would cause rivals to flee with their families, ensure the prompt repayment of overdue debt, or the uttering forth of formerly guarded secrets. They called him El Chivato, which is slang for a boisterous or unruly child, although he was far from unruly. His owner and uncle, a hoodlum who called himself Don Vincente Montez, found him in all ways easily bid and no trouble at all (except to his victims). He spent most of his spare time watching television and having sexual intercourse. His chief disadvantage from Don Vincente's standpoint was his insistence on being given time off for holidays, including Christmas, Epiphany, Easter (the whole week), the Feast of the Virgin of Guadeloupe, and the Feast of All Saints, as well as the birthdays of his mother and his sisters.

Don Vincente could live with that. After El Chivato had suppressed Vincente's personal enemies, the boy had become an important source of revenue, and was rented out to gangsters, politicians, and betrayed lovers throughout western Mexico and as far north as Nogales. He was not, however, pleased with the request from Jodón Obregon. In vain did he argue, as an uncle should, that the boy was not ready for such a trip, that he knew nothing of the ways of North America or of a big city. He had not been even to Mexico City above a half dozen times. Surely there were local boys, in New York, as he had seen many times on the TV? No, it had to be El Chivato. There was a place to stay, someone to supply all his needs. Well, in that case—but the cost, this would have to reflect the danger. Don Vincente named an outrageous figure, and to his immense surprise and disappointment (since he might have demanded more) Obregon agreed without cavil.

As he considered it later, the gangster felt it was for the best. If the boy was successful, there was all that money; if he failed to return, then the money from his many fees that Don Vincente held for him, which was by now well over a million pesos, would not have to be paid out. El Chivato expressed no emotion when told that he was going to New York, only asking whether it was farther away than Tucson.

FOUR

The door of the East Village Women's Shelter on Avenue C was made of eighth-inch steel plating and set into a steel frame. The windows of the storefront, which had once been a kosher deli and after that a bodega, were blocked with thick plywood under gray galvanized sheeting, Marlene rang the buzzer, and when the intercom box crackled the question, she told it who she was and the door buzzed open. After that door there was a short, well-lit vestibule and then another door, this one of glass with a heavy grille. A thick-bodied, dark-skinned woman behind a desk looked up from her book, then came around and opened the door.

"How's it going, Verda?" Marlene asked, entering.

"I ain't dead," said the woman. "You here to see her?"

"Yeah, is she free?"

"In her office," said Verda, and she sat heavily back into a swivel chair. Marlene saw that her book was a ragged high school math text. The door Marlene knocked on had been the entrance to a storeroom when the place was a retail establishment. Inside it was small office, as cramped as a lunar lander, but not as clean, lined on three sides by filing cabinets and green steel shelves loaded with cardboard boxes of paper and books. In the scant vacant center of this space, behind a scarred old schoolroom desk, sat Mattie Duran, the founder and genius of the institution. She was a blocky red-brown woman, with a flat, hard, bright-eyed *indio* face, and long, thick hair worn center-parted and braided. She wore a faded turquoise blue sweatshirt with a red bandanna around her neck, black jeans, and plain black cowboy boots

"What?" she said when Marlene walked in, looking up from a pad she had been scribbling on. "Oh, it's you," she continued by way of greeting. Marlene was not sure whether Mattie Duran liked her or simply tolerated her for her usefulness to the operation of the shelter. That Marlene had actually killed men was, she imagined, the main point in her favor. That Marlene lived with a man, in middle-class comfort, and was a loyal, if somewhat heterodox, Catholic, were all points against. For her own part, Marlene admired Duran and was to an extent fascinated by her. Marlene's partner, Harry Bello, had looked into Duran's past when Marlene first started to work with her. The woman proved to have an interesting background. She'd shot her stepfather down in Texas, blown a hole in his skull while he lay sleeping, and done a stretch in prison for it, and after that had hung with a bunch of guys who pulled bank jobs but never did any time for any of that. After the gang expired, in the violent way of such associations, she'd just shown up in New York with a hard face and plenty of cash money to start this shelter.

It was not an official shelter. It received no money from state or city agencies. It accepted only women and children who were in immediate grave danger of murder or serious injury. The official agencies frowned on the EVWS, because Mattie did not share paper with them. Women entered the EVWS and disappeared forever from the rolls of the social bureaucracy. On the other hand, the cops loved it, because it gave them a place to stash women who would otherwise have required twenty-four-hour protection, which was why Mattie never had much trouble with inspections.

Marlene did mostly transfers for the EVWS, and a little frightening-off work against the loved ones, although the guys who put their women into East Village often required more frightening than Marlene was comfortable in supplying at this stage in her life. Mattie was not sympathetic.

They had some brief business to transact, some details about moving a family, and as usual they got into an argument. It was hard to get through an hour with Mattie Duran without at least a few minutes of bared teeth and clenched fists. The woman extracted some kind of vital energy from combat, and Marlene was one of the few people in her life who was not crushed by her personality. This argument was about a woman named Kitty Valone, who, with her three children, was presently resident at the shelter. It was her fourth stay there. Each time she was placed, with enormous difficulty, at a new address, her estranged hubby, Ernesto, would find her. And she would take him in. After a brief period of bliss, Ernesto would try to kill her or one of the kids (again) and Kitty would wind up back at the shelter and Ernesto would do his stretch in jail and the charade (in Marlene's eyes) would start all over. Marlene felt she had enough work to do on behalf of women who *wanted* to escape. She declined to involve herself with women who lacked the sense to seek their own survival.

But Mattie never gave up. She would scream at women, threaten them, but every waif had an unlimited claim on her time and space.

"I should whack the fucker myself," muttered Duran after the argument had burned itself out.

"I didn't hear that," said Marlene, and left.

Karp sat in a straight chair in his kitchen waiting for supper. The room was a large area of a large SoHo loft that his wife had occupied for a dozen years, from before SoHo was invented. During Karp's brief period of wealth, when he had won some big ones for a tort firm, they had poured cash into the loft, nearly as much as would have made a down payment on a nice West Side co-op, which Karp would have preferred, truth be told, but Marlene loved her loft, and here they now dwelt in something approaching luxury, in a residence whose only connection with its past as a wire factory was an eight-hundred-gallon hard rubber electroplating vat pressed into service as a hot tub. The loft had climate control, and Swedish oak flooring (blood-colored Mexican tiles in the kitchen), dropped ceilings with track lighting, real walls with doors in them, and a kitchen out of *Architectural Digest*: a stainless double-door refrigerator, an immense Vulcan stove, and everything else white enameled, or birch, or butcher block, except (this typically Marlene) in the very center, huge, dark, ugly, and round, Marlene's immigrant grandmother's dining table.

Karp sighed and shifted uneasily. He was not allowed to cook. His few early attempts in the kitchen had resulted in injury to himself, the food, or, worst of all, Marlene's precious implements. He passed again through his mind the incidents of the interview in Williamsburg, which still rankled, and he felt, more than he usually did, the need for familial warmth and comfort. He looked about and attempted to derive some. Karp loved his family dearly, but if pressed in his secret heart, he would have admitted that it was the one he would have chosen if families were ordered out of glossy catalogs. His wife, stirring the bean soup with a traditional wooden spoon, might have been mistaken for a paragon of domesticity. Marlene was, in fact, a superb cook. Each weekend the kitchen filled with spicy steam, as she generated a week's worth of meals for the freezer as well as a feast for the Sunday. And a good mother too, of a sort. Karp cast his eye over his offspring. Lucy had a cutting board set up at the table and was making the salad, her usual chore. He watched her shave a carrot into thin sticks with a knife sharp enough to amputate a finger. She had been doing this since the age of seven, and Karp was well able to suppress his desire to snatch the thing out of her hand (and probably into his own carotid). Karp had been one of a family of three brothers and so had no direct experience with raising girls, but he still retained memories of girl cousins, and could not recall them being at all like Lucy. An odd child, an even odder girl child. She had never played with dolls, preferring from an early age guns and other implements of destruction. And there was an inwardness about her that worried him. You could never tell what she was up to, and so you could not extend over her the paternal cloak of protection as a dad should. And the languages. Karp, a confirmed monoglot, was amazed and somewhat pleased with his daughter's apparent genius in this area, but again, it was so . . . unexpected. When he looked at the girl nowadays he found himself wondering, What next?

"So, Lucy—learn any new languages today?" he assayed. "Polynesian?"

"Polynesian isn't a language, Daddy, it's a language group. There are over a hundred Polynesian languages."

"Uh-huh. How's the Chinese coming?"

"We're doing four-stroke radicals," said Lucy shortly, slicing. (She loved him, but she was not going to patronize him, or flirt. This was hard on Karp; he missed her being four.)

There seemed no reasonable comeback to that, aside from asking what such a thing might be, and Lucy telling him, at length, and giving him (prematurely, he thought) the creepy feeling parents get when their kids know more than they do, so Karp turned his attention to the boys. The two-year-old twins, Isaac and Giancarlo, called Zak and Zik, had, of course, been fed long since by Posie, the live-in nursemaid, and were currently on the kitchen floor amid a selection of their toys. Zak was hammering with the plastic hammer from his tool set on the heavy-duty snap fastener that Marlene used to secure the door of the cabinet under the sink. Zak's goal was to penetrate this forbidden space and drink deep from the delicious-looking bottles of poisonous substances kept there. Zak at two was, as they say, a handful. Zik was scribbling with washable markers on a large newsprint pad, and his hands and feet. Next to him, comfortable on the floor, was Posie, drawing mandala-like designs on her very own newsprint pad. Zik began to color on Posie's bare feet, prompting giggles. Marlene had picked the woman up out of some domestic-abuse fracas. She was a buxom, moon-faced innocent with long, straight black hair and bad teeth. She came from some obscure hollow in Pennsylvania and had been on the street from the age of fourteen until the night Marlene had given her shelter and a job. Karp had to admit she was a good baby-sitter, although a cool and elegant Swedish au pair would have been more to his liking. Yet another nodule of discomfort around the hearth.

Then there was the fount and source herself. Karp watched his wife work at the stove, as she bent to take a casserole out of the oven, specifically at the way her buttocks moved under the thin, worn blue jeans, still as solid and round as a nectarine. The outline of the pancake holster under her jersey, and the faint whiff of exploded gunpowder mixed with her Arpège brought forth another sigh. The gun itself sat in its gun safe, but there was the evidence that this was not your regular mom and wifey.

Marlene turned, casserole in hand, and caught his eye.

"What're *you* looking at?" she asked.

"You. Your ass, if you must know."

"Watch that mouth, buster," she said, thumping the dish down on the table.

"Hey, I can admire your ass. We're married."

"Not for long if you don't learn to behave. Posie: bath time. Get these horrible monsters out of my sight. Lucy: toss the salad and set the table, please."

"What should I do?" said Karp.

"Nothing. Just sit there like a pasha and thank your lucky stars for a house that runs like a clock. And clean up after, of course."

Later, in the relative peace of the kitchen, the dishwasher chuckling, they exchanged their news.

"Not that great," said Karp when asked how Williamsburg had gone. "He thinks I'm anti-Semitic." He said it derisively, meaning to solicit a supportive response from his wife, perhaps an incredulous gasp, but what she said was, "Maybe you are."

"What! How can you say that? Jesus, Marlene, the guy's a nut, a fanatic."

Marlene poured herself another shot of Medaglia d'Oro from the big steel hourglass espresso pot and said, "Probably is, but on the other hand, can you imagine anyone accusing me of being anti-Italian? Or anti-Catholic?"

"Why? Because you cook macaroni and go to church? I don't see you out there throwing rocks at abortion clinics."

"Don't raise your voice. Abortion clinics have nothing to do with it. It's not my fault you've cut yourself off from your own people—"

"My *people*! Since when did we get so biblical around here?"

". . . your *people*, if I could just finish, and it's not really your fault either. I have this big, warm, intact family, and in spite of my speckled past, I'm connected to my childhood, which includes the Church, and you're not, mainly because of your family, who you don't get along with, and who are also barely Jewish anymore."

"What do you mean, *barely*? My brother Richard is so Orthodox he gets re-circumcised once a year just to make sure."

"That's his reaction to the situation—burrowing in. Maybe your reaction is just as extreme in the other direction. Look at the situation, Butch. Your mother dies when you're just a kid, your father marries a . . ."

"Bimbo?"

"I was going to say uncongenial and not very motherly younger woman," said Marlene, driving on like a psychic bulldozer. "So all three of you go away from home. Your brother Dan becomes a clone of your dad, Richard marries a rabbi's daughter, you marry a nice Jewish girl, just like Mom, whom you ignore, and she runs off, and then you marry someone as little like your mother as you can find, who nonetheless has a great big family that you can slide into without having to think much about it, and in which no one expects much of you because you're like a permanent guest. Perfect, except I get these sly digs about my religion from time to time. . . ."

"I don't—"

"Shhh! Occasional sly digs, which I ignore, but which, if you notice, Lucy takes more seriously, and now this rabbi gives you a hard time and you come to me for sympathy. Which I would be glad to give, if I understood anything at all about your spiritual life, which I don't because that's all a kind of joke to you and you never talk about it."

"Thank you, Dr. Freud! What's to talk? I don't believe in that stuff, Marlene, I never have. And I don't believe in clans either, these little groups—this one's inside, the other one's outside. It pisses me off."

"Too bad for you, then," said Marlene. "They exist. It's like not believing in gravity. Oh, I'll just jump off this building, doesn't affect me, no, sir . . ."

"What're you getting at, Marlene?" Karp snapped, more violently than he had intended. "You want me to convert? You want me to lay *ts'fillin* in the morning? What? I don't understand."

Marlene finished her coffee, rose, and placed her cup and pot on the drain board.

"My point," she said, as if explaining something to a dull child, "was that although you yourself are miraculously free of the ethnic problems that affect the rest of us, it is a fact that you got yourself canned last year, from the only job you ever really liked, largely because you got yourself involved in a racial situation that was over your head, and now you're in another mess with this rabbi, who they sent you to see presumably because they figured you had some special understanding there. Everybody's on a team, Butch. People start getting anxious when they can't read the letters on your chest."

A long, uncomfortable silence. Marlene tilted her head to fix him with her real eye. Karp glowered at her, but as always, that tilt of her head, birdlike, interested, the symbol of her damaged body and its resident courageous spirit, charmed him and drained any resentment from his heart. "Well," he said dryly, "you may have a point. I will strive to do better in that department. And how was *your* day?"

"Oh, a day like all days, filled with those events that alter and illuminate our lives, as Walter Cronkite used to say. Girls and guns. Oh, and lest you think you're the only member of this family who doesn't live up to expectations, I got a tongue-lashing from Mattie about what a shitty feminist I am. Yes, you may well be amazed. She's got this goddamn woman who can't be made to understand that her husband is going to hurt her, that he's always going to hurt her, and every time we help her out she ends up getting back with him. I think she calls him, in fact, or lets it out where she is so he finds her. So I say there's so many woman desperately *trying* to break away, we don't have time to fuck with an idiot like this, cut her loose"—she made a helpless gesture—"but you know Mattie."

"Yeah. I wish I didn't."

"Oh, she's all right, really. I guess you have to admire her. She never gives up."

"Neither did Hitler," said Karp. "Marlene, she's a vigilante."

It was an old argument that Marlene did not at this moment wish to pursue. She shrugged off the comment and said, "You have to work with all kinds of people, and you have to take them for what they are, not for what you'd prefer them to be. That was Marlene's daily spiritual advice nugget, and I expect you to take it to heart."

"I will. You could put out a calendar."

"I could. The feminist failure date book." She stood and stretched. "What I need, and what I intend to have, is a long, perfumed, luxurious tub. Care to join me?"

"That's definitely the best offer I've had all day."

"Well, I should certainly *hope* so," said Marlene.

Hassan Daoud had been in the United States for ten years, since shortly after the Six Day War, in fact, when the famous lightning victory of the Israelis had convinced him that the Arab armies were never going to push the Jews into the sea and get him back into his grandfather's land in the Jezreel. He had a cousin in America. Transportation was arranged, he worked double shifts in a warehouse for seven years, saved every penny, and was able to send for his wife, Rima, his son, Walid, and his daughter, Fatyma. He started baking the flat bread of the Middle East, as his father had before him, in a borrowed oven, in a space rented in a friend's garage. He would bake the night through and then deliver the loaves before dawn to a string of Arab grocery stores in Brooklyn and lower Manhattan, using an old Pontiac station wagon, also borrowed. Again, every penny saved, until he had the down payment on the storefront off Atlantic Avenue he now occupied, and saw the lettering in real gold, in Arabic and English inscribed on the window, *Ahsen Foruhn*, BEST BAKERY (for it was nothing less), and his own name beneath it. A proud day, second only to the day his first son had been born.

The bakery prospered. Hassan worked like the devil, and Rima worked silently beside him, as a woman should, like a donkey. They had three more children, of whom only one, thank God, was a girl. The bread was in demand, not only among the Arabs, whose population in Brooklyn had exploded in the last decade, but also the specialty-food stores in Manhattan were buying, even some of the local supermarkets. He bought a large white GM step-in delivery truck. Each package of a dozen he sold for the equivalent of a day's wage in Palestine. He was rich, which was only to be expected. In America everyone was rich; why else live in so godless a nation?

What weighed him down, and made him curse, and stamp, and pull on his mustache, and beat his wife (although only with a very small stick) was the two older children. Walid, his firstborn, was involved in some stupid political thing, running with a group of worthless hoodlums who fancied themselves *fedayin*. This had attracted the attention of the police, and Hassan was waiting for the inevitable visit demanding a bribe. The boy had been beaten, of course, and given extra work to keep him out of trouble, but a father's eyes could not be everywhere. Still, politics, however stupid, was not disgraceful. Hassan could sit with the men and sip coffee and lament his worthless son. Many of the other men, of course, had worthless sons too, and it was pleasant to compete as to who had the hardest lot as a father, whose son was more ungrateful for the many benefits showered upon him. But of the other thing, the daughter, he could not speak. He could barely let it flow through his mind.

The fact was that Fatyma, at fourteen, was already a whore, or the next thing to a whore. Her head was filled with thoughts of fornication. She listened to the music of fornication on her radio (before he had smashed it) and went to American films (that were all fornication and blasphemy) and would have gone out of the house dressed as a whore, with a painted face (and had he not found actual whore's face paint where she had hidden it under her mattress?). He had stopped that for the time being by chaining her ankle to a radiator at night, on a long chain that enabled her to visit the toilet. This, however, was not a permanent solution. In the old country he would have paid a woman to slice out her sinful parts with a razor, as was done with uncontrollable girls, but the rules were different here. Hassan did not want to go to jail. Already he had a stack of letters from the truant officer, wanting to know why Fatyma was not in school. He did not think the truant officer would comprehend the problem. Americans had no idea of honor or of the responsibilities of a father. No, the solution was to marry her off while she was still marriageable, before she got with some boy and lost her honor, in which case he would have to kill her, jail or no jail.

So he had written letters and had found the right man, a prosperous importer in Baalbek called Zaid al-Habashi, who was fifty and looking for a younger wife to add to his household. The match was made by post, contracts were signed, passport and ticket purchased. In two days she would leave, escorted by a family going back to Beirut on a visit.

Naturally, when Hassan had announced this news, Fatyma had wailed, and cursed, and even an exceptionally severe beating had not stopped her noises. She was wailing still. He could hear her upstairs from the back room of the bakery where he worked, even over the rumble of the kneading machine. Eventually, he knew, she would stop crying and accept her fate, as all women did. But he was glad that it was only two more days.

In the night, in the short time between the preparation of the dough and the time the baking must begin, while the family slept, Fatyma worked. The chain that bound her to the iron radiator leg was long enough to reach the bathroom in the hallway, but was also long enough to reach into the next bedroom, where her brothers slept. She knew where Walid kept his knife, a long, curved dagger, old but sharp. It had been in the family for years, always in the possession of the oldest son. Walid was snoring like a pig and did not stir as she removed it from his bureau drawer.

Back in her room, she frantically scraped the soft, old wood upon which the radiator leg rested. It took her nearly two hours to chisel away a depression deep enough so that she could slip the loop of chain beneath it. Free now, she went to her closet and used the knife to pry up a floorboard. Beneath it, tightly rolled, were two pairs of jeans and four T-shirts, forbidden garments that she had shoplifted from stores in downtown Brooklyn. She dressed in jeans and a red T-shirt, pulled on socks and her cheap sneakers, and her ugly, knee-length gray tweed coat. The two suitcases her father had provided for the journey were packed with the clothes needed for her new life in Lebanon as the second wife of a fat old man. Choosing the smaller of the two, she spilled out the embroidered gown, the slippers, the headdress, the veil, and put in her scant American wardrobe.

"What are you doing, Fatyma?"

Her breath stopped in her throat. Leila, her little sister, was sitting up in bed and watching her. The child's eyes were wide and confused in the faint gleam from the street. Fatyma sat on her sister's bed and stroked her hair.

"It's late. You have to go back to sleep."

"But what are you *doing*?" the child insisted.

"Well, you know I am getting married, right? Well, my new husband is waiting outside for me. I have to climb out the window and meet him, and I have to be very, very quiet, because if anyone hears me, then I can't get married. That's why you have to be quiet and go back to sleep."

"But *why* do you?" asked the child.

"It's a tradition," Fatyma said, an answer the child had heard before.

"Will you come back?"

"Oh, sure," Fatyma lied. "I'll see you tomorrow. I'll wear my wedding dress for you, okay?"

When the child was settled under the covers again, Fatyma put her brother's knife in the pocket of her coat. She placed in the suitcase a plastic bag containing the lipstick and blusher (also boosted) that her father had not found, some underwear and toilet articles, and two paperback books, both heavily thumbed. One was called *Fountain of Desire*. These words were printed on the cover in swirling pink letters, over an illustration of a darkly handsome man embracing a woman in an old-fashioned dress. The other book was *Norma Jean*, a biography of Marilyn Monroe. Fatyma had stolen them from the public library. She believed they contained nearly all of what she needed to know to survive in her new life. Slowly, carefully, she forced up her window and slipped onto the fire escape, clanking faintly. She descended and walked quickly toward the Atlantic Avenue subway station. She stood on the IND platform for what seemed like a long time, with her hand on the knife in her pocket. A D train for Manhattan arrived, and Fatyma boarded it.

When the train doors swished shut, she sighed and relaxed some-what. At last she was bound for America.

Although El Chivato had never actually been imprisoned, he had visited jails many times, in Nogales, Tucson, and various places in Mexico. Many of his clients were incarcerated and wished still to conduct their businesses or to deal with difficult witnesses. The James A. Thomas Center, one of Rikers Island's ten facilities, was the largest jail he had ever visited. Passing through visitor clearance, the youth was conscious of a small uneasiness, which stemmed not so much from the precise venue, but from being in a crowd of strangers and unarmed. The guard who passed them in with the other visitors was, for example, staring at him insolently, and he could do nothing about it under the circumstances. This made him cross.

The guard had seen a good many odd couples pass through his metal detector, but even so, this one stood out. The woman had a big mane of blond hair done in the current Farrah style, or maybe it was a wig, and she had a coarse, lively face, with the eyebrows plucked into fine geometric parabolas and the wide mouth greased a shining reddish purple. She had on a wild jungle-print blouse with the top two buttons open. The guard didn't mind taking a look, and saw she had a red lace bra on, brim full of tan flesh, on which trembled a petite gold cross. She also wore shiny aquamarine slacks tight enough to show the slice of her vulva, tucked into white boots trimmed with fur, and had over her shoulders a fake fur coat of a bluish color not found among the furry creatures of the wild. Whore, was his thought, although she had signed in as the prisoner's wife. Maybe she was both—not an unfamiliar combo on the Rikers visit-ing list.

The kid was definitely in a different class of weirdness, however. He was a little guy, a Latino of some kind, and the guard was glad he was not an inmate, because he had the kind of girl's face and lithe body that would have had knife fights breaking out all over the joint on the first day. The hat was the first thing, a tall white cone with a wide brim, the kind cowboys used to wear in the old movies. His shirt was black and embroidered and had pearl buttons, and his neatly pressed whipcord trousers just brushed the tops of elabo-rately worked cowboy boots in black and white, which had tooled silver tips on them. He wore a peculiar loose pale coat, like a raincoat but made of a heavier material like canvas, that hung down nearly to the top of his boots.

People in the line were looking at him and some were making comments, and the guard could see the kid didn't like it. He passed them through with only a cursory examination of the woman's large leather bag. It was late in his shift, and he didn't want any trouble.

By the time El Chivato and Obregon's woman, Connie Erbes, were seated at the visitors' table, and Jesus Obregon was staring through the glass from the other side, the young man was in a foul mood. He had looked into a number of the faces of those who had mocked him, and should he ever encounter them again it would be too bad for them. Obregon greeted him effusively in Spanish, asked after his uncle and the rest of his family, uttered compliments and congratulations on hearing that they were—thank God—quite well, inquired about his flight, asked if he had encountered any trouble in getting to the apartment in Washington Heights and meeting Connie.

Then to business. El Chivato listened in silence to the story of the deal, the man Lucky, the betrayal, the lost product, the arrest, the failure of the bribe. The youth had heard such stories before. As the suspicious lump is to the surgeon, or the leaking pipe to the plumber, they were the basis of his trade. He listened further while Jesus Obregon explained what he wanted done.

"I understand," said El Chivato. "I find this man and I tell him, you must confess to the police that you have killed the *lahara* and not the Obregons. With them, I tell him, you go to jail, but if not, something worse."

"You will feed him his little *chile* chopped up in a tortilla," said Obregon.

"A taco," said El Chivato without inflection, as if correcting a minor point of technique, and then asked, "And suppose he does not confess, or dies somehow? Also, it may be that I can't find him. What then?"

"What then? You understand that while this is a comfortable jail, I would still rather be outside. So the most important thing is to get our release from the false charge. I would naturally prefer to combine this with fucking that *pendejo*, but if not, then not. There is the prosecutor. Perhaps a judge. You understand how these things are done."

"Yes, I do," said El Chivato, and for the first time he gave Jesus Obregon the favor of his remarkable, glittering smile.

The man who had murdered Ali al-Qabbani and thrown his weighted body off a Brooklyn pier was the product of a desert society and could therefore not have been expected to know much about tides and currents, especially the peculiar ones present in New York harbor and its various rivers. For the same reason he also was not overly familiar with the great increase in buoyancy attendant upon decomposition of the human body, or that to make sure a corpse does not float, you must make sure that the internal cavities are well punctured. Bloated like a young whale, Ali's corpse easily dragged the trivial weight of the concrete blocks that were wired to his ankles (which in any case soon fell away as the flesh softened and stripped off) and set boldly off upon the broad waters.

Arriving after many a tidal diversion at the Statue of Liberty ferry slip, the thing became the concern of Detective Al Carnera, who caught the new floater out of the First Precinct, within whose purview lies the southernmost point of Manhattan, including the slip. Carnera was, perhaps inevitably, known as Primo in the cops, although (perhaps because) he was not in the least like the late gigantic pug, but rather a rotund, balding, mild-eyed, scholarly-looking man of forty-eight, whose tastes ran to dull cardigans and comfortable cord suits.

He had a set of horn-rimmed glasses on his nose (the nostrils thereof having been liberally smeared with Vicks against the smell) as he peered over the dank ruin of Ali. Carnera had been with the First for twelve years and had seen all kinds of floaters. He was glad that this one was male and not mutilated in any way that he could see. Aside from that, he did not mind watching autopsies. He especially liked watching this particular assistant medical examiner work.

"Shot from behind, close range, four . . . one, two, three, four, no, I tell a lie, five times," said the M.E. He had a soft Irish accent and thinning red hair, and he was not as drunk as he would be later in the day. His name was Maher.

"A professional hit," said Carnera.

"Well, sure, you'd know about such things, being a detective and all that," said the M.E. "In my own professional capacity, however,

I believe I am almost ready to rule out both suicide and accidental death."

Carnera laughed, and Maher joined him, their noise echoing off the tiled walls.

"The entries are small," Maher observed, "and there are no exit wounds, which suggests a small-caliber weapon, the bullets bouncing around within the calvarium, doing great mischief. I expect a mere pudding when I come to crack his noggin open."

"How long would you say he's been dead, Doc?"

"Oh, a week, ten days, no more. He was slain in the dark of the moon by an attractive brunette with a Polish accent wearing Nuits de Paris and a pair of bloodred knickers. More than that I cannot say."

"How thick was the accent?"

Maher put on a look of mock affront. "Please, Detective, the profession frowns on rank speculation. But I was serious about him being killed in the dark. Take a look at this."

Maher went to the side of the exam table and lifted the corpse's shoulder slightly.

"A tattoo," said Carnera. "You're saying he shot the guy in the dark and stripped him and if he'd've seen the tattoo he would've cut it out?" Carnera thought for a moment and then added, "I like that. The clothes were stripped, but the fingers and the head weren't removed, which means the guy didn't have a sheet on him, or he was a stranger, so not much worry about somebody missing him or a bunch of people who could make an ID. It's night, the killer's in a hurry. Maybe he did it out in the open, some pier, or off a boat." He bent over and examined the tattoo.

"What do you think? Not a pro job. A jailhouse tattoo. Some kind of gang mark?"

"Possibly," said Maher, looking too. "But it looks like an inscription in Arabic to me."

"Yeah? You think the guy's an Arab?" They both looked at the corpse. It was grayish-white and the features were blurred and ragged, but it was not immediately out of probability that the man had once been numbered among that ethnic group.

Maher used an instrument to pry open the corpse's mouth. "A young man, but the teeth are carious and there's no dental work apparent except for one extraction. Thus unlikely to be an American, or a foreigner of the middle classes. Circumcised, as you see. So if it transpires that he is a Muslim boyo from east of Suez, Denny Maher for one would not fall off his chair."

Carnera watched as Maher sliced and sawed, scooped and weighed and talked into the microphone. The cop took prints from the dead man's fingers and used a Polaroid camera he had brought with him to photograph both the tattoo and the man's face. Maher removed the five .22 slugs from the brain, and Carnera put them in an evidence bag. Driving back to the precinct, he had a sudden thought and stopped off at a jewelry shop on Pine Street that he sometimes patronized, which was run by two Egyptian brothers. They told him that the inscription was indeed in Arabic and translated its meaning.

When he got back to the station house, the first thing he did was call Jim Raney at Midtown South homicide.

"Jim? Primo Carnera at the One. I got something here you might be interested in. You got those two Arab kids on the Shilkes thing—was there any suggestion that there could be more of them, like a gang?"

"Not a gang," said Raney carefully, "but there could be another guy. Why?"

"A floater yesterday. Five through the head with a .22, and he's got 'against the house of war' tattooed on his arm. Interested?"

"Yeah, you could say that," said Lucky Jim.

FIVE

This could complicate things," said Roland Hrcany. He was walking back and forth in front of his desk, breathing deeply, like a diver about to go under, and clenching and unclenching his fists, his biceps stretching his shirtsleeves into sausage skins. Neither of his visitors, the detectives Jim Raney and Primo Carnera, said a thing, but watched and listened with the blank, wary, patient expressions that were typical of their trade. Roland continued, talking as if to himself, "On the other hand, the only thing that connects this stiff to the Shilkes case is this tattoo. We have no evidence that he was even involved. So there's no reason to bring this in at all." He suddenly seemed to notice the detectives where they sat. He glared at Raney. "Is there?"

"Not especially," said Raney. "But somebody killed this guy. The case is up on the board. I'll be wanting to speak to Naijer and Hamshari. They've been saying all along that there was another guy along on the job. Maybe they got some idea of who whacked the John Doe. At least we could get a name."

"Yeah, but the problem is, let's say he was the lookout, he never went in. It doesn't matter. My problem here is these jokers find out their pal's dead, each of their stories is going to change to 'Hey, two guys did the job, sure, but one of them wasn't me.' I don't like it. It casts doubt."

Raney said, "We got Hamshari's print on the till. And the Shilkes ID on the two of them."

"Okay, the print, fine, although they'll argue that Hamshari was in the place before and left it then—"

"In blood?"

Roland frowned and made dismissive motions. "Okay, I take it back, maybe we got Hamshari, but that leaves Naijer. I want both of them. I don't want that little scumbag laying it off on a dead man."

Raney was starting to get irritated. Like most homicide cops, he liked Roland well enough, but there was something peculiar about this present line of argument, something nervous, a fussiness that was alien to the prosecutor's usual breezy and profane manner. Raney knew that Hrcany was taking the case himself, which was unusual for a bureau chief. Could he be worried enough about convicting the Arabs to try to suppress the John Doe homicide investigation? Roland was still maundering on: if this, if that, when Raney broke in with, "I don't understand where this is all leading, Roland, I really don't. I'm here talking to you because Carnera found a homicide and he came to me because it was connected to the Shilkes thing I caught, and we came to you because you're the D.A. and we need to talk to your defendants. I mean, it's a courtesy, Roland. We already solved the Shilkes killing. Naijer and Hamshari did it, and they're going down for it."

"How about letting me be the legal strategist here, Raney, okay?" said Roland testily.

"Great, I'll be the cop," snapped Raney.

"Oh, go right ahead, Detective," said Hrcany, flushing and clenching even more vigorously. "Be my guest! But if this case gets fucked, let me tell you, it's *your* ass that's going to fry."

Raney was out of his chair with warning strips of red popping out across his cheekbones. Carnera stood up too, however, and carefully positioned himself between the two men. "Yeah, well, we'll keep you up with how it goes, Roland," he said, "but if this conspiracy business heats up, you're going to be real glad we found this guy."

This stopped Roland short. "What are you talking about, conspiracy?"

Smiling, Carnera said, "Hey, I just read the papers, chief. Arabs kill a Jew, there's always a taste of this Middle East horseshit."

"Horseshit is right," said Roland contemptuously. "What,

you're listening to that fucking rabbi? He's got conspiracies on the brain."

"Yeah, right," agreed Carnera, "but, ah, Jim and I have been putting our heads together and, well, this John Doe kind of changes things in that department."

Raney could hardly keep a straight face, or rather, could hardly keep his scowl steady. Carnera was reflexively playing the good cop to his own bad cop, and Roland was going for it. Up to a point.

"Changes how?" Roland asked.

"The guy, the floater, was popped by a pro. These kids, we know, are not pros; they got no connection that we can find to any established terrorist group. But this guy had a tattoo that links him to this so-called House of War organization, which the perps are in too, so I'm asking myself, who whacked this guy and why? I'm getting a picture of another level. Somebody set these kids up maybe. Raney figures there was considerable planning went into this, but the perps are definitely in the short attention-span class."

Roland said impatiently, "Right, speculation is nice, but we have no evidence that these two acted on anybody's orders."

"Uh-huh." Carnera nodded. "Maybe that's why our guy took five through the head. Maybe he *was* that evidence. I mean, he was the contact. Maybe you should get serious about this, talk to the bosses, get some more juice into the investigation . . ."

"That's a lot of maybes," said Roland, waving his hand dismissively. "That's a big fucking balloon you're trying to blow up with about as much gas as a good fart. You got a floater with a tattoo, and all of a sudden we got Black September in town?"

Raney reached out and touched Carnera's sleeve. "Let's go, Primo, you're wasting your breath. This guy doesn't want to hear it."

"What I don't want is my case fucked up," Roland snarled.

The two detectives walked to the door. Raney paused for a parting shot. "Say, Roland—in the event somebody blows up a synagogue or whacks a couple more people of the Jewish persuasion, I'll remind you where you heard it first. It'll make a great story."

He closed the door on a burst of obscenity, and as they walked through the outer office of the Homicide Bureau, he remarked to Carnera, "What the fuck is it with him? He's turning into some kind of old lady."

Carnera shrugged. "He's the man now. It gets to some people. The big guy used to take the political heat for him. Now he's feeling the flames himself. I seen it happen before on the job, a million times. Guy passes lieutenant, all of a sudden he's Nervous Nelly. You want to go talk to these AY-rabs of yours or what?"

"Yeah," said Raney. He looked up and saw Karp talking to one of the clerks. "Speaking of the devil," he added as they left the office.

Karp was in the Homicide Bureau office on a routine administrative errand, something that he could have handled easily over the phone, but it had become his habit since starting his job with Keegan to descend without warning on the various bureaus or to stop in at courtrooms and view the proceedings there. Although Karp never interfered in any way, this was like poking an anthill with a stick; no one in the great warren of Centre Street was ever sure that at the next moment the long shadow of the D.A.'s guy would not fall across their doings. This had, in general, a salutary effect, as Karp was the furthest thing from a meddler or a spy, and the various satraps of the district attorney began to use him to convey messages, hints, suspicions, and trial balloons back to Keegan. Karp did not mind doing this (or not doing it, as he judged proper), but this was not his reason for roaming. It was simply that at unpredictable times of the day, it became unbearable for him to sit at a desk and talk on the phone or read. He was a large, healthy, athletic man, and sometimes he simply *had* to move, besides which he needed from time to time an actual immersion in the real life of the courts.

He had, of course, observed the two detectives leaving Hrcany's office, and had caught (as had everyone else within a hundred feet) the concluding sentiments of its occupant, and this, since he knew who Raney was and who Carnera was, made him curious indeed. He walked into Roland's office, after knocking and ignoring the shouted command to go away.

"Butch, I'm busy," said the bureau chief, glowering.

Karp ignored this too. "Something new on the Shilkes case?" he asked.

"What makes you think that?"

"Oh, you know—Raney's the guy on it and you're blowing a fuse at him. What'd he do, lose some evidence?"

"The case is under control," said Roland. Karp knew him well enough to know that had Roland really thought that, he would have screamed Karp out of his office, so he dragged a chair over with his foot and sat down.

"Make yourself comfortable," said Roland.

Karp waited a beat or two and said equably, "What is it with you, Roland?" Both of us worked for years for Jack Keegan. He trained us. We respect him. He respects us. I respect you. I *had* the job. Now you *got* the job . . . and you're acting like it's still the former asshole up there in the D.A. slot and I'm some kind of stooge. And I come in here, you just had a big fight with the detective on the hottest case you got, and I ask you what's wrong and instead of just fucking *telling* me, you get all coy. So what should I think? That for some weird reason you're planning on *concealing* something from the district attorney?" He paused. On Hrcany's face he observed the same petulant curl of lip, sidewise look, and wrinkled brow he had observed on his son Zak's face after the child had been caught in a misdeed. Not for the first time Karp reflected that raising baby sons gave him insights into how to deal with men like Roland Hrcany, a type with which the criminal-justice field was inordinately well supplied.

"Concealing is not a word I would use," said Roland with studied casualness, pursing his mouth. "There's nothing to conceal. It's garbage. Raney and Carnera found a floater who may or may not be connected with the two defendants in Shilkes, and I was trying to make the point that they shouldn't prejudice the case against these guys when they question them."

Karp pressed him for details, which he gave out, honestly but with as little good grace as possible, ending with the conclusions he had shared with the two cops.

After that Karp was silent for a long while, until Roland asked impatiently, "So, are you going to lay this shit on Keegan?"

"Not at the moment. Let's wait and see what Raney finds out from the suspects. But let's really keep in touch here, Roland. Let's play it straight up."

"Right," said Roland in a tight voice. "I just don't want my case soured behind this."

Karp suppressed a sigh. "Roland? Can I give you some advice? Ease up a little. Just run the case on the evidence you got, which is plenty. Don't try to control the externals. Lay as much as you can on your second seat. Who is it, by the way?"

"I picked Harris for it."

"Good choice. Tony's good."

The tension that Roland had felt since Raney and Carnera had come through with their news was now just starting to dissipate. Roland felt this, but did not understand why, or what Karp had done to make it so. He perceived that he had won something from Karp and thought he felt all right again because of that, because he was on top of things. He leaned back in his chair and clasped his hands behind his head.

"So—anything else you want to know?" he asked easily.

Karp, smiling, replied, "You're running like a clock, I hear, Roland. The Mexican brothers are scheduled?"

"Uh-huh. Late May, probably. Oh. Speaking of them, take a look at this." He picked up a sheet of folded lined notebook paper and handed it across. On it was written in ballpoint pen, in bold capitals: OBREGONS ARE INOCENT LET THEM GO OR YOU IN BIG TROUBEL WE MEAN IT!

Karp flipped the note back on the desk. "You talk to them about this yet?"

"Hell, no! I wouldn't give them the satisfaction."

"I don't know, Roland, threatening a prosecutor is no joke."

"Fuck 'em! I got a whole folder of those things. Don't you?"

"Some," admitted Karp. "But it's probably not at thick as yours."

At which Roland, after a suspicious scowl, laughed long and hard, and Karp joined in.

In the apartment in Washington Heights he now shared with the woman Connie, El Chivato dressed for work: his tooled boots, his white jeans (held up with a thick belt, its concha buckle set with turquoise), a white shirt buttoned to the collar, a tan sports coat in the yoked-front Mexican style, with slash pockets outlined in dark piping, and his long canvas coat over all. He examined himself in the mirror affixed to the back of a closet door. He walked back and forth, observing how the coat hung. He knelt, bent over, sat down on the bed, watching and listening carefully. Nothing clanked and the coat concealed what it had to.

El Chivato had experienced no difficulty in finding the material he needed in New York. Obregon had given him some names in the area, and Connie had access to sufficient cash. Therefore, in pockets cleverly built into the heavy canvas of his coat, the boy now carried a Colt King Cobra .357 Magnum revolver, a Winchester Model 1300

Defender twelve-gauge shotgun with a plastic pistol grip and an eighteen-inch barrel, a K-bar commando knife, and sufficient ammunition to start a small insurrection. He had a Model D-22 Davis two-shot derringer, loaded with magnum hollow-points, in his left boot. Satisfied, he put on his white hat and walked out into the apartment's living room.

Connie was sitting on a sofa in a black quilted robe, with a towel around her hair. She was applying red lacquer to her nails and watching a game show on a large color television set. She saw him and was a bit too slow in suppressing the smile that sprang onto her face. The kid did not like people smiling at him. Jodón had instructed her carefully on how she was to handle El Chivato and promised her an extremely large tip if all went well. He had also filled her in on his reputation in Mexico and Arizona. Don't offer unless he asks, he said. Get him anything he wants. Don't give him any advice. Never, never laugh at him.

Connie was the daughter of a Dominican woman, an illegal, born right here in the city. She worked out of a lounge on Broadway, girl-friending for a succession of Dominican and Central American bad boys, all with fairly short life expectancies. Not Colombians, though. The Colombians were known for going after the girls too, even before they hit the guys, as a form of warning. She had, naturally enough, encountered *chuteros* before this, but El Chivato was in a class by himself. When he fucked her (and of course he had fucked her, a number of times, immediately upon their return from visiting Rikers Island), it was like being in one of those movies with an animal. Connie had seen a number of such films (they seemed popular with the men in her circle) and she had always wondered what went on in the minds of the women in them when the burro or the dog was thrusting away. Now she thought she had some hint. There was nothing in his eyes when he did it, not that she saw much of his eyes. He liked it with her face pressed down in a pillow. What he looked at was the picture of the elderly woman in a silver frame that he kept on his dresser. That was another thing. Don't look at the picture. Don't say anything about the picture.

He was staring at her now. One problem was that he was so good-looking that it was a moment before you realized that what confronted your eye was not a small, sweet-faced kid, but something entirely outside your experience.

"What amuses you?" he asked. He had a soft, almost whispery voice.

"Ah, just something on the TV. You going out, huh?"

He kept staring at her for what seemed like a long time. She was finding it hard to breathe, and she could feel her pulse building in her ears. Finally he said, "Tell me how to find this place."

"It's in Brooklyn," she said. "You have to take the subway, or drive." In that outfit you better drive, she thought.

"I will drive," he said. He had been on the subway in Mexico. It was not to his taste. "Get me a car. Not stolen." He sat down in an armchair and directed his attention to the TV. She rose immediately, dressed in haste, with two fingernails left unpainted, and went out. At the lounge, which was on Broadway at 189th Street and called the Club Carib, she made an arrangement with Ramon the bartender. For two thousand dollars she arranged the rental, for two weeks, of Ramon's brother Felipe's 1975 Pontiac Firebird. Felipe had a large number of cars, many of doubtful provenance, but all lovingly repainted and maintained. While she waited, she drank two vodkas. She would have preferred rum, but she knew that El Chivato did not like the smell of liquor. As she drank, several of the local *guapos* passed the time of day with her, and one inquired whether she was back in circulation. She wished that she was. The Obregons were, she judged, even more stupid than the normal run of men and, besides that, had absolutely no idea how America worked. And they did not want to learn either, which made them different from the immigrants, legal and illegal, among whom she had been raised. And as bad as they were, they were nearly gringos compared to that little *pendejo* up in the apartment. Still, there was a good deal of money left, and she would stick it out while it remained. It never occurred to her to steal the money. Don't steal money, don't steal drugs: rules to live by up in the Heights and Inwood. She did not think that the *pendejo* would last long. Someone would push him, or say something, and there would be a killing and that would be that. The cops would not have much trouble finding somebody dressed like El Chivato in New York.

She finished her drink, and one of Felipe's boys came around with the car. It was black with a red vinyl interior. Connie drove back to the apartment and gave El Chivato the keys. "Do you know how to get there?" she asked helpfully.

He ignored the question and gave her the famous look. "Write

again to the *fiscal*," he ordered. "Say again the Obregons are innocent and say we are watching him and that we can reach him at any
time."

El Chivato then walked out, to locate a man he had never seen
in a city where he had never been. He had absolutely no doubt that
he would succeed in doing so, and that he would not be bothered
by the police or anyone else. This was because his mother was a
saint, and God naturally paid more attention to her prayers than to
the prayers of ordinary mothers. This had always been true and
was the reason for his great success, why he could walk through
guarded doorways and squads of bodyguards to do his work, and
also why he had never been arrested or even questioned. This is
what gave him his nerveless courage and confidence. (Of the subtle
networks of bribery and subornation that attended his assassina-
tions El Chivato was completely unaware.)

He drove south on the West Side Highway. He was a careful
driver, keeping under the posted speed limits and driving in the
right-hand lane. He was not in a hurry. Besides driving, his attain-
ments included a fair fluency in English, from his years in Nogales,
Arizona, and much watching of cross-border TV, and the ability to
read in both Spanish and English. He had an infallible memory for
faces and automobiles. He could also read a map and had a remarkable sense of direction.

It was somewhat after the noon hour and traffic was light. It
took him a little over an hour to drive from Washington Heights to
the bar on Court Street, Rudy's. This was a small, dim place under
the shadow of the Brooklyn-Queens Expressway, known by Connie
and the brothers to be a hangout of the man he sought.

Inside, half a dozen men and the bartender were watching a Gi-
ants game playing on a color TV suspended over the bar. There was
a brief silence when the kid walked in, a comment, a laugh, and
conversation and TV watching resumed. El Chivato stood at the
bar, and the bartender came over and stood there, waiting. He was
a middle-aged Puerto Rican with a pocked face and thinning
combed-back hair.

"I'm looking for Lucky," El Chivato said.

"Who?"

"Lucky. A big man, with a big nose."

"Oh, him. He ain't been around. What can I get for you?"

"Nothing. Where is he?"

The bartender sighed and rolled his eyes. "Hey, cowboy, this is a bar, not the fuckin' phone book. I *said* he ain't been around. So order a drink or take a hike."

El Chivato pulled the .357 out from under his coat and shot the TV. In Hermosillo he would have shot a dog, in the unlikely event that anyone in Hermosillo had spoken to him like that. A .357 makes an extremely loud sound when fired, and El Chivato now had the undivided attention of everyone in the place, especially that of the bartender, who was staring into the smoking muzzle of the pistol.

"Where is he?" El Chivato asked again. The bartender was shaking. Sweat pooled in the pits on his face.

"Honest to God I don't know! Jesus, man, take it easy!" cried the man.

"You do know. He comes in here all the time, I hear," said El Chivato. The pistol went off again, shattering several bottles and a beer-company mirror behind the bar. The flame of the blast scorched the side of the bartender's face. He fell to his knees behind the bar, clinging to the edge of the bar with his fingers as if hanging from a cliff; he wet his pants.

He looked up and saw the gun pointed down at him. He said, "Only on the weekends, Jesus, please, he only comes in on the weekends here, man. Please, he's a dealer, he hangs out at the Palm, other places, Jesus, man . . . that's all I know, I swear on my mother, man . . ."

El Chivato questioned the bartender as to the location of the Palm and the other places where Lucky might be found. Then he turned his back on them like a matador who has stymied a bull and walked out.

He paused for a moment outside the bar and looked both ways, as a cautious old man does before crossing a busy street. There were no pedestrians approaching and little traffic. He turned on his heel, went back into the bar. The six customers and the bartender had not moved. They stared at him, like mice paralyzed under a snake's jeweled gaze. El Chivato threw open his coat, unlimbered his shotgun with a smooth, practiced motion, and killed everyone in the place.

Fatyma's plan was a simple one: a young, rich, handsome man would fall madly in love with her and take her to Hollywood, where she would become a famous movie star, admired and loved by millions. Given her limited experience in the world and the narrowness of her literary sources, this seemed a reasonable goal. Every one of the heroines of the romances she had been able to obtain achieved the former goal, and the biography of Marilyn Monroe indicated that no particular ability was necessary to achieve the latter. It might be better to go to Hollywood and become a star first, Fatyma thought, for it was clear that Marilyn had plenty of rich, handsome men to choose from, but she was not entirely clear about how distant Hollywood was or how she might get there. She had on hand $28.35, in coin and small bills, pilfered over months from the family till. This might be sufficient to make the journey. She would discover this at the airport.

She rode the subway to the last stop, in the Bronx, and then back again to Manhattan. She saw a sign that said TIMES SQUARE and on impulse sprang up and left the train, clutching her small suitcase. She had heard of Times Square, but vaguely, as being the center of something exciting. Like Hollywood, the location had a symbolic ring to it, connoting romance, America, the mysterious pursuits of American adults, the life in which she desired to immerse herself.

The reality at four in the morning was mildly disappointing. The lights were alluring, the people less so. They seemed not too different from those in Brooklyn, especially the people in the sections starting a few blocks from her home, where she was not allowed to go. A large proportion of them seemed to be black or Spanish, which surprised her. She had imagined that once out of Brooklyn she would be in America, the land of the movies and TV, where the vast majority of faces would be white.

She walked around the periphery of the square for some while, from Forty-first to Forty-fourth, up Seventh and down Broadway, looking in the shop windows. This was disappointing too; she was not interested in cameras, electronics, or souvenirs, and she was shocked at some of the magazines on display, and at the marquees of the movie houses and at the places where men went to watch women undress. In fact, Fatyma had no information whatever about sex. In an Arab village she would have been ensconced in a community of women whose gossip and shared wisdom about the stupidity and perfidy of men would have provided her by her current (marriageable) age with knowledge sufficient to produce another generation.

As it was, she had only her mother, who had withdrawn into the morose silence of the deracinated immigrant, and Fatyma had been from too early an age denied the companionship of American peers. What she knew came from her reading and from snatches of movies seen in other people's homes, and the songs and chatter of her radio.

It passed briefly through her mind that her father's view of the world was correct, that outside the family and the narrow world of the Arab, there was nothing but what her father called fornication. And sin. Fatyma was not entirely sure what fornication was. She wished that she had been able to watch more television, since everything on television related in some way to fornication, according to her father, but this had not been possible. The Daouds had a TV, but the channel dial had been snapped off and it was exclusively devoted to service as a VCR monitor, playing tapes of Egyptian movies and sermons from Palestine and Syria. It had something to do with kissing, she had concluded, which you never saw them doing in the Egyptian movies. At any rate, she had gathered that a man and a woman were necessary, and that they couldn't be married, since clearly married people (in her experience) did not even kiss. It was also related in some way to love and passion. In *Fountain of Desire* Brent and Melanie were always kissing with burning lips, their hearts pounding as one. Also their loins were afire, and Melanie's breasts throbbed. Fatyma knew what breasts were, and as for loins, she could make a fair guess, although the book was short on the details of what occurred when you dissolved in a fiery embrace on the silken sheets. How this related to sleeping with men she could not decide. Marilyn, she knew, "slept with" a good number of men so that they would help her become a movie star and after she did become one, because she loved them. Fatyma thought that she could easily do this too: you went to bed and you awakened—what could be simpler?

The sky was now lightening above the eastward-facing urban canyons, and Fatyma found she was both tired and hungry. She had not slept at all the previous night, of course, and had dozed only fitfully during the subway ride. And she had hardly eaten anything since her father had told her about her forthcoming marriage to the old man. She went into an all-night place on Forty-third. It was harshly bright and steamy with the smell of bitter coffee, toast, and warm grease. She sat at the counter and ordered a double-hamburger basket, coffee, and a slice of apple pie. It was the first time she had ordered a meal for herself in a restaurant. It struck her suddenly that she would be eating like this forever after, in restaurants, although she expected that soon she would be eating in better places and that a man would be paying.

The meal came and it was huge, the pile of fries threatening to cascade from the oval plate. She ate greedily until she was full. The woman behind the counter filled the coffee cup without being asked, which for some reason made Fatyma feel particularly adult. Fatyma looked around the restaurant. Ten booths covered with beige leatherette, red plastic tabletops, a line of separate tables and chairs down the center aisle, a counter. A ragged man wearing many layers of clothing was sleeping in one of the booths. Another held four women wearing short pants and short fake-fur or suede jackets in unlikely colors. They were laughing and pointing out the window at some other women of the same type standing on the street. Another booth held a group of grimy-looking young people wearing black clothes. One of them had lime green hair, and another had his hair drawn into long spikes. Fatyma looked at these people carefully. The women she knew were whores, since they were wearing heavy makeup. What the other people were she could not tell. Perhaps they were insane or members of some sort of religion she had not heard of.

"Hey, are you going to finish those fries?"

The speaker was a young woman sitting next to Fatyma at the counter. She was thin, pale, and foxy-faced, and had thin, dirty white hair escaping from under a red acrylic cap emblazoned with the symbol of some professional team. She was dressed in a soiled denim jacket over a sweatshirt and blue jeans. Fatyma shook her head and pushed the plate a few inches toward the stranger, who brought it in front of her place, flooded the fries with catsup, and consumed them in thirty seconds.

Fatyma observed the woman closely. A whore, without a doubt, lipstick in a pale purplish shade, lavender eyeshadow, and powder above a neck that was not clean. When the woman had cleaned up the plate with the last fry, Fatyma pushed over her half-finished pie.

"Hey, thanks," said the woman. Then with her mouth half-full, she indicated Fatyma's suitcase. "You traveling somewhere?"

"Yes," said Fatyma. "I am going to Hollywood, California."

"Hollywood, huh?" She grinned and asked lightly, "What, you're gonna be a movie star?"

"Yes," Fatyma said matter-of-factly, and smiled.

The young woman looked at Fatyma to see if she had spoken sarcastically, but decided she had not. She asked, "When're you going?"

"I think today. Do you know how much it costs?"

"Oh, I don't know: a bus'll probably run you one-fifty, maybe. Air, maybe four hundred bucks, cheaper if you can get a special deal."

Fatyma looked shocked. "So much? I didn't know it costed so much."

"You don't have it, huh?"

"No. I have only twenty-two dollars."

"You could hitch," said the woman. She pulled a crumpled pack of Winstons out of her jacket and lit one, offering the pack to Fatyma, who refused with a shy smile.

"Hitch?" Fatyma recalled the word from songs but was unsure of the precise meaning.

"Yeah, bum a ride, Of course, twenty bucks'll hardly pay for your food, and they'll probably ask you to kick in for gas and all." She saw the effect this statement had on the girl and added, "Hey, it ain't that bad, kid. There's ways to make money."

"A job, you mean?"

The woman made a dismissive gesture. "Oh, yeah, sure a job! Look, nobody's gonna give you a job, you're on the street. I mean, you got to have an address, a real address, not a shelter or a crash pad. You got to have clothes . . ." She tapped Fatyma's little suitcase with her toe. "I mean more than you got. Also, there's what can you do? And how old you are. How old are you anyway?"

"Sixteen." Fatyma lied.

"Yeah, I'm eighteen and they won't look at me. I mean, face it, they're out to fuck you any way they can. I'm Cindy, by the way."

"I'm Fat—I mean, Franny. So what do you do? I mean to make money."

"Oh, a little of this, a little of that. Panhandle. Sell stuff. Boost from stores. How come you split?" Blank look. "I mean left home. You from out of town?"

"Brooklyn."

"Oh, yeah, Brooklyn. I'm from upstate. So . . . your folks give you a hard time, huh?"

"I am a whore, so my father was going to marry me to an old man." She shrugged. "I escaped."

"Wait a minute, you're a *whore*?"

"Yes, like you." She smiled.

Cindy's face hardened up. "Hey. I'm not saying I ain't done tricks, but I'm no whore, and I ain't gonna *be* no whore, let's get that straight."

"You do tricks?"

Cindy blew out a cloud of smoke from both nostrils, like a dragon. Fatyma looked on with admiration and wondered if she should have accepted a cigarette. "Yeah, everybody does it once in a while, on the street. The men're there. God, are they there! It's no big deal. Why, you thinking of tricking yourself?"

"You mean men? You . . . trick men for money?"

"Oh course, men! Who the fuck else's gonna pay for it?" Cindy cast an appraising eye over Fatyma. "You need to lose that coat, get you a little short jacket or something, a sweater. And boots." Her brow wrinkled and she shook her head. "On the other hand, you look like you just got out of fucking junior high. You can use that. Get your hair in like braids, little red ribbons or something."

Cindy went on, seeming glad to have a rapt audience for her fashion advice as well as her considerable street experience. Fatyma, while listening, was still running her mind over the novel notion of trickery. She recalled now something she had not thought about for years. She was in a kitchen, playing under the table while her mother spoke with two older Arab women, relatives perhaps, she could not recall exactly who. The conversation had to do with some man in the old country, a farmer, before the war, and some gold, and a cow. Fatyma couldn't remember the details, but she recalled the point, which was although men claimed all the power and made a great show of it, women were more clever and could trick men anytime they desired, and get them to do whatever they wanted. There was another story of a trick, something to do with a wedding night and blood on the sheets, and Fatyma remembered that here the women lowered their voices and glanced around to make sure no one heard, and this in itself made Fatyma ask her mother about the trick with the blood. Her mother ignored the question, and found fault with something the child did, which is what she always did when that sort of question arose, so Fatyma stopped asking.

Now her new friend was revealing the secret. The men come by in their cars, the girl gets in, and then the trick, and money. It sounded delightful. Fatyma was thrilled, more excited than she had been by anything before. She paid her bill and accompanied Cindy to the Port Authority Bus Terminal on Forty-second and Eighth, where they checked Fatyma's bag in a locker. By this time it was dawn. The city awoke, the terminal became crowded. Fatyma followed Cindy in what seemed like an aimless round of brief conversations with young people of unusual appearance. All of them seemed ragged and dirty and tired. They were in the habit of laughing when nothing was funny and engaging in brief spates of violence with one another, after which they seemed to forget that they had ever fought, although Fatyma heard words exchanged that would have demanded the heart's blood of the speaker had they been voiced to an Arab.

Cindy seemed to know a lot of people around the bus station and the neighboring streets. Several of these were black men, and Fatyma was amazed that Cindy would have conversation with *hubshi*, against whom Fatyma had often been warned in her old neighborhood. She supposed that here was another instance where her father had been mistaken, as these men seemed friendly, even jolly. Speaking with *hubshi* was clearly another part of being a whore, although when she was introduced to them by Cindy, they looked at her in a way she did not like.

The day passed in this manner. Fatyma bought food, once at the bus station café and once at a sidewalk restaurant window, and both times Cindy invited herself along for the meal. Nearly all of Fatyma's money was gone now, and she was starting to become worried. She voiced this fear to Cindy, adding, "Maybe we should try to trick the men tonight."

Cindy gave her a brief puzzled look, but the Quaalude she had just taken was working warmly within her, and her analytic abilities, never prime, were barely functioning. She shrugged and led Fatyma to the rest room at the Port Authority, where she braided the younger girl's hair into pigtails. Ten minutes later, they were standing at a corner of Ninth Avenue and Forty-fourth Street, looking out at the quickening downtown traffic.

"This is a good place," she explained. "It's not a regular stroll, so you don't get in trouble with the real pros or the pimps. But like guys going home to Jersey sometimes like to pick up a quick blow job before they hit the tunnel back to the wife and kiddies, you know?"

Fatyma did not know. "What is a blow job?" she asked.

"Twenty, twenty-five bucks, whatever you can get. Okay, open your coat and stick out your tits. Jesus, you look like you're twelve! Smile at the cars with single guys in them, and, like wave. That's it—smile and wave."

Fatyma smiled and waved. Several cars slowed to take a look, and at last a dark blue Ford LTD with New Jersey plates pulled over to the curb. The electric passenger-side window hummed down.

"Go over and stick your head in and smile," urged Cindy. "Remember, don't talk money until he's got his johnson waving, so you know he's not a cop. Go ahead, he's waiting! I'll meet you back at the Port Authority."

The driver, a balding man in his late forties, was looking nervously over his shoulder and checking his side mirror. Fatyma entered the car, and it pulled away.

An hour later, Cindy was sitting in the bus terminal café, sipping a lemon Coke to wash away the taste of the fellatio she had just performed on a truck driver, when Fatyma walked in, saw her, smiled, and sat down.

"How'd you do?" Cindy asked.

"Two hundred and twelve dollars," said Fatyma proudly, placing a thick brown wallet on the table.

"Jesus H. Christ! Fuck! How the fuck did you get this?"

"I tricked him," said Fatyma. She was glowing with excitement. "First we drove to the water, under where the road goes above . . ."

"Yeah, the West Side Highway—that's where they always go."

"He stopped the car. All the time I'm thinking how I will trick him, and I think I will say I am a poor orphan and need money. But he undoes his pants, you know, and . . ."

Here Fatyma looked away and her cheeks darkened. She lowered her voice. "He shows his . . . shameful parts to me . . ."

"His *what*?"

"His shameful parts. So I took out my knife—actually, it is my brother's knife, Walid—"

"Holy shit! You had a knife?"

"Yes, of course." Fatyma brought it out of her coat pocket and laid it on the table. Cindy gaped. The thing was nine inches long, hiltless and gracefully curving, three inches wide at the silver-mounted ivory handle and tapering to a needle point.

"Christ! Put it away! Put it away!" said Cindy in a frightened whisper. Fatyma did so. "And then what happened?"

"So then he said not to hurt him because he had children, and he gave me his wallet. It was a good trick, wasn't it?"

"Yeah, you could say that." Cindy looked at the girl opposite as if seeing her for the first time. "Jesus! You don't know dick, do you?"

"No. Who is he?"

"You never did this before, did you? Going with guys in cars?"

"No."

"Then why the hell did you say you were a whore?"

"Because this is what my father says, because I want to look like American girls, with makeup and listen to the radio music and go to movies."

Cindy sighed and rolled her eyes. "Girl, we got to have a long talk. But first, let's see what we got here." She riffled through the wallet. "Hot damn! A gold fucking VISA! Come on! If we move fast, we can score shitloads of stuff before the bastard calls it in."

SIX

The thin March afternoon sunshine trickled down through the leafless trees of Columbus Park, a small patch of green located between the New York County Criminal Courts on the west and Chinatown to the east. Lucy Karp and Tran Vinh sat together on a bench and watched a group of elderly Chinese people doing tai chi exercises. As they watched, they slurped noodles from cardboard boxes. This was the child's after-school snack. Marlene had instructed Tran to bring the girl here and wait while she performed some legal ritual in the courts. He was content with this. He was good at waiting. Lucy was not, nor was she looking forward to the afternoon's activity, which was the purchasing of clothes for Easter. Lucy did not yet see the point of clothes.

Tran's glance darted in a practiced pattern across the park, covered the full circle every minute or so. Columbus Park was among the safest patches of grass in the city, being a stone's throw from Police Headquarters, but Tran's wariness was by now as natural in him as a physiological function. When his gaze returned to his small charge, however, his face showed a flicker of disapproval. He thought new clothes were certainly needed. Lucy was dressed in the untidy fashion in which Americans allowed their children to go to school, a style with no respect in it, he thought, and they wondered why the children defied the teachers and learned nothing. Lucy was wearing white jeans, none too clean, scuffed Nikes, a maroon sweatshirt, with a somewhat grubby navy blue quilted parka over it. Her hair stuck out in its usual undisciplined corkscrew ringlets.

The girl was swinging her feet under the bench, scuffing the sneakers against the rough pavement, making a rhythmic and annoying sound. He had noticed this before too: Americans seemed not to be able to control their great bodies; even the adults bounced around like huge fowls in a yard, and the children were much worse. It came, he thought, from having so much space.

Lucy caught him looking at her and returned his stare. There were spots of grease on her nose and chin. "What?" she demanded.

In French he replied. "Nothing. I was merely observing you destroy your shoes, and reflecting that Americans can never keep still."

"I'm bored," Lucy said. "I hate clothes shopping, and I hate waiting around."

Tran ignored this and pointed across the park. "Look, do you see those old people? What do you think they are doing?"

"They are doing tai chi," Lucy answered in a bored tone.

"Yes, and do you know why? They seek to control their bodies, to let the vital energy flow along the proper channels, and so to control their minds and avoid confusion and stupidity. The mind controls the body, but the body also controls the mind. If you let yourself flop about like a mere puppet, you will also have clouded thoughts. You will say, 'I am bored,' for example."

"I *am* bored. And don't see *you* doing tai chi." She said this in English, which, given their history, was mildly insulting.

"Which leads, among other things, to impudence toward elders and failure in school. . . ." Seeing her firm little jaw tightening, he added, "Not, I think, will you ever learn to shoot properly."

She snapped her chopsticks down and turned on him, with her face contorted into a miniature of her mother's when enraged. The effect was so charming that he almost laughed but did not; she would not stand being laughed at, even by him, and Tran, although he had tortured any number of people, was not cruel enough to mock a child.

"That's not true!" she said. "I can so shoot." She had reverted to French.

"Anyone can shoot, but it is beneficial to also hit the target. Ah, now you are going into one of your famous blue sulks. You wish not to be treated as an infant, yet when someone gives you advice that will enable you to take on the duties of an adult, look how you behave! No, don't hang your head like a dog, look at me! If I thought you were only another brainless American girl, I would simply watch you like a sack of rice, but, you recall, at one time I trusted you with my life and you did well, and for that reason I have responsibility for the development of your interior qualities. Your life is not to be an ordinary one, as you well know, and if you wish to live and fulfill your destiny, you must endeavor to throw off all manner of stupidity."

Lucy's cheeks burned, and she found it terribly difficult to continue looking into the bottomless black eyes of the Vietnamese. She said in Cantonese, the language of their first communication, "I am sorry, Older Brother. I am stubborn unto death and a worthless person."

"That is true," said Tran, "but worthless is not hopeless. If you are sincere, something may be made of you in time. Here is your mother coming."

"Where?" Lucy looked around in all directions and at lost spotted Marlene walking into the Leonard Street entrance to the park. "Oh, there she is," she said, switching back to French. "You have good eyes, Uncle Tran."

"On the contrary, I have terrible old eyes, and one of them hardly works at all. However, I know how to look, which makes a difference."

"What do you mean? Looking is just looking."

"To ignorant girls, yes. To those who flop their arms and legs about and chatter like sparrows, it is just looking. But there is a way to look that lets you see what is important, for example, that lets you see your enemy before being seen."

"How?" This was beginning to sound interesting to Lucy, who had seen the *Star Wars* trilogy and had thus absorbed, along with the rest of the American population, a belief in miraculous powers taught (in a convenient seven minutes of screen time) by wizened, elderly beings.

But Tran said, "It may be possible to teach you when you have learned to sit properly and to breathe. And when your demeanor has become sufficiently respectful. Tell me, why do you dislike purchasing clothing with your mother?"

"Because she makes me buy things I don't like."

"You astound me. I am no great judge, but your mother appears to me quite chic, when she wishes."

"Oh, yes, *she* is, but she wants me to wear these little *dresses*. She doesn't care if I look like a dork."

"A *dork*? What is this *dork*?"

"Oh, you know, one who is not respected, like . . . like . . ."

"*Un fayot*, perhaps?" Tran offered. She shrugged. "In any case," he continued, "you appear to value the opinions of your school fellows more than the wishes of your mother. Thus you appear in the clothes of an unemployed laborer rather than those of a well-brought-up schoolgirl. I have seen this often in America, but fail to understand the reason for it. In my country, families would go without rice to enable their children to wear clothes to school that would not bring disgrace. In any case, you must honor your mother's wishes. Your friends will come and go, but nothing can replace a parent."

At this moment the irreplaceable arrived, looking chic enough in her best gray wool going-to-court suit, heels and stockings with a worn Burberry trench coat on top. After kissing her child and greeting Tran with the accustomed formal handshake, she passed him a slip of paper. It contained a man's name and address.

"An interview?" asked Tran mildly.

"Not at this time. Make your presence known and leave our cards in appropriate places. He needs to know someone is watching him, as he is watching our client."

Marlene and Lucy then took the subway to Bloomingdale's, where Lucy evinced an agreeableness so nearly angelic that Marlene readily consented to Lucy's request that she be allowed to go shooting with Tran on the weekend.

Which came, the clear weather continuing. Lucy disappeared with Tran, Marlene had a much coveted spate of concentrated mothering with her babies because Posie had the Saturday off, and Karp, as was his habit, went off to play basketball at the West Fourth Street courts.

Karp had been doing this nearly every Saturday for over a decade, with the only breaks coming during the year he had spent in Washington and the six months after he got his artificial left knee. He was well known, therefore, and always got some action, although he no longer played in the hottest games, which at West

Fourth are hot indeed: it is known among New York playground basketball fanatics as Death Valley. NBA players have been known to play there, and they do not have an easy time.

While Karp still enjoyed playing, he did not want to be knocked to the asphalt and he did not want to do a lot of full-court running and he could not jump at all anymore. He enjoyed instead intellectual half-court games with a rotating group of a dozen or so old farts who remembered the early Red Auerbach teams, and when City College was a basketball powerhouse, and when big-time basketball was not a contact sport like hockey. Karp liked position, passing, and floating long, graceful shots through the hoop from twenty feet out.

After his first such game that morning, Karp sat against the fence with a towel around his neck, sucking on an icy Yoo-Hoo, enjoying the loose, hot feeling in his limbs and the biting pain in his back teeth, and watching the more athletic contest that was now going on on one of the full courts. His attention was drawn to one of the odd mismatches common in playground games: an Irish-looking man of average height was guarding a black man with five inches on him and a full step of speed. The Irish guy was getting the hell beat out of him, but not as much as he should have, because he stuck to the bigger man like a cocklebur, his teeth gritted with effort. Karp could see the sweat flying off him in sheets, although it was a cool March day. And he was using his brains, psyching out the other man's fakes, countering to the extent he could the other man's superior athletic skills. His team lost anyway.

When the man came over to the fence to retrieve a towel he had shoved into the chain-link, Karp said, "Nice game," and realized that the man was Jim Raney.

"I got creamed," said Raney, wiping his face. He went out to the snack wagon parked outside the gate and came back with an orange soda.

"I'm surprised to see you here," Karp remarked as Raney sat down beside him. "I thought you lived in Queens."

"Just moved this month. I got a deal on a condo in Clinton, or Hell's Kitchen, as my old man still calls it. He thinks I'm a nut case. 'Jimmy, what is it, are you broke, have you lost your job?' They busted their humps to get out to Woodlawn, and here I am going back again. I like being in the city, though."

"The culture," Karp said.

Raney laughed. "Yeah. That and ten minutes to work instead of an hour."

They talked casually for a while, watching the games and commenting on the plays, in the careful, polite way that men do when one of them is a close friend of the wife of the other, as Raney was of Marlene. So, talking in this wary way, with a part of his mind focused on gently pumping the detective a bit about the sequel to the blow-up in Roland's office, and the identity of the floating Arab corpse, a memory rose up like a scrap of dirty paper in the gutters after a rain. Karp snatched at it and said, "Ali something, Ali al something . . . Haddad mentioned it. I don't know why I didn't think of it before."

Raney stared at him. "You mean Ali al-Qabbani?"

Karp smiled and snapped his fingers. "That's it! I just remembered John Haddad, this city councilman I'm supposed to keep in touch with, mentioned the name to me. He said the kid used to hang with our suspects, and he was missing. So you found somebody who knew him? In Brooklyn?"

"Yeah, it was no big deal," said Raney. "We went back to the garage where we found the other two, and the owner I.D.'d him off the morgue Polaroid. What did Haddad say about him?"

Karp thought for a moment. "Nothing much that I recall—just about being friendly with the perps and that he disappeared about the time of the Shilkes murder. He hinted pretty broadly that the Jews got him."

"What, he was thinking retaliation or something?" When Karp agreed, Raney asked, "What's your take on that?"

"It's possible but doubtful. This Ali disappeared the night after you picked up his pals, which was the same day as the murder. It would mean some Jewish revenge group found out the names of those assholes about the same time you did, figured out Ali was part of the plot, found him, and popped him in the very slick and professional manner in which he was in fact popped. So the question then becomes, do we have a Jewish revenge group around that's as stylish as that?"

"Lowenstein?"

Karp shook his head. "The will is probably there at some level, but not the ability. The rabbi likes to run his mouth and organize marches, and he's got a gang of black hats with clubs and walkie-talkies on neighborhood patrol. Does he have a secret death squad he runs out of a shul? Haddad probably thinks so. I don't."

Raney grunted in a noncommittal fashion and filed this away, together with the known fact that Karp was one of them too. He said, "So if not, we're back to either a personal thing or the famous shadowy terrorist mastermind that Roland hates."

That was a trailing cloak. Karp put out his large foot. "You sound like you don't. Hate the idea, I mean."

"Well, I'll tell you," said Raney, "I've talked to these mutts. These mutts are followers. Not original minds. They think they're like, some kind of fucking *soldiers* in this organization nobody ever heard of. Like they're under orders. They got the literature, the tapes. You ask me, and this is just my opinion, then yeah, somebody set them up, somebody they had no direct contact with, because these guys are not really swift enough to keep the guy out of it if they were pressed. And I did, and zilch. In which case, old Primo's idea that the mystery guy aced Ali to keep him quiet makes a lot of sense."

"So the next step is . . . ?"

Raney yawned and stretched elaborately. Some man on the court called out, asking if he wanted a game, and he stood up and shouted in assent. "The next step . . . I was thinking I could talk to Walid again, the bakery kid that tipped us. Maybe he'd talk if I could work with that conspiracy charge."

"That could be in play," said Karp carefully. It was still Roland's case. "You think he knows something?"

"Well, he's a dim bulb, but he used to hang with the late Ali. The problem is, all this is in Brooklyn, and Brooklyn North ain't got shit to spare for anything but that goddamn shotgun party in Red Hook. You heard about this?"

"Just on the news. It's Brooklyn. What's the story?"

"Oh, the usual. Some scumbag waltzed into a joint called Rudy's and took out six guys and the bartender with a twelve-gauge. Drugs, is what I hear. Rudy's was a place where guys who handled serious weight hung out. The six of them were in the business, and the bartender wasn't shy about holding product either. They find the perp, most of Brooklyn North'll probably pass the hat, give the bastard an award dinner. Look, nice talking to you—anything works out with this bozo, I'll keep in touch. Give my best to Marlene."

Raney trotted off. Karp rose creakily, tossed his drink bottle in the trash, and began to walk home. It had been a typical cop inter-action, of the give-a-little, get-a-little type. Raney got confirmation of the floater's connection to Shilkes and a little coverage if he wanted to work around Roland; Karp got some details without having to go through Hrcany. The mention of Marlene at the end there—just sociable, or was he being cute? Karp dismissed it from his mind; he had no jealousy at all in his nature. He thought about the shotgun killing and something nagged at him. Drugs. The Mexican brothers. Maybe a load of dope from a new source, dropped into the dog pit of the city's great dope exchange—always good for a peck of murders. Had the brothers been in Brooklyn? Had the dead cop Morilla? Something else to look at.

Marlene cooked infrequently, but when she did, she cooked on a heroic scale. Her neighborhood, the area just north of Canal Street, had at one time, before the tony restaurants and galleries made their appearance, been the center of the restaurant-supply business in Manhattan, and Marlene had furnished her kitchen largely with its wares. Two forty-quart cauldrons now bubbled on the vast black Vulcan, one containing a winey beef stew and the other basic to-mato sauce. A slightly smaller pot held furiously bubbling water, and on the fourth burner a dozen sweet sausages browned in a fourteen-inch cast-iron skillet, while in the oven roasted a free-range chicken and a pan of veal shins. Marlene herself was in a fine sweat, moving from pot to pot, stirring, prodding, shaking, leaving the stove entirely for strategic seconds while she worked up the filling and the strips for her famous Every Day of the Week Three-Cheese Lasagna, of which she planned to make about half a cubic yard.

Although she lived in the take-out capital of the habitable uni-verse, she refused to surrender her responsibility to provide her family with daily rations of the dense, nourishing, spicy food of her ancestors. And no Progresso-canned cheating either. It also gave her something to talk to her mother and her more domestic sisters and sisters-in-law about, and helped stave off the ever recurring pangs of guilt: children stuffed to bursting with lovingly made lasagna could not be considered neglected, even by a mother who was out a lot and at odd hours and occasionally shot people. She enjoyed, too, generating meals in a fury like this, alone, in charge, juggling ten balls with no audience but her own pride. It was a sim-pler version of the juggling she did every day: the emergency runs, the court work, the cases, endless cases, the long, slow crawl, like a maggot, through the dead body of romance. In the books and movies the private eyes worked only one case at a time. Marlene would have liked to try that. And they didn't have nursemaids who needed a day off either. (Marlene imagined Mike Hammer threatening one of his molls with his .45: "You're not going anywhere, baby. You're gonna watch these kids or I'll blow a hole in you big enough to park a grapefruit.") She tossed the raw lasagna strips into the boiling pot and set her unfailing internal stopwatch for six and a half minutes.

Marlene suddenly stopped what she was doing and cocked a suspicious ear. The living room was quiet. Too quiet, as your regular private eye was fond of saying. She put down her spoon and rushed out the door.

The TV was still on, purveying the usual mercantile indoctrination and cultural mores in the form of cartoons, but the twins were no longer propped drooling on the couch, happily rotting their minds, a dodge Marlene used only in the last extremity, as now. Murmurs emanated from beneath a side table. She stooped.

"What're you doing, boys?" she asked and then, seeing what they were doing, she made an ungraceful dive and dragged Zak out from under. All the baseboard electrical outlets were, of course, baby-proofed to the technological limit, but Zak had gotten hold of a teaspoon and had nearly managed to pry the gadget off. Interrupted in his quest for a 110-volt surprise, he squalled.

She hauled him into the kitchen. He made his objection known and turned pale blue. Zik followed under his own power. She plonked them both down under the table, set out some unneeded utensils for them to play with, scooped up some dough, sculpted two spiders, as nearly identical as she could make them, sat on the floor, invented a game involving the spiders, and a spider playground made up of bowls and spoons and strainers, sang "Itsy-Bitsy Spider" in a maniacal voice several times, and, with thirty seconds to spare, grabbed the lasagna pot and tottered over to the sink to drain it. At which point the intercom buzzed.

"Yeah?" Marlene snarled into the little box.

"D'Agostino's," said a cracking voice.

"That you, Robby?"

"Yo."

She pressed the red button that activated the outside elevator and heard the rattling thump of the mechanism spring to life. Check the oven, baste the chicken, turn the veal shanks. Turn down the beef stew, a little water, a little salt in the sauce, uncork the Gallo, cup of burgundy for the stew and a cup for the cook, Marlene's usual breakdown. Knock on the door.

Robby, a muscular youth with a ponytail and a team jacket that read HOLY FAMILY on the back, dropped a heavy carton on the floor of the kitchen. He looked around, stated that the place smelled real good, asked after Posie, took his tip, and left.

Marlene started to assemble the lasagna, alternating layers of fresh tomato sauce, chopped sausage, the cheeses, and the broad noodles. This was a curiously sensuous activity, requiring little dexterity, allowing the hands the comfort of immersion in warm food, food her family would consume, that would turn eventually into more child substance, that would fuel the enterprise of the family toward whatever fate awaited it. Although the various timers governing the other dishes she was preparing were still ticking away in her skull, this was the nearest thing to a break she had had in hours. She took another swallow of the indifferent red, and thought vaguely about what to have with the chicken tonight and whether she had it together enough to bake something.

Then an unearthly shriek burst through her reverie and she shot to her feet, hands dripping red like Lady Macbeth's. The boys, Zak actually, had managed to strip the top off a box of frosted flakes from the delivery carton and had spread them liberally over the floor, himself, and his twin. Zak was holding the box; Zik was wailing and holding his face. Further investigation was not necessary— this happened at least several times a day—Zik, the junior twin (by four minutes) always grabbed and Zak always slugged him with whatever object was at hand, in this case the cereal box, whose hard corner must have caught Zik on his tender cheek.

As she alternately cooed and kissed the boo-boo away, while staring daggers at her older son and chastising him, Marlene once again experienced that tremor of doubt that underlay her rearing of these two aliens. Where did it come from, that signal that made them crazy? It's always the mother, of course, the one who gets to sit calmly in the courtroom while Junior faces the music, but how does it happen? Marlene had seen it often enough in her work, the boys of mothers who got beat up become men who beat up women, and even acquired the added skill, more often than not, of finding women who would take it. Who even sort of liked it. A feminist heresy that, but she'd seen it, every cop had seen it—he's pounding her pretty good and the cop steps in to break it up and what does she do? She goes and cracks a vase on the cop's head. Not on the guy's head, the cop's head. The Valone woman, for example, heading for corpse-hood with a song ("My Man"?) in her heart, what to do about that, if anything, and Zik, sniff-sniff, need a diaper change—amazing, identical genes and they both ate the same stuff at the same time, but never did their diapers need changing simultaneously—and Oh, Christ! the oven . . .

She spun, still clutching Zik, and raced for the stove, slipping on masticated frosted flakes, banging her knee painfully against the table leg, put the child down, opened the oven, body-checking to keep Zik from the flames, grabbed a fork, rescued the roasting shanks (barely), at which point the dog, who had been lurking, waiting its chance, romped forward to scarf up the cereal, knocking down Zak with its mighty tail, who fell with a coconut-knocking sound to the hard floor and set up a howl, which got Zik started up again, of course. At that moment the door sprang open and Karp walked in, invigorated from his sport, and said brightly, "Wow, that smells good! When's dinner?"

Marlene gave him a look that could have fused quartz and said some disrespectful things about the Deity in Sicilian, a sure sign that deeds, not words, were required of the husband. Dropping his ball, Karp scooped up his sons and headed for the showers.

Some hours later, with the kitchen squared away, the table set, and no sound in the loft louder than the ticking of a clock and the eternal city rumble from outside, Marlene went into the bedroom and found the male units of her family sprawled on the big bed fast asleep, their tiny or gigantic limbs spread out and entwined, as in casualty photographs. He really was a darling man, thought Marlene, far better than she deserved, and what an amazing bit of luck to wind up with, considering her early track record with the other sex. A pang of guilt in there too, because she got to do exactly as she pleased, while he, natively a chauvinist of the true German-Jewish variety, had to cope around her. But of course, she told herself, there was all that nice food.

She leaned over carefully and kissed his cheek. He started awake, with a look of apprehension, just like Zak.

"What?"

"Food," she whispered, "and if we're extremely careful we can have a quiet meal by ourselves."

Which they did, with candles. Lucy burst in while they were washing up, cheeks red and eyes aglow and stinking of gunpowder.

"Look!" she crowed, "I got a Ballantine," and held up a shot-up silhouette target, pointing out the place where, indeed, three bullet holes merged into one.

"Very nice," said Marlene, Karp managing nothing more than a false smile. Marlene added, "Those don't look like .22 holes."

"No, Tran let me use the Tokarev. It was neat!"

"He did?" said her mother coldly. "Well, I wish he had asked me first."

Lucy clapped her hand to her mouth. "Oh, no! I was supposed to ask you, but I forgot."

"How convenient for you. Have you eaten?"

"Yeah, Tran took me to a Vietnamese restaurant. I had star shrimp and soup with limes."

"I thought they ate dogs," said Karp.

"They only eat dogs in the north, Daddy," Lucy explained, as if to a retarded infant. "Tran is from the south."

"Did you do your homework?" asked Marlene.

"I'll do it tomorrow after church. Can I watch *Saturday Night Live*?"

"Yeah, sure. Keep it down, though." Lucy darted away.

Karp said, "What the hell is a Tokarev? Who *is* this guy, Marlene?"

"Don't start," said his wife.

Late that night, after two, Marlene was awakened by the sound of the elevator motor, and the door, and crashing in the kitchen and a grizzling noise that sounded like crying. She put on a robe and went to the kitchen. Posie was seated at the table with the cooking Gallo and a full glass. Her crying had pooled her too-heavy mascara around her eyes, giving her the look of a bedraggled raccoon. Her dress, a thrift-shop red acetate number that was too tight and too bright for her hefty figure, was ripped at the sleeve and her long, straight hair was matted in patches by some sticky substance that Marlene did not care to identify. Marlene sighed. It was like owning a big dog that ran out in traffic and chased skunks.

The story emerged between gasps and snuffles. A guy had picked her up at a club. He had some good dope, and they smoked it in the alley and got wrecked. He had taken her back to his place and they had balled. More dope and some pills. And wine. Posie had found herself on a soiled mattress, naked, with a guy other than the original guy—no, it was two other guys. That part was a little vague. In any case, it hadn't been true love.

"All I want is a nice guy, Marlene," Posie said through the tears. "He doesn't even have to be cute. Just not a shit, you know?"

Marlene knew. Any number of improving lectures flashed through her mind: the Safe Sex one, the You Meet Nicer Guys in Places of Education Than in Clubs one, the For God's Sake Learn How to Dress one, the Don't Get Wasted with Guys You Don't Know one, but Marlene had not the energy for these at the present time and simply hugged the girl and promised her that someday her prince would come and tried to avoid stroking her hair.

Noise from the nursery. Posie rubbed her face on her sleeve and rose.

"Thanks, Marlene. I'll go take care of the boys."

"No, I will," said Marlene a bit too quickly. "Why don't you just get cleaned up?"

After their big score Fatyma and Cindy bought into a group apartment off Tenth Avenue in the high thirties, which they shared with a mutable population of people somewhat older than themselves, who had graduated to one level above the street. Some of them even worked at jobs, and of these jobs, some were even legal. Fatyma had a heap of new clothes and a bag heavy with cosmetics and perfumes. As against these riches she had been thoroughly deprived of her innocence. After a few days of Cindy's amused tutelage, she now understood not only what sleeping together meant, and what the cause of burning loins was, but she was also cognizant of the blow job, the rim job, the golden shower, and the Mexican three-way. She had learned, just through observation so far, the effects of nearly the entire bootleg pharmacopoeia. She had learned to avoid pimps and cops and to call Forty-second Street the Deuce. The sexual portion of this knowledge was as yet mere theory; she remained as intact, physically, as any good Arab girl should be, nor was she in a hurry to change that. Cindy had confirmed what she had known from the cradle, the value that certain men placed on what the older girl called the cherry, and her reading of the late Ms. Monroe's life story had convinced her that the actress, whatever her later success, had traded it too cheaply and far too early. It would be time enough for that when she got to Hollywood. Despite all, she retained her belief in true love.

The floating population of males who occupied the apartment and the drifters on the street had quickly learned that Fatyma was not up for a casual quickie, or even a longie; those who had persevered had discovered the Knife. Nobody wanted to mess with the Knife. Cindy helped out by spreading the word that Franny did not swing that way, which assuaged the egos of the males and which Fatyma did not mind, having learned also what a dyke was.

Fatyma still went on tricks with guys in cars, with the same result, although she never made a score like the first one again. After a couple of weeks she had over six hundred dollars stuffed in the change purse she kept under the waistband of her new red lace panties. She had a new coat too, lush brown leather with a fur collar, bought out of the trunk of a car from a twitchy little man who did not collect the required sales tax. She was wearing a short skirt and white tights and black plastic shoes with a strap across the instep and a white shirt with frills and a round girlish collar, and she looked like the sort of girl who carried Juicy Fruit in her coat pocket instead of a big knife, which was the point.

It was seven or so, already dark, and the traffic was thinning on Ninth. The weather had turned chilly again, and damp, which she was still not entirely used to, even after years in New York, and the cars were not slowing down for a look as often as they had. She decided to take a break at the Ham & Eggs on Eighth and Forty-third Street. There would be whores there, real ones (Fatyma having copped to the hyperbolic aspects of her father's nomenclature), but she didn't think much of that. Cindy had gotten stoned after explaining the mechanics of whoredom; she had not yet covered the economics.

Fatyma was eating a sweet roll at the counter when she felt presences on either side of her. Looking up, she saw that it was Carlotta and Daneesha, two regulars on the Deuce. Carlotta was a large yellowish woman with a blond wig like a pile of snakes and an intelligent harvest-moon face. Daneesha was bigger, darker, wigged with black braids and was not strictly speaking a woman at all.

"Oooh, honey," said Carlotta, "you better not sit with your back to the door. You in big trouble. *Big* trouble."

"What?"

"Trouble, sugar. Death type trouble. Kingman looking for you."

"I don't understand. Who is Kingman?"

"Kingman the mack," said Daneesha. "The pimp. He don't like what you been pulling out on the avenue there." She sat on the next stool and stretched out her long, lovely legs. They were encased in boots to the knee. "Let me explain, child, see if your little Puerto Rican brain can take this in—"

"Am not Puerto Rican. Am Arab."

"Whatever, you a fool. Listen up. Carlotta, darling, am I the ho with a heart of gold to explain this so this baby don't get herself killed?"

"Pure gold," agreed the other.

"So, what it is, you be ripping off the johns, sugar. With your little knife, dig? So the word get around, the other night this regular john tell the girl and the girl tell Kingman. Now Kingman, he got his business to run, he don't want no little girl scaring the trade away, taking off the johns like you been doing, dig? He be looking for you. He got his razor, he got his little bottle of acid. He find you, honey child, you gonna need a new face, dig?"

"I was you, girl," added Carlotta, "I'd get small real fast. That Kingman a *mean* motherfucker. Where you from anyway?"

"Brooklyn."

"No good. He *from* Brooklyn. Where you from before that?"

"Palestine."

"Where the fuck's that? Montana?"

"Is near," said Fatyma.

"Then you best get your young ass the fuck *back* to Palestine while you still got it, sugar," said Daneesha "And watch your back. You see a baby blue Cadillac in your rearview, thass the end." Daneesha turned away and began to study her reflection in the mirror behind the counter, adjusting her braids just so.

Fatyma waited until they had gone, so as not to give them the satisfaction of seeing her frightened, and then went back to the shared apartment, keeping her head down and staying, where possible, in the shadows. Although she was a remarkably courageous girl by nature, the exposure of her recent ignorance had shaken her self-confidence, and she felt a strong need for another tutorial.

When she arrived, she found Cindy where she usually was, on the sagging brown corduroy couch she used as a bed, eyes closed, the Walkman earphones stuck in her ears, singing a song from *Purple Rain* in the peculiar wavering manner that emerges when people are stoned with headphones on. Fatyma looked around the room and curled her lip. Fast-food bags and wrappers littered the floor along with beer bottles, glassine envelopes, the cassette tape boxes, filthy sheets and pillows. A lavender condom, used, poked its head out from under the skirt of the couch. Fatyma yanked the plug from the Walkman. Cindy opened her eyes and frowned, slowly focusing her gaze on the other girl.

"Wha'?"

"I need your help. I am in big trouble." Fatyma shook the older girl until she snarled and pulled away, and sat up, pouting like an infant, with a dirty red quilt hiked up around her.

The story poured out. Fatyma finished by asking, "Why does this mack want to hurt me, Cindy? There are plenty of joes. Every night they come in cars and cars."

"Johns, not joes," said Cindy. "And it's, like, the principle of the thing. It's his turf. He's supposed to, like, control it, make it peaceful for business and stuff. Enough shit like this goes down and the cops get pissed and start cracking down on the Deuce again, and worse than that, the other pimps get on his case, how come he can't take care of business and stuff. So he has to mess you up."

"But what should I *do*, Cindy?"

Cindy shrugged and sniffed, and started feeling, casually, under the quilt for her stash bag. "Well, shit, you got to stay off the street a while, that's for sure. And you can't go ripping off johns anymore. Like, see, Kingman might've just wanted to, like, scare the shit out of you. If you don't rub it in his face anymore, he might forget about it, you know?"

"But then how will I get the money? If I don't do this with the johns?"

"Hell, kid, you gonna have to sell your ass like the regular people do," Cindy said, with no small amount of satisfaction in her voice. She put the headphones back on and lay back again. Fatyma saw her slip something into her mouth and swallow.

Angry now, she walked out of the room and through the apartment to the kitchen. She had wanted to make herself a cup of tea, but the roaches and the smell and something a good deal bigger than any roach rooting through a plastic garbage bag drove her away. She couldn't understand these people. They were Americans! Those left behind in Gaza, those in refugee camps, people with *nothing*, lived better than this, and these fools seemed proud of it, as if it were an accomplishment to be filthy and lazy and whore and take drugs. It was a mystery, but one she did not care to pursue at any length. All these, Cindy and the rest, were going down, and she herself wished to rise.

It did not take her long to pack, since she lived out of her suitcase. Some of her things had been taken, "borrowed" in the local cant, but she did not bother herself with a search through the personal piles of things in the closets and corners. The drug Cindy had just taken was one that prompted a rosy emotional tone and gushing sentimentality, and so Fatyma found herself tearfully embraced, begged not to leave, showered with good wishes and advice.

"You should check out the East Village," Cindy said. "You might dig that scene better."

Fatyma furrowed her brow. The word "village" conjured up to her mind a cluster of mud huts full of women draped in black and children covered with flies. "The village?"

"Yeah, like Tompkins Square, around there. They let you crash in the park."

"I will go to Hollywood, I think," said Fatyma with firm resolve and, picking up her suitcase, which was a lot heavier now than it had been when she arrived, she walked out.

She set out for the subway. After half a block the cheap plastic handle of the thing was cutting into her fingers so painfully that she stopped, dropped it, and began to look around for a taxi. It was fortunate that she did so, for she was thus able to see the pale blue car that had been following her stop abruptly at the curb, and see the heavy, shaven-headed black man spring from the driver's side and rush toward her. Before she could move, he had snatched her up on his hip and was carrying her toward the car. The back door of the Cadillac opened, and a tan, tall man wearing a knee-length silver fox emerged and held the door open. Fatyma could see something sparkle in his mouth when he spoke. This must be, she thought, the pimp Kingman. He said, "Come on, come on, throw the bitch in here!"

But to the pimp's immense surprise, his assistant let the girl go and dropped to his knees. He seemed to be praying. The girl was running down the street toward the bright lights of Broadway. Kingman ran to the car, and from the glove compartment he took a huge nickel-plated .44 magnum pistol. He fired it at the girl's retreating back, missed, and was blinded by the enormous gout of flame the gun produced, rendering further shots nugatory. He took them anyway, doing considerable damage to street furniture, cars, and trash cans, but none to his target.

He went to check on his assistant, who was now lying on his side in the middle of a widening pool of blood. The blood pool glistened black as molasses under the sodium lights, and Kingman was not about to tread through it in his pale yellow glove-leather high-heeled pumps. The guy was obviously dead. Kingman heard the first faint warble of approaching sirens. He cursed, got into the car, and drove off, leaving on the pavement a corpse with the bone handle of a curved Arab dagger sticking out of its belly.

SEVEN

On the whole, Karp preferred Aaron Zwiller to Rabbi Mendel Lowenstein, and was more pleased than he should have been when Lowenstein's aide called and told him that the rabbi would not be venturing out into the perilous streets to attend this meeting, and that a substitute would be sent. Zwiller was a prosperous diamond merchant and a major financial backer of the Ostropoler Hasidim. Karp had decided that he was tired of meeting with the Arab and the Jewish representatives separately. Let them spend their energy yelling at each other instead of at him, was his thought. When Zwiller arrived, late, Karp realized that he had seen him before, during his ill-fated foray into Williamsburg, in Lowenstein's tiny office, the man at the adding machine. He was large and heavy, approaching sixty, broad and sallow of face, with a bushy gray beard and thick side locks shoved behind his ears and held in place by the frames of sturdy horn-rimmed glasses. His eyes were blue, large, hooded, glabrous, and intelligent, and they did not burn with fanatical fires—a negotiator, was Karp's take, and not on the ballot for the next Messiah.

He shook hands stiffly and formally with Karp and with John Haddad, sat with a soft sigh across the table from Haddad, and folded his hands. Just like fucking Geneva, thought Karp, and he launched into the story of the case thus far. It would go to the grand jury that week; they had been waiting for Mr. Shilkes to recover somewhat from his wounds so he could testify. There was no question that they would get an indictment and that a trial would be scheduled. The charges were murder, conspiracy to commit murder, and aggravated assault.

"First-degree murder?" asked Zwiller.

"It doesn't work that way, Mr. Zwiller. In New York state, first-degree murder is what we call the murder of a police or corrections officer in the line of duty. Second-degree murder is for—"

"For lesser beings like Mrs. Shilkes?" asked Zwiller. He had a gravelly, loud voice, compelling attention, or at least that was the one he used now. Karp imagined that he had others.

"It's what the law says, sir. That's how we play it. But I have no doubt we'll get a conviction and that the defendants will be put away for a very long time."

"What's this conspiracy business?" asked Haddad.

"That means—" Karp began, at which point Zwiller put in helpfully, "They're terrorists. That's what terrorists do. First they conspire, then they murder."

"That's what you call it," snapped Haddad, "but when a foreign occupying power is murdering innocent people every day, we don't have such an inflammatory name for it."

"Self-defense! Self-defense is the name for it against terrorists."

And from there they were off into history, back to the Hebron Massacre in 1929, up to '48 and Deir Yassin, to '56 to '67 to '73 and to the present antics of Black September and the Mossad and Shin Bet and al-Fatah. It was a form of boasting in reverse, each side competing to be the weakest, the most helpless, the most sinned against. Karp let them scream for a few minutes. This was part of the plan. They would yell and accuse, and after this meeting they would each come to him individually and try to make nice. Karp had used the ploy any number of times with scumbags accused of crimes and saw no reason why it should not work just as well with political types. Zwiller was just rolling out the Six Million when Karp rapped his knuckles on the table three times. They were very large knuckles, and they made a commanding sound.

"Gentlemen! Let me just say this once again. This meeting, and any future meetings we may have, are a courtesy of the district attorney's office. We don't *have* to do this, and we're not *going* to do this, unless we can keep focus on the case at hand. I don't care what happened in the Middle East back then or whose side is doing what to whom." He paused and glared at first one, then the other. "Now, we were discussing the issue of conspiracy. Conspiracy to commit murder is a crime in and of itself. We are charging all three defendants, Naijer, Hamshari, and Daoud, with conspiracy—"

Haddad broke in. "Wait a second: Daoud wasn't at the crime at all. He was in jail."

"Correct. But he conspired. He was part of the gang. That's a crime under Section 105 of the state criminal code. And he freely admits it."

"But he's just a kid!"

"They're all just kids, Mr. Haddad," said Karp. "Two of them are murderers."

"So what is this, guilt by association? He had political talks with people who were nuts, so he has to suffer? Look, Mr. Karp, I know this family. They're decent hardworking people, very strict, very old-fashioned—"

"Like the Shilkeses," rumbled Zwiller.

"Thank you, Mr. Zwiller," said Karp acidly. "Let's move on. I should inform you that Ali al-Qabbani has been found dead under suspicious circumstances. We're treating it as a homicide."

"Who?" asked Zwiller, and Karp looked at him very closely as he asked it. He seemed genuinely puzzled; that, or he was an extremely competent actor.

"So, the retaliation is starting," declared Haddad. He clenched his fists.

"What retaliation? What is he talking about?" asked Zwiller.

"Mr. Haddad thinks that militant Jewish groups may have had something to do with Mr. al-Qabbani's death," Karp answered, still watching Zwiller's face.

This reddened angrily, and the man snarled, "Yes, not only did we kill him, we used his blood to make matzos. Mr. Karp, I didn't come here to listen to blood libels from this man."

"What, it's so beyond belief that Jews are murdering Arabs?" Haddad shot back, yelling. "Get a television! Watch the news!"

"Gentlemen! Cut it out!" said Karp in an even louder voice. "You're supposed to be reasonable men. Act like it!" He waited for a few beats. He had their petulant attention. "Now, we've had one Jew killed, allegedly by Arabs, and we've had one Arab killed, by persons unknown. And I am going to press upon you, and I expect you to take this back to your communities, that we are not going to tolerate vigilantism, and we are not going to tolerate revenge, or incitement to revenge. This is not Beirut, and it's not the West Bank."

He let that sink in. "Returning to the matter of Mr. al-Qabbani: we have what looks like a professional execution-style killing. We also believe that Mr. al-Qabbani was a contact between the two defendants in the Shilkes case and someone else, perhaps someone who planned and directed this crime, and—"

"Oh, please!" Haddad broke in. "I can't believe you're bringing up that Dar al-Harb business again. I told you, there's no such group."

"Yes, you did," said Karp quietly. "So what groups *are* there, Mr. Haddad?"

That stopped him. "What do you mean?"

"Oh, just that every ethnic group in this city has its bad boys, and the respectable people know who they are, even if they don't talk about it much."

"That's nonsense! You're implying that I'm involved with *terrorists*? I'm a member of the city council, for God's sake."

"Did I say 'involved'? No. Let me explain something, Mr. Haddad. I was raised in Brooklyn, in a middle-class neighborhood. My father owned a manufacturing business. He had trucks. He had a lot of paper waste to dispose of. In those days, if you had trucks, if you had waste, you were in bed with gangsters. He used to complain about having to pay them off, but he did it. A good friend of his was a lawyer for some of the guys from Murder Incorporated. These are Jewish gangsters, by the way. Mr. Keegan down the hall, I bet he could tell you who's going around buying arms for the Irish Republican Army these days, or if not him, people he knows, in the Irish community. My friend Ray Guma knows half the Cosa Nostra in New York on a first-name basis. So, we know, and they know, and so do you, or people you know do. And if we assume, for the sake of argument, that this kid was killed by his own people, your people, in fact, then you could be real helpful."

"You want me to *spy*?" said Haddad. His nostrils had gone white against his olive skin.

"No, of course not," said Karp dismissively. "I just wanted to point out that you have the kind of access to your community that the police can never have, and that you probably know more than you think you do about this kind of thing."

He turned to stare at Zwiller, who was enjoying Haddad's discomfort rather too much for Karp's liking. "That goes for you too,

Mr. Zwiller. I'd be very disturbed if any further violence emerged from the group you represent."

Zwiller's mouth dropped open. "That's ridiculous! We are peaceful people."

"Who started a riot in which two police officers and several civilians were injured. I want to remind both of you that you have a positive duty to inform the authorities when you have knowledge of any plans to break the law. The state statutes provide six different levels of conspiracy, from misdemeanors to class A felonies. I'm sure we can find something to suit in the event it's required."

"Is that a threat, Mr. Karp?" demanded Zwiller.

"No, sir," said Karp, smiling. "I'm just expounding the law. It's an old Jewish tradition."

Marlene and her partner, Harry Bello, were arguing, as they had many times before, to little permanent effect, about the future of their security firm. She felt at a disadvantage in this argument because the changes that had come over Harry in the five years since they had launched Bello & Ciampi were almost entirely admirable. Then he had been a recently dried-out depressive detective, whose nickname on the Job—Dead Harry—was frighteningly apt. When she had first conceived of a security firm specializing in the peculiar problems of women, Marlene had brought him in almost as an afterthought. He was uncomfortable in the cops, she got along with him pretty well, and he was a terrific detective, as well as being personally fearless and devoted to her. Now, however, there was a new Harry, by almost any standard a better person, although for some perverse reason Marlene did not get on with him as well as she had with the former version. She had heard that reformed drunks often wanted to draw away from those who had known them during their degradation, and that those who had helped them often wished to retain the newly dry in their former condition of docile dependence. She expected that something like this was happening between Harry and her. It made her helplessly sad; more to the point, it promised to disrupt her business.

They were in the little firm's offices in a loft on Walker Street off Broadway, in Marlene's cubicle, which had room for a desk, a desk chair, two wooden visitors chairs, and a small bookcase, all from a Canal Street ex-used-furniture emporium. A dirty industrial-sized window glazed in chicken-wire glass looked out on Walker Street.

They did have one really great window in the place, a large semi-circular affair with the firm's name in gold on it, but that one served the large room where they met with clients, which was also where all their decent furniture was. Harry was finishing his latest, and thus far most disturbing, pitch, which was that Bello & Ciampi should merge with a larger, more conventional security outfit called the Osborne Group.

"I don't like it, Harry," she said. "I don't see why we can't just stay the way we are."

"Because nothing stays the same, Marlene. Businesses grow or they die, and this is our chance to grow. Personal security is one of the fastest-growing businesses in the country, and we should take advantage of it."

Marlene thought about this, studying her partner as she did so. Harry looked good; he had tossed his cheap, rumpled suits and his plastic raincoat and now wore banker's gray, and a sharp white-on-white shirt and crisp, patterned silk tie. His color was pinkish-tan rather than old-paper-bag dun, and much of the black had gone from under his eye sockets. Harry was still a somewhat scary figure, but no longer so in the Halloween sense. Whereas before he had hardly said a word from one day to the next, he was now fluent, a great talker on the phone, his speech freckled with statistics from *Fortune* and *U.S. News & World Report*. Somehow he had re-created himself as a go-getting businessman. She should have been pleased; she *was* pleased, and at one level of her mind she understood that he was right about the firm. But she still didn't like it. A vague picture of herself as a recalcitrant little girl being dragged away from her mud pies crossed her mind. She lit a cigarette and pouted silently, irritated at herself, and him.

After a pause he resumed. "Also, Marlene, you got to realize we can't go on the way we have. No way."

"What do you mean?" She bridled. "We're not making enough *money*?"

"Money's got nothing to do with it. I'm talking about the tricky stuff. Setups."

"I don't do that anymore," she protested.

"Yeah, you do. You can't work it any other way, Marlene, because you don't have the resources to guard all the women you're guarding, so you go talk to the guys, get them to lay off. . . ."

"What's wrong with that?"

"Nothing, except when they don't roll over for you, you set it up so you know the guy's going to come at the client, and then you what we used to call lie in wait, wave a gun at them, tune them up a little with a bat, maybe sic that goddamn dog on them. It's illegal, Marlene. And this business of giving the ladies guns—"

"It's legal. They're down as employees."

"It's a scam and you know it. I talked to the lawyer."

She gaped, shocked. "A *lawyer*? I thought I was the lawyer in this outfit."

"Osborne's lawyer," said Harry, and he had the grace to color slightly. "He said that wouldn't stand up worth a shit, anything bad was to happen. We could get sued, we could face charges. That's just what *you're* doing, and then you're still in there with that woman . . ."

She knew what woman he meant. "Look, Harry, don't hock me about Mattie, all right? She's cool."

"She's a felon, Marlene. She blew a guy's head off when he was sleeping, for chrissake!"

"She was sixteen, Harry, and the guy'd been raping her since she was eleven."

"Everybody's got a sad story, Marlene. The fact is, she pulls all kinds of shit out of that operation of hers. And then there's . . ." Here he reverted to the old Harry's telegraphic language and flicked his gaze back in the general direction of the area behind the offices proper, which included a small kitchen, a toilet, and a set of cubicles for emergency shelter, in one of which lived Tran Vinh Din.

"Tran," she said. "His name's Tran, Harry."

"Him. No green card, he's an illegal, *and* he's got an illegal piece on him. You're paying him out of petty cash, which is a violation all in itself."

"He saved Lucy's life, Harry. Your goddaughter, remember?"

"I know that, Marlene. Did I say *can* him? But you got to straighten out his paper, and you got to make sure he's under control."

Marlene puffed her Marlboro so hard it shone like a taillight and then jammed it hard into an ashtray. "Jesus, Harry! Okay, I'm sorry—but I didn't know we were running General fucking *Motors*! Since when did you get so bent out of shape about the bureaucratic details?"

Harry's expression remained as calm as a pallbearer's. "Don't get cute, Marlene. You know it's not that, just like it's not the money either. What it is, is, I'm too old to go to jail, and I don't want to get into a situation where I either got to rat you out or do time. I want to avoid that, Marlene, and it's definitely going to happen unless we stop this happy horseshit and start being a real business. Now, we go in with Osborne, they handle all the paper, the billing, payroll, referrals, bonding, insurance; we need to transport clients, they got cars and professional drivers. They have houses, apartments, we ever need to stash somebody."

"And so what do *we* do? Sit around and crack wise and drink scotch out the file drawer?"

"We do what we do, Marlene. We get out protection orders, we investigate, and we bodyguard, same like now but legit, and without all the chicken shit."

"And why is Osborne being such a sweetheart here? What's in it for them?"

Harry raised his chin a half inch in her direction.

"Me? I thought I was the *fuck-up*."

The thinnest possible smile stretched Harry's mouth. "They don't know that. And you're a star. There's a whole market opening in short-term protection of women, and there's the whole lady-celebrity business we got. We'll be in their publicity and like that. That's why."

Marlene blew out some air and slumped in her chair, digging her hands deep into her pockets. "Ah, shit, Harry, I don't know . . . it's not exactly what I had in mind when I thought this up. I mean, I could go work for a *law* firm if I didn't want to, like, freelance. I could wear nice clothes and mingle with a higher grade of scumbags. Can I think about it? Do I have to decide right now this minute?"

"Uh-uh. But not next year either. And, Marlene? The stuff I talked about? Lose it, okay? I mean it."

"I know you mean it, Harry," she said, staring back into his black hard eyes. "I said I'll think about it."

Evander Wilson, known as Train on the street, was the man stabbed and killed by Fatyma Daoud, and he was duly processed as a homicide by the Midtown South homicide unit. Mimi Aleppo and Jorge Fines caught the case in the usual rotation, and the first thing they did, after they learned the identity of the victim, was to go talk to the victim's employer, the pimp Jerol Kingman. Kingman was happy to help the police. Train had been a good man, and Kingman knew who had killed him. He described Fatyma, whom he characterized as a "little P.R. bitch," and explained what it was that Fatyma had been doing on the Deuce to ruin business and to upset the smooth flow of necessary vice. Kingman knew these were homicide cops, and had no interest whatever in the moral aspects of his business, so he spoke freely. He said he had sent Train to go find the bitch and explain why she could no longer rip off the johns.

"Just a talk?" This was Aleppo, a woman in her mid-twenties with a round olive face, large dark eyes, and coarse black hair cut short.

"Yeah, just a talk," responded Kingman. "That's why I sent Train. He real gentle. He never even packed a blade, you know? No piece, neither."

"Oh, yeah, gentle," said Fines. "Is that why he had ten arrests for assault?" Fines had a round olive face too, and black hair only a little shorter than his partner's. They resembled each other, in fact, and they both thought that the brass putting them together as partners was intentional. They were both the same height too, five-five, and had both entered the police department at the same time, Aleppo under an affirmative action program fostering the recruitment and promotion of women, and Fines under the terms of a consent decree removing the height requirement for police officers. This twin recruitment order was known uncharitably in the NYPD as runts 'n' cunts, and its beneficiaries were not popular.

"And no convictions," said Kingman. "Train's problem is he be so *big*, and he got this scowly face. Every time they's trouble, the cops pick up the first big nigger they see on the street."

"How sad," said Aleppo. "Where can we find this Puerto Rican girl?"

Kingman gave them an address on Forty-third and added, "She staying with another ho, name Cindy, skinny little blondie bitch."

"Okay, Kingman," said Fines. "We'll check it out."

"I hope you shoot the both of them," said the pimp sulkily. "Motherfucking bitch gut a man just for talking."

They did check it out, but no sign of either the P.R. girl or her friend could they find. The case therefore died a natural death; there is just so much energy in the police, and they are reluctant to spend it overmuch on the murder of an assistant pimp with a violence sheet on him. Aleppo was typing up what she expected to be the final DD-5 on the case when she became aware of a figure standing over her desk. Jim Raney was looking with interest at the large plastic evidence bag on her desk.

"What's this?" he asked, picking it up and examining it more closely.

"That? That's the murder weapon in Wilson. Hell of a knife, huh?"

"Yeah." He moved it in the bag and studied the long, curved blade. "What does it say here? Do you know?"

"Say? What do you mean, 'say'?" She peered at the blade, still gleaming where the steel showed around the brown-red stains. "I thought that was just decoration," she said. "Does it matter?"

"I don't know," said Raney. "There are a lot of Arabic inscriptions floating around recently, connected to murders."

Aleppo knew what he meant. "You mean the Shilkes thing? But this vic wasn't a Jew. It was a black pimp. The word we got, it was a P.R. whore, and this pimp sent his homey out to rough her up and she took him out."

"You got the girl?"

"No, not yet, but . . ."

"Then how do you know she's a P.R.? She could be an Arab."

Aleppo was about to say, "So what, it's a pimp killing, it's got zero to do with any Arab-Jew business." The thought had already formed in her mind when she stopped herself to think, and considered that she was at the low end of the pecking order and likely to remain there, picking up only the shit cases, and here was one of the more famous detectives in the house taking an interest in one of their cases, and so what she actually said was, "Yeah, it could be. You think we should check out the inscription," and she said it in a way where "we" did not mean her and Fines.

Raney picked this up, of course, and picked up the dagger too, and said, "Let's go. I know a guy for this."

The guy was in, as people whom Lucky Jim wanted to see very often were, and he stared at the weapon with horrified fascination.

"I am not an expert, but I would put this in the late eighteenth century," said Dr. Adouri. "Probably made in Damascus. On the blade it says, 'Neither slay anyone whom God hath forbidden you to slay, unless for a just cause.' It's from the Koran, Sura XVII, the Night Journey."

"A good thought," said Raney. "Who would own a dagger like that?"

"Oh, any Arab with some land or status, I think. The workmanship is, as you see, first-class, and it's custom-made, of course, for a particular family. These things are passed on from father to eldest son for generations."

"Not something you'd expect to find in a hock shop?" Raney asked.

"Not if it's genuine. And I think this is. I can't imagine any Arab man who owned this pawning it, unless he was actually starving."

Aleppo asked, "Doctor, how did you know it was custom-made for a family?"

The two men looked at her, and she felt her face warm.

"Yeah, how, Doc?" said Raney.

"The pommel here." He pointed at the silver boss on the end of the hilt. "This carving is actually a kind of monogram. The nature of the Arabic script makes it ideal for such uses. For example, in the Alhambra in Spain, there are mosaics in the fountain court where—"

"What does it say, Doc?" Raney interrupted.

"Oh. Just 'May God protect the family of David.' "

"David? I thought David was a Jewish name," said Raney.

A thin smile from the scholar. "Well, we are cousins, you know. Abraham, Ibrahim. David and Daoud."

Raney felt sweat break out on his forehead. In a voice louder than necessary, he demanded, "Are you saying that this knife belongs to a family named Daoud?"

The professor nodded. "That's a good assumption, Detective," he replied and then observed with some surprise the rapid and unceremonious exit of Detective Raney, with the other officer swept up in his wake.

They were halfway to Brooklyn before Detective Aleppo comprehended the reason for their haste.

"Just because of the name?" she asked.

"It's connected. Got to be. Guy's involved with the Shilkes thing, a stabbing, and then his name turns up on an antique knife in another stabbing. I don't believe in that much coincidence."

"Why? Daoud is a common Arabic name. I have cousins named Daoud."

He looked at her sharply. "You're Arab?"

"Not really, but my grandfather was Lebanese."

"Huh." He thought for a moment. "It doesn't matter. Manson's a common name too, but if Charles was loose and you found a bloody knife with that name on it, you'd check it out."

Hassan Daoud was no actor, nor was his son, Walid, which was clear from the moment Raney slapped the big knife down on the floured worktable behind the bakery shop. Hassan's eyes widened, and a slight noise issued from his opened mouth, a gasp, or perhaps it was a prayer, or a curse, while Walid actually made a physical movement to reclaim the blade. Still, even after that they tried, fatuously, to deny ever having seen the thing before. Then the silly lies: it was stolen. By whom? Didn't know—a thief. Did you report it missing? No—of no value, a cheap thing, didn't want to bother the police. After a good deal of this, Raney noticed two things: one, he hadn't seen the young girl who had tended the counter the last time he had been in the bakery, and, two, Mimi Aleppo was not in sight. He thought briefly of dragging the two men down to the precinct for a long, uncomfortable talk, but decided against it when the other detective came out from behind a bead curtain and gave him a look.

"What?" he said when they were back in the unmarked Cavalier.

"I talked to the wife," Aleppo said. "There's a daughter, Fatyma, age fourteen, left home about two weeks ago. She took the blade. He had her chained to a radiator."

"Why, what'd she do?"

"Wore makeup and listened to rock music was what I gathered, hence a whore, hence to be married off to some old guy on the other side. I got a snapshot of the girl, but she made me promise to keep her away from the old man and little Walid."

"She's worried about her."

"Not at all. The girl's dead for all practical purposes—to the family, I mean. She just doesn't want the husband or sonny boy to actually kill her and have to go to jail for it. She's got three little kids to feed. Unusual thing here—the Palestinians are the most educated and sophisticated people in the Middle East, taken as a group—next to the Lebanese, of course—but Hassan is pure country, real old-fashioned. Comes from a family that was some kind of big deal in the old days, very proud. In those circles, a girl goes bad, there's only one thing to do."

Raney snorted. "Fucking jerks!"

"Yes," said Aleppo, "but on the other hand, they don't get drunk and beat each other to a pulp in saloons, and run corrupt political machines, like some other ethnic groups I could mention. We should try to find that girl."

After the police left, Hassan snatched up a rolling pin and hit Walid on the back with it several times, and then threw it against the wall. His wife had retreated to the apartment above the bakery, where she sat on her bed, with her younger children huddled around her, until the storm subsided. After hitting Walid, Hassan sat down and put his face in his hands. He stayed like this for some time, rocking back and forth in his misery. Walid watched him carefully. When he judged the time was right he said, "Father, I will kill her myself."

Hassan looked up at his son. His eyes were red-rimmed, and this, combined with the white flour on his tan face, gave him a demonic appearance.

"Yes," he said, his voice a croak, "you will. But how will you find the whore? In this city?"

"There is a man," said Walid, "of whom Ali spoke, before the Jews killed him, may God send them to hell, a man who has power and many men who follow him. I don't know his real name, but Ali told me he was to be found at a café called the Palms. We should go there and find him, and ask."

"And why should this great man of yours help us, my son?"

"For honor! This thing disgraces the Palestinians, and he is a Palestinian, a freedom fighter. If he does this, it will be spoken of, and many will support him, and besides . . ."

He stopped, for his father was already shaking his head. "No, no, how can I expose my shame to a stranger? It is impossible!"

Walid stood up and said, "Then I will do it myself."

Hassan did not have the strength to object. He sat at his kneading board silently as his son strode out.

★　★　★

"Go see," said Chouza Khalid, "who is sitting in that white van. A bakery van should be making deliveries, in and out, down the street. But this one has been sitting there for over an hour. We should see if the bakery van has a baker in it." Two men rose from the group around the tables and slipped out.

Khalid had been out of town for some weeks. He had been in Beirut and Tripoli, and in Newport, Virginia, supervising the unloading of some cargo, which was now safe in the basement of the Park Slope house. The trip had gone well; the equipment was ready, and of the best quality; the paperwork was prepared, passports and the various cards and tickets necessary for travel; there was plenty of money from their various dealings; and best of all, there was no inkling of any suspicion from the authorities. The bearded man in the basement was pleased.

Since his return, Khalid had picked up the threads of his drug business, and of the other thing, for which the business was only a money source. He was sitting in the Palm, a coffee shop on Atlantic Avenue, with his back to the wall, at a table that was always kept free for him and his friends. These were a mixed group of Lebanese, Palestinian, and Syrian youths, some trained, others trainable, still others pawns to be used and discarded as the need arose. Bashar and Ahmed, the ones who had gone to see about the van, were among the trained ones, good tough boys from the south Lebanon camps.

Khalid sipped his sweet, sludgy coffee and watched his men cross the street to the white truck. Some minutes later, they returned, with the boy pressed between them like the meat in a sandwich. They brought him to Khalid's table and pushed him down in a chair. He was frightened and trying not to show it. Khalid questioned him, at first roughly and then, as the story emerged—the connection with the Shilkes murder, the vanished sister, the recent visit from the police—his manner changed and became more kindly, for it slowly dawned upon him that the fool represented a solution to a problem he had been considering for some time. Khalid called for coffee and pastries, and shared them with Walid. Everyone around the table seemed to relax, as the boy, having shared coffee and food, was now a guest and under the protection of their chief.

After the coffee had been drunk, Khalid said, "Now, listen to me,

Walid ibn-Hassan. Truly, God has brought us together, you in your need and me in mine. You say you wish to recover your sister, so as to wash the stain of her dishonor from the name of your family. I also desire this, for"—here he raised his finger and cast his eyes aloft—"I am aware of this disgrace already."

Walid goggled. "You are, effendi?"

"Indeed. Little happens among our people that I do not know. Your sister has been kidnapped by the Zionists, may they all rot in hell, and they are keeping her in a secret place, where even now they are committing dishonorable atrocities upon her. This is their object with all our women, as you well know, which is why God will curse and destroy them, with our help." A murmur of angry assent rippled around the tables where the Arabs sat.

"But we will find her and wipe out the dishonor with the edge of the blade, and when her violated body is found in the house of the Zionists, the cursed dogs, great will be the anger among our people, and even the Americans will be disgusted with the serpents they have pressed to their bodies. This I swear by God and our holy cause!"

Another rumble—cries of "On to them!" and "Death to the Jews!" and Walid was staring at Khalid, captivated, eyes glowing, mouth slightly parted.

"Effendi," Walid asked hesitantly, "when . . . when you find her . . . may I be the one?"

"Of course!" said Khalid, pounding on the table. "Who else? Are you not the brother? It is your duty. But the Zionists are clever, and it will take some time, I fear. In the meantime you must add your strength to the struggle. Are you willing to do this, upon your honor?"

"Of course, effendi. Whatever you ask," said Walid instantly.

"Excellent!" Khalid looked around at the other Arabs. "I told you this was a man." Murmurs of assent, compliments. "Now, you have a large truck. Sometimes it is necessary for us to move equipment or men from one place to another. Your bakery truck is well-known in this area, and it has a regular delivery route in other parts of the city No one questions a bakery truck driving around in the dawn hours, and so it is perfect for our purposes. Sometimes it may be necessary to modify the inside of the truck, in order to carry out certain operations. From now on you will drive for us, or make your truck available to us at certain times. If you behave in a satisfactory way, you will be sent for training as these others have, and become a true *fedai*. Are you willing?"

"Yes, effendi, with all my heart!" exclaimed Walid, the breath catching in his throat, his face aglow.

"I knew you would," said Khalid. Then the smile faded from his broad face, and his voice took on a grave tone. "Now, I must discuss something very serious. This is the need for secrecy. You will recall Ali al-Qabbani, peace be with him?"

"Yes, effendi."

"And Ali spoke to you about me, told you that I might be found at this place, described me, even?"

"Yes, effendi, but not your name."

"And now Ali is dead. Why is he dead? Because he spoke." He paused to let the import of this sink in. Then he resumed, in the same solemn voice. "The Zionists, death to them, are everywhere in this city. Truly it is said, two can keep a secret, if one is dead. If Ali spoke to you, then trust in it, he spoke to another, and they heard, and so the Jews killed him. Therefore, you must tell no one of this meeting, or of me, or of anything we tell you to do, or of the truck. Nothing! Not even to your father may you speak of this. All our lives are in your hands. Do you understand?"

"Yes, effendi," Walid croaked.

Khalid reached out and gripped Walid on the upper arm. His eyes bored into Walid's. "Then swear it! Swear silence unto death, swear it by God, the merciful, the compassionate, and by the honor of your family!"

Walid swore this with fervor, after which Khalid relaxed and smiled, and touched Walid caressingly on the side of his head. "Good. Now go, go with God. We will call for you when we need you."

Walid left, with many respectful words of thanks. Somewhat later, Ahmed looked inquiringly at his leader and asked, "Will he truly be silent, do you think?"

Khalid laughed. "Oh, he will babble like a girl, but that is all to the good. The police have their eye on him already, and they are still chasing the Duhd el Dar al-Harb, and so he is ideal. I should have thought of him myself before now. It also solves the problem of the truck. We need not rent one now. No, Walid is a gift from heaven. Let him talk. He will never know anything of any value."

Ahmed, a precise man with a scholarly air about him, said, "Well, in point of fact, he will eventually know everything, but by then he will be in no position to talk."

They both laughed then, about that.

EIGHT

El Chivato drove around the block again, checking out the Palm coffee shop with the edge of his vision. Two men emerged as he watched, and confronted, as he saw through his rearview mirror, the driver of a white bakery van parked down the street. This only confirmed his belief that his quarry was a vigilant man. Naturally, if his task was merely to kill the person the Obregons knew as Lucky, then there would have been no problem. He would have simply gone in the front door and killed them all. But he had been hired to talk to the man, in his special way, and convince him to exculpate the brothers. For this, however, he had to be alone, and he had observed that Lucky was a man who did not love solitude.

A difficult problem, and one unfamiliar to the young man. Previously, he had been told to go here, do that, and his imagination had not been greatly taxed. So he was uneasy. What made him uneasier still was the date. It was now mid-March. His mother expected him home for Easter, which this year fell on the thirtieth. El Chivato had never missed an Easter before, and if he had not been incapable of fear, the prospect of disappointing his mother would have made him afraid. Not that the old lady herself would have said or done anything, no: but the saints were the saints and God was God. Certain things were expected; it was necessary to do as one had always done, to keep the luck running, the protection strong. So it was necessary to be home by Easter.

He drove the black Firebird past the coffee shop for the fourth time. Through the shop window El Chivato could see the big man talking to a thin kid. He slowed almost to a stop, and cars honked behind him. He cursed and accelerated. Reluctantly, he decided that he would have to see Obregon again, which meant that he had to go into the prison again, which he hated like death—or no, he would send the woman to the prison with a message, and then Obregon would call him and they would talk. El Chivato would press upon his client the necessity of his being back in Nogales by the thirtieth. He drove east on Atlantic, heading for the Manhattan Bridge.

The peculiar maneuvers of the black Firebird were noticed by a man selling cheap appliances on the street. Observing the motions of vehicles and persons around the Palm was a more significant aspect of his work than moving toaster ovens, and somewhat later he reported it to Chouza Khalid's man, Bashar, who stroked his short beard and considered the news.

"Mossad, do you think?" asked the appliance vendor nervously.

Bashar gave the man a slow, contemptuous glance. "If it was Mossad, you would not have seen them." After he dismissed the appliance vendor, he went back to the Palm, but Chouza had already left. So, they were under some sort of crude surveillance: it has something to do with the drugs, he thought, with the Mexican thing.

Karp replaced the telephone receiver and leaned back in his chair and devoted himself to a moment of strategic thought. It had been a short conversation, Jim Raney letting him know about the odd connection between the murder of a low-life on the Deuce and a family drama involving one of the Arab conspirators. Raney had not mentioned conveying this information to Roland Hrcany, and Karp assumed that he had not done so. Yet it was also somewhat unusual for a cop to feed this sort of preliminary information to anyone in the D.A.'s office. Karp sensed that Raney was nervous about it, about the possibility of deeper currents roiling the flow of what had at first appeared to be a straightforward case, and was seeking cover. Which was fine with Karp. He did not intend to tell the D.A. about this latest development until things had clarified. The sister would turn up eventually, and then they would see what was what.

Today he was more concerned with the other nasty case on his plate, Morilla, which had gone to the grand jury the previous day.

Frank Czermak had gotten his indictment, as expected, but of course, the grand jury had not heard the entire story. Grand juries heard only what the prosecution wanted them to hear, in this case the discovery of the fatal gun in the Obregons' apartment, the status of the Mexican brothers as dope dealers, and the status of the victim as a narcotics undercover cop. QED, but Karp remained uneasy. Where was the heroin? Where was the money the Obregons said they had exchanged for it? Another thing: Morilla had been working one case for the better part of a year; the Obregons had only arrived in New York some forty-five days ago.

Restless, he made a brief call and left his office, descended to the sixth floor, to the Homicide Bureau, and tapped on the door of a very small private office. As a rule, A.D.A.'s worked in cubicles until they had accumulated considerable seniority. (This was because 100 Centre Street had been constructed when New York County suffered perhaps 280 murders per year instead of well over a thousand and when the people were less concerned with the self-medicating habits of their fellow citizens, so that drug cases did not strangle the courts.) Raymond Guma, at whose door Karp now knocked, was a very senior A.D.A. indeed, a contemporary of Jack Keegan, and one of the relatively few who had chosen, without any hope of promotion, to spend their entire careers laboring in these stony fields.

Hearing the expected growl, Karp entered. Guma was a squat, disheveled man with a deeply scored monkey face not unlike that of the former Yankee backstop Mr. Berra. His office resembled one of those sad apartments into which the police must break when the neighbors complain of the smell, there to find the rooms and halls filled with junk and papers dating back to 1923. Some of the pages sticking out from the piles on Guma's desk were absolutely yellow with age. Around these piles wafted the mixed scents of scotch whiskey, aftershave lotion, cigars, and abandoned hopes.

Karp liked Guma, and had from the first. He would not have recommended him for promotion into any slot requiring responsibility over others, but appreciated the man as a living museum of the hairy, nasty old days at the New York D.A. Guma was an enthusiastic sexist, a mild racist, not entirely incorrupt where he thought it served the greater good, and had never, as far as it could be determined, forgotten any detail of the thousands of cases with which he had been involved. He was also the resident guru on the Mob.

After brief pleasantries and a judicious discussion of the Yankees' prospects (not good, and not likely to improve, with that son of a bitch running the team) Karp said, "Morilla. I'm concerned."

Guma protruded his lower lip a full inch. "You're concerned? Maybe you should share your concern with Czermak. It's his case. Or maybe with our distinguished bureau chief. I could get a secretary to direct you to his office."

"I intend to," said Karp, "at the appropriate moment. This is not the appropriate moment. This is the moment when I go around to all my old pals, especially those whose ass I have covered and saved God only knows how many times, and pick up on the real stuff that nobody wants to tell the D.A." Karp smiled sharkishly and waited.

"Oh, *that* moment," said Guma. He grinned, showing a set of bone white false teeth, leaned back in his ancient wooden swivel chair, and placed his thumbs behind the armholes of his unbuttoned suit vest. The lip protruded again and then snapped back as he spoke. "Do you know Carrozza in Narcotics?"

"To talk to. What about him?" Karp spent as little time as he decently could in the Narcotics Bureau. It ran itself, like an abattoir, and he did not care for the smell.

"Mexican brown heroin. There's all of a sudden a shitload of it uptown, but mostly in Brooklyn. According to Carrozza it started showing up around about the time Morilla got hit."

"And . . . ?"

"There's not supposed to be Mexican brown heroin in New York. In L.A., yeah, but here we get it white from Turkey and the Golden Triangle through Europe. Everyone in the business is a little pissed off. There's all kinds of murmuring among the skells."

"What are they saying?"

"Well, the word around is that it all comes from a new kid on the block, not the *cugines*, not the uptown Zulus, not Jamakes."

"Mexicans?"

Guma shrugged, a slow and elaborate gesture. "It could be that's what the late Detective M. was trying to find out. Whether he did or not . . . you know how these undercover Narco guys are. They don't make contact for weeks, they live the role, they fucking *become* scumbag dealers. . . ." His voice trailed off. Karp indeed knew, and also knew about how easy it was for people in this kind of work to drift by imperceptible stages over the line between pretense and actuality. How far Morilla had gone down that road was something else they did not know. Karp thought in silence about all the other things. Why Obregon had killed Morilla, for one. The Obregons were not the new kids, being actually behind bars during the recent distribution of Mexican brown, and Morilla hadn't been investigating the brothers as far as anyone knew. And where was the dope? The Obregons had possessed serious weight of neither dope nor cash at the time of arrest. Who ever heard of drug lords traveling a couple of thousand miles to a strange city without either dope or cash? As he mused, he tugged idly at the top of a sealed evidence bag sitting in a box at his feet, the detritus of some case. He held up the clear plastic envelope. In it were several tiny vials with colored plastic tops, containing what looked like rock salt.

"What's this?" he asked.

"Crack cocaine," said Guma. "Somebody finally figured out how to make coke cheap. They smoke it in pipes." He indicated the bag. "Guy got shot over that. New kind of dope, new turf. It's funny, the homicide rate peaked in seventy-seven, and it's been dropping for a couple of years. Now, with this stuff, and if we start getting Mexican smack in here competing, it's going to be blood alley up in Zululand. That shotgun job in Brooklyn? Just a taster."

Karp smiled sourly. "Ah, Goom, you always make my day, a little inspirational message. But, seriously, on Morilla, frankly—what's your take?"

Guma shared a narrow-eyed glance. "Frankly. Well, I work for the guy, and he's a friend, but since it's *you*, and it's not gonna go any further . . ." He spread the fingers of one chunky hand and waggled the hand on a horizontal plane. "It's fucked. I don't know what Roland's thinking here, going with this case. Huerta's going to cream us."

Karp nodded. "Manny Huerta's on D?"

"Uh-huh. The little fuckers at least know to buy talent."

"Hmm. Roland tell you he's been getting threatening letters?"

Guma frowned. "No. About the Obregons and Morilla?"

"Yeah. It doesn't sound like Huerta, though, does it? He's a scumbag dope lawyer, but he's a stand-up scumbag dope lawyer. Christ, all he really needs is a couple of citizens confirming the Obregons' story about that phony police raid, and they walk behind the theory that the gun was a frame-up."

"Right, if the jury doesn't buy Netski's story," said Guma.

"Yeah, but Netski does not contribute powerfully to my comfort level." They were silent for a while, thinking about Ray Netski. Netski was a narcotics cop and, like many such, was often a witness in homicide cases. On a particular one of these occasions last year, Roland had caught him in a larger than usual fib, that is, a fib just outside the wire in the fairly wide sway given to police testimony by prosecutors and the courts. If a couple of cops followed a guy into an apartment to talk to him about an acquaintance recently slain with a sawed-off shotgun, and if during the interview a cop gently teased open the door of a closet and lifted up a dirty shirt with his toe, and discovered a twelve-gauge Remington with ten inches missing from the barrel, and thereafter swore on the Bible that the said weapon had been in plain view when they were invited in, as required by the Fourth Amendment in warrantless searches, the D.A. would not normally gag on the morsel. Netski's sin had been considerably greater than that, involving actually moving a weapon from one place to another. Roland, no stranger to such tricks, had caught him at it, had copped the suspect out to a lesser, and then had done nothing else, which is what he almost always did when he caught a cop lying. Roland liked to have cops on his gaff, and in Netski's case the hook was sunk good and deep.

Karp cleared his throat heavily, and said, "Um, Goom, you don't think that, ah . . . Roland . . . ?"

"Ah, shit, no! No fucking way!" replied Guma in outraged tones. "Nah, what I think is they found somebody else's setup and it was neat enough to believe it, and they sort of kissed each other through it. Roland fell in love with it—it's his first cop killer since he's been the chief, right? And he wants to show, like, *velocity* here, and Netski bought in for sloppy seconds, like he's saying, Oh, yeah, Roland, it turns out Morilla *was* closing in on a couple of Mexicans. What's he gonna do anyway, *contradict* the guy who saved his butt? It happens. Not usually with a guy who's as good as Roland, and as wised up as Roland, but since he took over, Roland's . . . what can I say? Not Roland. He don't have you to grab him by the belt anymore, maybe." He snorted and seemed, if such a word could be used in connection with Guma, embarrassed.

"Unfortunately, he does," said Karp, almost to himself. "So—anything else?"

"Not really. Carrozza says there's a name floating around. Lucky."

Karp snorted a laugh. "*Lucky?* Is that the one that hangs out with Lefty and Blacky?"

This forced another grin onto Guma's wide mouth. "What can I say? We're talking about an un-fucking-believably tight little dope operation. They came, they dumped, they scored, they're gone."

"They popped Morilla and framed the Mexican brothers."

"I didn't say that, Butch," said Guma after a meaningful pause. "The Obregons are the defendants in Morilla."

That was it, then, a lot more than he would have extracted from Czermak, who, unlike Guma, retained ambition. Karp rose and said, "Thanks, Guma. This helps."

Guma's eyes slid away. "Hey, don't thank me," he said, "we never talked about it."

Lucy Karp was thinking in Cantonese, something she did often, and with pleasure. It had been her first foreign language, almost a cradle tongue, and she still loved the sound of it in her head, the rolling burr and gong of it, and the music of the tones. It was in Cantonese that she first had discovered, almost as early as her memory went back, that when there was a different language in your head, you were a different person, you could think thoughts you couldn't think in another language. In Cantonese there was a whole world of puns and tone and syllable connections that did not exist in English. Her Chinese friends did not, to her surprise, seem to have this sense of wonder. Later, when she discovered that she could pick up other languages—to date, Sicilian, French, Spanish, Mandarin, Vietnamese—with hardly any effort, and that other people could not do this, and that they found it strange, even disturbing, it made her glad, and she had grown her odd little personality around this difference.

She was sitting in the backseat of the yellow VW reading a book her mother had bought her as a reward for being good about clothes (she was wearing a blue wool jumper over a yellow turtleneck jersey, with navy tights and Adidas, part of the recent raid on Bloomies). The book was *The Story of Language*, and from it she had learned that one could actually get paid for learning languages, and for thinking about how languages were connected and analyzing their structure, which information had blown all thoughts of other potential careers (cowgirl, detective, spy, nun) clean out of her head. Next to a loving family, such an early vocation is about the best thing that can happen to a child, and Lucy had become a happier person since: calmer, sweeter to her little brothers, more tolerant. The book was a permanent resident of her backpack, along with a Petite Larousse, an old red-bound Mandarin–English dictionary, a Vietnamese–English phrase book lent to her by Tran, and *The Catcher in the Rye*. Lucy read dictionaries and grammars like other girls her age read Judy Blume, and she never forgot anything she read.

Just now she was reading through a brief discussion of the history of linguistics in the nineteenth century, of, to be exact, the brothers Grimm and their discovery of consonant shifting among the European languages. Lucy was reading this in English, thinking about it in Cantonese, and listening, with a fragment of attention, to a conversation going on in the front seat between her mother and Tran, which was being conducted in French. She did this with no more thought than she would have given to the coordination of her various muscle groups while skipping rope.

The conversation was becoming somewhat strained: the parties had begun addressing each other as Madame and Monsieur. Lucy had noticed her mother's irritation on being picked up after Chinese school, and this seemed to increase after they had driven up to retrieve Tran from some mission in Clinton. When her mother was irritated, Lucy had noticed, she often expressed it by attempting to exert minute control over an unruly world. It was not pleasant being the object of such control, and Tran was becoming stiffer and colder in his locutions. Lucy paid more attention. It was, she gathered, a stupid argument about a surveillance Marlene wanted done. Marlene was giving him precise instructions instead of just telling him to do it, as she ordinarily did.

". . . take the whole roll," she was saying, "and make sure you get the license plate number. Can you use a telephoto lens?"

Tran made the hissing sound he uttered when he was annoyed. "Madame," he snapped, "I wish that you would stop treating me like an incompetent, and asking me if I can do this or that simple thing. It is insulting."

"I beg your pardon, Monsieur," replied Marlene in a similar tone. "I was not aware that you could do everything in the world."

Tran turned away and said something in Vietnamese to the side window.

"Pardon me, I did not hear that," said Marlene.

"It was nothing, Madame!"

"He said, 'I cannot yet menstruate, you foolish woman,' " supplied Lucy without thought.

They both turned and stared at her, gaping, and were called back to reality only by the blare of a car horn. Marlene had drifted over the center line and had narrowly missed a careening taxi. She cursed and dragged the VW back into lane, almost sideswiping a truck. More horns. Marlene pulled into the right lane, and at the next red light she said, "Jesus, I almost killed us! Tran, I'm sorry, I'm nervous and disturbed."

"I had noticed, Marie-Hélène," he answered dryly. "Is there something I can do to help?"

"No. I'm sorry, actually, yes, yes . . . but we must talk of it at length, without the presence of an injudicious infant."

"I am not an infant," said Lucy in French. "I am a linguist."

"Yes," said her mother, "but sadly, because of your unfortunate personality, probably unemployable as a diplomat. Are you enjoying that book?"

"Yes, thank you," said Lucy politely. She had noticed that her French self was more elegantly mannered than her regular self. She wondered whether this was a quality of the tongue itself, or because she was still not entirely comfortable in it, or because the language she had learned from Tran was not a street argot but the French of the schoolroom, with Tran's colonial accent. She was more polite in Cantonese too, but since her mother did not speak Cantonese, this was wasted on her. She continued, "In any case, I have no desire to be a diplomat. I intend to be like Mezzofanti."

"Who?"

"Cardinal Mezzofanti was the greatest linguist who ever lived. He's in the book. He knew a hundred and seventeen languages perfectly. Once he learned Swedish in forty-eight hours, so well that he spoke it better than most Swedes."

This was one of Lucy's apparently unlimited supply of conversation stoppers, so the three of them rode in a restful silence the rest of the way to the East Village Women's Shelter.

The first thing Marlene noticed when she entered the shelter was the new smell. Instead of the usual institutional pong of fry grease, disinfectant, and old tenement, there was a waft of fresh bread baking and an undertone of exotic spice, as of some oriental market. Tran slipped away to the kitchen to investigate the source. Marlene inquired of the proprietor.

Mattie Duran grinned and replied enthusiastically, "Yeah, ain't it grand? Every so often the street tosses up a pearl. The kid walked in last week, middle of the night, soaking wet. She'd been sleeping in Tompkins Square. Anyway, it turns out she's a baker, and the rest is history. I'm gonna gain thirty pounds."

"I thought you didn't take runaways. Or do you make exceptions for bakers?"

Mattie frowned. "Yeah, well, she's a runaway, but there's a difference. It took me a couple of hours to get the story out of her, she lied like a trooper, but you know me. . . ."

Marlene nodded; she did. Mattie never judged, but she would not be lied to by any of her wards.

"Her name's Fatyma, she's an Arab kid from Brooklyn. Her daddy sounds like he got him a *thing* about keeping her cherry in one piece. She says he chained her up every night as soon as she started growing tits and getting interested in boys. She wants to be an American in the worst way, but let me tell you, she knows nothing, I mean *zip*, about how things work in the States. Anyhow, the old man was about to ship her off to marry some old guy in the Middle East, so she lit out. Says she spent some time up on the Deuce ripping off johns."

"She was on the stroll?"

"Not according to her, and I believe her. She was an armed robber, technically. Fourteen years old." She snorted, as if to express her opinion of the way men had screwed up the world. "Anyway, she ran foul of some pimp and he sent muscle after her, and she stuck a blade in his gut and ran."

"So she's a killer? Is this, ah, *wise*, Mattie?"

"She didn't say she killed him, so she's not a killer in my book," said Mattie dismissively. "I got no reason to believe the cops are after her. Besides, she's not a resident—she's staff. I gave her a job and that's it."

Marlene had to chuckle. It was a typical Duran solution, full of humane criminality.

Just then the door to the little office burst open, and in came Lucy, breathless and leading, or rather, being led by, the black mastiff, which she had been walking.

She greeted Mattie enthusiastically, and they had a brief conversation in Chicano Spanish. Lucy and the Mexican woman were fond of one another. Mattie enjoyed the occasional presence of a sprightly child who was not the product of a marriage made in hell, which was all she usually got to see. For Lucy's part, Mattie was the only actual cowgirl-like personage Lucy had met so far and, in addition, knew a foreign language and was willing to teach it, nearly always a compelling recommendation. And there was one other thing.

"Can I see your Colt?" asked Lucy, as she always did.

"Sure, pardner," said Mattie, smiling. She reached into her desk and pulled out her family heirloom, an actual .44 Peacemaker.

Marlene was at the moment distracted by the troublesome thoughts that had clouded her mind since leaving Harry earlier that day, and so her shouted "No!" was somewhat too late. As soon as the big revolver appeared in Mattie's hand, the great dog growled and leaped across the desk, knocking Mattie off her chair and onto the floor, where she lay screaming curses at the ceiling, with her gun hand gripped in the vast, hot, spiky cavern of its mouth.

Marlene ordered the animal off and into a corner, and helped Mattie to her feet, apologizing profusely. Lucy was sent off to return Sweetie to the VW. The two women went off to the kitchen for some restorative coffee and pastry.

"I ought to sue you," said Mattie. "That fucking dog! Do you know a good lawyer?"

"An oxymoron. Honestly, thank God you're all right! I was in outer space, or I would never have let you pull that hog-leg Colt out. He doesn't need a command to take out anyone he thinks is pointing a gun at me. Is your back really okay?"

"I'll live," said Mattie. They entered the kitchen, which smelled like the anteroom to Paradise, and Mattie introduced the beaming, flour-spattered olive-skinned girl. Tran was seated at the table mashing pistachio nuts in a bowl. The two women sat and drank coffee and ate little cakes made with honey and almonds, light and delicate as blossoms. Mattie brought up the Valone woman again, and this time Marlene, feeling she owed one for the dog incident, relented and said she would help.

"So what's on your mind, *chica*?" asked Mattie. "What're you thinking about so hard I almost got ate by your dog?"

"Oh, just business problems. My partner and I don't see things the same way. He thinks we should merge with a big security firm and that I should lose all the fringe stuff."

"Fringe stuff like me?"

"Since you ask, yeah."

"Him's the one you should lose, *chica*. What you should do is come in with us, work full-time out of the shelter."

"Yeah, well, I need to think it through. My life in general . . ."

Mattie sniffed and struck herself solidly between her substantial breasts. "You think too much. There's women who need your help, who got nobody else. You know that in your heart. You should go with the heart. Fuck all the rest of it!"

Marlene had heard this speech before, of course, and had taken it in as the usual Mattie rhetoric, but now that Harry was pushing her into a decision, it cut more deeply. *Did* she really want to devote her life to this kind of work? She was a wife and mother with three children, after all. She was a feminist, whatever that meant nowadays, of course equal-opportunity and abortion rights and all that good shit, but she didn't follow it all the way, not by any means. She despised the whining about the oppressive patriarchy from privileged college professors. She didn't hate men, the poor saps. What she really liked was the tense, amphibious structure of her life, being *both* a good Catholic mom and an armed femi-semi-terrorist. This was hard to explain to the utterly committed like Mattie, or her husband. She thought briefly of the smug advice she had given him about picking his team and cringed inwardly; she was just as bad; no, worse.

Lamely she said, "I'll think of something," and after that they were mainly quiet, watching the baker girl. She was rolling out *filo* sheets by hand, something Marlene had never tried to do herself. As the girl worked, she hummed and sang snatches of a mournful-sounding song in what Marlene supposed was Arabic.

It was warm in the kitchen, and Marlene felt herself relax for the first time since leaving her office, with baking smells and the rhythmic rolling and grinding going on, and people drifting in to talk to Mattie or get coffee. The shelter seemed to run on its own time, in a slower and more traditional pace, like a tiny medieval court—the barbarians raging outside, and within, the inhabitants maintaining a precarious peace, preparing food, caring for children, having their lives. If, as Mattie urged, she followed her heart, Marlene thought that she would choose this over what she referred to privately as heavy metal: the high-technology guarding of the rich for some big firm. On the other hand, she had a brain, and a good one. This worldlet partook more than she liked of what Marx called the idiocy of village life, the dullness of the incompetent poor. She watched the girl roll out the translucent dough and wondered idly what *she* was thinking.

This is what: Fatyma was reasonably happy. She had endured a terrible fright and some miserable nights living out in the park with the weirdos, without even the knife to protect her, afraid to sleep at all. She had abandoned her suitcase, with all her recent purchases in it when she fled, and now owned nothing but the clothes she stood in, plus the wad of money sewn into a pouch inside her jeans. She missed her two books most of all, although she comprehended now that as a complete guide to the culture of the United States they left much to be desired. But she was safe; the woman had assured her of that, safe from her family and from the police. It was very much like living in the village in the occupied territories, better really, because there were no men ordering everyone about. Here there were only mothers and their children, fleeing as she herself had. This made her miss her mother and her little sister, but she thought there would be a way to get a message to them after a while, when she was far away and rich. The Duran woman paid her a good salary, and she had no expenses to speak of, so the savings would grow quickly. The baking was easy, although the oven was not right, not a true baker's oven; but she had been baking since she could stand, and she could work around that. Her English was improving. She could watch television all she wanted, real television, not just tapes, and listen to the radio too. She felt lucky to have stumbled on the place. She wondered what had become of her first friend, Cindy.

Lucy came in, seeming subdued, poured herself a glass of milk and took a pastry from a plate. Mattie was called away to handle some crisis. Tran finished grinding his pistachios and went out to smoke a cigarette. Marlene and Lucy chatted about school, until gradually Lucy became aware that the baker girl was singing in a language she did not recognize.

"What's that language?" she boldly asked, and when Fatyma answered, with some surprise, that it was Arabic, Lucy focused her considerable charm on the older girl and got her to teach her the words to the song, which was a simple repetitive ditty about girls and goats going up and down the hill, and the girl looking in the clouds to see the face of her future husband. In ten minutes, with much giggling on both sides, Lucy had the song down. To Marlene's ear there was no difference in accent or intonation between Lucy's and Fatyma's words. Fascinated, for she had never observed this process before, she watched Lucy attack the new language. How do you say this, how do you say that, in Arabic? and so on to every object in the room, and the basic verbs. By degrees Lucy spoke greater proportions of actual Arabic in her questioning (soon it was "*Tib 'a 'eyh* 'shoes' *bil arabee*?") and was corrected, laughingly, by Fatyma, and plunged on, never forgetting a correction, the ferocious throaty consonants of the language apparently posing no problems for her supple tongue. By the time Marlene dragged her away, complaining loudly, an hour later, she had a vocabulary of over two hundred words and a solid grasp of grammatical construction.

In the car, Marlene said, "Lucy, Tran and I have to go do something right now—it won't take long, but I'm going to drop you off at home. Set the table and make a salad—if I'm not home by the time your father gets there, throw a box from the freezer into the microwave. And don't forget your homework."

"Yes, master," said Lucy in sepulchral tones.

"Don't be smart. The other thing is—you know about Fatyma? I think it would be a good idea if we kept her between the three of us for now. She's in trouble, and she's safe at the shelter, but she might not be if word got out that that's where she's staying. Okay?"

"Not even Daddy?"

"I think *especially* Daddy. I hate to ask you to keep a secret like that, but it's probably only for a short time. Will it make you neurotic?"

"Probably. Anyway, Daddy and I have lots of secrets from *you*."

Lucy saw Marlene's eyes appear, startled, in the rearview mirror. "*What!*" exclaimed the wounded mother. "What secrets? What are they?"

"If I told you, they wouldn't be secrets, Mother," replied Lucy, cool as a peeled egg.

Marlene opened her mouth to fume but stopped. Hoist by my own petard, she thought, which I deserve. "Shut up, Tran!" she snarled, but he kept laughing, a soft, breathy clicking vibration, and Lucy started guffawing too, and after a while she joined in. After that, instead of driving straight home, she stopped off at Bello & Ciampi and told Harry that, as much as she hated to do it, she didn't think she could be quite as straight-up a security operative as he required, and that if he wanted to bail and go work for a slick uptown outfit, okay, lots of luck, and no hard feelings.

Harry looked at her for a long time, or so it seemed, not with his cop's eyes either, rather with the burnt ones, and Marlene realized how much all this was paining him, and she felt even worse, and so when he said, "Marlene, before you make up your mind, see the man, see Lou Osborne," Marlene sighed, and felt her eyes prickling in a non-hard-boiled way, a soft-boiled way, actually, and said, "Okay, Harry, set it up."

After leaving Guma's, Karp went back to his desk and ordered a roast beef sandwich and a soda from a take-out place. While he was waiting, he made a series of calls to people he did not want to speak to, but wanted to leave messages with. It was an old bureaucratic ploy, but one he was fond of anyway. He was laying a trail, weaving a web. Trailing a coat. The messages he left with Czermak, Carrozza, Netski, and Roland Hrcany would act as little crystals around which paranoia would form, and upon these might grow useful actions.

The problem was, he didn't have enough to go to the D.A. with, not enough to cause him to drop an indictment against a couple of putative cop killers. It would be a political disaster, and Keegan would never go for it, except if the folks who actually did the deed were waiting in jail and there was a plausible case against these new fellows all wrapped up. Karp realized he was far from that, and there was only so much he could do quietly to get there. He wanted other people to make the noise. He wanted Carrozza talking to Czermak about a missing load of brown Mexican heroin. He wanted Czermak to go to Roland, worried. He wanted Roland to lean on Netski so that Netski would get the cops stirred up, in the hopes that something would float to the surface, something fat enough to allow him to modify his lame tale about Morilla investigating the Mexicans. And the more they talked, the worse it would be, because word would get out—it always did. Every detective, every senior A.D.A., had a pet reporter to whom juicy tidbits might be fed, against the day when a sympathetic ear might be required among the jackal press. There would be a buzz, it would soon reach the ears of the defense, and so it would become imperative that Roland and his minions either uncover the reality behind the buzz, and use it in the People's case against persons now unknown or, if the buzz was actually false, learn enough to torpedo it in court and actually convict the Obregons.

This was Karp's thinking. He knew that the people he had called would not hurry to return his messages (or would call when they knew he would be out of the office—the ploy worked both ways), because it is an iron law of bureaucracy that when someone up the line or one who has the ear of the big boss calls and leaves a cryptic message (such as "what about this Lucky on the Morilla murder? The brown heroin angle?"), it is a foolish worker bee who calls back without having exhaustively researched the reason for the call. So they would call one another, and plot and plan, and Karp would observe and keep poking, which is what good staff is for.

Shilkes was meanwhile on the back burner. The girl might turn up, but Karp did not think, from Raney's story, that she was part of a conspiracy. That there *was* a conspiracy he now thought a reasonable bet, but this would not greatly affect the course of the trial of the Arab youths. Karp was mainly concerned at this point with the suppression of vendetta and the extraction of back-channel information from the hostile communities.

It came sooner than he thought. He was about to leave for home when John Haddad called, sounding both nervous and full of himself. There was someone Karp should meet. He gave Karp an address in Brooklyn, a law office on Washington Avenue. It had to be today or not at all. Karp called his driver, and in ten minutes they were in the car.

"Brooklyn," said Karp to Ed Morris. "Take the Manhattan Bridge."

"The rabbi again?"

"No, this time it's the Arabs," said Karp. "I'm an equal-opportunity schmoozer."

NINE

John Haddad's office was located in a small commercial building near Pratt Institute, old but well kept, a relic of the time when Brooklyn had been a major metropolis on its own. Karp took a creaky, mahogany-lined elevator up to the sixth floor. At the receptionist's desk in the waiting room of the suite, which seemed otherwise deserted, sat a dark-skinned man in a leather jacket. This person expressed a mien that made it doubtful to Karp that his ordinary task in life was uttering cheerful greetings to clients and fetching coffee. One of his hands was hidden beneath the desk, in a way that suggested it was not empty of lethal force. This person pointed silently at a door, and Karp nodded and followed the point.

Inside was a walnut-paneled office that might have belonged to any mildly prosperous lawyer, of the deeds, closings, trusts and wills sort, its panels decorated with the usual diplomas and awards. Since Haddad was also a politician, the walls also included photos of the owner with various big shots—the last couple of mayors and governors prominent among them. There was an old oak desk in the center of the room, set on a pale red oriental rug, behind which three large old-fashioned windows looked out on the avenue. Fort Green Park was just visible as a brown smudge in the distance. Haddad and another man were seated on a tufted green leather sofa set along one wall. On a low, ornately inlaid coffee table before them was a brass coffee service, brightly polished. Both men rose when Karp entered, and Haddad made the introductions: Mr.

Rahmali, Mr. Karp. Haddad's eyes shone behind his spectacles. This was a big moment for him, a far cry from bitching about street-cleaning schedules. They sat and Karp drank some bitter coffee and they exchanged pleasantries. Karp took this occasion to examine the stranger. Tired, was his take, maybe forty-five, but with a lot of hard miles, a small, compact, Peter Lorre–model fellow, a round, cropped head, clean-shaven, deep-set eyes, a bony, flaring nose, all set in a face brown as a grocery bag. Karp had spent a lot of time learning to tell the serious players from the bullshitters. Haddad was a bullshitter, more or less; Mr. Rahmali was a serious player.

There was a delicate pause in the light talk. Mr. Rahmali fixed Karp with his eyes.

"Mr. Karp," he began, "forgive me, but it is my understanding that you are Jewish, true?"

The voice was well modulated, the accent the familiar one spread by the British throughout their late empire, with the r's heavily rolled.

"What about it?" replied Karp.

"Then, I must ask you, what is your position on the current troubles in the Middle East?"

Karp took a deep breath and tried to suppress his annoyance. "Mr. Rahmali, my position on the Middle East is neither here nor there. My only purpose here is to advance the interest of criminal justice and, secondarily, to prevent civic unrest in this city. As a private individual, I would hope that the various parties out there would learn to live in peace."

A smile flickered across Rahmali's lips. "Yes, these are noble sentiments, which I, of course, share. Tell me, are you aware of what has been happening over the past few months in Lebanon?"

Karp ignored this and asked sharply, "Who *are* you, Mr. Rahmali? Why am I here talking to you?"

Haddad drew in his breath. Rahmali's face did not change in the slightest.

"Ah, I thought you had been briefed," Rahmali said. "Allow me to explain. In 1948, during the first Zionist war, Golda Meir came to the United States to raise money and proselytize the cause of her people. She collected over five million dollars in less than a month. I do not hope to do as well, but my cause is similar. If there were a Palestinian state today, I might hope to be its foreign minister. I have the honor to be one of Mr. Arafat's oldest colleagues. Is this sufficient identification?"

"You're with the PLO."

"Yes, and unlike the more fortunate Mrs. Meir, I am not here legally, which is the reason for our precipitous and surreptitious meeting. You will have understood that Rahmali is not my real name. May I continue? As to the Lebanese situation?"

Karp shrugged. "Just what I read in the papers. You've taken a big hit is what I gather."

"Yes. A complete defeat. It is essentially the end of the dream that we could, by means of guerrilla warfare, do to the Zionists what the Vietnamese did to you—extract political concessions from the gun. We have been driven out of Lebanon, eight hundred of our women and children massacred at the Sabra and Shatilla camps. Lebanon is now divided between the Zionists and the Syrians, Jordan and Egypt are both closed to us, and we cannot get any closer to Palestine than Tunis. So, we are realistic men. If armed conflict fails, we try political means. What are the political realities of the current situation? One, Israel depends for its existence on the support of the United States. Two, this support will be forthcoming only if Israel can pretend to be a just state, defending itself against foreign enemies. Three, Israel cannot continue this pretense while suppressing a million and a half Palestinians in the occupied territories. It is impossible. There will be atrocities, as in South Africa. Israel will become an international pariah. This they cannot stand, and so sooner or later they will deal with us. We will accept the existence of Israel, forgoing violence, and they will accept our existence, and after a great long while, your innocent hope will become reality. Meanwhile, however, there will be transitional difficulties."

"You mean like terrorist murders?"

A tiny nod of acknowledgment. "Just so. You understand that the Palestinian cause has always been used to further political ambitions that had nothing to do with the happiness of the actual Palestinian people. It is the great litmus test for Arab politicians—perhaps I should say for Muslim politicians now that Iran is what it is—just as communism was at one time for your country. It produces irrationalities as great. The Mideast is unusually rich in young, passionate men who have no serious education, no jobs, no future, and who are willing to sacrifice for a cause. Some of them are in this country, in this city. . . ."

"You mean like the suspects in the Shilkes murder?"

"Them, and others. These can be organized by . . . let us call them entrepreneurs of violence. They are by and large extremely clever and talented men who have lived underground for many, many years, who have been trained to kill and destroy by experts, and who have learned to love that mode of life. It is an addiction with them, like a drug. The Irish have them, the Basques have them, the Corsicans. And for various reasons they are not short of funding. Iran I have already mentioned. Libya. Syria. A Gulf prince or two. The Soviets, although they are perhaps more afraid of the ayatollahs than they are of the Jews. Give me two million dollars, Mr. Karp, a tiny sum on international scales, and I will launch you a terror campaign on behalf of vegetarianism, Esperanto, what you like."

"Mr. Rahmali, this is all fascinating, but could you make your point?"

Another ghostly smile. "I beg your pardon. Patience is a great virtue in the PLO, and perhaps I have too much of it. Or a cultural thing. We Arabs say, speed is of the devil. But you are, of course, American, so—to the point. There is a man. He was trained in al-Fatah, the striking force of the PLO. He was expelled for . . . let us say, excesses. After this he engineered, we believe, the assassination of a senior PLO official with whom he had political differences, an occurrence all too common, and one which our enemies have never been slow to exploit, which is one reason we are in Tunis rather than Jerusalem. He was briefly a Marxist and was resident in Moscow in the mid-sixties. Later he joined Black September. He fought in Lebanon for two years, in an operation funded by Iran. He calls himself Feisal Ibn-Salemeh. Does the name Salemeh mean anything to you? No? Well, then, Ali Hassan Salemeh was the mastermind behind the 1972 Munich attack on the Israeli athletes. Feisal started calling himself Ibn-Salemeh—son of Salemeh—as a commemoration when the original was blown up by the Israelis in 1979 in Beirut."

"Not a sweetheart, I gather."

"No. A dangerous man, and quite out of control. Of course, we tried to keep track of him, just as our opposites in the Shin Bet and Mossad did, but about eight months ago he vanished. He walked into the Hotel du Roc in Algiers one Sunday morning and never emerged."

Karp was getting antsy again. He didn't want to hear the details. "You're telling me this because you think he's here? Because you think he's somehow behind this dumb stabbing?"

Rahmali seemed unperturbed by the interruption and cruised ahead with his unveiling. "So there was great consternation among those who consider these things, on both sides. But there was nothing but silence—where Ibn-Salemeh had been there was a vacuum, as in outer space. Then some other quite interesting things start to happen. A man named Abdel Hussein Khalid, Chouza Khalid as he calls himself, who has a reputation in Beirut as a small-time arms and narcotics smuggler, suddenly begins to expand his horizons. He flies to Tripoli and meets with some senior Libyan military and state security people. He charters a small merchant vessel on a trip to Marseilles. He makes investments in several legitimate American firms dealing with the Middle East. On the strength of these investments he obtains a residency permit and moves to New York. He imports and exports. Recently, he traveled again to Libya and other interesting places, including the city of Newport, Virginia, where he met the vessel *Adouana*, Liberian registry, out of Marseilles, and arranged for the off-loading and transport of several large crates of cargo."

"How do you know all this? And what does Khalid have to do with this Ibn-Salemeh guy?"

Rahmali raised his hand in a mollifying gesture. "One moment, if you please, Mr. Karp. I promise it will all make sense. We know because one of the men close to Khalid has a cousin, who is close to us. Also from this cousin we know that something important is being planned, an outrage. What it is, we don't know, but from our Libyan sources we are fairly certain that Khalid took delivery of at least one 250-kilogram Soviet aerial bomb, from the Libyan military, plus a good deal of miscellaneous weaponry. Now, Khalid is a criminal, not a terrorist. He works for money, although I suppose it would please his vanity to be respected as a freedom fighter. It is inconceivable that he could or would mount an operation of this type by himself, or that the Libyans would even let him in the door without some major sponsorship or association with some important figure. Now, as you can imagine, we have a pretty good idea what the other groups are doing at any time—Hamas, the Hezbollah, Abu Nidal, and so on, and we have no indication that they have the will or the resources to mount an operation on American soil. Thus, we have an inexplicable operation, without an obvious leader, and a bold and ruthless leader who has utterly vanished. It gives one pause, does it not? And there is one other thing, which is why I am talking to you this evening. I said that Feisal was expelled from al-Fatah. Why was this? Because he preferred, in violation of the policy of concentrating on military targets, the organizing of little groups of boys to do stupid things. One group took over a school bus and crashed it, killing themselves and all the children on board. Another threw a grenade into a bathhouse on a kibbutz, killing three elderly women. They killed hitchhikers, they shot up restaurants. Every one of the boys he sent out was killed or captured. Every one! When we asked him to account for this failure, and for the stupidity of the targets, he laughed and said we did not understand how to wage war in this way. The point was to create rage in the target populations. Here he meant both the Jews and the Arabs. The Jews would be enraged by the choice of targets, and press more heavily on the Arabs under their control, which would enhance recruitment of *fedayin*, and so would the loss of the boys, because their families would require vengeance. He thought it was a *good* thing that his boys were killed, do you see? He recruited among the layabouts, the slow-witted, the dreamers. . . ."

"I thought that was precisely the point of terrorism, Mr. Rahmali. He sounds like a champ to me."

The man made a deprecating movement of his hands, a fluttering, as if brushing flies away. "Yes, we do terrible things, it is true, but we justify them by reference to a political purpose. There is at least—what do you say?—the *color* of a military action. Feisal was after rage for the *sake* of rage, unconnected with any political aim. Let me make myself clear, Mr. Karp. If I could achieve the freedom and dignity of the Palestinian people by detonating a nuclear bomb in this city, I would do it. I would hold the bomb on my lap and push the button. I am a fanatic, I admit it. But once I understand that such an act would not bring my goal closer, would make it impossible, in fact, then participating in violence becomes not a tool in a just war, but an insane fantasy which feeds on itself. This is the case with ibn-Salemeh. Now, you are involved in this situation because two or perhaps three Arab boys have killed a Jew . . ."

"And you suggest that the crime and the choice of the perpetrators is characteristic of this man's former style."

"Certainly. Ibn-Salemeh is missing. His presumptive associate,

Khalid, is in the city now. We have a crime, with implications of a wider conspiracy. I assure you that the PLO is not involved. Who else could it be?"

"Okay, sir, but if you're right, this is a matter for the FBI, not just the Manhattan prosecutor. I will be obliged to inform them of our talk." This brought a startled expression to Haddad's face, but the other man waved his hand dismissively and said, in a weary voice, "Of course, but your FBI has this information, and has for some time, through various sources. But whether they will stop the action or not is questionable. The FBI has difficulty in infiltrating Arab organizations, for obvious reasons. It would not be difficult to arrest Khalid—he operates quite openly—but this would accomplish nothing. It would not secure the explosives and weapons, and it would not catch Ibn-Salemeh."

"But what *have* they done? Anything? Do you know?"

"I know very little," said Rahmali evasively. "I am, as you can imagine, merely passing through. Mr. Haddad asked me to talk with you, and so I did."

"Why did you? What do you get out of telling me all this?" asked Karp, since Mr. Rahmali, the potential former would-be suicide nuclear bomber of New York, did not strike him as one ordinarily at the beck of the Haddads of the world.

Rahmali pursed his lips and smiled, making the sort of patient face one presented to a slow student. Karp saw him as he might have once been, a high school teacher in a dusty desert place.

"I thought I explained this. It no longer serves our cause to have the Americans see us as a gang of merciless fanatics, not specifically the PLO, I mean. We wish to separate ourselves from . . . others who are less discriminate in their actions. The Arab, the Muslim, population of the States is growing, becoming more powerful, not at present as powerful as the Jews are, but not inconsiderable in both New York, Michigan, and California, and these are important political states, as you know. So this is the battlefield of public opinion, and what we require is that when Americans think of Arabs, they think of people like Mr. Haddad here, not, as you say, rag heads with bombs and Kalashnikovs."

Karp allowed that this would be a good thing, checked his watch, and, after some desultory closing conversation, thanked Haddad and Mr. Rahmali, and made his exit. On the ride back to Manhattan, Karp was silent and emitting don't-bother-me vibes, so Morris left him alone with his thoughts. The councilman had, surprisingly enough, done the right thing, quickly and discreetly, although Karp had to wonder how much of the event had been constructed by the dangerous and anonymous "Mr. Rahmali." Assuming the man was more or less on the level, Karp now had confirmation of a conspiracy behind the stupid killing of an elderly food merchant. Karp was conscious of a roiled, slightly nauseated feeling in his belly that was not a result of bouncing over the corrugated surface of the Manhattan Bridge. Rather, it was the uncomfortable knowledge he now possessed. As a responsible citizen, Karp was naturally interested in preventing an outrage that would take innocent lives. As a prosecutor, even as the direct agent of a district attorney, he had, however, a much narrower interest, which was the preparation of an actual case, of a type that was ordinarily considered one of the most difficult to prosecute, a case of conspiracy. An Arab gentleman living in Brooklyn who might commit some violation of the New York criminal code at some future date was perfectly safe from the hand of the New York County D.A. except if, and only if, he had entered into an agreement with at least one other to commit a felony, that agreement being the "overt act" required by the relevant statute.

It would be a bear to try, which Karp would not have minded had he more to go on than a secret meeting with an unknown man, who might very well have some obscure political ax to grind against this Khalid character. So he was uneasy about that, but what really riled him was what he referred to privately as "foreign shit," the various ejecta from the world's trouble spots that happened to land within the jurisdiction of the County of New York. The Shilkes case and its dark surround certainly qualified as foreign shit. What to do with it was the problem.

The first duty of a staffer is to decide what is to be presented to the principal and in what manner. The staffer who goes to the principal with every little thing will not last long; if the big guy wanted to dick around with every little thing, he would not require the services of staff. On the other hand, the principal must never be surprised, so the staffer has to keep up a continuous flow of information, which, however, must be delivered in an appropriate form. Not "Oh, fuck, boss, what'll we do now?" but "I've done this and that, and it's fixed, boss." The staffer has no real authority, being a mere doppelganger of the boss, so the process of getting it under control can be a complex matter of threats and persuasion, with the great hole card being the level of information already slipped to the boss. Only the staffer knows this for sure, but naturally those he hopes to manipulate would dearly wish to know it too, so that they can slide by the staffer and sandbag him with the big guy. These conditions insure that most staffers are (or quickly become) sly, slippery, subtle rats.

That he understood himself to be becoming ever more ratlike, against the demands of his natural temperament, added no little to Karp's discomfort. Nevertheless, what he had learned and its implications needed sharing, and as he rode up in the elevator to his loft, he decided who were going to be the sharers.

Karp was a firm believer in the separation of church and state, and since his home and his family were the closest thing he had to a church, he almost never brought his business to his home. He made an exception only when privacy was of inordinate importance, as now. Somewhat after nine that evening, therefore, Karp sat at his round dining room table drinking Marlene's cocaine-strength coffee with three people, two of whom he trusted utterly and one who was merely a necessary participant. His wife, naturally, was of that number: Karp would not have dreamed of plotting anything in his home without including her. That this was not entirely reciprocated by Marlene, who had plotted things aplenty around this very table without including him, was of no moment. He was an officer of the law and she was not, and besides, Marlene was Marlene and came with a whole package of surprises, like a cereal box. The next was Jim Raney, who was necessary as the investigating officer in Shilkes. Karp understood that the foreign shit was way above the competence of a mere detective, but he thought that was Raney's problem. If he didn't want to carry the freight for something like a possible terrorist cell, all he had to do was inform his lieutenant and the thing would be whisked up into the fourteenth floor of One Police Plaza in a New York minute. That suited Karp well enough; whether it would suit Raney, or the other cop at the table, remained to be seen.

The other cop was Detective Lieutenant Clay Fulton. Fulton was Karp's oldest friend on the police force, had known him since his first stumbling days at the D.A., and had saved his young butt innumerable times. Karp expected him to try once more, and had confidence in his ability to do so, and since he was assigned to the

D.A. squad, and more or less worked for Karp, he would have the primary responsibility if Karp were to go ahead and institute some sort of conspiracy investigation. Fulton was at this time in his early fifties, his athletic body only slightly thickened, his pleasant mahogany-colored face smooth except for two deep lines at the corners of his mouth and three that shot down between his heavy brows, like arbitrary marks on a piece of expensive sports equipment. He was one of very few black detective lieutenants in the NYPD, and one of fewer still with a college degree. Fulton had broken a theater date with his wife to come here tonight, when Karp, as he had mentioned sourly, sent up the Bat Signal, and he was not charitably disposed.

Karp told his tale to complete silence. No questions were needed because there were few people in the country who could tell a complex story ex tempore better than Butch Karp. He gave them the Shilkes case from the beginning, as if opening to a jury: the crime itself; the scribbled slogans of a somehow not very real organization; Raney's discovery of the murder weapons and other evidence; the discovery of Ali al-Qabbani's corpse and what it implied; the peculiar incident of the pimp's assistant getting stabbed by a person who appeared to be the sister of a conspirator; and finally the intelligence garnered in Councilman Haddad's office.

After he stopped talking, there was a pause, which was broken by Fulton's deep chuckle, which, as it always did, made Karp start laughing too, and then they all started laughing. When the hilarity died down, Fulton said, "I knew this would be better than *Man of La Mancha*. You're in deep shit again, Chief, assuming what the rag head says is true."

"You think it might not be?" asked Karp.

"The *hell* I know! I wasn't there; you were. But . . . assuming that Mr. what's-his-name is what he says he is, a PLO guy, why should he be such a pal as to tell you what's really going on?"

"What, you don't believe that business about the PLO pulling back from terrorism against Americans?"

"I don't disbelieve it, necessarily," replied Fulton, "but there's also no reason I *should* believe it either. You got no independent confirmation, just the word of an anonymous alien that two other aliens you also don't know are some kind of bad guys, going to blow up the city. But just focus on the facts for a minute. What *do* we know for sure? One, a couple or maybe three punks kill an old lady in a robbery—"

"It wasn't a robbery—they left the cash envelope," put in Jim Raney.

"Okay, a *botched* robbery, then. Two, a week-old floater turns up, and you ID him off a slogan that he's got tattooed on his arm, which is the same slogan that your punks left at the murder scene. A professional hit, which feeds your idea that it's not just a couple of punks, but something wider, a 'conspiracy.' " Fulton said this last word in a tone he usually reserved for referencing Santa. He had their attention.

"Three is this Arab girl sticking the pimp. Again, you got one story about how she came to be wandering around in the Deuce and why she was packing a blade. No confirmation of that either."

"What's your point, Lieutenant?" asked Raney, his voice tending toward the tight. What Fulton was saying was starting to look like a criticism of the police work that had been done on the various cases, mainly by him.

"It's not 'Lieutenant,' Jim. 'Clay' is fine," said Fulton, smiling to show he meant it. "Believe me, this is so off the record and out of channels, we should've both left our shields out on the landing there. My *point* is, we got a bunch of apparent connections that don't add up to a whole hell of a lot, and don't give us a basis for any real police work, not to mention building any cases." Here he looked pointedly at Karp, whose motto, repeated to the point of tedium, was that it didn't matter who did the crime, but rather whether you could construct a case that stood up in court. Fulton drank some coffee, shuddered slightly, and continued. "But on the other hand, you got the possibility that Butch's Arab is on the level and somebody is planning a major crime. So the choice is, do we sniff around some more, just us, until we got a . . . a package, something that makes sense, that makes a case, or do we go to the brass with what we got and holler wah-wah-wah the *Ay*-rabs is comin'?"

"Holler," said Raney immediately. "This is too damn rich for my blood."

"I'm glad you said 'we,' " said Karp to Fulton.

"Oh, yeah," answered Fulton with a grin, "I haven't nursed you along all these years to see you screw up at this late date." He addressed Raney. "Okay, you holler to your watch commander—what does he do?"

Raney shrugged. "Hell, that's his lookout. Pass it up the line, I guess."

Fulton chuckled. "Really? Say I'm your lieutenant. What am I hearing? 'Uh, Loo, I just closed the hottest case in the zone, but see, the sister of the pal of the perps stabbed this pimp, but we don't have her in yet, and also we got a DOA ain't even on our chart that could've been a pal of the perps too, and, oh yeah, a city councilman arranged a secret meeting with the D.A.'s main man, and some guy we don't even know his real name says the Arab boys are part of a plot to blow up the city.' What's he going to do, Jim? Is he going to smile and stroke your hair?"

Raney shifted uncomfortably and felt a flush rise on his face. Fulton was perfectly correct; Raney would look like a fool going to his commander with a story like that, but he did not appreciate it being pointed out in this way, especially not in front of Marlene. And her husband. There was an uncomfortable silence, which Raney was about to break with something sharp and injudicious when Karp surprisingly came to his rescue.

"Yeah, but Clay, Jim's still in a crummy position. Some damn bomb goes off and there's another killing, and they find he's been sitting on all this, he's shafted. What do you expect him to do?"

Fulton considered this question for a moment, and replied with more gravity, "I don't have any expectations for him, and I didn't mean to make light of his problem. All I can say is what I'd do in his place, which is not to go up the line until I have the full story, or more of it than I got now. But that's just me, my style. That's what I've always done." He looked at Raney and smiled wryly. "On the other hand, I'm a fifty-one-year-old detective lieutenant, and I'm not feeling any big groundswell toward making me a captain in the near future. I'm almost ready to give up my boyhood dream of being chief of detectives. Playing it safe, going through channels, and dumping this heap of shit on somebody else is one kind of career move. Trying to *solve* the goddamn thing, taking the chance that it'll blow up—ha! Bite my tongue!—that takes a different kind of cop. You got to decide which kind you are."

Marlene followed this colloquy with fascinated interest, but kept her face neutral. She already knew which way Raney would roll, and wondered whether Fulton was manipulating him. Probably not, she decided; Fulton was like Karp, a straight shooter, unlike herself. What an odd little group the four of them were! Sitting around a civilized table spread with coffee and chocolate biscotti, tied to one another by bonds formed of dreadful violence, with her as a kind of center. She had once saved Raney's life, Raney had saved her daughter's life, she had saved Karp's life, and Karp had saved Fulton's on information she had developed. What kind of people were they? Not the kind that flourish in organizations. When Raney, for example, had discovered that bakery robbery, he should have slipped away and called for backup instead of barging in there and killing four people, in which case he might not have been the kind of cop who would have head-shot a thug holding the infant Lucy with a knife to her throat. In any case, he must know that having killed more people in line of duty than probably any currently serving NYPD officer was not going to contribute to his rapid advancement. Fulton was a hero too, but clearly the brass, while they admired heroes, did not want them as fellow brass. She could see the thoughts roiling behind Raney's freckled forehead. He was going to cast his lot with the crazies; what else could he do?

"Ah, shit!" said Raney under his breath and then, louder, "Okay, how do you want to play this?"

Fulton nodded and replied, "The main thing is this terrorist business. Butch, you had a guy at the FBI?"

"The son of a bitch retired on me. Before that, he sort of dirtied the nest up there. If Carlos the Jackal was hiding in my bathroom, they might tell me, but otherwise . . ."

"Okay, I got a few contacts in the Bureau," said Fulton. "I'll check it out, see if there's any buzz. Meanwhile, it might be a good idea to turn the heat up on this al-Qabbani killing. Someone must have seen him with this Khalid guy or his home boys."

Raney said, "Yeah, all right, we could do that. We could even have a talk with Khalid himself, if he's really operating in the open like Butch's guy said."

Fulton and Karp exchanged glances. Karp said, "True, but the last thing we want is for this guy to spook and disappear with a load of weapons and explosives. Let's leave him alone until we see what kind of coverage the Feds have. And let's keep this tight. If we're assembling a conspiracy case, then it's critical that the bad guys don't catch on until we're ready to go in with wiretaps and warrants."

They discussed details and coordination for a while after that, Marlene listening and not saying much, until Raney brought up the girl, at which point she stopped saying anything at all. Of course, Fatyma, the pastry queen of the women's shelter, was the girl involved; Marlene knew that as soon as Raney had told his story, but she'd said nothing then and would say nothing now, knowing it was stupid, knowing the risk.

She thought about this later, at two-thirty in the morning, sitting in the lightless kitchen, as she was getting into her terror outfit, which was built around a black, rip-stop nylon coverall, with many pockets and zippers. She hadn't slept at all, but had tossed beside the warm, roughly breathing bulk of her husband, playing endless self-recrimination and self-justification tapes through her head, the usual double feature. Had she been a less scrupulously fair woman, she might have blamed it all on Harry Bello, who in forcing upon her a decision she had carefully avoided making for years, had upset the finely balanced segmentation of her life, those layers of licit and illicit activity she had maintained with the force of her own will and warped conscience, like some elaborate poussecafé. Without knowing it herself, she had already made her decision *in re*: Bello & Ciampi, which was why she had not betrayed the Arab girl to the police.

She finished tying up her hair and stuffing it into a rolled-up black silk ski mask perched on top of her head, and bent to pull on her black Converse high-tops. This done, she walked silently down to her office at the end of the loft and took her pistol from the gun safe. On the way back, she looked in on her children. Lucy was sprawled in her usual horizontal frozen leap with her Italian-flag-striped duvet half kicked aside. Marlene covered her again, extracted the little clutch of foreign-language dictionaries that had become tangled in the bedclothes, and replaced them on the bedside table. In the next room she found Zak with his butt up in the air and snuffling, Zik rolled up against the crib bars like a prisoner straining for freedom. She carefully adjusted their positions and kissed them both, inhaling their powdery odor. She secretly thought that at some level they recorded this attention and would count it to her credit as a mother and, when they came necessarily to hate her, would hate her somewhat less.

In the street, Tran was waiting, dressed as Marlene was, smoking and sitting crosswise on the seat of his old black Jawa motorcycle.

When he saw Marlene, he flicked the cigarette away and kick-started the motor. Marlene got on the pillion seat, and they rode off north on Crosby.

There was little traffic at that hour, and in ten minutes Tran had the motorcycle parked at Eleventh Avenue and Forty-seventh Street. From there they walked to a six-story apartment house on Forty-seventh. Some minutes later, Marlene having easily picked the locks of the street and apartment doors, they stood, with their ski masks down over their faces, and surgical gloves on their hands, in the one-bedroom apartment of Ernesto Valone, estranged husband and tormentor of Kitty Valone. Marlene brought out a pencil flashlight, and by its beam they entered the bedroom. Few people are capable of resisting an armed attack when awakened from a deep sleep in the small hours, and Valone was not one of them; with Marlene's gun in his face, he gave, after a few strangled protestations, no trouble. In two minutes they had him trussed hand and foot with the kind of plastic restraints the police use in riots, with a strip of duct tape over his mouth. Valone was a squat, blocky man in his mid-thirties, with a nascent beer gut and a brush mustache. He slept in a T-shirt and Jockey shorts.

Marlene kept the flashlight in his eyes as she spoke. "Mr. Valone, we're here to give you an intelligence test. We want to see if you're smart enough to stay alive, or if you're so stupid that we have to really hurt you. The test is, can you stay away from your ex-wife? So far it doesn't look good, Mr. Valone, I got to tell you that. You've violated the terms of your restraining order fourteen times in the last year and a half. You've been arrested twice. Something is not getting through. This is where we come in. You want to know who we are? The Mafia. The CIA. We're from outer space. We know where you live, we know where you work, we can get you anytime. We're always watching. We're *stalking* you, Mr. Valone, just like you're stalking your ex-wife. We can do anything we want to you anytime we want. We could break your arms and legs. We could cut out your tongue. We could cut out your eyes. How would you like that? It'd be real hard to bother your ex-wife if you were blind and couldn't talk. But we won't do that, not yet, because this is your first warning. It's also your last warning. Bother your wife one more time, and unbelievably bad things are going to happen to you. Things like this."

Marlene had been speaking in a low, caressing voice, with her mouth close to Valone's face. She could see his eyes bulging with terror and hear the breath gushing heavily through his nostrils. A rank scent rose from him. Now she let out her impression of a crazy person's giggle and moved away from the head of the bed. Tran moved deliberately onto the bed, straddling the prostrate man's knees. From a pocket he brought out a straight razor. Marlene shone her light onto Valone's chest. When he saw the hideous glitter of the razor, he made a strangled, high-pitched noise deep in his throat.

Marlene said, "I wouldn't move if I were you, Mr. Valone. I would try to be very still."

Slowly, Tran ran the razor down Valone's chest, slitting the T-shirt and then the Jockey shorts. The shorts were soaked with fresh urine. With short, precise strokes Tran shaved off Valone's pubic hair. Then he got off the bed, held Valone's jaw, and shaved off half his mustache, as much of it as he could reach over the tape. There was very little blood. Valone was shaking like a man in a fever. He made another high-pitched noise when Tran rolled him over, but all Tran did was nick the plastic restraints with his blade. The man could struggle free of them in a half hour or so.

"We're going now, Mr. Valone," Marlene said. "I hope you got the point, I really do. We're bad, but we don't want *you* to do anything bad. Just obey the law. Leave your ex-wife alone and you'll never see us again."

They slipped out. On the street, Marlene staggered away from the doorway, leaned against a lamp post, and threw up. Tran gave her a clean handkerchief, which she accepted and used to wipe her mouth. Tran always brought along a number of clean handkerchiefs on these expeditions, because Marlene always threw up. As they walked back down the sleeping street to the motorcycle, Tran said, in French, "Forgive me, Marie-Hélène, but I fear you are not suited to this work. Perhaps next time you should stay away."

"This may be true," answered Marlene wearily, for they had this conversation every time, "but if you will forgive *me*, your English is not yet sufficient to allow you to make the proper impression upon those whom we must interview. In any case, it is my responsibility, and so I must attend." They walked a little farther, Marlene muttered something, and Tran said, "Pardon?"

"Just talking to myself, the mark of a collapsing mind. I was thinking, all this, and what if it fails to work."

"Oh, I think it will work, more or less. Of those whom the law does not dissuade, very few will resist this kind of interview."

"You're the expert," Marlene said sourly, and immediately regretted it.

"So I am. There will, of course, be some in whom folly is so deeply seated that even this will not root it out, and these will have to be disposed of in some other way. All this is quite remarkable to me, you know. We do not have this problem in my country."

"What! That's absurd. In a—a . . ." Marlene closed her mouth.

"You are embarrassed to say, 'a male-dominated society where women are mere chattels.' In truth, my dear Marie-Hélène, Vietnamese women are not particularly oppressed, by Asian standards. But what I meant was that in a society where the family is paramount, a man would not be allowed to molest a woman in this way. Her brothers or her uncles would do to such a man far worse than we have done to that filthy specimen just now. The Americans have abandoned the family, however, in the name of freedom for the individual and put their hope of protection in the law. Which, as we have seen, is incompetent in such cases."

"You should talk to my mother," said Marlene.

"I would be charmed, of course. Here is the motorcycle. Do you care to mount, or are you still sick?"

"I am still sick, but I will mount nevertheless. And, Monsieur, if it ever occurs that I am not sick after such an excursion, I beg that you will shoot me."

"My pleasure," said Tran, and booted the machine into roaring life.

Marlene slipped into the loft and undressed in the bathroom and washed her face and her mouth as quietly as she could; it was just past three-thirty. But to her dismay Karp reached out and touched her and said sleepily, "You were out."

"Yeah, Sweetie was whining. I forgot to walk him earlier," she said.

A pause. He said, "Next time you walk the dog, you should remember to take the dog. He was tromping around while you were gone."

A longer pause. "Am I going to get *grilled* now?" she asked stiffly.

Karp rolled into a more comfortable position. "Uh-uh. I din see nothin'. I don' know nothin' and I don' *wanna* know nothin'. Let's just get some sleep."

"Could you hold me?" she asked, her voice near breaking. "I need to be held."

"Sure," he said, and wrapped his long, long arms around her, pulling her close.

"That's nice," she said.

"It *is* nice," he agreed. "It's the nicest thing there is, just about, but just so we're clear on this, if it should come to my official attention that you're breaking the law, I will put your ass in Bedford, *this* ass"—here he grasped the literal naked, warm globes—"which will break my heart, but my kids are not going to have both parents in jail at the same time. Just so we're clear."

"That sounds fair enough," said Marlene, who now threw her leg up over his hip, their usual signal, for the desire she now urgently felt for a certain kind of oblivion could not be turned off by any amount of legal warning.

TEN

In the pre-dawn darkness, Chouza Khalid watched his men load the material into the Daoud bread truck. There were four large wooden crates marked in Arabic, French, and English as industrial ceramics, with the appropriate customs tags and seal still affixed to them, and one long tan fiberglass shipping cylinder, marked as a compressor unit carrying the logo of a French firm. The men grunted as they lifted the cylinder into the truck, which was fortunately low to the curb. Khalid had men with radios posted on the surrounding streets. They reported no sign that the house in Park Slope was under observation.

Ibn-Salemeh had ordered the move immediately upon hearing Khalid's report that the Palm coffee house had been under observation, and at the same time he also instituted what he called Beirut rules governing communication and the movement of people and supplies. Beirut rules meant coded telephone and radio communications and elaborate route-changing and car-switching routines. Chouza grumbled at this, for like most professional criminals he was lazy and ill-disciplined, but he grumbled inwardly and carried out the orders. He was afraid of Ibn-Salemeh, which was not something he could say about any other man he had met. Fortunately, their connection would not last much longer. The other man would have his victory here in New York, and Khalid would be gone, with a good deal of money, provided he could extricate himself safely. Ibn-Salemeh controlled the papers and the preplanned escape routes, and Khalid was cognizant of the possibility that he himself might be as dispensable as the young Walid. It was like holding a jewel and a scorpion in the same hand; the trick was to get rid of the scorpion without losing the jewel, and without being stung.

That was, however, a thought for tomorrow. Tonight all he had to do was to transfer the goods to a warehouse in Manhattan that he had leased in the name of one of his dummy corporations. He would drive the truck himself, with Bashar and Ahmed to help unload. Bashar and Ahmed were, of course, Ibn-Salemeh's boys, but that could not be helped. The man was not going to let him drive off with his goods without them along. The four of them were the only ones who were supposed to know the location of the drop.

When the truck was loaded, Khalid drove off, and during the ride he naturally paid exquisite attention to all the traffic regulations. Weaving around the truck, sometimes passing, sometimes hanging back (Beirut rules), were three other cars full of their men, checking for followers. In this way they proceeded northwest, avoiding the elevated highway, sticking with the surface streets, which gleamed wet and nearly deserted at this hour. At the Brooklyn Bridge each of the escort drivers informed him that they were unobserved, and Chouza sent them away, proceeding up the west side of Manhattan, under the shadow of the old highway with only Bashar and Ahmed for company. This was a district of old industrial buildings and warehouses around what remained of the great rail-freight-handling district that used to cover much of the middle west coast of Manhattan. It was undergoing redevelopment, and Khalid had gotten a good deal on the lease of a depot scheduled for demolition. He arrived at the building, a four-story concrete structure with an enclosed loading dock secured by a corrugated steel door. They unloaded without incident. After that they drove back to Brooklyn and returned the truck to Walid, who had been waiting, impatient and confused, in a back room at the Palm. Walid received the grateful thanks of his comrades, together with many assurances that "after his training" he would be allowed to take a more active part in operations, and he was sent off. Then Khalid and his associates prepared coffee and sat down to plan how they would determine the identity and the resources of whoever was spying on them.

"That's one hell of a story," said the district attorney after a long, thoughtful silence. Karp had just finished relating to the D.A. what had transpired around his dining room table the previous night, and thought he might actually light the long green cigar he habitually played with, but while he did not do that, he appeared more worried than he had ever been in Karp's long connection with the man. Karp agreed that it was one hell of a story, and the D.A. said, "You think it's wise to keep it close like you're doing?"

"Shit, *I* don't know, Jack. I don't know if it's wise or not. We're not set up to make decisions like this. What I want Clay to come back with is something like, oh, yeah, the Feebs have this covered up to the nostrils, go back to sleep, girls. Failing that"—here Karp made a helpless gesture—"I await your orders, sir."

"I could go holler to the police commissioner," said the D.A. speculatively, "and he would crank out the Red Squad."

"I don't think they call it the Red Squad anymore, Jack."

Keegan rolled his eyes. "I *know* that, wiseass." He leaned back in his big chair, creaking, and sighted up at the ceiling along the length of his unlit cigar, as if watching the rise of smoke. He said, "You know what I do not love? I do not love the district attorney who goes on crusades where the interests of important constituencies are concerned. Do you know a fellow named Zwiller?"

"I met with him. He's Lowenstein's guy. Why, has he called you?"

"Persistently. I told Marcie to refer him to you. Why's he trying for an end run? Aren't you keeping him happy, bless his little Semitic heart?"

"I thought I was," said Karp. "Unless he heard I met with the opposition and he thinks I'm ready to sell out my people for Arab gold."

"Well, go stroke his balls for him, but we definitely don't want Lowenstein hearing about this business, not until we get it sorted out. As to that . . . did your mysterious Arab gentleman make any indication as to the urgency of his warning? Any date mentioned?"

"No, it was all very general."

"None of that 'there's not a moment to lose, the bomb is ticking under Fifth Avenue' kind of thing?"

Karp shook his head, and Keegan put the cigar down, drumming his fingers on his desk, which Karp knew was an indication that he had come to a decision. "Okay, that being the case, and since I have no intention of going off half-cocked, we'll leave it at least until Fulton gets back to you, and should our pals at the federal level not have an operation going, *we* will investigate so as to either uncover a prosecutable conspiracy, or let our minds rest that there isn't one. In the meantime I will slip a discreet word into the ear of our friends down the street, just so we're covered."

That meant the cops, or rather the police commissioner, their political head. Karp thought this was a reasonably good idea.

"Meanwhile, where does Roland sit in all this?" asked Keegan.

Karp had been waiting for this one, and answered uncomfortably, "I haven't actually brought him into it yet. I figured he had enough to worry about, just the cases and running the bureau, and until I had it more solid. . . ." He trailed off. Keegan's eye did not miss his discomfort. He did not press the issue, but let Karp off the hook by saying, "Well, why don't you let me fill him in?" Karp assented, feeling grateful. They understood one another very well. The staffer must convey information to the boss, but if the staffer routinely rats out his friends, he will soon have no information to convey, because no one will talk to him. Thus between a staffer and the very rare boss who knows how to handle staff there develops a nuanced set of signals as complex as a pas de deux. Keegan changed the subject a little. "Speaking of Roland, how's the other festering boil?"

Here Karp could be blunter, because he knew more, and because he had already expressed his doubts about the case. "Sometimes even scumbags tell the truth," he said, "and this is one of those times. The Obregons came in with brown heroin, major weight. They claim they got ripped off, and sure enough, the town is flooded with Mexican brown, but most of it hit the streets only *after* they were arrested. There's no real evidence Detective Morilla was chasing the Obregons. He was chasing someone else—who we don't know, but the name Lucky comes up a lot."

"*Lucky?* You can't be serious?"

"Yeah, me too, but it's all pretty vague at this point. Netski, the cop in the case, backs up the party line pretty good, and we've got the right gun. The only real question is, Can you believe a conscious, planned frame against a couple of out-of-town nogoodniks? Roland and I have a difference of opinion over that, as you probably know already."

"I do," said the D.A., "and I don't like it, but I can't walk these cocksuckers until I have something to put in its place."

"I understand that and I'm not suggesting it," said Karp, "but there's another angle. Roland's been getting letters, death-threat-type letters, about the Obregons. They're innocent, if you don't let them go you die, Yankee dog, that kind of thing. Not what you would expect from a couple of guys who didn't do it."

Keegan's face clouded. "I hope Roland's taking this seriously."

"No, he's not, as a matter of fact. I was hoping you'd mention it."

"I'll do that." A moment later, "Why isn't he? His famous macho image?"

Karp had given the matter some thought, and he replied, "That, but it's mainly that none of us have much experience with a criminal class that operates against law enforcement authorities directly. The wise guys never do that here, although the Sicilian Mafia does it all the time, and it's practically the national sport in Mexico, bribe 'em or kill 'em."

"You're thinking some segment of our colorful immigrant community is bringing in those kinds of customs?"

"I don't know, but it's probably safe to say it's not all knishes, pizza, and shish kebabs. Face it, I just got finished talking about people who might be planning to blow up something in New York to make a point over in the Middle East. Threatening a prosecutor seems like spare change compared to that. And we know *somebody* executed a police officer."

"Something else to talk with my friends down the street about," said Keegan, rapping his knuckles lightly on the desk. "Meanwhile, keep doing what you're doing and keep me informed." He picked up the cigar again, twirled it, replaced it carefully on the desk. That part of the conversation was over. Karp waited for the next shoe to drop, but the D.A. only leaned back, smiled, and asked, "So, who do you like in the playoffs?"

Marlene sat upright in bed, instantly awake, her heart pounding, her stomach clenched, in the sort of dreadful rising that occurs when we have overslept an appointment, or fallen asleep at the switch, or suffer from a bad conscience. She wiped her eyes, which were blurred with tears shed during sleep, an evil sign. It was full morning, and the loft was silent but for the whisper of the heat-pump fan and the noises filtering up from the street. She got out of bed, groaning as the events of the previous night re-occupied her mind and she distinguished them from her unhappy dreams. She checked the bedside clock, which bore the unlikely message that it was ten forty-five. Throwing on a silk robe—her whore's robe, as she thought of it, a wrapper printed with green leaves and pink flamingoes—she stomped out of the bedroom.

Complete silence: no clattering of utensils in the kitchen, no baby voices, no TV, no Posie singing or talking to herself or to the boys, nothing. In the kitchen, which was spotless, the breakfast dishes put away, the counters wiped, she found the notes. One from her husband read, "Sleep in, Tiger. I'll bring Chinese home. Love, B." The other was in Posie's third-grade dyslexic scrawl: "Took the boyes to the zoo. Buctch siad OK," signed with a little heart with a curly P in it.

Marlene sat down at the table and fingered both notes. Had she been a certain type of woman, familiar from the movies, she would have clutched them to her breast and wailed tears of gratitude. Instead she dragged the somewhat grubby sleeve of her robe across her face a couple of times to stem a certain dampness, loaded the espresso maker, showered, washed her hair, dried it, and lolled about with her mind more or less blank, as the sages of the Orient advise, until the enticing odor of the finished coffee brought her back to the kitchen, where she had two big cups of jet fuel with plenty of warm milk in them, with (her secret vice) a couple of sticks of the boys' zwieback, which she dipped biscotti-style into the brew, and a single cigarette smoked free of poisoning-her-children guilt and thus superbly delightful.

She then strolled down to her little home office and called Bello & Ciampi, where she found all in order, the miraculous Tran having covered her neglected responsibilities of the morning, and the messages not that urgent. Sym reminded her that she had an appointment at one at Osborne uptown.

Ah, yes, Osborne. She walked back to her bedroom and threw open the doors of her wardrobe closet. She noticed the heap of black rip-stop nylon she had worn the night before and, wrinkling her nose, tossed it and the underwear that went with it into the hamper. No terror clothes for Osborne, she thought. No, instead she would give him the full KL, see what he was missing and eat his liver out. She took down her one genuine Karl Lagerfeld suit, an item that must have cost five grand new, but which clever little Marlene had picked up for $450 in a consignment shop belonging to a woman whose persistent ex Marlene had discouraged, and who had given her the first crack at it. It was made of wool mixed with cashmere, had a hand like a baby's kiss, and was colored the darkest possible shade of plum. The jacket was cut lush too, with wide shoulders, which meant the pistol didn't break its line, probably not something old Karl had in mind, but welcome. The $250 perfectly matching fuck-me pumps that Marlene had bought new to celebrate this bargain and an ecru silk blouse completed the outfit. She did her face and hair, popped in the glassie, checked her image in the full-length mirror, declared it not bad for an aging, one-eyed, mother-of-three felon, and, lusting after the now unobtainable *noir* look, wished she had a black mink and one of those little velvet hats that sat cocked on one's head like a bird, with a half veil. It was while unashamedly primping in this manner that the solution to her problem with Harry popped into her mind, as if the diversion of cerebral blood to the fashion lobes had somehow released a blockage in the region of sneaky creativity, something that may happen more frequently than neuroscientists suspect. Grinning and chuckling, she grabbed up her beloved trench coat, one of the old Burberrys, from before they changed the color, and her gun, and left.

El Chivato waited for the phone to ring three times before he leaned over and picked it up. The woman was watching him. He glared at her and made a shooing gesture, and she went immediately into the other room. It was the elder Obregon brother on the phone, as arranged by Connie during her recent jail visit. The conversation lasted the full ten minutes allowed by the jail authorities and was not pleasant for either party. El Chivato put, as he thought, the very sensible case for modifying the contract, since the man Lucky was guarded in such a way as to make capture and subsequent modification of his attitudes impossible. As an alternative, El Chivato would be happy to simply kill the man and his associates and, if desired, the mysteriously unbribeable prosecutor, but in any case, the business had to be finished before the end of the month, as he had pressing business back in Mexico. But this plan Obregon absolutely rejected, as it would not accomplish his main purpose, which was to win release from jail. Lucky *had* to be captured and made to confess. Here Jodón Obregon made the tactical error of suggesting that El Chivato's talents were overrated, that perhaps he was losing his nerve. El Chivato objected in the strongest terms to this analysis, hinting also about how relatively easy it was to get at people who were incarcerated. Jodón withdrew his comment. In the last few minutes of the call they cooked together a compromise: El Chivato would make one last attempt to snatch Lucky, and failing that, he would directly approach the blond prosecutor and use his justly famous skills to win an appreciation of the innocence of the Obregon brothers, all by the end of the month, of course.

When El Chivato hung up, he was in a fury, not only because of the conversation and the insulting remarks (which he would remember) but also because, for the first time, he was experiencing a vague feeling that things were going on that he did not quite get. The way his quarry was being guarded was remarkable. He had, naturally, studied the various methods of bodyguarding available to him thus far, as a cheetah may be said to study the herding patterns of antelope, but he had never before experienced a system so elaborate, so multi-ringed and impenetrable. There were never, for example, any free parking places in front of the Palm café, and there was always a car full of men double-parked outside. He had spotted any number of lookouts on the streets surrounding the place, although these were changed in a pattern that he had not yet been able to figure out. Lucky arrived and departed according to no fixed schedule, and when he left it was in one of never less than three vehicles. Several times El Chivato had tried to follow one of these cars, and each time it had led him in a meaningless loop, at the end of which a different set of men would emerge than had entered it at the origin of the ride. He was, in fact, competing against a system designed to foil the most aggressive and efficient counter-intelligence operation in the world, bringing to his mission only what he had learned in rural Mexico, where the authorities were well bribed and lax. He was out of his league, and the growing apprehension that this was so was making him crazy, or to be precise, more crazy than he already was, which was crazy indeed.

El Chivato cursed, picked up a straight chair, smashed a table lamp with it, then battered the chair into sticks against a door frame. Holding a chair leg in his hand like a club, he kicked open the door of the bedroom through which the woman had passed, but Connie, being familiar enough with the behavior of men conforming to El Chivato's type when they were angry, had silently slipped away. The young man smashed one of the bedroom lamps and beat the cosmetics and perfumes laid out on the dresser into a mash of glass and scented mud. Ticking like a bomb, he threw on his gun-heavy canvas coat and went out.

"Karp, you complete shit!"

"Good morning, Roland," said Karp brightly into the phone. He had been expecting this call since his meeting with the D.A., and while he had not looked forward to it, he was, in the event, glad that it was a telephone call and not a red-faced, jaw-tightening in-person visit.

"You bastard, how could you rat me out like that!"

"I didn't rat you out at all, Roland, unless you're referring to the threat letters. That's not ratting, that's reporting the commission of a crime, perpetrator unknown. I'm supposed to do that." And you too, schmuck, was the implication, but Hrcany, if he caught it at all, was off on another grievance.

"And what's all this crap about the terrorists? You're running your own little private investigation and you don't see fit to tell me? How the *fuck* do you think that makes me look?"

"Probably like someone who has problems listening to advice. If you recall, I discussed the possibility of a wider conspiracy in Shilkes, and you pissed all over me. So did Raney and Carnera, as I recall, and you pissed on them too."

"Oh, yeah, if I didn't have the facts, what the fuck was I sup-posed to do?" was Hrcany's response to this, inane but very loud. Karp moved the phone some inches away from his ear and let the screaming issue into the air for a moment or two. When he brought the earpiece close again, he heard, ". . . balls in an uproar! All of a sudden, because the great Butch Karp has fucking *concerns* about my case, Keegan thinks I don't know what I'm doing. Well, I'll tell you something, *buddy—*"

"What did he tell you to do?" Karp interrupted.

"Oh, like you don't know."

"I don't know. Jack just said he'd talk to you, period. On a personal note, I hope he told you to take the threat business more seriously."

"Oh, fuck that! I can take care of myself."

"Yeah, right, but are you going to get the cops in on it?"

"Yeah, shit, I'll get Ray Netski to check it out. I'm telling you, you're both acting like a couple of old ladies on this thing—"

"Netski?" said Karp without thinking, and then, a second later, realized why: that the very last policeman to send to investigate something Roland did not consider important was Ray Netski, who lived to confirm Roland's suppositions.

"Yeah, Netski. Something wrong with him? Or are you taking over *all* the fucking investigations in this bureau?"

Karp sighed. "No, Roland, he's fine, great. How are you going to proceed on the Arab thing?"

"I'll let the district attorney know if I find anything," snapped Hrcany, and hung up.

While Karp was mulling over this conversation, and wondering how many more friends his job was going to cost him, the phone rang again, and it was Aaron Zwiller, speaking in what seemed an unusual tone for him, nervous and confidential. He had heard some disturbing things, which he would not like to relate over the telephone. Would he like to come in to the office here? No. Karp volunteered to drive out to Williamsburg. No again. Zwiller mentioned the name of a dairy restaurant on Second: could Karp meet him there at one on Sunday afternoon? He could. After that Zwiller seemed anxious to end the call, but Karp asked, "Could you give me some idea of what this is all about, sir?"

"Terrible things, Mr. Karp. Such terrible times we live in, I would not have believed it. They have forgotten *pikua nefesh.*"

"Pardon?"

"The most important principle in the Torah, Mr. Karp: *pikua nefesh*—the preservation of human life. I'll see you Sunday, at one on the dot."

The Osborne Group was housed in a new building on Third, in the high Sixties, just slightly out of the posh-most district of Midtown, but still an acceptable place for a Beautiful Person to visit without losing caste. In the suite itself, of the two acceptable upwardly mobile decors, they had opted for the Starship Enterprise rather than Ye Olde Cozy English Barrister. What was not glass and chrome was matte, all in colors that ended in the letter e: taupe, mauve, beige. The magazines on the glass-chrome coffee table in the reception area were either upscale or security-trade rags. The receptionist was the usual sort of decorative young person in crisp linen (beige) who offered coffee or Coke (declined) and a seat (taken). Marlene read the company brochure and learned that the principal had guarded the president of the United States for nearly twenty-five years, and had lost only one of his clients, and that he staffed largely with ex–Secret Service. After that she amused herself with an article on the relative merits of night-vision equipment in the latest *Industrial Security* and had just about decided to go with the Meyers Dark Invader 3000 when Osborne's secretary (non-decorative, chunky, forty-ish, frosted flip, black pants suit) came out and led her to the boss's office for her appointment.

Osborne had gone for oak, red leather, and the oriental rug as a way of differentiating the captain's quarters from the rest of the interstellar vessel. Both he and Harry Bello rose when she entered, and she shook Osborne's hand. Osborne was a tall, well-set-up man with a rugged pink face, blue eyes sharp and cool, and a remarkable thick crop of snow-white hair, which he wore *en brosse* in the manner once favored by Chancellor Bismarck. He was wearing navy blue suit trousers, white shirt, blue and gold rep tie, and dark blue suspenders, which she was glad to see were unadorned by any cute little devices indicating his profession, tiny eyes perhaps. This disposed her well toward him.

Marlene was ushered to a comfortable red leather Windsor chair, the two men sitting in similar chairs across a low table, coffee was offered again and declined, pleasantries were exchanged, and then, smoothly, Osborne began his pitch. The Group (as he called it) worked mainly for corporations and non-governmental organizations of a certain size, specializing in large-meeting security. They offered a complete package, including venue inspection, travel arrangements for the officers, and operations during the event, whether convention or corporate annual meeting. In this work they often used local security firms—Osborne believed in keeping a small central staff and contracting out much of the grunt work. The system had worked well, and he expected major growth in the next few years, but he also wanted to extend his business into celebrity personal security, which was why he had contacted Harry. Bello & Ciampi would, if they agreed, become a subsidiary of the Osborne Group. The parent firm would handle the business paperwork, billing, bonding, personnel, record keeping, and supply expertise and hardware for specific jobs. Osborne had the numbers prepared on paper, in slick plastic binders, which he presented to both of them.

Marlene flipped through the pages, not really reading. She understood that the deal was a good one, with many advantages for both her and Harry, but she was starting to resent the smooth tone of the pitch, as if it was already a done deal. She cleared her throat and said, "Mr. Osborne, one thing I didn't hear you mention is what Osborne gets out of the association. I mean, why us?"

"Oh, I would've thought that it was obvious," he said, smiling. "You're good, we're buying your rep on stalking cases, and, frankly, it doesn't hurt with female clients. I mean you personally."

"Uh-huh. And this is notwithstanding my approach to stalking cases?"

Osborne cocked his head slightly in inquiry. "Your approach?"

"Yeah. You know the standard security book says, harden the target. Throw up a screen, use the courts, report the perp to the cops, and so on. In heavy cases, where you don't have a public figure, you move the client, make her vanish, and so on. I have problems with that approach."

"Oh?"

Marlene spared a glance for Harry, whose face was unreadable; at least he was not rolling his eyes and squirming. "Yes, my position is that after you've done the legal, and the client is still being harassed, you have to go after the stalker, the harasser. You have to make them cut it out."

"And how do you do that?"

Marlene shrugged. "Harsh words. Powerful arguments . . ."

"She beats them up," said Harry. Osborne started to grin, believing this to be a light remark, but then he saw that Harry was not joking.

"That's right, I do," said Marlene. "I do what I can to make their lives more hell than they've made their victims', and when that doesn't work and they use deadly force, then I take them out, or I make it possible for my clients to do so. Let me be straight with you, Mr. Osborne—"

"Please, it's Lou."

". . . Lou, frankly, I tend to pinch the law a good deal. I take the risks when I think it's right to. You may not, your bonding and insurance people may not, be comfortable with that. But I've been giving this a lot of thought, and so let me make this counter proposal. You go absorb Bello & Ciampi and cut me in for a piece. I'll meanwhile set up a separate d.b.a. for the work I want to do on my own. I'll make myself available on an as-needed basis, consulting, individual contracts, showing my lovely face to the famous clients, whatever. Strictly cash and carry, and when I work for the Group,

I'll play it your way straight up, no horsing around. Harry will supervise me; he's been dying to do that for years anyway. So—that's the best I can do. That do you any good?"

Osborne pursed his lips and stared at nothing for about ten seconds. Gradually, he started nodding his head and then said, "Okay, okay. It could work. I'll have to let the legal eagles mess with it, but we can at least start moving forward under the setup you described. In fact, I sort of like it. Harry?"

Harry said, "I told you she was smart."

By the time El Chivato got down to his car, his anger had largely dissipated; this was how he was, his emotions, even the most violent ones, no more than squalls on a very shallow sea. He drove in his usual careful fashion down the FDR and across the Brooklyn Bridge to Atlantic Avenue. There he resumed his watch on the Palm. He parked around the corner on Tompkins and walked past the café several times on the opposite side of the street. Lucky was in there, with his associates and guards. There were two more of the guards on foot, and there was the ever-present ready car, a blue Ford LTD, double-parked. At a little past five, a white Mercury Montego pulled up in front of the ready car and waited there, its motor running. El Chivato walked quickly to his Firebird, cranked it up, and raced around the block, coming out on Atlantic in time to see his man enter the Mercury with another man and the driver, and pull away, followed closely by the LTD. El Chivato followed both cars west on Atlantic and over the Brooklyn Bridge, up the Bowery to Canal, left on Canal and down to the waterfront. The traffic was fairly heavy, but El Chivato had no trouble keeping a few car lengths behind the white car and its companion. At Varick Street, to his surprise, the LTD cut away and vanished, leaving the Mercury alone. That was all right. He had actually seen the man get into the white Mercury. That meant that when they got to where they were going, he would only have to get rid of two men to be at last alone with the bastard.

They turned left on Washington Street and wove in and out among a maze of narrow streets among low-built brick buildings, the remains of the old meat-packing district, deserted this late in the day. El Chivato moved his car closer; he no longer cared whether they saw him or not—ah, they *had* seen him. The Mercury roared and sped away, tires screeching, and cut right down a narrow street. El Chivato tromped on his own gas pedal and followed the turn. To his surprise, the white car had vanished. He slowed to a crawl, peering down each of the many service alleys that led off the street.

Suddenly, he heard the roar of several engines and the squeal of accelerating tires. In the street in front of him a Buick sedan and a gray van with Jersey plates had appeared, running side by side, blocking the street. He instantly threw the Firebird into reverse, but when he checked the rearview, there was the LTD slewing across the roadway to block his path. Men boiled out of all three vehicles and closed in on his car, pointing a variety of firearms at his head. Ahmed, a big, flat-faced man with a shaved skull, yanked the Firebird's door open and dragged him out.

Two men threw him up against the car and stripped the weapons from his coat, exclaiming in a tongue he didn't understand. Ahmed knocked him to the ground with a blow from the flat of his pistol. The hail of blows and kicks that followed was interrupted by the blare of a car horn. They dragged El Chivato to his feet, and he found himself looking at the man he knew as Lucky through a haze of blood and pain.

The big man looked at him curiously and without apparent anger. He said something to the men around him and got a laugh.

"Who are you and why are you following me?" Khalid asked in English, still smiling.

"I am Fernando Zedillo," said El Chivato. "I was hired to find you."

"And you are a Mexican, yes? So you were hired by those Mexicans, the . . . what were their names?"

"The Obregons," said El Chivato.

"Yes. The Obregons. And what were you going to do once you found me, little man?"

"I was to get you to confess to the killing of the policeman, and also to give the Obregons back the drugs that you stole from them, or the money."

This information and the calm, matter-of-fact way in which it was delivered brought forth more and heartier laughter from the Arabs.

"And why," Khalid asked, "would I do something like that?"

El Chivato shrugged. "Perhaps I would make you see that it was the smart thing to do."

"How, by the offer of your sweet little ass?" More laughter. Khalid resumed on a more serious note: "So where are the others?"

"There are no others," said El Chivato. He seemed bored with the conversation. "I work alone."

Khalid smacked him across the face, leaving a livid mark on the smooth tan cheek.

"Don't lie to me, little girl! You see this big man who's got you? He's going to ask you some questions, and if you lie to him you'll get worse than a smack on the face."

Khalid beckoned to Bashar and drew him away from the others. "Listen," he said, "this boy is clearly nothing but a throwaway, testing our security. He probably knows nothing, but get as much out of him as he has and then get rid of him."

"The water?"

"No, no . . ." said Khalid quickly, thinking of the floating Ali. "Take him to the warehouse, get some lime and concrete—you know what to do."

"The warehouse—are you sure, effendi?" It had been deeply impressed upon Bashar that only four people were to know the location of that place and what was in it.

"Yes—look, we don't have time to secure another location and I don't want this boy found until afterward, so it's better we don't dump him. Besides, it's isolated and it has thick walls. He's going to scream like a baby."

Bashar nodded and looked grave. He understood the necessity, but still he was glad that Ahmed was the expert in that department.

Ahmed tossed El Chivato into the trunk of the LTD. They were less than a quarter of a mile from their destination. Bashar drove the car up to the loading dock, and Ahmed raised the steel door. They opened the trunk and frog-marched the young man up a flight of steel stairs into a vast, dark, chilly hall. Bashar threw a switch, and a row of fluorescent fixtures high above came on. Many of the tubes were out, however, and the light seemed swallowed by the great, dust-speckled volume of the room. El Chivato could make out receding lines of thick concrete pillars and a concrete floor littered by industrial trash, piles of steel pipe, tangles of wire, broken glass, stacks of old wooden pallets and, in a far corner, an angular mass covered by tarps.

Ahmed had hold of El Chivato by the collar of his canvas coat and by his right arm, which was hammer-locked behind the Mexican's back. He leaned over and said caressingly, "You're going to tell us all about your friends, but first we're going to have some fun, yes? I'm going to split your little girl's ass like a peach. How about that, little faggot?"

El Chivato said, "I told you I work alone, you ape."

Ahmed snapped his arms out and threw the youth against a pillar, hard. El Chivato took the impact on his shoulder and crumpled at the base of the pillar.

"Take your clothes off!" ordered Ahmed. Bashar walked a few steps away and sat on a convenient stack of pallets, first brushing the dust off with his handkerchief. He lit a cigarette and watched. The boy took off one of his fancy boots, then the other. He rose, staggering slightly, and Bashar thought he saw him extend his arm, as if to reach out to Ahmed for support.

There was a sharp pop. To Bashar's immense surprise, Ahmed fell down. Blood was gushing from a wound in the top of his skull. The boy turned toward Bashar. Something small shone in his hand. Bashar sprang to his feet and reached inside his coat for his pistol. He saw a flash and heard another pop He felt a hard blow strike him in the chest. He touched the place and looked stupidly at his hand; the fingers were tipped with blood. He had his pistol out now and pointed it at the boy, but the boy was no longer there.

Bashar took a few steps forward. He could not catch his breath, and his vision was going gray. He looked down at Ahmed. The blood had stopped spurting from the wound in his head. Bashar noticed the hole above his upper lip. The boy had pulled a small gun from his boot, that was it—it had all happened so fast! Bashar felt his knees soften, and he leaned against the pillar for support. He caught a movement out of the corner of his eye and tried to bring his pistol around to face it, but now everything was too slow, as in a dream. He fired once, and then a steel pipe hit him square across the temple.

When he came back to consciousness, he was naked, spread out on a pallet, tied with lengths of electrical wire. The kid was kneeling by his side. He had stripped to his undershorts, which seemed to be half white and half red. He wore around his neck several gold chains, from which depended a large cross, a gold medallion, and a small enamel portrait of a saint, and also a leather thong holding a small square canvas pouch, much stained. From this the young man took a roughly S-shaped shiny object, somewhat smaller than a playing card. It had a wooden handle along the base of the S and a curved and pointed razor-sharp blade on the upper limb of the S: a skinning knife.

Bashar had been tortured by the Israeli Shin Bet and beaten by the Syrian police in Lebanon and he thought that he was pretty tough, but he had never been skinned alive by an expert. In the interminable hour before he died, he told El Chivato everything El Chivato wanted to know, about the house in Park Slope, about the details of Khalid's security arrangements, about Ibn-Salemeh's plan, about what was in the crates under the tarpaulin in the corner of the warehouse.

ELEVEN

He had never been shot before, shot *at* plenty of times, but always before this the bullets had gone wide, diverted by the miraculous protection of the saints, and it was this demonstration of his vulnerability rather than the wound itself that wrapped a chilling hand around the heart of El Chivato. Of course, it still hurt a great deal, but he was actually glad of the pain, since it served both to remind him of his recent stupidity and as a warning that he must not overstay his time.

There was an employees' washroom at the back of the warehouse that had cold water running in it, and here he washed off the spattered blood from his job on the Arab, and also washed, as best he could, the bullet wound, which was a long, deep groove in his left side, right above the hip bone. He cut a clean strip from the old-fashioned roller towel in the washroom to make a bandage, which he wrapped tightly around his waist, like a cummerbund.

Nude but for this binding, he went to inspect the crates the Arab had mentioned. One of them had already been opened, and the top layer of excelsior and ceramic parts had been removed and set aside. El Chivato rummaged through the contents for a good while, selecting some items and placing them on a tarp. His weapons had been taken from him by the Arabs, and here was a new supply, and of a better sort as well. He was used to this manner of providence, and he thought it was possible that the protectors had not entirely deserted him: the wound was a warning, then, and not abandonment.

When he had laid out as much as he thought he could conveniently carry, he wrapped up the tarp, slung it over his shoulder and brought it out to the loading dock, where he placed it next to the LTD. Then he got dressed, took the car keys and the two pistols from the dead Arabs, distributed the various items from the crates in appropriate places, and drove off.

Chouza Khalid said, "Perhaps the little thing was tougher than he looked. I can't think of anything else that would be taking them so long."

The man known as Ibn-Salemeh did not look away from his television, which was playing a rerun of *I Dream of Jeannie*. He said, "Perhaps they discovered another spy. You should go and check. In fact, you should have interrogated him yourself."

"I was preparing for tonight," said Khalid, trying to keep the resentment out of his voice. "As it is, if they don't show up soon, we will have to call it off."

"We will not call it off. This is interesting, here, I've noticed on many of these programs: the man is a moron and the woman is the clever one. Even without magical powers. And this one is especially blatant. We have the familiar orientalism: the submissive woman, the harem pants, the little waistcoat with sequins, but in fact she is entirely in control. What do you suppose it signifies?"

Khalid shrugged. The only things he watched on television were wrestling and soccer. He said, "We cannot do this operation without Ahmed and Bashar. In fact, I don't understand why we are doing it at all. The Daoud boy is not going to take his truck back if we don't give him his sister."

For the first time Ibn-Salemeh turned away from the screen. He gave Khalid a long, slow look. In the darkened room Khalid could make out nothing of the man's eyes but two black pits, in each of which there burned a tiny flickering spark. He felt a chill, and was about to make leaving noises when the man spoke.

"It has nothing to do with the Daoud boy or his sister. It is a political issue, a political decision, and you know I don't discuss political issues with you. However . . ." and now the bearded man did something he had never done before. He rose and switched off the volume on the television set, and courteously gestured to a chair near the old couch on which he spent almost all his time. Khalid sat, not knowing what to think.

". . . however, this time I will make an exception," the man resumed, when he had seated himself at the far end of the couch, facing Khalid, with his legs curled up underneath him, like a cat. "You are, after all, an Arab, and although you are a mercenary, you are still part of the struggle. So: what have I done? You notice that at the center is our plan. What is the purpose of this plan? To harm the Zionists and their Jew allies in this country, of course. That is the obvious purpose, but not the only one, perhaps not even the chief one. You also notice that I improvise with the tools at hand. I arrange for a group of Arab boys to kill a Jew. A stupid, meaningless act, you think. But no, its very meaninglessness, its triviality, is its virtue. The Jews howl, and the Americans think, these Arabs are capable of anything, any of them could have a knife. Now this raid tomorrow. Another outrage. The police descend on the Arab community, looking for the murderers, the kidnappers. Jars are broken, women are insulted. The Daoud family will be arrested, but, as we have arranged, they will have been in mosque, with many to attest to their presence. The police will not believe these distinguished men perhaps. More insults. Then our centerpiece occurs. There is true terror now. Now the U.S. government is called in. There are mass arrests of Arabs, but even more important, the Americans strike at the Arab community. Who are these foreigners, these aliens? Again, jars are broken, and women are insulted, perhaps now heads are broken. More insulting cartoons are published, on the television, on radio, the voices are angry—at the Arabs, of course, but also at the Jews. Why have you involved us in your quarrels, so many dead in an American city? And so on."

He paused here, and Khalid felt he was required to say something, to demonstrate that he understood. But he did not. He wet his lips and asked, "But if the Americans hate and fear the Arabs, why will they help us in Palestine?"

The other man made a harsh, breathy noise, like escaping steam. "No! You have missed the point. The Americans will *never* help the Arabs in Palestine. The Jews here are too powerful. You should watch more television, Chouza: watch the little names flash on the screen, read who is in control of what the Americans believe. But there are perhaps a million Arabs in this country. And they, of course, are so busy getting rich that they have forgotten us, forgotten their struggle and their honor, so we must remind them what it is to be despised and abused. Many of them will become our allies as a result. With this base we can mount more actions, have even greater freedom of movement, and this in turn will create even more oppression upon the Arabs here. It builds like that, do you see? Finally, the Americans, who have no stomach for such suffering, who want only to enjoy their wealth and watch this kind of nonsense"—he gestured to the TV screen—"the Americans will say, *enough!* Let the dogs fight it out between themselves and leave us alone. And thus we will win."

"We will?" asked Khalid spontaneously. He had seen Israeli jets and tanks in Lebanon, and thought that, all in all, the Zionists could take care of themselves.

"Of course! Can you doubt it? How could the Arabs, the most heroic people in history, seventy million Arabs, be defeated by less than four million Jews, people who for thousands of years let themselves be killed like sheep? How is it possible? It is *not* possible, for it is the Americans that have done it. *And this I will stop.*"

Khalid had, of course, heard this argument before, many times. It might well be true, for all he knew, but he was not interested in politics, and he was quite indifferent to the fevered patriotic psychopathy of Ibn-Salemeh and his associates. He waited, saying nothing, and after a while the other man seemed to emerge from the reverie into which he had apparently been placed by the sound of his own rhetoric, and he rose and turned up the volume again. A laugh track filled the room, which seemed appropriate, in a way, to Chouza Khalid. He rose himself, said he was going to try to find the two missing men, and was dismissed with a flick of the hand.

After leaving the Osborne Group, Marlene boarded a southbound Lexington Avenue train and got off at Bleecker Street, from which she walked to Old St. Patrick's Cathedral on Mulberry and went inside, putting a black lace scarf over her head as she did. Today the nave was draped for Lent, in the old-fashioned way, with dark purple palls on the altar and the statuary, suiting perfectly Marlene's present mood.

She chose to go to Old St. Pat's instead of to St. Anthony of Padua, where every other Italian in lower Manhattan went, or Transfiguration, which was closer to her home, for reasons both aesthetic and spiritual. Old St. Pat's was a venerable Gothic Revival pile, parts of it dating back to the War of 1812 (which antiquity she thought gave worship there an almost European style) and full of the ghosts of departed poor Irishmen and the present bodies of poor Latinos. The spiritual reasons were more complex. In general, Marlene did not hold with parish shopping, as smacking of the Donatist heresy, which held that the character of the priest influenced the efficacy of the sacraments. Marlene did not go to church for the Christian fellowship, the style of the services, or the brilliance of the sermons, nor was she particularly bothered by the policies of the current pope. She went for the magic, because, she firmly believed, if it wasn't magic, the whole affair was so much gilt horseshit, and if it *was* magic, the personality of the priest was the last thing to bother with. It was like believing that because the president of a bank was a son of a bitch, the money that came out of the cash machines wasn't any good. Old St. Pat's was run as closely as possible to the old devotional style that Marlene had grown up on, and which the current parishioners, Latin American and Caribbean types, also seemed to prefer. The fresh breezes of Vatican II did not penetrate very far up the nave of Old St. Pat's, which was fine with Marlene, whose deeply held opinion was that Vat Deuce had got it mainly wrong, changing the stuff that didn't need changing and leaving alone the stuff that did. Marlene thought the Tridentine Mass had been just fine as it was, and in Latin (and if you couldn't understand it, tough shit, Mac, you could look it up), and the rosary, and the stations of the cross, and the clunky statues with the red lamps—candles, incense, mystery, old ladies in black mumbling on their knees—that was *church.*

The pastor of Old St. Pat's was a man who supported this view. Father Raymond was a genial, sheep-faced Irish gentleman of a certain age, as Pre-Vat II as it was possible to be without getting actually defrocked, and without a brain in his head. His sermons concerned, in ascending order of frequency, foreign missions, the evils of communism, and the certainty of Hell for anyone participating in any sexual behavior whatever except for the express purpose of peopling Heaven with new souls. Marlene, although for long an enthusiastic participant in the non-peopling sort of behavior, accepted these clerical commonplaces as she did the wafts of incense and the music, without resentment, with fondness even, as representing something familiar and calming, like the sound of surf.

Lately, however, Marlene had acquired yet another reason for attendance here, and it was for this she had come on the present occasion. The curate, Father Dugan, was hearing during this slot, and Father Dugan was interesting enough as a human being for Marlene to suspend her notions about it not mattering who was on the other side of the little grille. He was, to begin with, a Jesuit, uncommon enough among diocesan clergy, but also, in former days, one of the Church's high flyers. He had once been on the very small staff of the Jesuit Superior General in Rome. How an aide to the Black Pope had been busted down to a curacy in a second-rate New York parish was a mystery that Marlene had not solved. The usual priestly errors—Punch or Judy, a weakness for choirboys— did not seem to fit what she had been able to gather about his character, but his personal glamour added to the already very great appeal of sitting in a dark box and whispering secrets to a strange man who could never reveal them to anyone. Since her first communion Marlene had been an enthusiastic patron of the confessional, and had, during an unusually libertine adolescence, expanded the sexual horizons of any number of celibate gentlemen. She told the truth, of course, took the penance, was genuinely sorry, and always did as she pleased thereafter. This was how the system was supposed to work, in her opinion, and very well it worked too, especially nowadays, when she had so much on her soul.

She entered the confessional and, after the ritual words, began an account of her week's transgressions, concentrating on the various tortures and death traps she had involved herself in, ending, as usual, with the statement that she found it impossible to believe in God.

"When you were torturing this man, did you feel any pleasure?" asked the priest.

"No, Father. I was sick. I was literally sick outside afterward."

"I see. Don't you think that's odd? You do something you have rationalized is necessary, and yet your very body rebels."

"The spirit is willing, but the flesh is weak."

"Clever and mocking as usual," said the priest. His tone was not angry, or contemptuous, but tired, exhausted. Marlene felt an instant pang of shame. "But cleverness and mockery won't give you the peace you seek, which is why you come here. Why do you come here since you say you don't believe?"

"I hope that adherence to the forms will prepare my heart for the grace of faith," said Marlene with sincerity.

"You still hope, then?"

"I do, Father."

"That's something, anyway. Tell me, do you consider that breaking the law as you do is the only way to prevent the deaths of these women?"

"I do, Father."

"That seems unlikely. You could hide them, for example."

"I could, but that means condemning women to a lifetime of hiding and subterfuge, with still no guarantee that the man wouldn't find them years later. Why should they? Give up their lives, their careers, their names, when they've committed no crime? Just because some guy has decided to make their lives hell—"

"You've answered the question. It is your choice rather than actual necessity. Do you know this verse: 'All things have I seen in the days of my vanity; there is a just man that perisheth in his righteousness, and there is a wicked man that prolongeth his life in his wickedness. Be not righteous overmuch, neither make thyself overwise: why shouldest thou destroy thyself?'?"

"No. It sounds like Ecclesiastes."

"It is. It's a good warning. The world is full of inexplicable and incurable evil. That's why the Lord told us that our responsibility was to the care of our own souls and the extension of loving kindness to our neighbors, and not the elimination of evil. That's also why we render unto Caesar. You know all this. Even your body knows it. Look at yourself now. Your partner has left you. You can't speak to your husband about what you do. Your children are endangered. Your only companions are either fanatics or those with damaged souls and no moral compass. If you continue as you've been going, you will either become a monster or you will be destroyed in some awful disaster. And I don't think you will become a monster."

Marlene thought, he's talking about himself too.

"Your heart is full of pride," he went on after a pause, "so full that there is no room for faith, and because what you do is for the good of others, and at some sacrifice to yourself, you think it doesn't matter, that it's not really pride. But that kind is the worst kind. Do you think the Devil only tempts us with sensual lusts?"

"No, Father," said Marlene meekly, regressing to childhood, as she often did here.

The priest caught her tone. "All right, all right: when you're ready. I pray that you are not one of those who has to be smashed to pieces before the light dawns. Your penance is to read the *Spiritual*

Exercises, let's say through the first Meditation. If you insist on being a warrior, you should learn something about discipline."

"You know nothing about discipline," said Tran, "which is normal among people with remarkable gifts, such as yourself. Without discipline, however, all your gifts will come to nothing."

Tran was sitting with Lucy on a bench in Tompkins Square Park in the East Village. Lucy had just failed for the third time to recall, with her eyes closed, the costume and characteristics of every person visible from her vantage point. The park was crowded in the mild late afternoon with the sort of exotics who normally populated that well-known roofless after-care clinic.

"*You* do it, then!" said Lucy irritably. Tran sighed and closed his eyes, and rattled off concise descriptions of a dozen people, until Lucy said, "Okay, okay, I believe you. But I'll *never* get it." She slumped and started kicking her leg. "I don't see why I have to do it anyway."

"No, you do not, because all your energy is going into worrying why you must do it. And squirming. Sit straight! Calm yourself! Breathe as I have told you! One . . . two. One . . . two. Yes. When you learn how, you can stay quiet all day, like a stone."

"No one can stay quiet *all* day," objected Lucy. "What if you have to pee?"

"For that there are bottles. Once I lay on a roof for twelve hours without moving, just watching."

"What for?"

"To shoot someone," replied Tran blandly. He did not believe in sheltering children from the realities, especially not this child.

"A bad guy?"

"An enemy. There are neither bad nor good in war, only friends and enemies."

Lucy thought about that for a while. She was vaguely aware of something called the Vietnam War, which her mom also called, when she thought Lucy was out of range, That Fucking War, mainly because of her Uncle Dom. His service therein was the explanation given by her mom for Uncle Dom's odd walk, and for his peculiar and frightening behavior at family gatherings, or his absence from them, both of which made her nonna cry. She knew Tran was a Vietnamese, she knew there was a Vietnamese language, but until that moment she had not fully realized that the Vietnam of Uncle

Dom's war and the place that Tran came from were the same place, rather than being, like Joan of Arc and Noah's Ark, two entities whose apparent congruence of name did not denote a true connection.

"Was that in the Vietnam War when you shot that guy?" Lucy asked to confirm this insight.

"Not as such," said Tran delicately. "It was another war, before that one, against the French."

"I thought you *liked* the French," exclaimed Lucy in surprise, speaking French, as they had all afternoon.

"I *love* the French," said Tran. "I love them in their own country, however, rather than in mine, just as, let us say, you love horses, but one suspects you would not like ten of them living in your bedroom."

Lucy was examining Tran with new eyes; it is one of the great revelations of childhood, this comprehension that our elders have a past prior to their connection with ourselves. "Is that where you got that dent in your head?" Lucy asked with characteristic bluntness.

"No. That was given to me by my own former comrades. I fought for twenty-five years against three armies and received not so much as a scratch. After the war was over, I was imprisoned and there, in the midst of peace and victory, I received all my wounds. This on my head comes from a beating."

"But why did they? If you won."

Tran watched the smoke from his cigarette whip away through the maple buds and considered that question, which was one he had spent, naturally enough, a great deal of time contemplating. "They thought I was too good at fighting, perhaps. Especially against unpleasant and oppressive regimes. It is a long, sad story."

Which Lucy was not that interested in hearing, truth to tell, and so she asked, "Uncle Tran, when will you teach me a martial art?"

As if in answer, Tran threw his arms around her and placed his hands over her eyes. "Maybe. When you can tell me who was the last person to walk by on this path, from the right."

"Old lady, short, not too fat, brown coat, glasses, pulling a cart, blue wool hat."

"And before her?"

"Two black teenagers, one fat, one tall and skinny, fat one with a Raiders coat, gray baggies, tall one with blue track pants, Monsignor Ryan jacket, Nike gym bag, both wearing Nikes. Hey! I did it!"

Tran pulled his hands away and hugged her, beaming. "Yes, you did. Without knowing, which is how you must do such things. I will buy you an ice cream."

"What about my martial art?"

"Ah, as to that, I regret that I know no martial arts other than the few holds I learned in the army. Unlike the Koreans and the Okinawans, we Vietnamese have never developed any unarmed combat of our own."

"Why is that, Uncle Tran?"

"Because we have always made sure we had arms, I suppose. This shouting, this kicking, are for people without swords, without guns." He rose from the bench, stretched and yawned like an old dog, and held out his hand, which she took. They proceeded eastward on the path out of the park.

Khalid knew it was a disaster the moment he saw that the steel gate of the loading dock was raised and the LTD was gone. What he found inside the warehouse merely confirmed it. Khalid had an extremely strong stomach, and he had seen a lot of corpses, but what had been done to Bashar brought up his gorge, and he had to flee back to the dock for some deep breaths of air. The entire front half of the man's skin, from the wrists to the ankles, had been removed in a single piece, which object had been neatly laid out on a pallet next to the former owner's body. Khalid had not much liked Bashar, but he felt a pang of sympathy nonetheless, and understood instantly that whatever Bashar knew, back to his earliest retrievable memories, and certainly including the details of Ibn-Salemeh's plan, was now in the possession of the Mexican youth.

He went out onto the dock and sat down on its lip, and smoked a cigarette and considered his options. Option one was to get in his car, drive to the house he had rented in Crown Heights, take the considerable trove of cash he had sequestered from the dope deal, drive to the airport, and get out of town. The disadvantage of this was that for the rest of his life he would have to protect himself from the revenge of Ibn-Salemeh and his many admirers, which span, given the reputation and talents of that body of men, was likely to be quite short.

Option two was to go back to Ibn-Salemeh and explain that a boy who had appeared to be a mere pawn, whom any reasonable man could not have imagined to be anything else, had turned out to be a frighteningly dangerous monster, one who was now at large and, it could not be doubted, in possession of all of Ibn-Salemeh's deepest secrets. As the word *possession* entered his mind, Khalid felt a still greater pang of fear and leaped to his feet. He trotted back to where the crates were stashed and did a quick inventory. Some small arms missing, but the cylinder and the other specialized equipment had not been disturbed. Khalid leaned against a crate, sighing with relief, and continued with his train of thought.

Option two also left something to be desired. Ibn-Salemeh would blame him for the debacle, and for the loss of two prized subordinates. This also was not conducive to a long and peaceful life.

Option three . . . Khalid was not experienced at creative thought, but he found that the prospect of facing the wrath of his employer concentrated his limited faculties to a wonderful degree. He thought it through, then thought it through again, taking a walk through the warehouse as he did. Yes, it would work; it would be a close thing, but it would work, and might offer the best chance of getting out of this miserable association alive.

He went back to the dock and drew down the corrugated door, locking it with his key. Then he drove to a building-supply place on Eleventh Avenue and bought a four-by-eight-foot sheet of rough plywood, several plastic tarps, a length of one-by-two fir, a circular saw, an extension cord and work lamp, a garden hose, a cheap plastic wheelbarrow, four bags of ready-mix concrete, a box of plastic bags, a box of nails, and a hammer.

Back at the warehouse, he stripped to his underwear, wrapped his shoes in plastic bags, wrapped Bashar's corpse and his former, now stiff skin in a tarp, and hauled it and all of his materials to the building's elevator shaft, using the wheelbarrow. He raised the freight car to the second floor and walked down. He hooked the hose up to a wash sink in a nearby janitor's closet and plugged in the work lamp. He had worked construction in Israel as a youth, before discovering that smuggling paid better, and he was reasonably skilled at this sort of rough work. In an hour he had ripped the plywood into one-foot-wide strips, from which he built a shallow four-sided form, using the fir as bracing.

He climbed into the bottom of the shaft, carrying the form, and set it on the bottom. He brought the wheelbarrow down and, using the hose, mixed up a bag of ready-mix, and poured it into the form. He added the tarp-wrapped carnage and then covered it with the rest of the concrete, finishing the task by dumping assorted debris into the shaft and bringing the car down to the first floor again. He loaded Ahmed's body into the wheelbarrow and took it to a small room off the main bay that had previously been used as some sort of office. He placed the body in an empty closet and nailed the door shut.

Khalid sprayed water from the hose onto his sweating face and then had a cigarette, contemplating the next steps. This was going to work.

Marlene walked back home from church, feeling a good deal better than she had earlier, despite Father Dugan's grim tone, accepting this as yet another proof of the efficacy of the sacraments, and burying the moral lessons in the corner of her mind where she kept such things between her religious visits. There was no one in the loft, but the dog was gone, which meant Posie had taken them all for another outing. She changed into jeans, boots, sweater, and leather jacket, and left, whistling gaily, for her car.

She spotted them on Canal Street, the boys in their stroller, hideously covered with chocolate ice cream, Posie flirting with some Con Ed workers, while the dog heaved at its leash in an attempt to grab a morsel of decomposed matter in the gutter. Marlene honked and ordered them all into the VW. Then they drove to the East Village Women's Shelter.

Marlene's boys loved the women's shelter. It had action. It had a large playroom covered with industrial carpeting and full of decrepit toys, cardboard cartons to crawl into, a varied and changing cast of other kids, and all manner of interesting filth. After hosing off the chocolate, Posie left them in the playroom and went into the kitchen to socialize.

Lucy had also looked forward to visiting the shelter. She wanted to speak Arabic with Fatyma, for while she had memorized the relatively simple conjugations of that tongue already, there was nothing like conversation with a native speaker to flesh out the bones of a language, to clothe it in idiom and nuance, to generate in the seemingly infinite partitions of her mind yet another person, one with the thoughts and concepts of an Arab. Failing that, Mattie was always willing to fill in her knowledge of racy Texas Spanish, but now, in the kitchen, she found that even this was not about to happen. The three women—Mattie, Marlene, and Posie—and the Arab girl were sitting around the table, eating honey cakes and drinking coffee and talking in boring old English, and their subject was the most boring one of all.

It had begun with Marlene ribbing Posie about her flirting with the Con Ed men, after which there were passed remarks about "laying cable" and "getting your pipes reamed out" that provoked wild witch-like laughter, which Lucy didn't care for, because while she followed the double meanings (for, of course, these had to be explained to Fatyma, which occasioned even more chortles), she didn't see what was so funny. Then Posie told a story about how this guy had taken her home with him and they were "balling," as she said, on a bed, and a woman had walked in and changed into a pink waitress uniform and walked out without saying a word.

"I go, like, 'Who was that?' " said Posie. "And he goes, 'Just my wife, but don't worry, she works all night.' Then he says he loves me. Then he goes, do I have a job? I guess he's fixing up a schedule."

Loud laughter at this, more from the expression on Posie's face than the story, so similar to those Posie had told often before, and Mattie and Marlene hummed the first two bars of "Isn't It Romantic," which cracked them up, and then explained the thing to Fatyma, and laughed some more.

"I'm about ready to get, like, a cucumber," said Posie. "I must be doing something real wrong, but I'm always thinking, this is the one, you know? But it never is."

"Hell, no! What you got to do, girl, is get 'em young. Young and hung," said Mattie. "Use 'em and lose 'em. Get 'em young enough, you can break 'em and train 'em: a little pussy, a little taste of the whip." Marlene snorted and rolled her eyes. Mattie's actual sexuality was something of a puzzle to her friend. Marlene had assumed at first that the woman was aggressively lesbic, because she'd at least mentioned lovers with female names and also from her general attitude toward the other sex, but from time to time over the years she'd noticed young men hanging about, usually possessing a slim cowboy beauty and a hangdog expression, and from that she had gathered that Mattie practiced a bluff bisexuality, the key to her heart apparently being the understanding that she was always entirely in charge.

Of course, in Marlene's opinion there was not a chance that someone like Posie was going to benefit from this sort of Amazonian pep talk, and said so, and they got into a not entirely humorous argument about dominance in relationships, which made Lucy even more uncomfortable, because her dad's name was brought up and used to demonstrate various points on either side, and then Posie said she didn't care about any of that, but that all she wanted was a good fuck a couple times a week, and then, remembering Lucy's presence, she said, "Oops, sorry!" and then Fatyma said, "You should meet my brother. All the time with his dumb friends, all they are talking is sex, sex, but they never have girls, you know?"

And after that they talked about Fatyma's family, which Lucy found sort of interesting, and she passed around little photos of her sibs (Posie pronouncing Walid gorgeous) and then they started talking about *really* gross stuff, whereupon Lucy walked out.

She stopped by the playroom first and messed around with the twins, mainly to continue her secret experiment, which consisted of speaking to Zak only in Cantonese and to Zik only in French, to see if they would start speaking those languages to each other, or invent a new one, hybridizing the two, or drive themselves crazy. It didn't seem to be working, although she noted, with some interest, that they each seemed to make sense of the other's babble, and they jabbered at one another in a sort of imitation conversation, with the appropriate tonalities, just as she used to imitate adult writing by making looping squiggles on paper before she learned cursive.

There were no girls her age in the shelter at the moment, and no one with an interesting language to convey, so she trotted up four floors and climbed the narrow stairs to the roof. There, as she had expected, she found Tran, leaning against the roof parapet and smoking. She stood next to him and joined him in watching the street below. It was chilly on the roof; she had come up without her jacket, but after a few minutes Tran seemed to sense this, and un-buttoned his pea coat and drew her to him, enfolding her in his left arm and the thick, stiff wool. He smelled of tobacco, damp wool, and, more faintly, the peculiar combination of odors Lucy associ-ated with Asian men: fish, frying oil, and the scented hair tonic they all used in Chinatown. She liked it. She slid her thin arm around his waist and nestled closer to his wiry body, feeling con-tent and safe, as she did with her dad, but also slightly excited. It was like hugging a wolf.

"What are you watching, Uncle Tran?" she asked after ten min-utes of silence.

"Look yourself, Little Sister. What do you think I am watching?"

"That gray van, Jersey plates. It drove by and let two men out, and drove away. The two men didn't go into any stores. Then a white car came up, and one of the men talked to the driver and it went away. Then the two men went into the building next door to the shelter."

"Yes," said Tran. "And what do you think about this?"

"Dope, or something. I don't know. Or maybe they're going to rob the check-cashing place. What do you think?"

But Tran only shrugged, and then suggested that it was getting too cold, and took her back into the shelter.

Down in the warm kitchen, the little group had broken up. Fatyma was busy with something at the stove, some women needed Mattie's urgent attention, and Posie had been called away to the playroom by some unusually loud squalls from the boys. Marlene helped her settle the twins and played with them for a few minutes, and then went to Mattie's office.

"We have to talk about Fatyma," she said without preamble.

Mattie came back with "What about her?" switching to her truculent self, and Marlene struggled not to roll her eyes and sigh, or put out any of the other silent signals we use when a pal is being a pain in the ass.

"The cops are after her. She really did whack that pimp on the Deuce, and they know who she is. There's a warrant out on her, and this'll be one of the places they'll check."

"So? When they come, she'll get lost."

"Uh-uh, Mattie. This isn't some woman who's hiding her kids from a man with a better lawyer, or a parole jumper. This is an A felony. As of right now you're liable on a charge of hindering prosecution, and technically, so am I, for not speaking right up when a cop told me they were looking for her and I knew where she was."

"So . . . what, you're going to rat us out?"

"Of course I'm not going to rat you out," Marlene snarled. "Will you just *listen*? One of two things has to happen. One, she has to turn herself in, tell her story, and cop out to a self-defense plea. That's what I would recommend to her, and I'll represent her in that if she wants. She's a kid with no record, and they're not going to drop the courthouse on her head for wasting a lowlife who tried to hurt her."

"I bet," said Mattie. "You forgot dear dad's gunning for her too. And the brother. Once she's in the system they're going to send her back to her loving family, and it's good-bye, baby. What's the other thing?"

"She has to disappear. Out of town, gone, never existed. I know you've got some kind of network you move women through. You could place her with a family until she's grown."

"Okay, I'll think about it."

"You have to do more than think about it, Mattie. You could wind up losing this whole place."

"I *said*, I'll think about it!" snapped the other woman. Marlene saw the warning signs, the clenched fists, the bar of darker color on the broad cheekbones, the eyes becoming hot, and she was about to marshal her forces for a knock-down hair-puller when Lucy burst into the room.

"Mom! Fatyma says I could stay over with her tonight. Can I? Can I?"

"Well, I don't know, Lucy—" Marlene began.

"Puh-leeze? It's a Friday."

Marlene looked at Mattie for some indication, hoping that the woman would say no, but of course Mattie grinned and said it would be fine, and Marlene, who had just tossed away a brilliant career opportunity to be able to continue to work for places like EVWS, could not bring herself to articulate her thought that the actual place was dangerous and rather dirty and not the kind of place she felt comfortable leaving *her* little girl in. So she relented, but assuaged her conscience by having a few discreet words with Tran before Posie stumped into the kitchen with a squalling, damp-diapered brat on each hip, and she had to clear out. Tran was an exception to the EVWS rule about no men on the premises. He was a hell of a cook, willing to whip up exotic delicacies for the semi-imprisoned ladies, and make cheerful jokes and himself useful in various other ways, including (which Mattie well understood) as a guard beyond compare.

Khalid inspected his troops by the light of a yellow street lamp on a deserted lane near the Lillian Wald project on the lower East Side of Manhattan. He had only six men instead of eight, which meant that he would have only one man to secure the rear entrance, and that he would have to participate directly, which he did not at all like. This could not be helped. He went down the row of black-clad armed men standing in front of the gray van and questioned them each for the last time about what they were supposed to do. Rifaat, Abdel, Jemil, and Big Mahmoud were all Palestinians and experienced *fedayin*, and he expected them to do their parts well. The other two, Hussein and Little Mahmoud, were immigrant boys who had never been on a real operation before, but they would probably suffice for front and rear security. They were, or should be, already in position at the target. He did not expect serious opposition in a house full of women taken by surprise.

It had not been difficult to determine where the girl had gone to ground once they started to make serious inquiries. Professor Adouri had been his usual helpful self, with a timely phone call about the Daoud dagger and the police interest in it, and from there it had not been hard to find the name of the victim in the case with the funny knife, which had led to the pimp, Kingman, who had been delighted to supply the name of the blondie ho the girl they were looking for used to hang with, and it had not been hard to lift Cindy one evening at the bus station, and a quite brief conversation with her had led to the EVWS being mentioned as one of the places Cindy had recommended someone like Fatyma could run to. They had then paid a woman to go in there with a story and a couple of brats, and this person had confirmed Fatyma's residence and its precise location. So far, so easy. On the other hand, his confidence had been badly shaken by the affair of the Mexican. Nevertheless, he clapped each man on the back and cried, as expected, *"Usrub! Aleikum!"* with his fist raised. Strike! On to them! And they all echoed. He hoped it raised their spirits, as it did not his own. They climbed into the van and drove slowly off.

TWELVE

Tran was dozing in a stuffing-gushing armchair in a hallway on the second floor of the shelter when he heard the thump from above, a thump and then the squeal of bending metal. The origin of these noises told him that the place was being raided by people who knew what they were doing, because you assault any urban structure from the roof down. Then you can set up your kill and capture zones at the more easily controllable street-level exits. The only question now was, were they just good, or very good? If they were good, he had ninety seconds, and that must be the case because if they had been very good he would have heard nothing; he would have been dead already. He moved quickly into the bedroom behind him, snatched up the sleeping Lucy in her blankets, and slipped into the clothes closet.

Lucy jerked awake and stiffened. Tran placed his hand over her mouth and whispered in Cantonese, "Do not make a sound. Someone is attacking the shelter, and we must be very silent. You must hide under this blanket at the back of the closet, and do not move! Understand?"

Lucy made a faint noise and curled into a ball, with the blanket over her. She wondered if she were dreaming or if this were real life.

Tran cracked the closet door a half inch. Three men dressed in dark track suits and ski masks entered the room. The first two were armed with machine pistols. The third carried nothing but a large sack of some thick cloth. He had strips of duct tape stuck to his chest. This last man leaped upon Fatyma as she slept, mashed a strip of tape over her mouth, spun her around, secured her hands behind her with tape strips, got her thrashing legs under control and taped them too, and finally pulled the sack over her head and shoulders, securing it with additional taped strips. The man spoke to the others briefly in a language Tran did not know. He hoisted the girl up on his shoulders like a rolled carpet, and the three men left.

Tran, who knew a good deal about the subject, thought it a fairly competent snatch, a little noisy perhaps, a hair slow, but certainly sufficient against a site that was prepared to deal only with the random violence expected from estranged boyfriends. He put his pistol away and got Lucy to her feet.

"What happened?" she asked, now sure that it was not a dream.

"Your friend Fatyma has been kidnapped by several men."

"*What!*" The girl rushed into the room, saw that it was true, and turned angrily on Tran. "Why didn't you stop them?"

"Because they were many and heavily armed and I am one, and besides it is my duty to protect you and not others. Put your clothes on. We must leave instantly."

Lucy was about to object, but something in Tran's look dissuaded her from doing so. "Don't look!" she said. Tran turned his back while she yanked off the T-shirt she'd slept in and pulled on her clothes. As she did, she heard heavy footsteps from above, a shout, the report of a large-caliber handgun, more shouts, screams, the peculiar ripping roar of an automatic weapon, a slamming door, a woman crying for help. These sounds accelerated her dressing. Then she was being pulled and pushed through hallways full of frightened women and children out into the chilly street. Tran hailed a cab on Avenue B. Sirens sounded in the distance as they drove off. Shortly they were back at the loft, confronting a white-faced Marlene, who, surprisingly, was not in bed but up and in the process of getting dressed as they entered.

"Where are you going?" Lucy demanded, after she had blurted out her version of the recent events, and Tran had delivered a less emotional précis.

"I have to see a client," said Marlene. "It's an emergency."

"But what about Fatyma?" cried Lucy.

"Who's Fatyma?" asked Karp, staggering into the kitchen in his robe and pajamas. "What's going on, Marlene? It's three in the morning."

"I'll explain later," said the wife. "Could you please put Lucy to bed?"

"Yeah, sure," said Karp sleepily. Then he noticed that Marlene was dressed. "Wait a second . . . you're going out? What's happening?"

"Joan Savitch just shot and killed her husband," said Marlene. "A client. I got to go walk her through the system, and I have to leave now. Please, just get Lucy to bed and I'll call you later today." She kissed him and left, followed by the Vietnamese. Karp sighed and led his daughter to her bedroom, where he watched her undress with perfect modesty under her nightie, and then tucked her in, and comforted her while she cried about Fatyma, in the process learning a little about who Fatyma was, and, putting the night's events together with what he knew about an Arab girl wanted for a killing and connected somehow with a terrorist operation, he experienced (and suppressed) a wave of white-hot rage against his wife.

"What will happen to Fatyma, Daddy?"

"Don't worry about it now, baby. Just try to get some sleep."

"No, tell me! I can't sleep because I'm *worried* about her."

"Okay, look: the cops will come, and maybe the FBI too, because it's a kidnapping. They'll check all the people she knew to find out who would want to kidnap her. Maybe the kidnappers left some clues. They'll find her. The main thing is, it's not your worry. You're ten years old, Luce. You're a little girl. Just 'cause your mom's decided to be Batwoman, it doesn't mean you have to get sucked up in all this stuff. All right?"

"They were Arabs," Lucy said sleepily.

"Who were, honey?"

"Those men. The kidnappers. They were talking Arabic." She yawned. "He said, 'Abdel, you go first, Rifaat behind. Let's go!' "

Detective Ray Netski had this Saturday as his regular day off, but he was working anyway, and he was not going to put in for overtime either. For the last few days Hrcany had been on his butt about Morilla, which seemed in the process of becoming seriously untied. Then there was this business about the threats. Netski could not imagine who would be so stupid as to threaten a prosecutor; in his experience such threats were entirely the province of wackos. Professional criminals like the Obregons simply did not do such things, although twenty years on the job had taught him that there was an exception to nearly any rule.

Which was why he was now standing alone in front of the door to an apartment in Washington Heights, on his own time, preparing to brace the woman, Concepción Erbes, and find out whether she was the source of the threatening notes or knew who was. Netski knew from looking over the jail's phone records that Jesus Obregon had made numerous calls to this apartment. He had interviewed Connie Erbes several times way back when the case was fresh, and had found her in possession of only limited gun-moll knowledge of the criminal doings of her pals (although she had confirmed their phony story in every particular, sad to say), but he had to start someplace, and there *were* all those calls.

He knocked on the door. Some seconds later it was flung wide, not by Connie but by a thin young man who was snarling, "Where the *fuck* you been . . ." as he opened the door and stopped, scowling, when he saw that the person at the door was not the one he had anticipated.

Netski flashed his shield. "I want to talk to Connie Erbes," he said, looking this character over. He was dressed in white jeans and socks, and had a wide bandage wrapped low around his bare abdomen. There was a spot of brownish red about the size of a nickel soaking through just over the hipbone.

"She ain't here," said the young man, starting to close the door.

"Know where I could find her?" asked Netski, moving his foot and his body forward.

"No," said the young man, and Netski said, "Mind if I come in and wait?" clearly a rhetorical question, since he had already pushed his wide shoulders and solid hips through the door. Netski was a big guy, well over two hundred pounds. He had a meat-slab face, graying blond hair, and pale eyes. These took in the immediate scene in the apartment's living room. Some smashed furniture. Stacks of take-out containers on the coffee table. Wads of bloody dressings strewn around. An assemblage of first-aid supplies—antiseptic, bandages, gauze pads, tape, scissors.

"Looks like you got hurt, fella," said Netski. "How'd it happen?"

"At work. Is construction job. I fell on a nail."

"Oh, yeah? Where was that? I mean, what job?"

"Some job. Downtown."

"Uh-huh. What's your name, fella?"

"Fernando Zedillo."

"And what're you doing here, Paco? I mean, excuse me, but you don't look like you work much construction. You keeping the old bed warm for Obregon? A little snuggle with Connie while the big man's in the *calaboza*? I tell you what, Paco, let's you and me take a tour of this crib, see what we can find, all right?"

Netski gestured to the hallway that led from the living room. The young man hesitated a moment and then walked off docilely enough. The first door led to the kitchen—dirty but otherwise innocent. The next door led to a bedroom.

Netski had no sense of danger. He was there to interview a woman; the real bad guys were in jail; there was this pretty boy who looked like maybe somebody stuck him, which in Netski's experience was an occupational hazard of pretty boys.

So he didn't have his gun out, he didn't have his hands on the kid, he didn't kick the doors open, holding the kid in front of him like a shield, which is what he would have done had he had any sense of danger.

The kid walked into the bedroom and over to the bed, which was unmade, and picked up a pillow. Netski just had time to take in what else was in the room, in the corners, stacked, the machine guns, the rocket launchers, the magazines, the little egg pile of hand grenades, and time to feel the first thrill of fear and reach for his pistol, but not enough time to do anything useful before El Chivato shot him three times in the chest through the pillow.

Marlene came back to the loft shortly before eleven on Saturday morning, having shepherded Joan Savitch through criminal justice system hell, and then visited Mattie Duran in the hospital. Of the two women, Marlene thought that Mattie would recover sooner, despite having taken 9mm rounds through thigh and collarbone.

The Savitch business had, fortunately, been a perfectly straightforward case. Gerald Savitch, ex-husband of Ms. Savitch, having been released from prison the day before, had used a wrecking bar to break into Ms. Savitch's apartment, thus gaining entry illegally during the hours of the night, upon the discovery of which Ms. Savitch had confronted him and ordered him to leave, whereupon, he refusing and advancing toward her in a menacing fashion with the wrecking bar, and she in fear of her life or grievous bodily harm, she had fired five .38-caliber hollow-points into his chest, killing him instantly. Marlene had managed to get the woman released on her own recognizance even given the charge of homicide, the authorities being fairly sympathetic to householders who shoot guys who break in at night. Savitch would have to appear before a grand jury at some future time and explain the death, but Marlene had little doubt that the jury would find the shooting justifiable homicide and no crime.

Yes, the legal part was dandy. What Marlene was dragging behind her like a sack of dead mackerel as she entered her home was the other stuff that always surrounded death by violence, especially death by violence by loved ones, especially messy death by violence by loved ones, with big hollow-point wounds, *not* as seen on the TV, blowing great gouts of estranged-Dad flesh over the tweed couch and the framed picture of the kids and the nice blue shag rug, and the blood actually gurgling and hissing out of the blown aorta, another thing (besides, of course, the smell) that the media are reluctant to depict, blood mist filling the air and spraying a fine carmine airbrush-like pattern over the table and the chairs and the ceiling, and over Mom with the smoking gun and the two little boys, seven and ten, standing there, watching.

And, inevitably, the various horrified feelings, the real, the ancient gut-ripping feelings, which turn out to be not at all ameliorated by all the hundreds or thousands of dramatized killings we have all seen, but are just as vivid as they were the day Clytemnestra whacked Agamemnon, king of men, those feelings, after taking some twisting caroms around the psyche of the formerly abused lady, popped out at—who else?—the author of the event, the supplier of the deadly weapon, the enabler, Marlene herself. And Marlene had to take it, the blame, the rage, the shame, the horror, the dumping, because what could she say? Congratulations? Ding-dong, the witch is dead?

Baby giggles and a peculiar shuffling sound greeted her as she entered the loft. Her husband had brought out a four-foot-high plastic basket and backboard into the wide, smooth hallway, and he was on his knees playing b-ball of a sort with his twin sons, using a six-inch green Nerf sphere. Much of this game consisted of wild heaves by the boys and scrambling after the loose ball, but occasionally one of them caught a pass or hit close enough to the backboard so that Karp could flick it in and crow, "Swish! Two points!"

Ordinarily, this scene lifted Marlene's heart, but not today, with the faces of Savitch's two boys occupying her interior TV. And there was the unfinished business with the shelter and the Arab girl that would have to be thrashed through with Butch and, God knew, she didn't have the energy just now. She waved at Karp and got a wave in return, a formal one, like a salute, and then she went into the bedroom and stripped. She hooked up the thick, old-fashioned Koss headphones to the cassette deck of the bedroom's stereo and slapped in Glenn Gould doing *The Well-Tempered Clavier*. Wrapped in her sleazy kimono and trailing the twenty-foot cord that was pumping heavenly order into her ears, she marched to the huge rubber hot tub, dropped the robe, and submerged up to her neck. Hot tears leaked from her eyes and dimpled the black surface of the water.

As for Karp, contrary to appearances, he had not spent the morning entirely in fatherly Saturday a.m. pursuits. Posie had left him with cleaned and fed twins before departing for her regular day off. Lucy was sleeping in. Plopping the boys in front of the most lurid and violent cartoons on offer, he had worked the phones. As the district attorney's sole deputy, and as a former homicide bureau chief of some luster, Karp still drew a good deal of water in the murky channels of Manhattan's criminal justice system. Cops from working-stiff detectives to precinct captains took his calls, and fed him more or less the straight line. He managed to grab the Fifth Precinct night-shift detective lieutenant, a man named Eric Schenck, before that tired fellow had gone off duty, and extracted from him the full story of the women's shelter raid.

"Funny business," Schenck said, his voice husky with smoke and coffee and the end of a Friday night East Village shift. "They came in through the roof door. Looked like a pro job, but nothing taken—hell, nothing there *to* take. The director there, that Duran woman, blasted away at the perps with that big Colt she keeps, and they returned fire from some kind of nine-milli auto weapon, the proverbial hail of fucking lead. She got hit twice, but lucky. She's stable at Saint V's. What's your interest here?"

"Couple of angles," said Karp. "One, my wife works with them—a kind of volunteer, so I was concerned. The other thing is that Arab girl that got lifted—she's connected to a couple of homicides I'm looking at. . . ."

"Wait a second! What Arab girl? Nobody said anything about an Arab girl."

"Yeah, I guess. I imagine you know, the shelter being on your turf and all, that Ms. Duran sometimes pinches the criminal code of the state of New York when it suits her."

A short, hollow chuckle sounded on the other end. "Oh, yeah. Mattie and I go way back. We've been known to look the other way, and she does what she thinks is right, which if you want to know, most cops would agree with. We cut her a lot of slack because she's a fucking indispensable resource. Harboring a homicide suspect is a little rich even for her, though. Who was she?"

"Name's Fatyma Daoud," said Karp. "Age fourteen, around there. The story is she's a runaway, the dad is an old-fashioned kind of guy, wanted to marry her off, kept her chained up. Yeah, literally. This is the kind of daddy who when the girl acts up figures death before dishonor. In any case, she runs, ends up on the Deuce, with the usual results. Oh, yeah, when she split she took the family dagger, and apparently when some pimp tried to get heavy with her, she stuck him with it. That's how we traced it was her. Then she headed for the shelter."

"Okay," said Schenck ruminatively, "this stuff is coming back. There was a circular about this girl a little while ago. So she whacked a pimp on the Deuce—this is not the focus of your interest, I'm thinking. I mean, it's not the kind of case you guys usually go after teeth and claws."

"No, we usually handle those with a framed certificate of appreciation and a nice dinner," said Karp. "The interesting part is the Daoud connection. The girl's brother, Walid, was the guy who fingered the perps in the Shilkes case. You remember Shilkes?"

"Who could forget?" There was a brief silence on the line as Lieutenant Schenck engaged his experienced and highly paid, if exhausted, detective brains. "Um. So . . . brother Walid has, could I say, terrorist connections? The family wants the sister back, and suddenly we have the sister kidnapped by a well-drilled team carrying automatic weapons. You're assuming that Arabs grabbed her? That there's an operating Arab terrorist cell in New York City?"

"Oh, it's more than an assumption. There's no question she was lifted by Arabs."

"What do you mean, no question?"

"My daughter happened to be staying in the same room as the girl. She was hiding when the snatch went down and heard the perps speaking Arabic. By the way, according to her, you're looking for an Abdel and a Rifaat."

"Your daughter speaks Arabic?"

"Among other things—it's a long story. Meanwhile . . ."

"And—wait a minute—she was, like, pals with this fugitive . . ."

"Well, Lieutenant," replied Karp, dropping his tone down half the Kelvin scale, "of *course* no one in my family *knew* she was a fugitive. What do you take me for?"

"Yeah, sure, but . . . okay, let's see here. Tell you the truth, Mr. Karp, I got a lot of expertise chasing P.R.'s down stairways in Alphabet City. Black fucking September is a little out of my line. I'm open for suggestions. I mean, there must be other parts of the system plugged into this."

"Yeah, there is, sort of. The key guy is Jim Raney up at Midtown South. You know him?"

"Oh, yeah, everybody knows Pistol Jim. He was through the Five a couple years back. He's got the Shilkes thing, right?"

"Right. What you need to do is give Jim a heads-up on this raid, share your material with him, the ballistics and other forensic stuff. My sense is this is going to end up in a city-wide task force, operating out of the fourteenth floor, and you might as well start laying it off on Raney."

Karp knew that neither Schenck nor his watch commander would have to be nudged very hard to get rid of a file like that, and his casual mention of the deck of One Police Plaza where the chiefs of the NYPD dwelt in their glory could not but accelerate such a movement. After Karp had finished with Schenck, he called Midtown South and, on being told Raney was at home, used Marlene's Rolodex to get Raney's home number. The detective listened without comment as Karp filled him in on the night's events.

"That's what we know so far," Karp said, "and the obvious next step is to talk to the Daouds, dad and junior."

"Yeah, I'll get on it," Raney said. Then, after a thoughtful pause, "Well. It's out of the closet now, anyway. That ought to make Fulton happy. Have you heard from him on the FBI angle yet?"

"Not yet," said Karp. "I got to go now, Raney. I have to call the D.A."

Which he did, and informed that gentleman about what was indeed out of the closet: that an armed, skilled body of Arab terrorists was in fact operational and at large in New York City.

*　*　*

Khalid owned nearly a dozen separate identifications, only some of which were known to his employer, and he selected one of the unknown ones, which conveniently had an Hispanic surname (Jorge Gomez) for his Saturday visit to Rikers Island. Jodón Obregon did not know any Jorge Gomez, but he assumed that this was a pseudonym of his agent, El Chivato. He was therefore astounded to discover the visitor's chair on the other side of the glass occupied by the man he knew as Lucky.

They stared at one another for a moment, each of them maintaining the calm visage required in such meetings. Khalid spoke first, in English, their common tongue. "That's quite a boy you sent after me."

Obregon allowed himself a tiny smile. "Yes. He is really the best."

Khalid shrugged. "Well, he has succeeded in disturbing my business, and I can't afford to have my business disturbed. I underestimated you, I admit that. I thought you were a chicken; it turns out you are a tiger. So, I was mistaken, and I have to pay for the mistake. The main thing is for both of us to return to business with no hard feelings."

"I'm listening," said Obregon.

"Hard feelings are not businesslike. I figure, your interests are elsewhere, my interests are elsewhere too. We started out on the wrong foot, but we could make it right. On the other hand, you could say, hey, this guy Lucky, he fucked me, I have to get revenge, but in that case we have war. Maybe your guy gets me, maybe I get you, maybe we're both dead. This don't make sense, agree?"

Obregon nodded.

"Okay," Khalid continued, "here's what I see the fix is. The guy who killed the cop Morilla is named Ahmed Falani. As it happens, he's dead too. Now, suppose the police find his body, and on this body they find the policeman Morilla's identification—"

"And the fingerprints," Obregon interrupted. "Tell me, did this Falani really do it, or is this another story?"

"No, really. Morilla was too close to our operation, and . . . what did you mean about fingerprints?"

"My lawyer tells me that besides my idiot brother's fingerprints on the gun there are others, on the bullets in the magazine. This was to be a point in our favor at the trial, a weak one, but you know, if your man's really match these . . ."

"Of course. Also, there is a little man I know, a small-time distributor who informs for the police. Sometimes these people are useful, as now, do you see? Let us say, he goes to the police, he says, ah, this Ahmed Falani, he was boasting to me how he killed this Narco cop and blamed the Obregons, and of course, he will have the whole story, with many details that only the police know, as if from the mouth of Ahmed. So that confirms the story, and you will be released. Now, as to the money . . . let us say our original agreement, the two million, plus, oh, ten percent for this . . . trouble, and to ensure good feelings. You are now—how should I say?—*whole*, with something extra, and free to go your way. This is satisfactory?"

Obregon did not answer immediately. He had imagined this scene many times. He had planned it, of course, and now it was bearing fruit. The problem was Lucky himself. He had expected to encounter a man terrorized, helpless, not the calm and confident figure who now faced him. There was not enough suffering here, and that made him suspicious. Ten percent, that was fine, but did it really pay for the indignity? No, of course not, but revenge could wait. In fact, it was better to wait, until this *chingada* would be off his guard, relaxed, enjoying himself, at which time Jesus Obregon would repay. He smiled at the man and nodded. "Yes, satisfactory, as you say. My lawyer is named Manuel Huerta. He will accept the money. When it is in his hands and your arrangements have made them release me and my brother, I will call off El Chivato."

"Is that his name? Yes, but there is one other small thing. This man, he has taken something of mine, some information, which he must not have. It is not a matter of money, but political. You must arrange for him to be . . . delivered to me. Or else there is no deal—we go back to start and either your boy gets me or I get him, but either way you're in jail and broke. So decide."

It took little additional thought. Getting rid of El Chivato would represent a substantial savings for Jodón on the boy's fee, as well as putting Lucky off his guard. There were any number of boys working the same trade along the border, and if none of them had quite the style of El Chivato, one or another of them would do just as well: when he returned to Mexico he could send them against this Arab in squads.

"All right," Obregon said. "When the money is paid and we are released, I will give him to you."

"When you are released, but before the money is paid," said Khalid.

"Half the money first," said Obregon, "and half after."

"As you like," said Khalid.

It was one of the chief virtues of the Karps' marriage that in times of stress, when the fan was roaring and spraying the local volume with innumerable fragments of shit, they could suspend the usual who-struck-John business that occupies so much of married discourse, and drop together into the sort of cool collegial space in which they had both been trained to function.

It was by this time about two in the afternoon, on the Saturday before Palm Sunday. The boys had been exhausted, fed, and laid out for their naps; Marlene had finished her healing music and her bath and taken a nap of her own; Lucy had emerged around noon, made some calls and been picked up by a gaggle of Chinese-American girls of her own age, and was off watching a Bruce Lee marathon at the Chinese movie house on Canal, discreetly trailed by Tran; Karp had made a large number of calls, nearly all of which were unwelcome to the recipients, and was taking his ease in front of the TV, desultorily watching Wake Forest play a basketball game against Syracuse, and toying with some notes for the meeting he had set up for the Monday.

His wife entered the living room and plopped herself down next to him. She was warm and smelled of roses, and he put his arm around her.

"What's the score, counselor?" she asked, snuggling in.

"I'm just calculating that very thing, counselor," Karp replied. "I believe the bad guys are ahead at present, but the good guys are tanned, rested, and about to come out swinging." Whereupon he reviewed the calls and arrangements he had made, she commenting intelligently and making several good suggestions, and, by way of coda, adding, "I note you did not rat me out on the Fatyma thing. I appreciate it."

"Your appreciation is noted and stored away for when needed," said Karp.

"Short-term, my big worry is Fatyma. She was a nice kid: born yesterday, but a good spirit. Luce was really down about it."

"Clearly a priority for the cops. Raney's on it as we speak."

"Yeah, well, good, but I intend to look around myself too," she said, glancing at Karp significantly.

"Look away, Wonder Person," said Karp blandly. "I wish you luck."

"Hmm, a changed fellow," said Marlene. "No lectures? No furrowed brow?"

"Not a furrow," said Karp. "And I also get points for not saying a word about you leaving our precious little girl in environs where automatic weapons are likely to be discharged."

"I noticed. So what's up? You changed your medication?"

"Not at all. Just the calm resignation that comes with maturity. Now that I'm semi-retired, I have time to take the long view, and also recent events have reconnected me with the ancient Talmudic traditions of my people. I'm married to you—that's not going to change. As I've often said, either you'll get nailed or you won't. If not, fine, life goes on. If yes, I will visit you every weekend at the Bedford Correctional Institution, I'll bring you from Dean and DeLuca, I'll bring you from Zabar's. I'll take videos, the kids shouldn't forget what you look like. When you get out, I'll help with your rehabilitation, find you a decent job—maybe food service, maybe transportation . . ."

"Gosh, what a prince!" said Marlene. "I'm throbbing with gratitude."

"As well you should be. As for the rest, the risks, the kids, I figure, you live in Kansas, it's tornadoes; in California, it's quakes; in New York, it's my wife's chosen lifestyle, so I'm either going to live in fear forever, or just live, and forget this Jewish mother catastrophe business. I'm overcoming my cultural conditioning is what it is."

"I thought you were getting closer to the traditions of your people."

"Closer, further, what's the difference? It's a mystical thing. It's hard to explain."

"To a shiksa, yeah. Is this where you start going dy-da-dee-dee-dee-deedle like in *Fiddler on the Roof*?"

"If it would make you love me more."

"Um, let me pass on that," she said. "As a matter of fact, though, I can't recall a time recently when I *did* love you more. Understanding always makes me throb. Do you think that there's the remotest chance that we could sneak in a hot quickie without waking up the twins?"

The phone awakened Roland Hrcany out of a sodden sleep just past noon on Palm Sunday. He cursed and pulled the pillow over his head and let the machine pick it up.

But when he heard the message, he cursed again and rolled over and grabbed the phone. Into it he growled, "Timmons, it's Palm Sunday, why aren't you in church?"

An unenthusiastic chuckle on the line. Detective Inspector Pat Timmons was a Police Plaza suit known to be close to the chief of detectives himself, and the man especially charged with following cases of particular interest to the NYPD in the County of New York. Like cop killings.

"Roland, yeah, I'm sorry to bother you at home, but we got a situation here. It's going to reflect on Morilla."

Roland was instantly awake and alert. "What happened?"

"Last night the Six logged an anonymous call, there's a body in the trunk of a car under the highway. They checked it out and there it is, late model Firebird, New York plates, a stiff in the trunk, dark-complexioned male, late twenties, took one shot, small-caliber, in the face. The preliminary from the M.E. says dead a couple of days. They search him and find Morilla's shield and ID in his pocket. So naturally, their attention is drawn."

"No shit. Who was he?"

"No other ID, but a little later, this'd be around five this morn-ing, a skell picked up in a drug sweep in Brooklyn last night calls a detective named Melville out of the Seven-seven. This mutt's Melville's snitch, been feeding him stuff for years, named Cren-shaw, Kibble Crenshaw. He's got a story. Apparently he's in a bar last week talking to one of his associates, an Arab named Falani, supposed to be muscle for some kind of dope gang, and this Fa-lani tells him the whole story about how he whacked Morilla, and ripped off these two greasers, and planted the murder gun on them. Melville figures this is worth checking out, so he calls Ray Netski. He doesn't get him. No Netski. It turns out nobody's seen Netski since Friday, when he told his squad sergeant at the Two-five he was going to look into something for you. You got any idea where he went, by the way?"

"Not a clue. He didn't call in or anything?" Roland felt his stomach start to roll into a hard, painful knot.

"Not that I've heard," said Timmons. "In any case, Fuller, the sergeant there, tells Melville to drive the mutt over to the Two-five and Netski'll talk to him when he shows. Meanwhile, Fuller fields another call for Netski from Detective Alfasano at the Six, who's holding Morilla's ID in his hand and what should he do? After that this shit fucking *flies* up the chain of command, and I get a call at about seven this morning. Let me cut to the chase. One, Crenshaw ID'd the stiff positively as Ahmed Falani, the guy he heard the story from. Two, the plates on the Firebird are stolen, and the VIN's etched off. Three, Netski's not at his apartment, he's not at his girlfriend's apartment, and his kids don't know where he is. We got a bulletin out on him, city-wide. Four—you're gonna love this . . ."

"Let me guess," said Roland. "The unmatched thumb prints on the unfired bullets in the Morilla murder weapon are from the dead guy."

"You got it, son. Speaking of bullets, I think you just dodged a big one. You would've looked like a piece of shit this stuff had come up during the trial."

"Yeah," said Roland weakly. "Lucky me."

"Look, I got Fuller coordinating all the paperwork, the forensics, the snitch's statement and so forth, and he'll ship that over to your shop. I'll have our P.R. people get with your P.R. people, and we'll work up a joint statement for the press."

The conversation dribbled away in details. Roland hardly listened. For some reason, all he could think of at the moment was Karp.

Somewhat to Khalid's surprise, Ibn-Salemeh was perfectly calm when he heard the story Khalid had concocted. Bashar and Ahmed were gone, and they had apparently taken two point two million dollars from one of the cash drops the organization maintained.

"The other drops are safe?"

"I checked them all and moved them in case they thought to come back. Nothing else is missing." He watched Ibn-Salemeh stroke his beard. The man's eyes never left the television set, which was showing *Jeopardy*.

"Will we cancel the mission, effendi?" Khalid asked.

"No. Why should we?"

"If they betrayed us in this, why not in everything?"

"Pah! Ahmed and Bashar did not betray us. Clearly they were tortured into revealing the hiding place of the money, and they are surely dead now. This is the work of those Mexicans. I see now that it was an error to have cheated them. We must find some way of eliminating that pressure."

Khalid could hardly believe what he was hearing. Controlling his elation, he said, "That would be a wise move, effendi. If you will allow, I will take care of it myself."

Karp arrived at Moiseh's Second Avenue Dairy a little before one on Sunday. The place was jammed, and he had to wait for a table. The customers appeared to consist of a minority of actual eastern European-derived Jews enjoying their native cuisine and a majority of assorted goyim having an exotic experience of a vanishing culture: bagels, lox, blintzes, and the famously rude waiters. Karp hadn't been here for years, and although himself an assimilation cheerleader, the transformation of Moiseh's from a living cultural institution to a sort of museum de cuisine made him inexplicably sad.

Aaron Zwiller's arrival, punctually at one, in his full Hasidic regalia, caused a minor stir, a raising of heads and a murmur from the tourists (Is that a *Jew*, Ma? Shh, dear!), and when the tan-coated elderly waiter came by, slamming a basket of rolls down on the table, they ordered. Karp went for the cold borscht with sour cream with a boiled potato in it and the blintzes; Zwiller ordered the white fish plate and a glass of tea. After ordering, he excused himself, and Karp figured he was going to wash his hands, as required by ritual.

The food came, Zwiller returned, sat, and murmured a *borucha*. They started to eat. Zwiller did not seem in any hurry to convey information. To make conversation, Karp commented on the goodness and authenticity of the food, and that he did not get much of it anymore.

Zwiller raised a set of bushy eyebrows. "Your wife don't cook?"

"She cooks very well, but not this. I married an Italian."

Zwiller frowned. "You know, this is an interesting thing, Mr. Karp. People like you marry outside and become goyim, and at the same time completely assimilated Jews, people very much like yourself, return to orthodoxy. *Baalei teshuva*, they're called."

"I know," said Karp. "My brother is one."

Zwiller nodded. "Yes. Some of these simply wish to be reunited with their people, and to live and raise their children in holiness and piety. Others . . . others are angry, full of rage—it gives them a kind of reason for living, to think of themselves as defenders of embattled Israel. Perhaps it is part of the poison left over from the Holocaust; perhaps it is from some mixed-up notions about the state of Israel. You know, there are many orthodox who believe that we must rebuild the temple in Jerusalem before the Mosiach will return. In any case, many of these Americans make the *aliyah*, and in Israel they join the radical right parties, Kach, for example, and build settlements in Judea and Samaria, and carry guns, and beat up Arabs, and behave like people in cowboy movies. I find this very distressing. My reading of Torah is that it is all about peace and justice and the respect for human life."

"I take it Rabbi Lowenstein doesn't agree."

Zwiller put his knife and fork down and directed a blue glare at Karp. "I didn't say that. Rabbi Lowenstein is young. He is about to inherit the leadership from a genuine saint, a *tzaddik*. Reb Lowenstein, whatever his talents, is not a *tzaddik*. I believe this gnaws at him. He has great energy. It may be that, in confusion of spirit, this energy flows into areas that may not be in accord with the spirit of the Law."

"By law," asked Karp, "do you mean those of New York state or the Talmud?"

Zwiller sighed and twirled a finger in the fringes of his beard. Karp judged that he was a man in some discomfort, pulled between his loyalty to a tight-knit group and his sense of righteousness. "Both," said Zwiller. Almost to himself, he added, "It is better to betray a city, so that the city fall, than to be false to the Lord, blessed be He."

Karp felt there was no good response to this statement, so he waited. After what seemed a long time, it came. "As you may know, I handle various financial duties for our community. In this regard I've noticed recently, the past few months or so, certain transfers of funds for which I have no good explanation. Through Israeli banks. Not a lot, but enough to be troublesome. Then just in the last week we have had visitors. From Israel. This is not unusual, of course: between Williamsburg and Israel there is naturally a continual going and coming, our people visit the holy land, those who have made *aliyah* return to visit relatives and so on. But these boys . . . I don't know, Mr. Karp. They are supposed to be teachers, in our yeshivas, this is the story, but they don't look like yeshiva teachers to me. Also they have bags, big green military duffel bags, that maybe are not full of clothes." He paused and checked to see that Karp was following this somewhat oblique account.

Karp said, "You think the rabbi is assembling a group of hard guys and serious weapons."

Zwiller seemed to ignore this statement. "You know, first it was the Guardians of Israel, a few boys in cars, patrolling the neighborhood at night with radios. They discourage burglars, nogoodniks from the other areas—we had break-ins, rapes, people are incensed, and the police don't seem to be able to stop it. Then the boys start carrying clubs, bats, they chase away the schvartzers, the Spanish. Then I hear they're quoting Talmud: if anyone comes to kill you, you are permitted to kill him first. So it follows from this, why wait like lambs for them to come after us? Why don't *we* go where they are, make them fear us, like in Israel. They don't wait to get attacked, they go in, they clean out the nests of terrorists in Lebanon. . . ."

He stopped. More beard twirling. His food was forgotten, but he took a deep draft of sweetened, lemony tea. Karp said, "Mr. Zwiller, if you have any information about a specific illegal act these men are about to commit, or even knowledge that they plan to break the law, you're obliged to tell the authorities."

Zwiller nodded. "Yes, I know, but I've been careful to hide my eyes, Mr. Karp. I'm not a policeman. I have nothing that could be used as evidence in a court of law, not even, I bet, enough for you to get a search warrant. Do you know, in ghetto days it was a crime under the Talmud to denounce a Jew to the *goyische* authorities, whatever the offense. A *capital* crime, Mr. Karp."

"Do you think you might be in danger yourself, Mr. Zwiller?"

He smiled. "From the rabbinical court? I don't think so. Times have changed. On the other hand, I have this fear. There seems to be so much anger, it seems so easy for it to slip over into violence. And so I think, yes, I'm in danger, you're in danger, we're all in danger."

THIRTEEN

They held the meeting in one of the conference rooms on the top floor of NYPD headquarters, first thing after lunch on Monday afternoon. The room was paneled with light wood and carpeted in blue, and it had blue drapes that were pulled back to reveal tall windows that looked out on Police Plaza. There was a flag stand against one wall holding the national banner in the center and the flags of the state, the city, and the NYPD flanking. On the opposite wall was an oil portrait of the Police Commission, circa 1910, six plump and whiskered Irish gentlemen, who stared out at their successors with bland confidence. The center of this room was occupied by a long table in pale oak trimmed with a darker wood, in shape a near oval with the ends truncated, and around it sixteen comfortable blue-upholstered swivel armchairs.

Each of these chairs was occupied, and several more people, of lower rank or more peripheral to the meeting's purpose, sat in straight chairs against the wall. The highest-ranking person at the meeting sat at the head of the table, closest to the window, so that he was enveloped in an intermittent glory of afternoon sun flowing through the great panes and anyone addressing him was illuminated, as by a searchlight. This was Chief Inspector Kevin X. Battle, a silver-haired, pink-faced man in his late fifties, urbane, smooth, careful, the epitome of a fourteenth-floor suit. Chief inspector is the highest regular rank in the NYPD, and this particular chief inspector was even more exalted, since he served as the uniformed chief of staff for the police commissioner, the political appointee who ran the Department. Battle's presence at this meeting attested to its significance, and also explained the presence in the room of a number of people who had little to contribute and no direct knowledge of any facts germane to the meeting's purpose, which was to determine the likelihood that New York was in danger from a band of Arab terrorists. They were there in obeisance to the bureaucratic law that states, in effect, that a subordinate shall not meet privately with his boss's boss. The subordinate in this case was Detective James Raney, and since he was meeting a boss at a stratospheric level, this meant that every level between him and the police commissioner had to show. Thus he was accompanied by his watch commander, his precinct commander, his zone commander, the commander of all the detectives in Manhattan, and a deputy chief inspector from the office of the chief of detectives. Since the affair extended to Brooklyn, there was a contingent too from that proud borough, and a man also from the Brooklyn District Attorney's Office. Since the affair involved political groups, the head of the Bureau of Strategic Surveillance and Intelligence (the former Red Squad) was there, looking not at all pleased. In addition to these worthies, and their accompanying fuglemen, there were also present the two people besides Raney who knew what was going on: Butch Karp, representing the New York D.A., and Clay Fulton, representing essentially himself. As one of the Department's few tolerated eccentrics, Fulton had, in practical terms, neither superiors nor subordinates. Everyone in the room knew who he was, and everyone thought someone else had invited him.

Chief Inspector Battle looked sourly around the table. He did not like such meetings interrupting his intolerably busy schedule, and his assumption going into it was that it was either a bout of hysteria on the part of the district attorney who had demanded it, or, more probably, a ploy by that gentleman to generate political support and money from the Jews. Battle naturally understood who the real players around the table were and who the merely ritualistic attendees. Karp was a well-known crazy man, yet another smart Jew, but reportedly unreliable with respect to supporting the Department. Raney was a trigger-happy hooligan whose remarkable streak of luck was going to run out one day and leave the Department probably facing a nasty lawsuit (Cop Shoots Nanny, Three Kids). Fulton was untouchable because of his race and record, but was not, nor had he ever been, a team player to Battle's standards and would never, as a result, see captain's rank. Battle's instinct was to can this as quickly as possible, while establishing a foolproof ass-covering apparatus. Battle's own ass was protected by (figuratively) four inches of molybdenum-vanadium steel, a barrier he had worked for decades to develop, and there was not the slightest chance that he would endanger it, not for a legion of putative sand-nigger bombers. While demonstrably loyal to the commissioner of the day, Battle had as his primary loyalty the Job, and, a thin little hair back from that, his own career. He reasonably hoped to retire a super-chief (of Patrol, for choice), and after a stint as police chief of a smaller city, it was not out of the question that he might return to the Apple as the big cheese.

He got the meeting under way, paying due attention to bureaucratic courtesy, which meant that the bosses had to give their completely hollow and noncommittal opinions before the working cop who knew something got to speak. The burden of this guff was that if there really was an Arab terror cell in operation it would be a bad thing, but that the Department (and My part of it, of course) was fully capable of dealing with it, under the wise orders of the brass.

Then it was Raney's turn. He was wearing a dark gray suit, a gleaming white oxford shirt, a blue tie with tiny pale Nixonian dots, and his black wing tips were mirrors. He had never been on the fourteenth floor before, had never, since leaving the Police Academy, been in a police building that did not have pea-soup green walls, brown linoleum on the floors, and a pungent aroma of tobacco, Lysol, and acidic coffee. He thought he could get used to this kind of class pretty soon.

He was not in the least nervous as he began his presentation. His closest experience to what he was now doing was his service as an altar boy. There was God down there at the end of the table, and all you had to do was go through a set of well-rehearsed motions and he would be happy and you could go off back to regular life.

Raney was a decent enough presenter (he had learned much from Karp's style in covering similar material the other night), bold enough to eschew the heavy circumlocutions of police jargon, and he told his story smoothly and succinctly. The Shilkes killing; the idea of a violent conspiracy wider than four boys; the discovery of the floater Ali and his tattoo; the business of the Daoud sister and the knife and the stabbing of Train Wilson on the Deuce; the raid on the East Village Women's Shelter and the kidnap of the sister;

the discovery there of 9mm shell casings with Czech military markings; the interrogation of Hassan Daoud and his son, Walid (they both had alibis); the evidence for Arab participants in the raid.

"*Who* was that who said they were Arabs?" Battle interrupted.

"Lucy Karp, sir, age ten," said Raney. "She was sharing a room with the kidnapped girl and hid in the closet. She overheard them talking."

Battle looked at Karp. "No relation, I presume," said Battle.

"My daughter," answered Karp.

A soft murmur in the room. "Excuse me, your *daughter* was in a battered-women's shelter?" asked Battle.

"Yes, my wife does volunteer work for them, and my daughter occasionally befriends some of the younger residents, as apparently happened in this case. Fatyma Daoud was teaching her Arabic." Incredulous stares. "My daughter is something of a language prodigy, Chief," Karp added.

"I see," said Battle. "So, is that it? A stabbing, a floater with a tattoo, another stabbing, a kidnap from a shelter by 'Arabs' of some kind on the evidence of a ten-year-old?"

"Not quite," Karp said, and related the story of Ibn-Salemeh and Khalid, as he had heard it in John Haddad's office.

Battle was skilled at keeping his face unrevealing of his thoughts, and so no one saw how truly irritated he was at these revelations. A city councilman had been involved in this stupidity, which meant that even greater circumspection was required. John Haddad could not be hauled into a precinct and sweated for more information about the shadowy Mr. Rahmali; nor was it wise to launch at this time a major roust of the Arab community, not until the P.C. had worked the mayor and seen how much clout Haddad exercised on issues critical to the Department. His suspicion was confirmed that this was some kind of political thing that the Department would do well to keep at arm's length.

"Very interesting, Mr. Karp," Battle said icily. "It's always fascinating when the New York D.A. extends his investigatory reach to the outer boroughs." He turned to the BSSI chief, whose name was Richard Bailey. Bailey was an elderly desk-jockey inspector with a lot of pals among the brass, who was filling his present post as a sinecure before retirement. Battle said, "Dick, you have anything on this?"

Bailey cleared his throat. "Not a thing, Chief. In fact, I spoke to

Don Herring at the Bureau this morning when I got the heads-up for this meeting. He said, and I quote, 'it is extremely unlikely that there has been significant penetration of the continental United States by Middle Eastern terror organizations.' So . . ." He shrugged elaborately.

Battle grunted and looked down the table, straining for a way out of this garbage that would cover the Department and let him get back to serious work. His gaze lit upon the one face that stood out in the ring of pale, attentive, respectful ovals around the table. This face was not particularly respectful or attentive. It was bored. It had an expression on it that might even be called insubordinate. And it was deep brown. Chief Battle well understood that in this year of 1981, the slightest taint of racism was an absolute career killer, and so he never, even among his closest friends, allowed a word disrespectful of minorities to pass his lips. On the other hand, if one had to stick someone with a tar baby, so to speak . . .

"Lieutenant Fulton," he boomed, "perhaps we could have your thoughts on this, and why don't you begin by explaining your connection with the case?"

Fulton explained that he was there at the request of the district attorney's office, and that he had reviewed the case at the request of same, he being a legitimate member of the D.A. squad, and there being some sense that there might be a suspect involvement of a public official, Mr. Haddad. Which, he was happy to say, there was not. But having reviewed the case material presented by Detective Raney in some detail, he had to respectfully disagree with Inspector Bailey. It was his professional opinion that there was sufficient evidence to suggest the existence of an alien conspiracy of unknown capability and extent, certainly enough to warrant a full-scale investigation.

"Thank you, Lieutenant," said Battle, smiling faintly. That was what he had expected and desired the man to say. "Since you feel that way, why don't we put you in charge of the investigation? Say, you and Sergeant Raney for starters, and other resources as required. You'll report through BSSI and Inspector Bailey here, if that's all right with you, Dick? Good. And please—watch the overtime, people. We're getting killed on it this year." He got to his feet. "Gentlemen, thank you for coming," he said crisply, as if attendance had been voluntary, and then strode out, followed by two junior suits who had been sitting in chairs along the wall.

★ ★ ★

"Well, wasn't that a rat fuck?" said Raney, who was sitting in Karp's office with Fulton. All three men had their jackets off and were dabbing themselves with wads of paper towels. It had started to rain heavily while they were walking the few blocks from Police Plaza to Centre Street, and they had gotten soaked, which did not improve their moods.

"It's more or less what I expected," said Karp. "The cops don't like D.A.'s telling them they're asleep at the switch."

"Speaking of sleep," said Raney, "am I crazy or did Inspector Bailey actually doze off while Fulton was talking? Are we really going to report to that crock?"

Fulton said, "Absolutely. We will generate paper and send him every scrap of it, at least a ream every day, tabbed and indexed. He's not going to read any of it, but it'll cover our butts with the chief. Meanwhile, we'll do what we need to do."

"And he's going to give us what we need?"

"No, and we're not going to ask him either, unless we want to dick around until Christmas. Me, you, White, maybe we can steal some people from the D.A. Squad, I can call in some favors uptown if we need to, but that's going to be it. We'll get a piece of paper with Battle's name on it we can wave around the precincts so they don't laugh in our faces if we need a canvass or something."

"That's not enough," said Raney.

"No, but it's what we got. So, where do we start?"

"What did your FBI guy say?" Karp asked Fulton.

"What Bailey's guy said, more or less. The Bureau is real careful nowadays about setting up intelligence operations against domestic political groups, or so they tell me. What, *us* spy on a peaceful businessman of Arab heritage? *Us?* Also, it's well known in the Bureau that local cops, when you can drag them away from beating up minorities and collecting graft, can barely tie their own shoes. The idea that *we* picked up a terrorist cell that *they* missed . . ."

"Got it, " said Karp. "So, no help there. Suggestions?"

"Get on the kidnap," said Fulton. "It's the most recent crime. Go over the scene, check the forensics, do a canvass. There were a bunch of guys involved, somebody must have seen something, recognized a car, seen a license plate."

"We should have a talk with this Khalid character, what's-his-name, Chouza," said Raney.

Fulton frowned and shook his head. "Yeah, you said that the other night. But like I said then, what if he spooks? These guys are probably pretty good at that."

"If he spooks, at least we know he's dirty," said Raney.

"Uh-huh, and then him and an unknown number of associates are loose in New York with—what was it, Butch?—a two-hundred-fifty-kilogram bomb. We don't know shit about what they're doing yet. It's way too early to brace Khalid."

"We could follow him, low-profile."

"Yeah, we could if we had the troops," said Fulton. "It takes eight people to provide full-time one-man surveillance, and if you want to set up a moving surveillance on anybody who's likely to be looking for it, you need at least three cars. Also, if we're going to concentrate on anyone, I'd rather concentrate on the Daouds."

"Oh, fuck the Daouds!" snapped Raney, who was getting a little tired of being told his business by this guy, whatever his rep. "The Daouds are patsies. The kid is a dim bulb; the father is a straight-up bakery guy who barely speaks English."

Fulton's genial smile did not break. "Right, Jim, but if they're such nobodies, why did a slick bunch of guys with automatic weapons go through a lot of trouble to lift the daughter?"

Raney opened his mouth to answer this and then realized he didn't know the answer, that the answer to that particular question would be one of the prime goals of any investigation. He subsided, cursing under his breath.

"Yeah, right," said Fulton sympathetically, "me too." He looked over at Karp, who was gazing dreamily out the window and slowly drying his head. "Say, Ace—you got any ideas here, now that you got us into this shit?"

Karp said, to their surprise, "I guess you noticed who was missing from the meeting today."

A moment's thought and Raney answered, "Roland?"

"Yeah, Roland's having a bad day all around," said Karp, and he told them the story, widely circulating now through Centre Street, of the weekend's developments in re: Morilla. "I'm concerned about the supposed gunman here," Karp concluded. "The late Ahmed. I hate it that he's an Arab."

This dangled for a moment, and then Raney bit with a puzzled grimace "So he's an Arab—you're not saying there's a connection?"

"Not yet," said Karp, "but you might want to touch base with

Alfasano in the Six, see if he's got any more story on the deceased. There could be a link."

Raney nodded agreeably, not desiring another argument. "Yeah, okay. So they're going to spring the Mexican brothers?"

"Probably walking free this minute," said Karp.

Two hours after his release from Rikers, Jodón Obregon was reclining on a comfortable bed in a West Side hotel. Next to the bed stood the large suitcase that had been delivered that morning to the offices of Manny Huerta. Huerta had turned it over to him upon the brothers' release, pointedly not inquiring what was in it. The delivery of such suitcases was not an uncommon event in Huerta's practice. The lawyer had been paid, in cash.

Jodón had enjoyed a long, hot shower, several cool drinks, and a cigar, and was awaiting the arrival of a blond whore he had ordered from the bell captain. There was one item of business remaining before he could fully relax, however. He picked up the bedside phone and dialed a familiar number.

El Chivato answered on the fourth ring. Jodón was effusive in his praise—all had worked out as they wished. They were free, and the money was promised. Lucky was terrified and willing to do anything to stave off the attentions of El Chivato.

Who listened to this without comment, saying only, "I have to get back to Nogales."

"Yes, you can go tonight. But there's one last thing. You have to pick up the money."

"From Lucky?"

"Yes. I arranged for you to meet him in Brooklyn, five-thirty this evening. Take down this address." He read out the address of a garage on Fulton Street that Lucky had given him. "Okay, this is a car-repair shop, but it'll be closed for the day. There's an office you can see from the street. He'll be there, sitting in the office. With the money in a suitcase. You go in, pick it up, and get out. You got that?" Jodón asked.

"Yes. How much is it?"

"Two point two million. That's something, huh?"

"Yes."

Jodón waited for the kid to say something else, but there was nothing but the hiss of the line. He said, "So, again, a good job. I'll recommend you to all my friends. Maybe I'll see you back in

Mexico . . ." Another long pause. For some reason the kid didn't want to hang up. Then he heard the click of the broken connection, and with a feeling of relief and a vague unease, as if something had been left undone, he hung up the phone.

It was not until over an hour later, with the blond whore on top of him, bouncing vigorously away, that he understood, and the understanding drove an icy spike of fear through his vitals and drew the stiffness from his organ, causing the girl to break her rhythm and look down at him with a confused expression.

He heaved the girl off him, wiped himself with a corner of the sheet, and grabbed instinctively for the phone. But who to call, what to do? José was no help, the lawyer was no help—a plane ticket out? Yes, but to where? Nothing could be planned until he had assurance that the little *maricón* was truly dead. He put the phone down and tried to think how he had come to do such a stupid thing. The excitement of being released perhaps, the strong drinks after long abstinence. This was what had caused him to tell the most dangerous man in Mexico to pick up over two million (imaginary) dollars without also telling him where to deliver it.

"The car is about as clean as a car can get," said Detective Joe Alfasano to the two detectives who had come by to check out the dead Arab and his rolling sepulcher. Alfasano was an overweight, balding fellow who sported the last Adolphe Menjou mustache in New York. He had no problem talking about this case to two strange cops because this was not an ordinary case; the brass was interested in this one big-time, and these two, Raney and White, had hinted broadly that they were working for the fourteenth floor. He did not have much to share as yet, but he was sharing for all he was worth.

"It's been wiped and vacuumed. It smelled of Windex when we cracked it. The stiff was in the trunk, by the way, naked, no bloodstains on the trunk carpet."

"So killed someplace else, he bled out, and they stuck him in there," observed White. "You got a previous owner on the car? I understand it had stolen plates."

"No, that's what I mean by clean," said Alfasano. "The VINs were ground off, not just the ones on the engine block and the chassis, but the ones on the axles too, which they don't usually bother with. Whoever sold the killer the car was a serious pro. Nice car too. A '75 Firebird, black, with red interior, got the stencil on the front and everything."

"A Firebird, huh? In good condition, is it?"

"Perfect. Runs smooth, the engine's been steam-cleaned. The upholstery's in good shape. Why, you in the market?"

White smiled briefly and said, "No, just that why use a nice car like that for a dump car. Why not steal a car from a dentist, or use the vic's own car?"

"Maybe it *is* his car," said Alfasano.

White exchanged a look with Raney and said, "If it was his car, why would it have phony plates on it? Why would the killer bother? No, this is a special kind of car. This is an armed-robbery getaway car, bought or rented from a chop shop. It's like Avis uptown: you pay your money, you get a clean, fast, good-running car for the job. After, you take it back, the guy wipes it, paints it, dumps the stolen plates he supplied, and it disappears. It never was. If for some reason you got to dump the car, nobody can trace it back to you or to the guy you got it from." He paused and explained, "Eight years on the heavy-crimes unit out of the Two-Eight. Now, the guys who do this kind of work tend to be a close-mouthed bunch, or they're out of business, or dead. However . . ."

"What?" said Raney and Alfasano almost simultaneously, provoking a chuckle from White. "There's one guy up in Inwood I recall," said White, "used to specialize in muscle cars, Firebirds, GTOs, Mustangs. A Dominican guy, real precise, a perfectionist. He used to grind the VINs off the axles too. And he owes me a favor."

As it turned out, Felipe Valdés, the chop artist, did not mind giving up the name of Connie Erbes to Detective Alonso White. Erbes was not a regular customer and was unlikely to take violent revenge if busted. Also, White had sworn to him that he would not have to testify, and White, Felipe knew, was not only a man of his word, but had, in the old days, placed his bulk between Valdés and any number of "accessory to" charges.

Ramon Valdés, when questioned at the Club Carib, said he hadn't seen Connie for a while. The word was she was laying low, trying to shake a troublesome boyfriend. And yeah, he had an address for her.

The door to the apartment Connie Erbes reportedly occupied was unresponsive to knocks and, surprisingly, unlocked. The detectives entered, therefore, with drawn guns, crouching. They found a place unkempt, piled with take-out debris and smashed furnishings, but unoccupied. Raney went to check out the bedrooms, White to cover the rest of the apartment.

One bedroom had clearly not been occupied for a long time, and Raney ignored that one. The other showed signs of recent occupancy. The bed was rumpled, the sheets stained. There were some women's clothes on the floor of the closet, and the smashed ruins of a dressing table. In a wastebasket he found wads of blood-stained cotton wadding. Raney looked under the bed. A brassy gleam attracted his eye, and he reached the little thing out with a rubber-covered hand. He was examining the cartridge closely, although he had known what it was the instant he had it in his fingers, when White came in, looking gray.

"Find something?" asked Raney.

"Oh, nothing much," said White. "Ray Netski's stuffed into the refrigerator with a bunch of holes in his chest. Besides that . . ."

"Oh, Christ!"

"Yeah, the beat goes on. Looks like he's been dead a couple of days. We need to find this woman."

"Uh-huh. Look at this." He stood up and handed White the cartridge.

White peered at it. "What is that, Russian writing on the base?"

"Uh-huh. They were thick on the ground in 'Nam. That's a Soviet-made 7.62mm round for the AK-47 assault rifle."

"Roland," said Karp, "you're acting like a baby," knowing it was the least calming thing he could say, and not caring anymore, not caring if the red-faced man who had just barged into his office cursing and screaming had a stroke, launched himself across the desk at which Karp sat, fists flying, or vanished through the earth like Rumpelstiltskin.

Roland didn't seem to hear, however, but, standing by the open door, continued his diatribe. ". . . and didn't think to even fucking inform me, a meeting at police headquarters, on *my* case. Who the fuck died and left you king shit? Huh? You trying to *ruin* me? You son of a bitch!"

Karp had on his desk a paperweight, a heavy piece of Lucite enclosing a rifle bullet once removed from his shoulder. Right next to it was a regulation baseball bearing the signature of Mickey Mantle. Instantly Hrcany's last words were out, Karp sprang to his feet, grabbed the paperweight, and flung it at Roland's head. It grazed his ear and slammed into the wall next to the door, making a sizable dent. Roland's jaw dropped, and he went pale. He touched his ear and looked at the claret on his fingertips. Then he looked at Karp, who had the baseball in his hand and was in the final stages of a serious wind-up.

Roland ducked the bean ball, which flew through the doorway. A sound of shattering glass and a woman's short, shrill yelp. Roaring, Roland took two long steps and a leap, and threw himself across the desk at Karp's throat, bearing the larger man down behind the desk.

Karp had not had a serious physical fight (except once with his wife) since age thirteen, and it quickly crossed his mind that he could be in serious trouble in this one. Roland's hands were on his throat, cutting off air and blood supply. He had once seen Roland, on a bet, actually bend a horseshoe with his hands. Things were starting to go gray when a deluge of cold water fell on both their heads, followed by a sound like the clang of a cracked bell.

Karp coughed water from his nose and slid out from under the spluttering Hrcany, the side of whose face was now covered with blood. Marcie O'Malley, the D.A.'s secretary, stood over the two of them, holding the galvanized one-gallon watering can with which she maintained the small rain forest of houseplants in the D.A.'s suite. This was the source of the flood, and also of the sound, for she had whaled Roland a couple across the skull.

"Jesus, Marcie!" said Roland, exploring his head with a cautious finger.

"Don't you Jesus me, young man," said the fierce O'Malley. "I've never seen anything like it, carrying on like a couple of mutt dogs on the street. How could you, right in the district attorney's office! Broken glass! You should be ashamed of yourselves. And the both of you *attorneys* . . ." The enormity of this last fact overwhelmed the woman's reserves of outrage, and she left, closing the door behind her.

Karp got to his feet, righted his chair, and fished a couple of clean paper napkins out of a bottom drawer. He handed these to Roland, who held them in a wad against his bleeding ear. He got to his feet too and collapsed into Karp's visitor armchair.

"Christ, Butch," he said, probing gently, "you almost tore my ear off."

"I was aiming to split your skull," said Karp huskily. There seemed to be something wrong with his vocal cords.

"Why, 'cause I was yelling at you?"

"No," Karp croaked, "because a man is dead, a cop is dead, a cop who was supposed to be a pal of yours is dead, and what's on your mind is your status, your *goddamned* ego, whether Butch Karp is fucking with you or not. That's why. I couldn't stand it anymore, Roland. It's fucking *unworthy* of you. And you've been poisonous like that ever since you took that damn job."

Hrcany was studying his fingernails intently, as if a remarkably engrossing novel had miraculously been imprinted on them.

"I mean, fuck it, Roland," Karp added, "it's okay to be wrong. Everybody's a schmuck sometimes. The difference between the occasional schmuck and the incurable schmuck to the bone is, do you fucking *cop* to it and drive on?"

Roland shook his head sharply from side to side, like a man discouraging a small flying insect. "Okay. On this Netski thing—I do feel bad about it, especially since he probably got it looking into this thing for me, these threats. I think we should pick up the Obregons again. That was his girlfriend, the Erbes woman, who rented the car the Arab who killed Morilla was found in."

"You think she killed Netski?" asked Karp with a hidden sigh. That "okay" was all the acknowledgment he was going to get on the subject of Roland's errors of judgment and his atrocious behavior over the last weeks. It was back to business, with Karp hoping faintly for a less abrasive relationship with the Homicide Bureau chief in the future.

"I doubt it," said Roland. "There's another guy involved. Who knows, maybe a third Obregon brother we don't know about. I'll have them picked up. The cops are already looking for the woman."

"And the Arab connection, the Russian bullet in the apartment? The Czech bullets in the women's shelter?"

Roland tossed his hand, fingers spread, a gesture of bafflement. "Fuck if I know, man. We're back to zero on this whole thing. Let's reserve theorizing until we get more information."

"A wise policy, Roland."

"And fuck you too," said Roland, a hard smile cracking his face. He got up to leave.

Karp said, "Roland, I want to apologize for trying to kill you."

"Ah, shit, that's okay," said Roland. "My dad tried a lot harder than that about a million times. I'm surprised I made it this far. What can I say? I'm a fucking pain in the ass."

"You are not paying attention," chided Tran. He was trying to teach Lucy how to spot a tail by dashing across busy streets just before the traffic started, and then observing the results in a plate-glass window set perpendicular to the direction of travel. It was a simple enough dodge, but the child seemed uninterested, dull, and recalcitrant.

Lucy was about to offer a reflex denial of this charge, as kids do, but then a little flower of maturity chanced to blossom in her soul, and she came out with what was on her mind, in Cantonese:

"That's right, Elder Brother, I am not. I am worried about Fatyma. I still cannot understand how you allowed this to occur. It is confusing. I think it was cowardly to allow her to be taken without a fight, although I know you are not a coward."

"You are mistaken, Little Sister," said Tran. "I am a great coward. This is the proof: in my country there are one million dead heroes, but I am alive after twenty-five years of war. I am very good at running away."

"And you are not ashamed of this?"

"No. Shame is for when we act inappropriately. Sometimes it is appropriate to fight like a demon, and other times it is appropriate to run like a rabbit."

Lucy thought assiduously, trying to digest this odd lump of notions, so alien to the popular culture in which she had been raised. At length she remarked, "I think I understand, Elder Brother, although I cannot see how you can tell what is appropriate and what is not, when to run and when to fight."

Tran smiled benignly. "Well, as to that, that is the study of a lifetime, which you have barely begun. For now you should accept the guidance of your elders."

Oh, right! thought Lucy, who could only absorb so much Confucian wisdom at one time. Changing the subject somewhat, she said, "Still, I would very much like to get Fatyma back from whoever has stolen her."

"Surely this is a matter for the police."

"Oh, the police! If the police find her, they will return her to her horrible father, and he will make her marry that old man or else kill her. No, she must be found by her friends."

"And how will her friends do that? She is hidden in so large a city, or maybe she is already taken to another country."

Lucy's jaw firmed up in a way that reminded Tran powerfully of the same expression on Marlene's face. She said, "I don't know how yet. But I will ask my mother."

"That is always a wise way to begin any enterprise," said Tran.

Marlene was at her kitchen table drinking coffee when they hit her with this. Hearing it, she didn't know whether to laugh or cry, for she was exhausted with overwork. In the first place, Harry was moving out of the office for his new life with the Osborne Group, leaving Marlene to cope with all their various protective operations. She had spent the morning in court, filing orders and representing several abused women at hearings, then up to St. Vincent's to see Mattie, who had prevailed upon her to watch the shelter while she was laid up. The shelter was, naturally, in an uproar. Verda and the rest of the small staff were trying hard, but Mattie had kept the operation of the place very close, especially the financial end. The records were a mess, Mattie apparently having filed much of the comings and goings of the residents in her head and in piles of loose papers stuffed in folders. Marlene had worked in the tiny office for hours, interrupted by continual crises—fights between residents, sick children, and the necessity of convincing thirty-odd women that the place was still safe, that they were better off in than out, despite the recent gunplay. Cops were, of course, in and out, interviewing the residents, collecting bits of evidence, and generally stirring things up. She had ordered her calls forwarded to the shelter's phone, which, of course, never stopped ringing.

A miserable day, and now this. "Ah, Lucy, darling," she said weakly, "I'm sorry, but I got my hands full already. There is no way we can mount a search for Fatyma."

"I thought you were a detective," said the implacable child. "I bet her father knows where she is. I bet he's just waiting to do something bad to her, and it'll be your fault."

Marlene groaned and looked around the room for support. Tran was sipping coffee with his usual neutral expression, looking remarkably like a feeble, retired clerk. A tiny Frenchified jerk of the mouth and eyebrows was all she got from him—what can one do? it said. Posie was supervising a finger-food meal with the boys—

cooked carrots and bread-and-jam slivers—giggling with them and spilling sunny personality around the room.

"Or the brother," Lucy added contemptuously, "Mr. Gorgeous."

"Walid," said Posie. "I never dated a Walid. I bet he's got a great body."

"Posie, you could think about something *else* for one minute, you know," snarled Lucy, and she got a sly giggle back.

An idea drifted lazily into Marlene's exhausted brain. She looked at Posie more closely. The girl was wearing oversized USMC fatigue pants that hung nicely on her broad hips, and over that she wore a sleeveless garment of some shiny silver-blue fabric, a retro-shop find, that stretched tightly over her cantaloupe-sized breasts, solid as round shot. She was on one of her interminable diets (grapefruit and yogurt), and this one actually seemed to be doing her some good. She'd dropped some suet (with the resilience of youth), and the arrival of spring had allowed her constant excursions with her small charges, which had toned her legs and put some color into her formerly doughy complexion. Her best feature was still her hair, which ran like a river of hot tar, straight as a die, down her back to her buttocks.

No, I can't do that, was Marlene's first thought, it's evil; and then, no, it wouldn't work; and then, no, it'd be too dangerous. But of course, once it had been reduced to a protection problem, it was a done deal as far as Marlene was concerned, since she knew a great deal about protecting people and had every confidence in pulling that part of it off.

"Um, Posie . . ." said Marlene.

Posie turned to her, her gigantic smile pumping out innocence and animal sensuality in equal measure, and Marlene, thinking, oh, my, what a piece of work I've become, said, "You know, Posie, maybe it's time you dated a guy named Walid."

FOURTEEN

In the older sections of Brooklyn, anciently prosperous and some still well-off, the houses stand separately and are brick-built, and each one comes supplied with a ready-made dungeon, for until the clean-air ordinances of the mid-sixties, these houses were all heated by coal. Twice a year the filthy, huge trucks would back into the alleys that bordered each house, and out would come the steel chute, to be inserted into the cellar hole that stared blackly from the side of the house. Then the sooty man would haul on the chain, and with a rattling roar the coal cellar would fill with a couple of tons of number nine anthracite. With the coming of oil and gas heat, each householder had found himself with a small, brick-walled, uncleanably filthy room having a small outlet to the sky and a door leading to where the coal furnace used to be. Most of these coal cellars vanished behind the pine paneling of rumpus rooms or dens, their chutes bricked up, their doors replaced by gypsum-board walls.

In the house at 308 Sterling Street in Crown Heights owned by Chouza Khalid, the coal-cellar chute had indeed been bricked up, but the space had otherwise hardly been changed since the last load of coal had gone up the chimney. The house itself was a ninety-year-old three-story yellow brick town house with sandstone facings, set back from the street, the former front garden grown up with weeds and ailanthus and maple trees ten feet high that seemed to be trying hard to obscure the weathered realtor's sign. The windows were boarded up with plywood. In its semi-derelict condition it had been a good deal for Khalid, who wanted a cheap place that no one else knew about, a bolt hole, and a hide for various liquid assets.

Naturally, the place had been used as a shooting gallery by the local addicts for some time, and Khalid's first task, even before having the electricity, gas, and water turned on, was to discourage these people. This he did with a savagery unusual even in Brooklyn, and the word soon spread on the junkie grapevine that people who went into that house emerged seriously messed up or did not emerge at all. So they avoided the place. Khalid restored one bedroom and one bathroom to use, and put a thick, solid-core door on the coal cellar, doing all the work himself.

Fatyma lay on a mattress in this former coal cellar. A razor-thin bar of light came from under the door, dim during what must be the hours of daylight, and sharp on those occasions when someone turned an electric light on in the room outside the coal cellar. Otherwise, it was dark. And damp. The mattress was supplied with a gray wool blanket, and she spent most of the endless hours huddled in this. Twice each day (she thought) the light would go on outside, she would hear the sound of the bolts sliding out, and a big man would come in with a plastic box and a plastic bottle. He was very quick. He removed the old plastic box and bottle and left, locking the door behind him. Once, Fatyma had flattened herself next to the door frame and tried to dash out, but he had caught her easily, then he had hit her so hard on the jaw that she had blacked out for a moment. Her face still hurt from the blow. She had not tried it again; nor had she bothered to scream after the first day, when she had screamed until her throat was raw. She had no idea what he had planned for her, and this was perhaps the worst part of her captivity. Besides that first horrible moment in the car, when he had felt every part of her body, he had not molested her at all. This did not, however, assuage her fears for the future.

The light came on. The big man came in and made his switch of box and bottle. She heard him sniff. It was the smell from the portable toilet in the corner, a sharp chemical smell that did not quite cover the foetor of her waste. Then he left. Fatyma did not bother checking the food box. It was always the same: two hard-boiled eggs, two large, flat Arab loaves, a handful of olives, a sliced tomato, and a little paper packet of salt. Instead, she lay down flat with her cheek against the floor and took the thin, pointed sliver of slate she had found and dug. She was digging away at the thick layer of compressed coal dust that former decades had deposited on the floor of the coal cellar. For the past day she had dug a shallow bowl-like hollow, filling it up with loose dust so she would not be found out. A few more scrapes and she was able to set the side of her head into the space so that her left eye was just level with the crack between the new door and the old uneven brick door sill. She could see a room harshly lit from overhead and the bottom of a large, dirty gray cylindrical form. The man's shoes and ankles. Then his knees. He was kneeling before the gray structure. She heard the squeal of a metallic door opening, a scraping sound. She sighed in frustration. The angle was wrong for her to see what he was doing. A dull clang: he had closed the metallic door. She saw his feet move away, and nothing but utter blackness as he switched off the light.

Khalid was thinking about the girl as he washed his hands in the bathroom sink. He was reflecting about the time just after he captured her when he had run his finger into her warm little slit and found, to his great surprise, that she was an actual virgin. Khalid had dabbled in pimping during his Beirut days, and had occasionally engaged in the specialized aspect of the trade that involves the procuring of virgins for wealthy elderly men, in the course of which he had done that sort of probing enough to know what was what. The business had been enormously lucrative, but risky and a great deal of trouble, and after a while he had drifted into the more sensible and straightforward drugs and guns trade. The problem, in Lebanon, at least, was the Arab attitude toward their women. Even extremely poor families would not sell girls, so they had to be lifted, which was risky. It was not something one wished to get a reputation for doing. The usual practice was to import them from Albania, or buy them from Italian gypsies, or (more commonly) ship them in from the Far East, where apparently they grew on trees. The problem was that an eleven-year-old Thai or Filipino girl, although certified intact, was not an object to inflame the lusts of the average wealthy Arab customer. This girl was another thing entirely—a full woman's body, a face like a ripe peach, and she spoke Arabic. Such an item could command any amount of money from one of a half dozen men that Khalid knew in the Gulf, and more than that, the girl offered *as a gift* (for Khalid had plenty of money now) to one of these men would go a long way toward securing sanctuary, a new identity in some air-conditioned villa in Kuwait or Bahrain where Ibn-Salemeh and his friends would not find him. He would have to think about how this might be accomplished.

Khalid drove the white Mercury carefully through the Brooklyn streets, just beginning to fill with the afternoon rush—east on Dean to Saratoga, left to Fulton, west to Ralph, where the gas station was. It had once been a Mobil station, and one wall still bore a faded mural of the old-style flying horse. The illuminated logo signs and the pumps were gone, but not the pump islands and the concrete roof that hung over them. Behind these stood a concrete-block three-bay garage and a small office. The place was now used as a brake and transmission shop. Four miscellaneous sedans were lined up on the apron to the left of the former pump island, in front of the wide bay doors, which were shut. A large red-painted wrecker was parked at the curb. A long, high pile of old tires stretched along the right side of the property, from near the street back to the rear lot. Khalid parked in this rear lot, a good spot, giving access to both Fulton Street and Ralph Avenue, at ten minutes before five and went into the office carrying a white Samsonite suitcase, Pullman size. He turned the light on, placed the suitcase on the counter, and sat down in a plastic chair to wait. From where he sat, he could not see Jemil or Hussein or Big Mahmoud, but he knew they were in position and armed with automatic weapons. As soon as the boy passed into the shadow of the pump island's overhead shelter, there would be a brief spurt of fire from the Dodge Dart parked on the apron and from the shadows among the piles of tires. Hussein, he knew, was crouched below window level in the seat of the wrecker. If the boy became suspicious for any reason and tried to get back to his car, Hussein would roar out in the wrecker and block his move. So they waited for the Mexican.

Who was at the moment parked several streets away, in his Ford LTD, reading a sort of comic book with great interest. The comic book, a simple four-fold, was printed on thick, oil-proof paper, and its illustrations, drawn with the uncompromising clarity of Socialist Realism, showed how to set up, aim, and fire the RPG-7 rocket launcher. El Chivato had taken one of these weapons from the warehouse, together with a rack of three missiles for it, attached to a convenient backpack. He finished the comic book and compared its illustrations to the fat green, pipe-like device on his lap. After a little study he was able to load and arm the thing. The illustrations seemed to assume that two men would operate the weapon, but it was also clear that it could be loaded and fired by one. He flicked up the sight assembly and peered through it at the peaceful Brooklyn street. He returned the arming lever to the safe position and placed the rocket launcher on the passenger seat beside him.

As El Chivato drove off, he was extremely angry, actually more than angry (since he was angry most of the time), rather in a state beyond anger, a kind of single-minded, icy murderous calm. It had been a long time since someone had tried to set him up, and then it had been an extremely clever trap, involving a woman and occurring in a place where he had every reason to feel secure. He had killed four people for that (including the woman, who was, in fact, the first person he had actually skinned entire), and so no one had ever tried it again. To be set up in this incredibly clumsy way not only required vengeance as a professional matter, but involved a personal insult as well—did they really imagine him to be *stupid*? Beyond that, he was angry because, naturally, he would have to kill Lucky and all his party, *and* search out the Obregon brothers and kill them too, which meant, unless he was extraordinarily fortunate, a long search in New York, and perhaps Mexico, which meant that he might miss Easter with his family. And he did not feel fortunate anymore. His side ached. The wound was puffy and swollen. He had not had a bath in several days, having left the apartment where he killed the policeman. Now he lived in the car. This added to his anger, for he enjoyed being neat and clean.

At five-thirty, right on schedule, El Chivato pulled into the gas station. He did not drive up to the vacant pump island as if buying ten gallons of ghost hi-test, but parked just in from the street, turning the car so that the passenger side faced the island and the station structures.

Khalid saw the car stop, saw the boy get out. He hoped that his gunmen would wait, as he had instructed, until the little shit was well within the shadow of the pump-island shelter before opening fire. Then he saw the flash and instantly thereafter heard a peculiar flat, whooshing noise.

To anyone who spent the seventies in Beirut, as Khalid had, that particular flash and noise were nearly as familiar as the sound of traffic. Every one of the innumerable contending parties of that sad town had accumulated Soviet rocket launchers in numbers and used them with enthusiasm. They were not as common as Kalashnikovs, but common enough. Khalid had never had one fired directly at him before: it was like a tiny approaching sun with a black dot in its center. Almost without thought he dived over the counter and lay flat on the floor, with the Samsonite suitcase pulled close over his head and his knees drawn up in fetal position.

The rocket smashed through the plate-glass window and the double wallboard wall behind the counter. Anti-tank rockets need to hit something massive before they will explode, and this particular rocket found it in the rear concrete wall of the garage. Khalid heard a dull boom as the warhead blasted a foot-wide hole through the wall and sprayed the area behind it with molten steel and concrete.

A long ten seconds of silence. Khalid heard the sound of a submachine gun opening up—Jemil in the car out on the apron, from the sound, and then another from the Dumpster—Big Mahmoud, leaning on the trigger as usual. He would spray only the clouds and the trees shooting at that rate and probably a few bystanders as well. Khalid did not intend to stay around to find out which. He crawled through broken glass to the door that led from the office to the repair bays, and scuttled, bent nearly double, to the rear door of the garage.

The Mercury was there, smoking gently, no longer white. It had not received the full blast of the rocket's charge, but a by-blow had been sufficient to render it permanently undriveable. Khalid said *"Elaghkna!"* (shit) and ran for the left side of the building. Poking his head around the corner at knee level, he observed that Jemil was still directing controlled fire at the Mexican's car, which he now recognized as the Ford LTD Bashar had used. It was doubtful that he was doing any damage to the man, however, not with 9mm Parabellum. Khalid could not help but admire the positioning of the Mexican's car, blocking lines of fire from the parked cars and all obvious cover on either side of the building. He really should have put someone on the roof with a Kalashnikov, he thought, but who could have imagined . . . ? What should be happening now was for Jemil to lay down a base of fire from the Dart and for Mahmoud, who was pouring slugs senselessly into the wreckage of the LTD, to work his way among the old tires to take the Mexican on his right flank, but Mahmoud would not have the sense to do this. When Mahmoud's firing paused, Khalid yelled out in Arabic the order to do just that. Back came the shout, "I have no more ammunition." Perfect. Then there was another flash-whoosh. Khalid ducked back behind the building and covered his head with his arms.

This rocket penetrated the engine block of the Dart and did what it was designed to do, which was to turn a small mass of solid steel into white-hot liquid. The car turned instantly into a fireball. The cars on either side burst into flame. Thick, choking black smoke poured into the air. From where he stood, Khalid could no longer see the Mexican's car. He assumed that the Mexican could not see him either, and made his move. Pistol in hand, he raced around the rear ends of the flaming cars and, with a step on the running board, dived into the open window of the wrecker. There he found Hussein, crouched in the well of the driver's side, holding his submachine gun like a teddy bear. There was white showing all around the pupils of his eyes as he stammered, "Effendi, I did not know what to do."

"Then I will tell you what to do, Hussein," said Khalid slowly, gasping for breath. "Start this vehicle and drive away."

Enveloped in thick smoke, El Chivato did not see Khalid make his escape, but he heard the engine of the wrecker roar into life and saw the red blur as it pulled away from the curb. He heard sirens from many different directions. Even in Brooklyn, it is not possible to have a battle involving serious military hardware without attracting the attention to the authorities. El Chivato loaded his last rocket and carefully placed it with the rest of his equipment in a green duffel bag. He slung its strap across his chest, bandoleer style, and walked out of the smoke.

Cars were slowing down on Fulton Street to view the fire. No one took any notice of the slim youth as he walked quickly up the center line of the roadway. He could see the high red crane of the wrecker several streets ahead. At the first red light he walked up to the driver's side of the first car in line and stuck dead Bashar's 9mm Smith in the driver's face.

The car was a black Chrysler New Yorker. As soon as El Chivato was in the driver's seat, he gunned the engine and took off after the wrecker, cutting through the intersection of Fulton Street and Ralph Avenue against the light and causing a chorus of horns and two minor traffic accidents.

This maneuver caught the attention of the RMP called Seven Frank, manned by patrolmen Ed Graves and Manolo Echeverria. Seven Frank was a Seventy-ninth Precinct RMP, and it was responding to the "shots fired" call as a matter of routine. Seeing the smoke and hearing the fire engine sirens and seeing a large black car zoom through the intersection created a picture in the minds of the two patrolmen, a non-routine picture. Without a word Graves, who was driving, hooked a U-turn on Fulton and took off in pursuit. Echeverria called in the action and gave a description of the vehicle and its heading.

El Chivato swerved around a line of cars, driving down the center line of Fulton Street until he was directly behind the wrecker. He saw the flasher and heard the siren of the police car behind him, but paid no attention to it. He steered with his left hand, and with his right worked the wire-stocked AK-47 out of the duffel bag and placed it across his lap. After a moment he reached in again and brought out two Soviet RGN hand grenades and placed them in the cushioned rectangular hollow between the front seats that most drivers use to hold coffee cups and toll change.

Ahead, Hussein checked his rearview and spotted the Mexican tailgating them behind the wheel of the black sedan. Hussein was a much better driver than he was a street fighter, and he had a heavy, powerful vehicle to demonstrate it. He swerved from side to side, keeping the Mexican from coming up on his flank, and incidentally driving a half dozen cars into crashes of varying severity.

In Seven Frank, Patrolman Echeverria was working his radio, talking to his dispatcher, impressing upon her that this was something out of the ordinary. The dispatcher was responding, calling other RMPs in the area to set up a block somewhere up ahead.

"Holy shit!" said Patrolman Echeverria. This was not a phrase recognized in NYPD radio parlance. The dispatcher came back with, "Say again, Seven Frank."

Echeverria said, "We're taking automatic fire! A white male on the tow truck ahead of the black Chrysler, he just leaned out the window and fired an automatic weapon at us."

The dispatcher acknowledged this and fielded calls from RMPs Three Eddie and Eight George, who said they were converging on the junction of Fulton Street and Bedford Avenue. They intended to close Fulton eastbound to avoid more civilian casualties, and wait for the fleeing vehicles to arrive. The dispatcher also fielded a call from Boy Sector ESU, which declared itself rolling toward the scene. The emergency service unit consisted of twelve heavily armed, specially trained police officers wearing attractive black costumes, Kevlar vests, helmets, and face shields. The dispatcher, hearing this, declared a "no further" on the call, on the reasonable assumption that this unit and the three RMPs represented enough police power to handle a couple of cars full of bad guys.

On the wide running board of the wrecker, Chouza Khalid fired another four rounds from Hussein's Model 25, and cursed as they went high, shattering the light bar of the police car following. It was an impossible shooting task: he had to hold on to the door frame with his left hand and try to fire one-handed with his right, while the wrecker swerved this way and that and bounced wildly on the decrepit surface of the thoroughfare. He gave up and swung himself back into the seat, just in time to hear Hussein shriek, "What should I do? What should I do?"

Two police cars with their lights flashing were parked athwart the street, partially blocking all four lanes of the thoroughfare. White-helmeted police crouched behind the cars, and beyond these Khalid saw the flashing lights of a large blue and white van, which must mean reinforcements.

"Right turn!" screamed Khalid. "Don't stop, smash through!"

This is what Hussein did: he floored the gas pedal, swung right, struck Three Eddie, the right-lane RMP, behind its rear wheel and knocked it skidding out of the way like a child's toy. The two officers sheltering behind it, Joshua Rollins and Paula Nolan, were both dashed flat. The officers from Eight North fired after the wrecker but did not damage the massive vehicle.

El Chivato stepped on it too, roaring through the hole the wrecker had made in the roadblock like a running back following a guard. A bullet smashed through the left rear window of the Chrysler, spattering the back of his neck with sharp flakes of glass. He cursed, grabbed one of the grenades, pulled the pin, and tossed it backward out the window.

The grenade bounced twice and rolled, spending its forward velocity. After four seconds it exploded, three feet from the driver's-side door of Seven Frank as it raced through the roadblock in hot pursuit.

Echeverria saw the flash and felt the heat of it, and heard the enormously loud sound. Something hard and hot slapped him on the side of the head. He looked over at Graves, who had no face and was on fire. Echeverria noted that he himself was on fire too, and that there was something that looked like a human lower jaw on his lap. Then Seven Frank crashed into the side of a parked truck.

Patrolman Lou Kravitzki of RMP Eight North sprang into his vehicle and grabbed the radio handset. He was the only cop available to do this at the roadblock, because his partner, Tom Parmignano, was giving CPR to Joshua Rollins, who looked to be going into shock with a cracked skull. Into the handset he shouted, "Eight North to Central. Ten-thirteen! Ten-thirteen! Officers down! Three . . . no, four officers down!"

As these magic words hit the air, the police world of north Brooklyn was transformed. The dispatcher pressed a button that generated a rapid, high beeping on all channels, and she repeated the message that police officers were injured at the junction of Fulton and Bedford. Kravitzki told his story over the air. Grenades. Machine guns. The cops in every RMP within five miles dropped what they were doing and sped forthwith to join the pursuit.

Bedford Avenue turns one-way north of Fulton Street, four lanes of normally fairly sedate traffic feeding commuters toward the Brooklyn-Queens Expressway and trucks toward the Brooklyn industrial zones. Into this flow, at just past six on a Tuesday afternoon, a nodule of chaos inserted itself.

Hussein, having crashed through a police barrier, having heard the bullets strike his machine, now had his blood well and truly up, and he hit on the plan of slowing down the pursuit by strewing wreckage across the avenue. Therefore he proceeded to slam his heavy wrecker into the cars he overtook, in the manner of small boys playing bumper cars at Coney Island.

Unfortunately, the traffic was moving too slowly to allow the creation of any really horrendous pile-ups, although nearly twenty people were injured and one was killed. Behind them, their pursuers, the Mexican and the cops, were indeed slowed by the wreckage, but not entirely stopped.

Khalid was an experienced criminal and a wily man, and so he realized that one could not long escape pursuit in the streets of a major city in a large red-painted tow truck. It was clearly necessary to ditch the thing, and in such a way that they could escape unobserved. Accordingly he gave orders to Hussein.

As the wrecker crossed Flushing Avenue, it bulled its way into the center lane. In the rearview mirror Hussein observed that the black car had done the same, and also that there were now three police cars visible, lights flashing, sirens screaming, besides the large van, in pursuit.

A few seconds later Khalid shouted, "Now!" and Hussein whipped the wrecker into a screeching right turn across two lanes of traffic and onto narrow Hayward Street. They were going forty as they made the turn into the heart of orthodox Williamsburg.

Khalid's plan was to quickly make another right, and then, out of view of all pursuers, ditch the wrecker and lose themselves on the streets, get to a subway, steal another car. . . .

Two RMPs, far enough back in the parade to do so, peeled off to follow the tow truck, but El Chivato missed the turn. Screaming curses, he pulled right and made the next turn, onto Rutledge. The ESU van and four RMPs followed him. Williamsburg is not a good neighborhood for exciting car chases, however. The Hasidim who live there are very densely packed, and reasonably well-off, and there are lots of vehicles, both private and the property of religious organizations. They line the streets; they double-park with other-worldly disdain for the NYC traffic code; they move slowly in the narrow roads, which are typically jammed with pedestrians, many of whom cannot be counted upon to focus on the here and now.

The ESU van tore around the corner of Rutledge. In its front seat the response team leader, Lieutenant Paul McElroy, saw what was happening ahead and said to his driver, "Slow it down, we got him," and shouted to the troops behind him, "Lock and load! We're rolling out."

The junction ahead, at Lee Avenue, was solidly plugged with ve-hicles. El Chivato did not, however, slow down. There was a short gap in the line of parked cars left open for a fire hydrant. He jerked his wheel, bumped over the curb, clipped the hydrant from its base, and shot along the sidewalk, scattering pedestrians like duck pins. A jet of water twenty feet high sprang into the air and quickly turned the street into a shallow canal.

People were screaming. A dark van in front of the ESU immedi-ately stopped, blocking the street, and spilled a dozen Hasidim, who started giving succor to the injured people in the Chrysler's wake.

"Get up on the sidewalk!" McElroy ordered the driver. "Follow the bastard!"

The driver inched by the Hasidic vehicle, mounted the curb, and was instantly blinded by the torrent of water falling on his wind-shield. He turned the wipers on, and when the window cleared, McElroy saw that the black sedan had stopped thirty yards ahead.

A meat truck had been making a delivery to a butcher shop and had run two wheels up on the sidewalk so that the driver could set up a roller chute leading into the basement of the shop. The basement entry was the common New York type (quite unknown in Nogales) in which two steel doors set flush with the sidewalk could be raised to give access to underground. The sedan had crashed into this arrangement and buried its right front wheel in the cellar opening.

McElroy ordered his van to stop, yelled for his men to deploy, and leaped from the van himself, taking cover behind its open door. He saw the front door of the black sedan open. McElroy had run a squad in a Marine rifle company in 1967 in Quang Tri province, so he knew just what he was seeing. He wasn't sure he believed it, quite, but he knew what it was. He screamed a warning—"Spread out, take cover, incoming, *incoming!*"—and raised his M-16, to try to shoot the son of a bitch before he got a round off.

It was too late. He saw the flash and heard that unforgettable sound. He scrambled for a doorway and crouched there. The rocket struck the front of the ESU van, which had quarter-inch steel plating over the radiator to protect it from the odd bullet. This armor was enough to trigger the warhead, sending a gout of superheated gas and incandescent metal through the length of the van. Its body burst like a toy balloon, and then the gas tank (full with thirty-two gallons of regular lead-free) exploded, and then, at intervals, off went the remarkable range of explosive devices normally carried in ESU vehicles—tear-gas rounds, shotgun rounds, rifle and pistol bullets, concussion grenades.

McElroy got to his feet and put his gas mask on. He could not see more than a yard in front of his face, so thick was the combined fog of smoke and gas. He stumbled along in the general direction of Bedford Avenue, hoping to find an intact RMP so he could get back in communication. He had no idea if any of his men had survived.

He heard coughing all around him, and the sound of hopeless retching, and the crackle of things burning, the continuous wailing of sirens, the weirdly discordant splash and rush of water from the broken hydrant, the pop-bang-pop of miscellaneous ordnance exploding. Someone in dark clothes blundered by him coughing, but he could not see whether it was a Hasid or an ESU cop. Then a new sound, the *wacketa-wacketa* of helicopters, more than one, he was sure. It was exactly like Vietnam, was his thought—we get creamed on the ground, the bad guys book out, and the choppers come in to dust off the survivors. McElroy found his RMP and began the slow process of rallying his troops and coping with the awful mess on the street.

But within twenty minutes the sun went down and an evening breeze sprang up from the East River nearby, which blew the gas away, at the same time fanning the dozen or so fires that had broken out in buildings on either side of the van explosion, when white-hot chunks of debris flew into shops and apartments. It took another half hour to clear the fourteen RMPs back out of Rutledge Street so the fire trucks and the ambulances could enter. The clearer air brought shocking sights. McElroy had, of course, seen a good deal of bad stuff in his work, and during the war; this rivaled the worst of that. All down the street Hasidim were stumbling through the ruins, screaming for their relatives in Yiddish and English. Hasidic ambulance-society men were cruising with stretchers, occasionally arguing with the regular paramedics over possession of the wounded. There were enough for both; they lay thick on the street, black and limp like shot crows. He recalled the old grainy black-and-white films and photos he had seen, and decided that, the helicopters apart, it looked less like 'Nam than like the Warsaw Ghetto.

El Chivato had not stopped to enjoy the havoc he had caused, but immediately after the rocket had left its tube, he had shoved his assault rifle into a deep pocket of his canvas coat, filled the other pockets with grenades, and walked down Rutledge to Lee Avenue. He still hoped to find the man he was chasing. He had to push through crowds of the curious, running in the opposite direction, trying to see what was happening around the corner, and as he did so, he could not help noticing that nearly all the men he was passing were dressed almost exactly alike, in long, shiny black wraparound coats and black hats trimmed with red fur. He found this somewhat strange, but not that much stranger than many other aspects of this accursed city. Several police cars raced up Lee, sirens wailing. One stopped across the street and two officers emerged. El Chivato kept walking, searching the storefronts for a place to hide. Many of the signs were in a language he could not read. This made him nervous.

One shop caught his eye. In the window, garments like the ones he saw on the street were displayed, coats and hats and other cloth objects, whose purpose he could not guess. He went in. There was a bearded man in black behind the counter who stared at him in open-mouthed surprise. El Chivato looked around the little shop. There were no display dummies—caftans of different sizes were hung on the walls and from hooks depending from the ceiling. Hasidic hats in various styles were stacked on shelves along one wall.

Without a word the youth pulled a largish caftan from its hanger and tried it on over his canvas coat. It reached to the tops of his boots and made him look heavier than he was. He went to the hats and tried on several, choosing a fur-trimmed one with a wide brim that shaded his face. The shopkeeper still had not made a sound.

El Chivato went to a mirror and looked at his reflection, turning this way and that. He had not shaved in over a week, so that was to the good, although he could do nothing about the tone of his skin. Something was missing, though. He went to the counter and confronted the shopkeeper.

"How much?"

The man cleared his throat and cocked his head to one side appraisingly. His glasses glinted. "You want this? It's a little tight across the shoulders."

"I don't mind," said El Chivato. "How much . . . no, wait, I want this too."

"What, reading glasses?"

"Yes." El Chivato selected a green-tinted pair from a dusty rotating rack on the glass counter and slipped them on. If he pulled them down on his nose a bit, he could avoid seeing blur through the lenses.

The shopkeeper totted up a bill. "Four sixty-eight seventy-two, with tax."

El Chivato paid with twenties from the roll in his pocket, waited for his change, and walked out.

He walked north on Lee past knots of excited people, past squads of police searching every building. There were now a score of police vehicles of all sizes, RMPs, vans, buses, parked on Lee and the streets surrounding. No one stopped him. He walked up to Broadway and west, over the Williamsburg Bridge into Manhattan. Looking back from the center of the bridge, he saw a thick mantle of smoke hanging over the district he had just left.

On Columbia Street just off the Manhattan end of the bridge he found a white van driven by a black pimp who was running a mobile two-whore brothel for the early trade. El Chivato approached him, got a nice gold-cap smile, which turned to an expression of fear and dismay as the putative Hasid shoved a big pistol in his face.

"Anything on the tube tonight?" Karp asked just before eight.

"The usual crap, I guess," answered his wife from her position on the living room couch, which was supine, with a glass of red wine handy. "I'm too tired to watch, and I still have some calls to make. Sit down here and stroke my brow."

Karp did so. Karp was a plain vanilla erotic arts sort of guy, but over the years she had taught him a thing or two, brow stroking being one of them.

"Poor baby," he said sincerely (since she really did look frazzled), "they're pounding you into the ground. Can't Harry take some of the freight?"

"Oh, Harry! Yes, in fact Harry can take some of the freight, as long as I do what he and Osborne want me to do. He volunteered, so to speak, to pick up some of my stalking and abuse load if I do a chore for Osborne. Some meeting-security horseshit."

"So? What's the problem?"

"A little back, over the ear, please. No problem, except I hate meeting security, and also it's a dick-head two-day job that a couple of square badges could do in their sleep, and they only want me because I'm the girl on the team and it's a girl's club that's having the meeting. Nice Jewish girls, as a matter of fact."

"What, like Hadassah?"

"Not *like* Hadassah, Hadassah," said Marlene. "I have an appointment with an Amy Weinstein tomorrow. Is that a sketch or what?"

"It'll broaden your cultural horizons," said Karp. "What's the matter, they couldn't get a Jewish girl? Jewish girls don't pack heat?"

Marlene struck a pose, wrists bent, fingers splayed, and said in thick Lawn Guyland syllables, "What, you want me to break a nail?"

Karp laughed and continued with his stroking. "Oh, good, it's remarks like that'll win their hearts over by Hadassah. This has made my week, Marlene. I only wish my mother was here to see it. Remember, when you go up there, you should bring a little something, a cake from Babka, maybe a nice challah . . ."

Marlene suddenly shook herself and sat up. "No, no, Marlene," she said, "we can't sink into mere animal luxury until we've made all our calls. Are we a Sacred Heart girl? Are we imbued with the twin imperatives of the Mesdames, guilt and high achievement? Oh, yes, we are!" She rose groaning to her feet and walked out of the living room toward her office.

Alert as only a mother can be, she picked up all the evening noises chez Karp: Posie playing R.E.M. at top volume through her earphones, singing tunelessly along; tiny soft snores from the boys' room; a strange droning mumble from Lucy's.

Marlene was a firm believer in the principle that children deserved privacy and a life of their own, although in practice she spied like the KGB every chance she got. She pressed her face up against the door frame and peered through the gap. Her daughter was sitting tailor fashion on the bed, rocking back and forth.

"Tomorrow," she chanted, "*bukra,* tomorrow morning *bukra e-sub 'h* tomorrow afternoon *bukra e-dohr* tomorrow evening *bukra bil layl* the day after tomorrow *ba'ghkd bukra* see you tomorrow *ashoofak bukra* tongue *lissan . . ."*

Marlene stopped looking and continued down the hallway, feeling odd. Her daughter was memorizing an Arabic dictionary. It was something she did, memorize dictionaries, for amusement. One time through and she had the whole thing. She'd done it with a French one and a Spanish one and a Mandarin one. Marlene knew this, but every time she observed the actual process, she got a little chill, as if watching something beyond the ordinary realm of human achievement, something one could not do oneself in a million years, like watching Nolan Ryan pitch. If the genetic sweepstakes had thrown up such a weird ringer (for she herself, although reasonably competent with languages, was nothing out of the ordinary, while Karp, though a natural mimic, was entirely monoglot), what else was in store, what other mysteries would play out, for Lucy and the boys? And she felt the half-shameful irritation that even a good parent feels when the kid has gone beyond her in some way.

At her desk, she shook off these thoughts and turned to business. She was looking over her list of calls, trying to decide which ones would take the least time, when the house phone rang. She picked it up, and it was Clay Fulton.

"Hey, Marlene. Butch there?"

"Yeah, I'll yell. How's it going?"

240 / Robert K. Tanenbaum

A rueful chuckle. "Oh, I've been better, lady. I've had better days."

"Why, what's the matter?"

"*What's the matter?* Don't you people have a damn TV?"

"Yeah, but it's not on. What's happening?"

"Oh, not much," said Fulton, and now Marlene picked up the absolute exhaustion in his voice, "just that a couple hours ago Arab terrorists burnt down half of Williamsburg, and killed about twenty-five people, seven of them cops."

Ibn-Salemeh was watching the news, for the news had preempted nearly every channel, and he was fascinated.

"I should be angry with you," he said. "This could have jeopardized everything, and yet . . . it was so brilliantly done, I cannot find it in my heart to criticize you. You say it was entirely spontaneous?"

"Yes, effendi," answered Chouza Khalid. "When I thought of what the Zionists, may they roast in hell, had done to Bashar and Ahmed I could not control myself. I had to strike back at the Jews. I am sorry if I did wrong."

"Well, killing a few Jews is never wrong, but please, no more until after the operation. It is truly amazing that you were able to escape after doing this."

"Yes, effendi, but . . . who can explain the will of God? Jemil was martyred, and I escaped, and Hussein and Mahmoud."

"Yes, the will of God is truly inexplicable," said Ibn-Salemeh, and he went back to watching the scenes of carnage.

Khalid sat back in his chair and discreetly dabbed at the beads of sweat on his upper lip. Perhaps God *had* been involved. It was certain that he was enjoying a remarkable run of good luck, both in the world and in relation to satisfying Ibn-Salemeh. He would, of course, have to go completely underground after this, to disappear from his usual haunts. The police were stupid, but after this business, they would grab up every Arab who hadn't been in the country for fifty years, and some of them too.

It was certainly what the man next to him wanted. Perhaps, Khalid having performed (as he imagined) this unexpected outrage, Ibn-Salemeh would be accommodating about the girl. If not, he would have to fall back on initiative. With luck it would all work out. And his luck had always been good, always left him one up. Like there being a hand truck and an oil drum in the bed of the wrecker. They'd loaded the oil drum on the hand truck, Khalid had picked up a clipboard with some old invoices on it, and they'd walked away from the thing, a couple of working stiffs making a delivery down an alley. In that way they'd gone through to Lynch Street and by that back to Bedford Avenue. Nobody expects fleeing felons to be hauling a fifty-five-gallon oil drum. This was abandoned when they entered the subway at Flushing Avenue. An hour of riding back and forth, and they'd made their way to Grand Army Plaza and walked back to the house on Tenth Street.

Khalid turned his attention back to the television screen. He was not, naturally, as happy with the chaos as his employer was, first since he knew the absurd origins of the thing, and second because he thought that the present carnage and the attention it would draw from the authorities would make it nearly impossible to carry out the original mission. Which the madman next to him would in no way consider postponing. He turned his inner thoughts away from the television, away from Brooklyn, to the villa on the Gulf which he would one day occupy, to the girl Fatyma, her round brown body, and to his luck, which had not so far deserted him and which, God willing, only needed to hold out for a few more days, less than a week.

FIFTEEN

Despite a good deal of history tending to the contrary, the United States of America remains a union of sovereign states, to the extent that an official of the executive branch of the federal government cannot give orders that an official of one of the several states is obliged to obey; nor can he fire said state official or have him shipped off to an unpleasant place. Foreigners (and not a few federal officials) often do not understand this, but Karp understood it very well, and appreciated, not for the first time, how well little Jemmy Madison had wrought. Therefore, he was not overly impressed with the aggressive mien of Carl J. Anderson, the special agent in charge of the New York office of the Federal Bureau of Investigation.

"And you didn't think to report this . . . this 'interview' with a terrorist leader?" asked Anderson, his voice heavy with contempt.

"I did report it," answered Karp mildly. "I reported it to the district attorney."

"Oh? And what action did *he* take?"

"None to my knowledge," Karp said, and added, "None was required, Mr. Anderson. Membership, claimed or real, in the Palestine Liberation Organization is not a crime in the state of New York. We had no evidence that this person or anyone associated with him had committed any crime within our jurisdiction."

"How did you know that? Because the guy said so?"

"Yes, as a matter of fact. I believed what he said."

Anderson literally threw up his hands, riffling the papers before

him. He looked around the table at the others, soliciting acknowledgment of the insane stupidity this last statement of Karp's represented, and he got some nods, from the other FBI people there, of
course, but also from Ed Kirby, the Brooklyn district attorney and
from Chief Inspector Kevin X. Battle.

"On what basis, pray tell?" Anderson asked, gently mocking as
to an idiot child.

Karp replied, in the same neutral tone, "On the basis of fourteen years' experience distinguishing truth from bullshit. It's what I
do, Mr. Anderson."

Anderson had the sort of eyes usually referred to as steely blue,
and these he locked on Karp's eyes, which were non-metallic gray-
yellow, but could be just as hard, and held the stare for what seemed
like endless seconds, until it passed the borders of silly, and the person who might have been considered the senior person in the room,
Thomas Colombo, the United States attorney for the Southern
District of New York, cleared his throat and said, "Let's move on,
people."

Karp was ignored for the moment as everyone looked at Colombo, a bony, hawk-faced gentleman of precise habits and dic-
tion, a brilliant prosecuting attorney, and ambitious as Satan. He
looked without sympathy upon SAIC Anderson and said firmly,
"This transient PLO man seems to be neither here nor there. The
name I keep hearing is Abdel Hussein Khalid, a.k.a. Chouza Khalid.
He actually seems to be a legal resident alien, and in the city at this
time. Has anyone talked to him?"

No one had, but both the NYPD and the FBI had well-rehearsed
excuses why not. They had, of course, searched for him since yesterday's horrific events, but had come up empty. The man had
vanished. Karp ignored this blather, sat back, and looked around
the room. This was located in the FBI command center at 26 Federal Plaza, and it was even more generously appointed than the
analogous room at One Police Plaza in which Chief Battle had
lately palmed the Arab terrorist menace off on a detective lieutenant and a corporal's guard of cops—shit-canned it, in fact, and
didn't he regret it now? Karp thought Chief Battle looked bad; his
pink had gone gray, and he seemed to have shrunk a little, especially compared to the police commissioner himself, who was sitting next to him, deep in a dull rage. P.C. Bill Mallory was a very
big and very smart Irishman who had devoted his stint as P.C.

mainly toward technical modernization and management improve-
ments, both of which the NYPD badly needed, of course, but
which did not seem relevant to the present crisis. The NYPD had
never lost seven officers in a single day, not even during the New
York draft riots of 1863, when most of Manhattan was ablaze for a
week, not during the race riots of the sixties—never. Seven LOD
deaths was a bad *year* for the NYPD. It was the worst thing that
had ever happened to the Department, and someone was going to
get the worst punishment the Department had ever meted out.

Karp thought he knew who that someone was. Down at the end
of the table, several seats away from the others, at the back of the
bus, was Detective Lieutenant Clay Fulton. Karp could not imagine why Fulton had been ordered to attend, except as Battle's public sacrificial lamb. Fulton had his head down over one of the legal
pads the federal government had supplied at each place (together
with two sharpened yellow pencils), and he also had his own steno
pad open on the table. He had been scratching away since the beginning of the meeting. Karp suspected that he was calculating his
pension should he be forced to take early retirement commencing
tomorrow.

Karp felt bad about this, and resented Kevin Battle on behalf of
his friend, but he also could not help feeling at least some fellow
bureaucratic sympathy for the poor schmuck, whose famous ass
covering must feel like tin foil now, like Saran Wrap. He moved his
gaze past Battle to Ed Kirby. The Brooklyn D.A. was a short,
stocky man with a flat, unattractive, pugnacious Irish face and the
slightly bulbous, dark, wide-set eyes of a Boston bull terrier. Like
that breed, he had a tendency to snap, and a barky high-pitched
voice. He met Karp's glance, scowled, and looked away. In the
shuffle before the start of the meeting he had expressed surprise
and disappointment that a mere representative rather than his fellow D.A., John Keegan, had shown. Karp had not repeated the remark of that official when he had directed Karp to attend in his
stead (*It's fucking Brooklyn: you go!*) but had made a transparent excuse and then listened while Kirby whined about the Hasidim. No
Bushwick Irishman could hope to be elected and reelected Brooklyn D.A. without the support of the Jews, but these particular Jews
were not being helpful. Within an hour of the catastrophe the
agents of Hasidic burial societies had seized the corpses, loaded
them onto stretchers, and carried them off, despite the efforts of

the police to protect the crime scenes. They were gone, to be interred (as required by Talmudic law) within twenty-four hours and no autopsies either, so Kirby had, in principle, over twenty homicides for which he did not have a legal *corpus delicti*. He could (also in principle) get a judge to write exhumation orders for each of these. The chance that a Brooklyn judge, an *elected* judge, would sign such orders and dig up twenty-odd dead Hasidim—it was to laugh! No, the perps in this one—when found—would be nailed for first-degree murder, for the seven cop killings. The Jews would have to be satisfied to come along for the ride. It would be far and away the biggest trial of Kirby's career, and the reason he was here was that he did not want anything, however tiny, to screw up the investigation.

The investigation! A stir moved around the table, like an unexpected breeze on a sultry day. The attendees were being informed that, remarkably, an investigation of Arab terrorism was *already* under way, under NYPD auspices. Mallory said this because Battle had informed him that such an investigation did exist, although he had been vague about its structure and progress, and Mallory had carried that message to the press on the evening of what everyone was already calling Black Tuesday. "A major investigation under way, sir," Battle had said, hoping that the big boys would take this statement on faith so that the word would not leak out that the NYPD had been caught, so to speak, flat-footed, and then the worker bees could come up with something that he could feed to Mallory, who could feed it to the TV jackals at the press conference he had scheduled for noon.

But Anderson said, "I didn't know you had anything going on terrorism, Commissioner. Do you mean Dick Bailey's operation?"

The other FBI suits around the table barely concealed their smiles. They knew Bailey. That dim bulb had not even been invited. Mallory turned an inquiring eye to Battle.

"Kevin?"

Battle was already shaking his head in denial. "No sir, no, not at all, this is a special investigation, a major investigation. Um."

A delicate silence followed, at which point Clay Fulton stood up, cleared his throat, a sound like the rattle of musketry, and said, "Chief? If I may. I could summarize the facts and figures in a few minutes."

If Battle was surprised, he did not show it. With a magisterial wave he bade Fulton proceed.

"Thank you, sir," said Fulton. "Briefly, on Friday last, a women's shelter in Manhattan was subjected to a well-planned, well-executed raid by Arabs carrying automatic weapons, during which an Arab girl was kidnapped. This girl came from a family involved in pro-Palestinian political violence. When put together with information arising out of the Shilkes killing and other crimes, together with the interview Mr. Karp has already mentioned, it strongly suggested that an Arab terrorist group was operating in New York. We brought this evidence to Chief Battle, and he, of course, took it very seriously indeed, tasking me to plan a major investigation, involving over seventy-five detectives, over fifty support personnel, two hundred and fifty uniformed officers, unlimited overtime, rental space for the unit, et cetera, reporting to Inspector Patrick Timmons, in the Office of the Chief of Detectives, and with myself as executive officer. Naturally, the unit is still organizing itself, but we've already made significant progress."

He took a breath. Battle was staring at him, as a drowning man might stare at a cork ring. Fulton resumed. "First, we have a photograph of Abdel Hussein Khalid, sent from Interpol. The French have been after him for years for arms and drug smuggling. Using this photo we've positively identified Khalid as one of two men driving the wrecker involved in the chase in which officers Graves and Echeverria were killed. Civilians observed them escaping the area pushing an oil drum on a hand truck. By now every RMP, detective, and foot patrol in the city has that photograph. Second, we have confirmation from the owner of a brake shop on Atlantic Avenue that Khalid was the man who arranged to rent his garage for yesterday evening, with the story that he was setting up a dog fight. The garage was clearly the origin of yesterday's events. There was a gun battle between two factions, and two rockets were used. One man was killed. The shell casings found at this scene had communist-bloc military stock markings identical to the ones fired at Officers Graves and Echeverria, and also identical to ones fired during the kidnapping at the shelter. Third, we've located the firm Khalid bought into when he entered the country. It's a legitimate import-export firm, but the owner, a Mr. Hashim Moulari, explained that Khalid does a lot of independent importing on his own. We're checking their records now, and of course we'll apply for the usual taps and mail covers, at the firm and at the mail drops Khalid uses. Some interesting things about Khalid. According to available records, he doesn't have a phone, doesn't own a car, has no bank accounts, doesn't have a driver's license or a Social Security number, and the only address Moulari had for him was one of the mail drops. A very, very careful man."

Fulton spoke briskly for another ten minutes, mainly on organizational details, and then threw it open for questions.

The first one was from Anderson. "Lieutenant, didn't you think to inform the Bureau about this operation?"

Fulton smiled. "But we did, sir. It's department policy that all liaison with the FBI go through BSSI. Dick Bailey went through his contact and was informed that there was no Arab terrorist organization in New York. So . . ."

So, indeed. Into the silence that followed this the police commissioner put in a dab of political balm, assuring Anderson that the NYPD would continue to work closely with the FBI and that, of course, nothing could replace the expertise and experience of the Bureau in tracking down evildoers of foreign origin. Color had come back into Chief Battle's face. Owing a big one to this fancy shine was well worth it, given the disaster thus averted.

The meeting broke up soon thereafter, with many more expressions of goodwill and promises of full cooperation. In the elevator lobby, after the P.C. had sped off to meet with his press people, Battle gripped Fulton's arm and held him in what appeared to be a most earnest conversation. Their heads were almost touching. The car came, they descended in silence, and then Battle was scooped up by his driver and bodyguard and vanished, leaving Fulton and Karp alone on Federal Plaza, under a long, ugly steel wall sculpture. They watched it rust for a moment, and then Karp looked at his friend and touched his own nose, after which he brought his pinched fingers slowly about a foot distant. Fulton laughed.

Karp said, "You keep that up, boss, you're not ever going to be a real boy."

"I resent the implication I lied to that august group of public officials."

"Seventy-five detectives . . . ?"

"Chief Battle has on his desk the administrative order authorizing a task group of the size I described, dated yesterday. I expect he'll be happy to sign it when he returns to his office. You saw him talking to me. He didn't say one word about this not all being his idea, and he never will. History has been changed, my friend, just like Russia."

"What about Timmons? He wasn't even at the meeting yesterday."

"Oh, Timmons! Timmons is cool too. Pat Timmons and me, we go *way* back. He was in the bag at the Three-Oh, the year I got my gold tin, another, as we say, paddy motherfucker, dropped in amongst the Negroes to dispense law and order. Pat was a little sharper than most, no, be fair, a lot sharper. He made detective in record time. Not that I helped much, him having the kind of rabbis he had downtown, but I did him some favors. When this shit broke, I called him and told him what the situation was and what I thought needed doing, and he said go ahead and work it out and him and the Chief of D would back me all the way. So I did."

Karp looked at him in amazement. "Jesus, Clay! It hasn't been twelve hours since Brooklyn blew up. How the hell did you get all that done?"

Fulton chuckled and rubbed his face as if he had a thick towel in his hands. Karp looked at him closely and saw how tired the man was. Clearly he had been up all night.

"Yeah, well, as to that," Fulton said, "I started on it as soon as you got me into this. I figured if there was a terrorist group, and they did something major, we'd need a task force like this. If there wasn't, well . . . compared to working homicide, working for you all, I got plenty of time."

"And that other stuff, about Khalid and Interpol—that's legit too?"

Fulton waggled his hand from side to side. "There I indulged in a somewhat jive version of the truth. We do have a snap of the scumbag, but it's not a mug shot. It's a surveillance photograph, grainy as hell. Not that great for ID, but at least we know he's not a bald midget. The brake-shop guy didn't see Khalid, but we got him working up an Identikit sketch of the guy he did see. We'll have that out by noon. As far as the getaway went, yeah, some people did see a couple of guys with a barrel, but we don't have a positive ID yet. In fact, the whole canvass is a disaster. The block is all Satmar Hasidim. The men won't talk to P.W.'s, and they won't let the women talk to male officers. Needless to say, we are not going through this particular neighborhood in the kind of balls-to-the-wall shit storm like we would've if this'd happened uptown. And don't think I'm not bitter."

"In that case, I apologize to you on behalf of the Jewish people and the entire white race," said Karp. "Meanwhile, how the *fuck* did this happen? And for that matter, what *did* happen? I'm still unclear."

"Okay, let's walk," said Fulton. "I got to get to One Police to meet with Timmons and then over to Brooklyn to review my legions."

"There won't be any problem with that, I presume. Resources—"

"You got to be kidding. The sky's the limit on this one, Stretch. I'll need four people just to handle the calls from guys volunteering their off-duty time. These fuckers are doomed."

They walked across Foley Square, a broad, unattractive plaza that, since it was home to the criminal, civil, and federal courthouses, contained more lawyers working at their trade than any other in the City, and thus in all probability was accursed of God. It was swept by freakish Canadian winds in the winter and baked like Chad in the summer; today it was raw, with a light chilling rain.

Fulton said, "Here's how I see it playing. Khalid and company rent a garage for the night. Why? Obviously to set up a meeting, a meeting with a guy or group they don't trust or who doesn't trust them; otherwise they'd go to a bar, or where they lived. The meet comes off, but one of the parties does a double-cross, and a firefight breaks out. The other group's got rockets, so Khalid and his people book. One escapes on foot, after shooting off about a hundred rounds of nine mil. One dies in a car. And Khalid and another guy take off in the garage tow truck. The other party, number and composition unknown, disperses on foot, because the car they came in is totaled. But one of these characters wanders out onto Atlantic and steals a black 1979 Chrysler New Yorker from a tile salesman on his way home to Bensonhurst. We got him on an Identikit too—a young kid, thin, good-looking . . ."

"An Arab?" asked Karp.

"Probably. They didn't converse much. The kid had a duffel bag on him, and he's the source of the grenades and the rocket that did all the damage. We would really like to catch this particular scumbag."

"He just walked away after he blew up the ESU van?"

"Just walked away. You got to understand the kind of shit that was going down on that street after the van went up. There were bullets cooking off, shotgun shells, slugs and pellets flying off buildings, concussion grenades exploding, plus the gas. If he'd've been King Kong nobody would've noticed him, and the cops back on Rutledge Street were blocked by a wall of flames and gas. Why did you ask if he was an Arab? What else could he have been?"

Karp's step halted for a moment, and he gave Fulton a hard look, leavened with appreciative humor. "You never stop detecting, do you?"

"You weren't tying to slide one by me, were you?"

"Not really," said Karp. "I had a meeting with Aaron Zwiller the other day, one of Lowenstein's people. He thinks Lowenstein is assembling a little army. Guys from Israel, Israeli weapons. It was pretty vague . . ."

Fulton frowned and chewed his lip. "Shit, man, I don't even want to think that some Israeli guy working for the Hasidim killed seven cops."

"Yeah, tell me about it. Maybe I'll put in a call to Zwiller. Maybe he knows something. Meanwhile, maybe you can get Kirby to ask for a warrant to toss the Ostropoler shul."

Fulton cackled and waved good-bye, heading south for One Police Plaza. Karp went into the Criminal Courts through the D.A.'s entrance and ascended directly to the sixth floor. He hung his raincoat in his office and went to the D.A.'s suite.

"Is he free?" Karp asked the O'Malley.

"He's got Roland in with him, but he said to send you in." Her glance turned narrow. "You'll behave yourself, now?"

"Yeah, Marcie, we kissed and made up," he answered and pushed through the door.

Jack Keegan was on the couch in his shirtsleeves, with his arms flung out along the back of it, talking to Roland Hrcany, who sat easily in the wing chair opposite. They both looked up when Karp entered, and Keegan waved him over. Karp thought Keegan looked tired. Roland, however, looked better than he had appeared in some months. Perhaps the blow to the head, Karp thought.

But no, it was a break in the terrible Mexican brothers case. Roland made this known, with glee.

"I was just saying to Jack," Roland said, "if it hadn't been for this Arab thing, they might have gotten away. As it is, there must be a couple hundred cops wandering around Kennedy and La Guardia, guys off duty, whatever—the cop bars are going broke, I hear. They're all out looking for the Arabs, but of course, they could spare some attention for a couple shitheads who only killed *one* cop."

"This would be Ray Netski," Karp ventured. Roland caught the tone of hesitation in his voice, but being the new Roland and the D.A. being present, he did not bridle.

"Yeah, at least it's our working theory. The scene is full of prints. The two Obregons, this girl, Connie Erbes, a semi-pro whore, who we're still looking for, and a third guy, who right now is pretty much a mystery, but we like him for Ray. Oh, and another thing: we found the pad that the notes threatening me were written on—the old ballpoint-pen impression routine. These guys don't watch spy movies, apparently. Unfortunately, nobody but the girl and the Obregons got a good look at him, and we don't have the girl and the Obregons are going, 'What other man, señor?' "

"What are we holding the brothers on now?"

Roland did some nervous flexing. "Well, there's the 240.30, with me as the complainant, and the 135.65, also me. I threw in conspiracy to commit murder, on the assumption that they were in on Netski's murder, that this guy was acting as their agent, but without more evidence, or testimony from the girl . . ."

Keegan said, "The harassment charge is a misdemeanor, and the coercion won't hold up as a felony. The threats in the letters are too vague, and also we dismissed the damn charges against them on Morilla. So it's oh, your honor, my girlfriend, she knows I'm innocent, so she writes to the prosecutor. We are simple people, your honor, and so forth, bumped down to a misdemeanor or tossed out. And the conspiracy charge is pure horseshit. You better find that third guy."

To Karp's surprise, Roland was nodding along with this. "Yeah, otherwise it's *hasta la vista*, Mexican brothers. Speaking of which, I got to go . . . unless there's something else?"

Keegan said there was not, and Roland got up. Karp had in his mind the image of loose ends flapping in the wind, intensely disturbing, but not articulable at present.

"Just a second, Roland," he said, "what about the dead Arab, the shooter in Morilla?"

"You mean, who did him? Well, the smart money's on man number three, him or the girl—she rented the car he was found in, and mystery guy's prints are all over it. Did the Obregons put out a contract on the Arab? Possible, but again we need the guy or the girl."

"What about the Russian bullet?"

Roland shrugged. "It doesn't match anything else in the case. Netski was killed with a nine, American made. Hell, it could've been there from the last tenant."

It could have been, Karp thought as he watched Hrcany leave, and doubted it tremendously, but there was nothing solid to make a point upon.

"So? What transpired at our federal government?" Keegan asked, and Karp told him, Keegan laughing aloud at Fulton's coup.

"Anderson was not amused," noted Karp.

"Oh, Anderson will get over it. He's a grown-up and Hoover's still dead. Four GS-13s, including Don Herring, will get transferred to Butte, and the Feds'll dive into this with both feet. My Lord, seven dead cops and the Hasids too! Kirby must be shitting himself, I hate to say it, but thank God it's Brooklyn. You going to the funeral?"

"I hadn't intended to. I haven't gone to an official funeral since Garrahy died."

"Go. You'll drive out with me. It looks good, they're cops, we're on the same team. What the hell is that?"

The phone was ringing, and clearly Keegan had told O'Malley to hold calls. He stumped over to his desk, picked up, said, "Okay, put him on," listened for three minutes, pounded his fist once on the desk, muttered something to the other party, and hung up.

"I spoke too soon," he said. "Let that be a lesson."

"What?"

"That was the police commissioner himself. It seems that at approximately five this morning, a Hasid shot three black kids uptown, killed two and wounded one. With a machine gun. Crowds are gathering. Black Muslims are standing on cars with bullhorns."

"My God! What happened to the Hasid?"

"Escaped apparently, covering his retreat with a hail of lead, as they used to say."

They were silent for a moment, and then Karp said, "Well, this sucks," and they both laughed hysterically, and a little too long.

In the nervous, sober moment that always comes after such an outburst, Keegan picked up his toy cigar and said reflectively, "It's so thin, really, what keeps it all together. Society. The law. You know, we talk lightly about the asphalt jungle, crime is out of control, it's anarchy. Well, it's not. Cops can go anywhere in the city, and they almost never get shot at. That's why it's such a big thing when a cop gets it in LOD. But I was with a military government unit in Italy in the last eight months of World War Two, and I've seen what breakdown *really* is. Say all you want about the cops, they're brutal, they're corrupt, the courts don't work, criminals go free—but even a real bad criminal justice system is better than *any* military government, and you have to move to military government a lot faster than most people think when you've got gangs of people running around with heavy weapons aimed at the police."

"We're far from that," said Karp.

"Are we?" Keegan shook his head, as if to clear it of old thoughts of cities in ruins. "Oh, I guess we are. I'm just pontificating, because I'm so pissed off at this Arab–Jew thing, and I hoped we could slide by it this time, but I guess not. Watch this for me, Butch. Bird-dog the cops. Find out what's going on. And let them see our flag."

Karp put on his still damp raincoat and called Ed Morris, and they drove up to Harlem in the dark blue Plymouth Fury. While they drove, Karp got on the radio, was patched into a phone line, and made inquiries of Zone Five homicide, which had caught the case. This was Fulton's old yard, and Karp knew most of the people working murders up there, and when he heard who was covering these murders, he was about as relieved as he could get, given the circumstances.

At 110th Street, Central Park West becomes Eighth Avenue and loses its class, becoming just another seedy New York avenue, wet and greasy today, broad, lined with heavily barred shops, with most reachable surfaces on the buildings, doors, and street furniture covered with spray-painted gang tags. Despite the thin rain there seemed to be more people than usual on the streets, groups of ten to twenty-five, mostly young men, dressed in team jackets and hooded sweatshirts, hanging around convenience stores or moving like migratory herds up and back on the avenue.

A can flew through the air and clanged against the Plymouth's fender. Karp heard a bottle smash behind them. Morris picked up the pace a little.

Morris said, half to himself, "We'll be fine, we're almost there," and Karp said "What you mean 'we,' white man?" Morris laughed.

The Two-Eight was located at 2271 Eighth, off 135th Street. Karp walked up the stairs to the bay where the homicide cops sat. Detective Second Grade Lanny Maus was at his desk, typing. He was wearing a dark purple shirt with an antique 1940s wide tie bearing a painting of firecrackers exploding, and baggy cream linen and wool trousers held up by thin woven leather suspenders. Maus had a blue-eyed, blunt, dull-looking white working-stiff–type face, a wide mouth, uneven teeth, a low forehead. His shaggy blond hair fell over his collar. It was the kind of cracker, redneck, peckerwood face that showed up in old photographs of lynch mobs. In fact, however, Maus loved working in Harlem, loved what remained of New York black culture, and might have joined the Black Muslims if they let white guys in. He had a black girlfriend and lived on 103rd Street. This did not increase his popularity with other white cops.

He caught sight of Karp and waved him over. "You're a college graduate—how many s's in aggressive?" Karp told him and he finished his line. He looked up at Karp and said, "So they busted you down to riding D.A.?"

"Nope. I'm still a big-time desk jockey. Who was the riding D.A. for this abortion?"

"Name of Womroth. Thirteen years old, braces and acne, I gave her a spanking and sent her to bed without her supper. Why? She fuck up?"

"No, given what's going on, Jack wanted me to watch this one. What happened?"

"Who the fuck knows, like usual. I haven't had a chance to hit the snitches yet, so all we have is the statement of the surviving kid, who's in Harlem Hospital, and statements from the kind of mopes you expect to be wandering around Lenox and 'seventeenth at five in the a.m.; they all back Roscoe's story."

"Roscoe being the survivor."

"Right, Haroon Roscoe, nineteen, a.k.a. Rough, a.k.a. Shane. Not a choirboy. A mugger, a hype. Now a hero of the downtrodden black race, a model citizen cut down in his youth along with his dear friends, also model citizens. The vics are Jermane Metcalf, eighteen, a.k.a. Doughboy, and Pierre Claussen, seventeen, a.k.a. Bose. According to Roscoe, these fine lads were just minding their business in front of the Ro-Lo convenience stores at five-ten this morning, you know, discussing contemporary French literature and the latest advances in molecular biology, when this Hasid walks in, buys a carton of o.j., some rubbing alcohol, and some shaving and first-aid stuff, pays, and walks out. Metcalf approaches this person—"

"Right there, in front of the store?" Karp asked.

"Ah, you catch on!" said Maus, grinning. "No, it seems the boys felt the need of some exercise just then, and they headed down Lenox about thirty yards, down to where this Jewish fella had parked his van. He had a new white Dodge van with tinted windows. Metcalf politely asks if he's got a light, and the fella pops open his coat and blows Metcalf practically in half with a burst, and then sends another burst at Claussen and Roscoe, who wun't doin nuthin'. Then he drives away. We got a city-wide out on the van."

"So what really happened?"

"Oh, that's easy. These three guys are a strong-arm crew; they're all graduates of Spofford Prep and Rikers. They're hanging out there, just about set to put it away for the evening, when the vic from heaven shows up—a skinny little Hasid with a brand-new van and carrying Allah knows how much cash, because it's well known that the Jews are all loaded. It's practically a direct deposit in their bank. So they follow this fool back to his van, maybe play with him a little, tell him to give it up, cash and keys, and then—surprise! He pulls a fucking Kalashnikov out and mows them all down."

"A Kalashnikov, hm?"

"Yeah. We found nineteen 7.62mm casings at the scene, Soviet military markings and all. And Roscoe knows what an AK looks like. They're hard to miss."

Karp said, "You know . . ." and paused so long afterward that Maus said, "What?" and then Karp said, "Just thinking out loud. You know, Jim Raney found a Kalashnikov bullet with Soviet markings in the apartment where Ray Netski got shot. It'd be interesting to see if they match up. You know, same batch marks and all."

Maus knotted his brow, puzzled. Given the character of his face, he looked like he was trying to figure out what number came between four and six. "Netski? I thought that was Mexicans. Where does a Hasid fit in?"

"Well, as far as that goes, what we have for sure is a man wearing Hasidic clothes. Everybody in a Santa Claus suit isn't Santa Claus."

"Oh, now you're really fucking with my head, Karp. Let's try to keep some things sacred, okay? Also, I'm trying to think why a guy would want to run around Harlem at night dressed up like that, unless he was looking for trouble." He stopped. "Uh-oh . . ."

"Right. If the guy was halfway legit, then there's a possibility that somebody's trying to get the word out on the street, don't fuck with the Hasidim." He told Maus what he had told Fulton about Zwiller's fears.

"Oh, shit," said Maus. "That's all we need, Jewish vigilantes. Did you notice what's going on in the street?"

"A little. You think it could get bad?"

Maus humped his shoulders. "This was August, I'd say no question. The X-men are hot over this, and they're hot over this Arab business too. Solidarity with the Arab brothers, even though actual Arab Muslims think they're full of shit. Still, it's something to get pissed off about through a bullhorn. We better pray for a couple weeks of cold, chilly rain."

El Chivato lay in a dry bathtub and poured rubbing alcohol into the festering wound in his side. He was biting on a washcloth so he wouldn't scream, but he made a noise anyway, arching his back and writhing, washed with waves of agony such as he had never imagined. He rested for a while and then, staggering to his feet, turned on the shower.

While the hot water beat down on his head, he thought about his recent misfortunes and the various stupidities he had committed. He had, naturally, no remorse for shooting the three *negros*, only that he had not made sure that they were all dead at the scene. Nor had he killed the pimp and the girls from whom he had taken the van; nor, worst of all, had he taken out the man with the black Chrysler. So there were people alive who could identify him as the cause of a good deal of death and damage. In Mexico, he thought ruefully, this would not have happened. On the one hand, he was well known—mothers pulled their children in off the streets in both Hermosillo and Nogales when he walked by. On the other hand, the police were bought off. The law belonged to the man paying the highest *mordida*, and El Chivato had always worked for that sort of man. But here in New York the rules were all different.

The police were bribed, as everywhere—drugs and prostitution were much in evidence, openly pursued, and this was clearly impossible without the connivance of the police. But the Obregons had not been able to buy their way out of jail. Why? Because they had killed a cop? Or because they had tried to buy the wrong person or hadn't offered enough? It remained a mystery, and one that he would never decipher, because he was not going to be there very long.

El Chivato left the shower and dried himself, as he did so examining his wound in the mirror. It was still vividly red on both sides of the gouge, and swollen and dripping a pale, unpleasant fluid, and it throbbed, sending a bolt of pain out with each heartbeat. He bound it up with the material he had purchased, padding it heavily with gauze squares and absorbent cotton. Then he wrapped a towel around his middle, lay down on the bed, and switched on the television.

He drank orange juice with ice and flicked through the channels. At five-thirty the local news came on. Several of the items were of interest. A black man in a suit and a bow tie was shouting to a crowd about the shooting of three black boys. It took a while for El Chivato to understand that these were the boys he had shot. This confused him. The man seemed to be saying that there was something wrong with shooting the thieves, that the Jews were to blame, that the police should arrest someone for the shooting, but that they would not, because the thieves were black and the man who shot him was a Jew. Pictures of the thieves appeared on the screen, and then a drawing of himself in the black costume with hat and glasses. He understood now, a little. The word "Jew" had meant little to him; it was like "Toltec" or "Aztec," a name for people with odd customs who lived long ago. They had killed Christ, he recalled, and then, as far as he knew, had vanished. But it seemed they were still around, and he had inadvertently disguised himself as one of them. El Chivato had very little sense of humor, but this made him smile.

The smile vanished during the following story, which showed a picture of police officers leading the Obregon brothers away in handcuffs. The announcer said they were being held as material witnesses in the murder of police detective Ray Netski. A picture of Netski appeared on the screen, and although he was younger and in full uniform, El Chivato recognized him as the man he had shot and refrigerated. He was more interested, however, in the next snippet, which showed a group of reporters and a muscular blond man identified in white letters at the foot of the screen as Roland Hrcany, Chief of the Homicide Bureau, N.Y.D.A. He was saying, "We are holding the Obregons as material witnesses in the shooting of Detective Netski. That's all I can say about an investigation that's ongoing."

"Are they suspects?" asked a reporter.

"No, not at this time," said Hrcany

"Do you have any suspects in this case?" asked another reporter.

"We're following a number of leads."

Another reporter: "What about the rumor that Russian weapons were found at the murder scene?"

"No comment."

The same reporter: "Is this killing connected in any way with the recent terrorist violence in Brooklyn in which Soviet weapons were used too?"

"I can't comment on that."

The picture changed to show a hefty, well-dressed Latino man, identified as Manuel Huerta, who was representing the Obregons.

". . . this is harassment pure and simple," Huerta was telling the reporter. "First there was a trumped-up charge, and now, when these innocent young men are preparing to return to Mexico and their families, the state tries to pin this *other* cop killing on them. Well, I'm not going to allow it, and I'll tell you that the Latino community in New York is not going to tolerate it."

"Have the Obregons been returned to jail?"

"I have no idea where the Obregons are. That's another thing— I'm being denied access to my clients."

The man was cut off as he opened his mouth to expand on his outrage, and the reporter finished by saying that, according to the D.A.'s office, the Obregons were being held at an undisclosed location for their own safety.

The anchorman came back on and introduced the next story, which was about the Brooklyn disaster. First some tape of the previous night's catastrophe—smoke, flames, flashing lights, firemen, medics—then grieving Hasidim, flocking into an emergency room, then Chief Inspector Kevin Battle, with a grim account of the police carnage and the medical status of the injured officers, then FBI Special Agent in Charge Anderson, with just a few lines about every law enforcement resource being directed at capturing the dastards, and finally, two faces above telephone numbers to call if you saw them: one a grainy enlargement of the face of Abdel Hussein Khalid, whom El Chivato recognized as his own Lucky, and the other a police artist's sketch portrait of what the television was calling Arab terrorist number two, himself.

SIXTEEN

They buried the seven slain police officers, six men and a woman, on Holy Thursday. The day was appropriately overcast, but the rain stayed put in the heavy ash-colored clouds. Every police officer killed in line of duty in New York gets what is called an inspector's funeral—the Emerald Society pipe band, the flag on the coffin, the rows and rows of police in their dress uniforms, with medals, the volley of shots over the grave, the eulogies. These particular obsequies made the usual inspector's funeral look like the quick cremation of a friendless drifter. The cortege was nearly ten miles long, stretching almost from the Williamsburg Bridge down Brooklyn Broadway and Myrtle Avenue into the borough of Queens and out to Cypress Hills Cemetery, in the center of New York's vast suburban necropolis. Usually, out-of-town police departments sent a few representatives. This time there were whole squads, an unusual number of horses, including a band of Texas Rangers and a group of actual mounted Canadian Mounties in traditional scarlet, a whole pipe band from Chicago, and literally thousands of out-of-town cops demonstrating solidarity with the Finest, with the mourning bands wrapped around their arms or draped on their badges. Police chiefs in full regalia came from all the major American cities, as did the mayor and the governor of New York, and the director of the FBI, and the vice-president of the United States.

Stands had been set up for the dignitaries, so they could see the elaborate ceremonials and hear the eulogies, not one of which adverted to what was on the minds of a great number of participants—

that here were seven Christians who had perished in a war between Jews and Arabs during Easter week. The Israeli consul, and the consuls and U.N. reps of a number of Arab nations had volunteered to make an appearance, but these offers had been firmly turned down by the Department fathers. A lone piper played "Amazing Grace," which had been edging out the traditional Celtic laments in recent years. Karp, from his position in the rearmost ranks of the VIP stands, saw tears flow down the faces around him. Beneath the genuine sorrow stirred something nastier; he could almost see it rising from the ranks of dark blue, like the heat shimmers from the slowly moving cars of the cortege. For the next few days it would not be pleasant to be an Arab in New York, or a Hasidic Jew. The honor guard was shooting volleys into the air, three for each of the slain. Karp wondered idly why they fired over the graves. Speeding the souls bullet-like to paradise? Doubtful. Perhaps a sacrifice, a little powder burnt instead of an ox. The shots rang on, echoing. Then the flag ceremony, the stars and stripes removed from the coffins, folded into triangles with jerky, precise motions by the honor guard, and handed by its commander to the grieving widow or, in three cases, the mother. At this even Karp felt his throat contract, his eyes sting. He thought of his boys, grown into their twenties, killed. And of Lucy, which did not take as much imagination, the girl clearly out of control and headed for an early demise. Losing a child—how could you live past that? People did, however, which was either a miracle or a horror, depending on how you looked at it, your philosophy. . . . Taps sounded and then it was done, as was Karp's speculation on the great themes, his ability to shut down unpleasant thoughts being one of his major psychic characteristics. The VIPs left, in order of precedence, which meant that Karp, as a mere appendage of a district attorney, had long to wait.

Thus Clay Fulton had plenty of time to locate him as he stood by the feeder road to the parking lot, near a clump of cypresses, overlooking the endless rows of graves and monuments. Karp had seen Fulton in his dress blues only when the detective was receiving some sort of official award, and as usual he was impressed, despite his genial contempt for the appurtenances of the military. Fulton's breast bars rose from the gold shield on the left side of his chest almost to his shoulder straps, capped by the star-spangled green bar of the police medal of honor. Karp noted with surprise that he was wearing double silver bars on his shoulders.

"Congratulations, *Captain* Fulton," said Karp, shaking hands.

"Yeah, well, it's acting jack so far. I got lieutenants galore working for me on this task force, and the rank helps. It could get made official if we pull this business off."

"And how is the business going?"

"Pretty well, considering we've been at it a little over a day. One team is going over every piece of paper Chouza Khalid touched since he's been in the country, the overseas calls from his office, hitting all the phone booths, even, in the neighborhood. Another team's going through little Arabia like the wrath of God. Every restaurant, every coffee shop. This place, the Palm, was the big hangout. We got the owner in, the waiters, their relatives. Another team's going after the politicals, anybody ever said anything nice about the Palestinians. The FBI and some folks from the INS are pulling entry visas, checking out the green-card people, the students."

"Observing all legal safeguards, I assume."

"Oh, my, yes," said Fulton, grinning. "You take a drive down Constitution Avenue today, you might hear a wailing sound coming from the National Archives, the Constitution getting pinched. Let me tell you, son, the Force is cranky, very cranky. Some Arab illegals decided to take off from a sweep last night, they tripped and hurt their faces something fierce. Oh, we also pulled Walid and his dad in for another exchange of views."

"Anything there?"

"Yeah, something. He was in contact with Khalid. Was going to be trained as a freedom fighter. The most we can figure he did was lend the bakery truck for moving stuff around. When we vacuumed it, we came up with a couple of scraps of packing material and a lot of bread crumbs. We sent the packing material down to Quantico for analysis."

"What's your take on them?"

"The father knows from nothing. The kid is obsessed with politics and his sister. He admitted going to Khalid for help in getting his sister back. He was surprised as hell when we told him that his pals already had her. Anyway, a patsy. Not a player. We've got their phone and mail covered but . . . we don't expect much."

"Speaking of the girl . . ."

Fulton shook his head. "No luck there. Not a trace. My feeling is, she's gone. Plastic bags. Our thought was they told the kid they'd get his sister back for him if he'd let them borrow his truck. They paid off and then they whacked her."

"Seems like a lot of trouble to go through for something they could buy from U-Haul for a couple of hundred."

"Yeah, right, but these people play by their own rules. And they're good, man, too fucking good. They make Colombian dope kings look like impulse purse snatchers. Their whole operation is all celled out. Nothing leads back to a location or any of the main characters. Wherever they're living, they're paying cash. We've got another team going around to realtors in Brooklyn, checking for big cash transactions. They don't use phones. However they've got their vehicles registered, there's nothing traceable back to any name we've got. And so on."

"How about the Jew side?"

"Oh, Kirby's still being delicate about searching the Ostropolers. The paddies are not pleased with this, nor are my racial brothers. A lot of them figure the Hasids have been getting a free ride for a long time, and you know, plenty of them thought Hitler had a point a long time before this all went down. We might see a situation there in Williamsburg, something don't break pretty soon." His face brightened. "Oh, yeah—the big news! Yitzhak Schneider came through. A credit to your race."

"Yitzhak . . . ?"

"Runs a clothing store on Lee, Hasidic garments and so on. On the re-canvass, we sent a team of nice Jewish cop-type boys through, yarmulkes on. Yitzhak says that on the day of, a thin dark kid walks into his place and buys the complete rig, pays cash, and walks out. Guy thought he was a Yemeni Jew rediscovering the true faith."

"Same guy who took the Chrysler and shot the muggers?"

"Absolutely. We're dealing with Lon Chaney Junior here."

"So, one of the Arabs," observed Karp with some satisfaction. "That should annoy the Nation of Islam."

"Well, not so fast, son. He could've been an Arab, in which case we have to ask why was he in a fight with a bunch of other Arabs? He could've also been one of the rabbi's troopers, or from some Israeli operation."

This gave Karp pause. He had himself been involved in an Israeli covert operation some years ago, unofficial to be sure, but . . . He made an eye-rolling, hand-spreading gesture, of the type New

Yorkers make when, once again, the metropolis has thrown up a number beyond all comprehension. He spotted the D.A.'s Lincoln oozing through the drive and, bidding Fulton good-bye and good luck, went to pick up his ride.

Rashid ibn-Ali al-Halim al-Qayuayn was the ruler of a small emirate on the Persian Gulf, the proverbial patch of sand with few citizens and a great deal of oil, and so when his eldest son was neatly lifted off a street in London, he was prepared and able to pay a great deal to get him back. When the call came, he was therefore surprised that the kidnappers did not want any money.

A few miles from the police funeral, at Kennedy International Airport, at around the time that taps was blowing, a stretched white Cadillac limo with smoked windows enters the freight area. The driver shows the proper identification, and the limo is allowed onto the apron. There it waits. Some minutes later a large twin-engine Gulfstream jet lands and taxis over to the customs building. A customs agent and an INS agent board the plane, which they have been told to expect. The passengers receive VIP treatment; the emir Rashid is a friend of America and of American automobiles. Their passports are, of course, all in order: they identify the emir himself and six of his entourage, all in their traditional robes. The customs man and the INS smile. They do not quite bow, because Americans don't do that, but isn't this, they think, so much nicer than rousting Nigerians who have swallowed condoms full of heroin? They leave, wishing the emir a pleasant stay.

The white limo pulls up to the plane. It departs. The plane refuels and parks. The crew leaves. No one notices that no one else has actually left the plane. The white limo, containing a uniformed driver and seven Arabs in white robes, with headdresses and ceremonial daggers, drives out of the airport, the chauffeur showing the proper papers, naturally, and back to the city, to 35 East Seventy-sixth Street, where its passengers check into the Hotel Carlyle. The Carlyle has been cabled to expect the party, and has reserved the entire eighteenth floor for the emir.

Chouza Khalid felt like a fool in the white robes, which he, a native of a Palestinian refugee camp, had never before worn, but he liked the suite and had to admit that Ibn-Salemeh had been clever. Hiding in plain sight, he called it. Every policeman in the city was looking for evil Arabs, and so the best disguise was this—as Arab as you could get. No one ever studied the face of a man in a robe and headdress. He made himself a drink from the bar, Chivas and water, drank it, washed out the glass, ate a breath mint, and went through the connecting door to Ibn-Salemeh's suite.

Ibn-Salemeh, in a somewhat more luxurious costume, in which he seemed far more comfortable than Khalid, was watching television with the sound off. There was a contented, almost a benign expression on his gaunt face, like that of a dairy farmer watching a line of plump Jerseys trooping into the barn to be milked. The TV showed an official funeral in progress.

"Sit down," said the terrorist. "This is worth watching. Do you ever wonder why the Americans show civil disorder over and over on the television? You would think the government would suppress it, but no. They seem to delight in it, even though showing it must surely spread the disorder."

The television showed a group of police trying to arrest a young man, an Arab, while fending off a crowd of outraged neighbors and friends. The camera shook. A long shot down a street. More police in riot gear deploying. A shot of police pushing back a mob of angry protesters. A shot of an Arab youth holding a cloth to his bloody head, being hustled roughly into a police vehicle. The anchor back now, a look of professional gravity on his craggy face. His lips moved. The screen changed to show a man in a black suit and a hat, haranguing a crowd of similarly dressed people in a broad plaza backed by the trees of a park.

"This is our ally," said Ibn-Salemeh.

"A Jew?"

"Yes, he is telling everyone who will listen to him that every Arab in the city is a terrorist or a harborer of terrorists or a potential terrorist, which we also wish people to believe, especially the Arabs. I only wish we had more time in this city to amuse ourselves with this man. However, after Sunday we will leave behind a fertile field from which I hope will grow a permanent organization, in fact as well as in this fool's imagination." He turned away from the set, which had gone over to selling a car. "That is for the future, God willing. Now, as to the present, what is the situation with the Daoud boy?"

"He was questioned, with the father, then released. One of our runners reached him. He is angry because the police told him that we have his sister."

"Good, let him be angry. Send a message back. Say it is a test of his discipline. Family is important, but not so important as the cause, and so on and so on. You know the words. He will, let us say, be with his sister on Sunday. Say that Ibn-Salemeh himself promises this. God willing."

Ibn-Salemeh seemed to recall something and smiled at Khalid. "The girl is well? Safe?"

"Yes. It would be wise to check on her, however. She has proven to be resourceful at escape."

"No, the risk is too great. Brooklyn will be swarming with police, Williamsburg, and Atlantic Avenue and Crown Heights especially. You have a good arrangement. She will keep until Sunday."

Posie looked at her image in Marlene's full-length cheval glass and goggled.

"Holy shit!" was her thought, expressed in a high-pitched, child's voice.

"You look like a million bucks, kid," said Marlene, the apprentice whore monger.

"Jesus, I should—you spent a million bucks." She turned and twisted, looking over her shoulder in the instinctive manner of women who wish to see the impossible—how they look walking away. She was wearing a dark mid-calf-length russet-colored dress in thin wool. It buttoned all the way up the front, had a scoop neck and thin straps. Over this she wore a shoulder-padded black jacket in shiny, slinky black oiled cotton. Little black close-toed sandals on the feet, over lacy white anklets. The final accessory was a checked cotton Arab scarf, loosely tied around her neck. Freshness not unavailable, and sympathy with the oppressed Third World was the effect Marlene had sought, and she thought she had achieved it. It was pathetic, really—no one had ever bought clothes for the girl before, not since she had, at thirteen, grown a Body and started attracting the attention of her boozy step-dad. After that there had been the street and odd rags. She'd had her hair done too, a razor cut that gave her the shaggy lioness look currently popular among TV action heroines.

The purchases were, however, the easy part. The requisite girl talk would be a good deal harder.

"Posie, dear," said Marlene. "We need to talk."

They sat on the bed and talked. Marlene told Posie that she was to attract the target, that she was to engage him in conversation, that she was to enter into a friendly relationship with him, of the type that might allow the sharing of confidences, that she was to find out whether Walid knew anything about what had happened to his sister, and finally, that she was not under any circumstances to engage in a sexual relationship with Walid Daoud.

Posie's jaw, never quite firm, gaped wider still. "How come, Marlene? I mean, you know, if I like him and all."

"Two reasons, kid. One is, I can't send you out to engage in sex as part of an investigation that may end up in court. It's illegal and I could lose my license. Two, the thing is, with this particular guy, you have to play it cool. He's not from our culture; he might not react the way you think he will. It could get dangerous."

"Oh, yeah, for sure, I know what you mean," said Posie, now on more familiar ground. "I balled this guy once from Canada? He was like French? I never could tell what he was going to do. He had an old, like a Nash or some car they don't make anymore. He was totally out of it."

Marlene smiled weakly at the girl. "Uh-huh, right. Well, this guy could be even weirder than a Canadian, Posie. So, no balling, okay? Just a date."

Posie nodded seriously and then broke into a grin. "Also, I don't want to get this new stuff all, like, gummy, you know?"

Marlene left the girl to a spate of renewed primping and went back to the kitchen, where Tran was entertaining Lucy and the boys by pretending to be a duck, in Vietnamese. When he saw Marlene, and the look on her face, he rose, dropping the clown act. Lucy was set to watch the toddlers, and Tran followed Marlene into her office.

"Well?" she said.

Tran brought a creased street map of New York out of his jacket pocket and spread it on her desk.

"He always follows the same route for each run, one every morning but Friday, with bread, and one in the afternoon on Saturday, Tuesday, and Thursday, with cakes." Tran pointed at the map, tracing the web of streets with a Bic. "A dozen or so stops in Brooklyn and somewhat fewer in Manhattan." He had marked the two routes in blue ink, neatly circling the stops. Marlene gave the map a cursory look. She was thinking of other things. "Is he followed?"

"Yes, but not continuously. There was a car with two dark-skinned men in it, twice, earlier this week. Yesterday, he was followed by an obvious pair of police, but they were not there this morning. I think they have lost interest."

"Maybe, or maybe you missed them."

Tran flicked an eyebrow upward but made no comment.

"And he stops in Washington Square every afternoon?"

"Yes, he parks and has a soft drink and a cigarette and eyes the college girls with a hungry look."

"But does nothing?"

"Nothing, if burning looks are nothing. He has no money and his English is clumsy, and he is very proud and cannot bear rejection. Also, he thinks these girls are sluts, loose, because of their dress and their easy ways, yet he desires them. He hates this in himself. He wishes to be at the same time an Arab, faithful to his tribe, and an American boy, walking, laughing with his arm around some girl's waist."

"You know this all, huh?"

"I was once an immigrant boy in a student quarter in Paris, with no money for the girls, and I was far, far more sophisticated than Walid," said Tran confidently. "There were Arab boys there too, and it was very much worse for them. Once or twice during the term there would be a suicide, or a stabbing after an error in the sexual communication. The same in Moscow, although there was a good deal more supervision."

"I bet," said Marlene, her eyes widening. "When were you in Moscow?"

"In 'sixty-five. A kind of terrorists' convention, although we were all freedom fighters then. I was a speaker. My subject was, as I recall it, *ba giong thac Cach mang,* the three currents of revolution present in every people's war: the ever growing socialist camp, the armed struggle, and the progressive forces within the imperialist nation. It was well received. There were a large number of Arabs— Algerians, Lebanese, Syrians, Palestinians. The Palestinians, I recall, were rather lonely, since the rest of us spoke French and they did not, not most of them anyway, and we spoke little English. The Americans had not arrived in numbers large enough to teach us their language. It is quite possible that some of my comrades from those days are loose in New York this minute. That would be amusing, would it not?"

"Hilarious," said Marlene stiffly. She was simultaneously fascinated and repelled by her associate's past. Tran dropped his eyes and there was a moment of uncomfortable silence. Then he said, "You must tell her to be careful, eh? He will not tolerate any insult. Also, there will be his guilt."

And mine too, Marlene thought.

At first Walid did not believe that the girl was smiling at him, and he instinctively looked over his shoulder to see whether there was someone else there, but since he was leaning against his truck, this was impossible. He felt a flush of embarrassment rise to his cheeks. He looked away, examined his cigarette, and then risked a cautious glance out of the corner of his eye, wishing that he had a group of friends around him. The girl was still there, still smiling. With mixed horror and excitement he watched her approach.

He really was gorgeous, Posie thought as she approached him, asked for a light, got one. This was the most thrilling thing she had ever done. The new clothes seemed to make her into a new person, and doing a . . . she had to call it a *mission* for Marlene: it made her head swim. Marlene had filled that head with cautions, orders, strategies. These swam away like small fishes. She smiled harder. "Neat van!" she said. "Can I see inside?"

Walid did not object, and she stepped past him into the van. She was close enough for him to smell her perfume. She actually brushed his hip with hers, and showed him a long stretch of white leg as she mounted the step. He followed her in, closing the door behind.

"Oh, wow! This is cool! You could fix this up to travel in, you know? What's on the shelves?"

"Bread. Arab breads. We are in bakery business."

"Cool! You're an Arab?"

"Yes."

"Far out! I never met an Arab before." A pause. She strolled back and forth in the bay of the van, seemingly fascinated by the bags of stale and unsold bread that Walid had retrieved along his route when he made his cake run. He could not take his eyes off her. She was an American girl, free, smelling of flowers, but not whorish like the ones who strode brazenly through the streets in their underwear. They exchanged names. She sat herself down in the passenger seat and asked him what he did for fun. He said he worked all the time. And he had political interests.

This stimulated a frayed bookmark in Posie's brain. "That's great," she said. "I'm, um, real sympathetic to the, you know, the Palestinians." She flicked her scarf.

"You are?"

"Oh, for sure. Hey, you want to go in back and do some dope?"

"Dope?"

"Yeah, like grass. Pot? Reefer?" She brought a plastic baggy out of her jacket pocket and waved it at him.

Light dawned. "Ah, hashish."

"I don't know about that, but it's pretty good Colombian," said Posie. She walked into the back of the truck, sat down with her back against the rear door, and began to roll a number on her lap. Marlene hadn't said anything about this, but she hadn't told her not to either. They smoked, Walid coughing a good deal. Afterward, they chatted, giggling. She found he knew nothing about rock music, or movies, or TV shows, the only subjects in which she had any expertise. Get him to talk about himself. That was one of the things Marlene had said. His family, especially his sister. She wished there was some music. They guy wasn't putting any moves on her, which was unique in her experience of stoned young men. She moved closer to him and said, looking into his face, "You know, you have a great mouth."

"Yes?"

He was just staring at her. Incredible! Don't let him right away, Marlene had ordered, you have to string him along, allow him to get comfortable. Well, yeah, but this was ridiculous. She planted a good one right on that luscious mouth, with plenty of action behind it. Then she stood up.

"Got to go, Walid," she announced. "I'll be around here about this time tomorrow. Maybe we could, like, do something."

Karp returned to the bosom of his family with more than his usual gratitude for its shelter from a heartless world. He had not had a meal at home since Monday.

"Don't ask!" was the response when Marlene inquired about his day.

"Still bad, huh?"

"You're not watching the tube?"

"Cartoons. And I've been in and out. Lucy's been holding down the fort, haven't you, dear?"

Lucy made a grumping noise. Lucy was at the kitchen table with a math workbook, using her precious Easter vacation hours doing work she should have done during the term, instead of participating in the nonstop excursions and sleep-overs with her more dutiful pals, and her mother, who claimed to love her, was actually making her do set portions of this work before being allowed out, not only that, but was taking advantage of her confinement to demand baby-sitting. They were not speaking.

Marlene was doing what she did instead of cooking when she was working, which was heating a brick of material she had previously cooked and frozen. The microwave ticked away, measuring out her domestic slavery. The boys were climbing the vast belly of the mastiff, who was delighted to serve as a hill provided it could lick them as they rolled off. They had been fed earlier, and were covered with yummy bits. Karp, surveying his hearth, noted an absence.

"Where's Posie?" he asked.

"Out," said Marlene quickly, and got a covert sneer from her daughter, who knew very well where Posie was. To draw attention from this she said, "I haven't seen you—did I say I went to see Hadassah? No? Amy Weinstein was very nice. Turned out they wanted me because they found out, somehow, I was your mom's daughter-in-law. I didn't realize she was such a heavy hitter up there. There's a plaque on the wall of honor and everything, and it was, 'Oh, I'm so glad to meet you *finally*. Dora Karp, may she rest in peace, was a *saint*. And how *is* Roger—we never hear from him.' You should be ashamed."

"I am," Karp said lightly, and then realized that, faintly, he actually was. "What's the job like? Making sure no goyim get in?"

"No, but it's not much. Honestly, I think they *were* just being nice. It's basically a square-badge job for the meeting they're holding over the weekend. All their youth organization leaders, and on Easter weekend, no less—they may be making a tiny point there—our ways are not your ways. Anyway, it's checking credentials, keeping out crashers, controlling demonstrators, if any."

This caught his attention. "They expect demonstrators?"

"She said it was a possibility. With the city like it is, a big bunch of Jews from all over the country, some celebrities. Do you think they should be worried?"

Karp blew out a long breath, like a horse. "Hell, Marlene, I don't know anymore. I've never seen it like this. The cops are essentially out of control. Since Tuesday night we've logged over forty complaints of police brutality, and that's just in New York County—God only knows what's going down in Brooklyn. There was a riot and a lock-down out at Rikers today, the Muslims acting up. The Daoud family had their bakery firebombed. You know Zwiller, that old guy I told you about I had lunch with? Yeah, nice guy, trying to do the right thing. Dead."

"What, just today?"

"No, on Tuesday, but we just found out about it today. They're still investigating, but either he got caught in the Williamsburg mess directly or he died of natural causes because of the excitement. Or, and I hate to think this, somebody found out he ratted on Lowenstein and took him out. But the way Kirby's handling it, we can't get a straight story. With no Zwiller, he says he has no probable cause to search Lowenstein's operation. It's still kid gloves, and the more he soft-pedals with the Hasidim, the worse the Arabs bitch and moan, and the X-guys uptown start throwing heavy objects off roofs. Meanwhile the rabbi is still running the Warsaw ghetto tape. Jews, arm yourselves, the *schvartzers* are coming! It escalates. It could start shaping up into a black-white thing. I don't know—if we don't break this, we could have another situation like with the Haymarket bomb, like the Frick bombing, another red scare. We could see thirty years of civil liberty law go down the drain."

"As millions cheer, including us," she said lightly. But Karp was not in a light mood, not on this subject at any rate.

"Yeah, right, I know we like to act tough, oh, look at all the bad guys getting loose because of Warren and the Supremes, but you know and I know that not that many really bad guys get loose. In fact, the reason everybody thinks they do is that it's so unusual that it makes headlines when it happens. You want the average cop acting as judge, jury, and executioner? I don't. I don't even want to do it myself."

Marlene said, "You know, I think you're tired, and I think you're exaggerating. Lucy, time to move. We need the table." She started dealing out plates and silverware. Lucy closed her book and began to lay out the settings.

"You'll eat, you'll feel better," Marlene added. "You get exhausted like you are now, you always think it's the end of the world."

Karp bristled. "Marlene, don't patronize me! If I say it's bad, it's bad. You haven't been out there. I'm telling you—we don't find this Chouza Khalid guy and the kid with the rockets in the next couple of days, something unbelievably terrible is going to happen."

Marlene brought a steaming tureen of veal stew with mushrooms and a jug of red wine to the table. "Eat!" she ordered. "Drink! Forget about Chouza Khalid for an hour . . ."

"Daddy," said Lucy, "why is he lucky?"

"Who, baby?" asked Karp, digging gratefully in.

"That man, Chouza Khalid. Why is he lucky?"

"I don't get you—who said anything about him being lucky?"

"That's what his name means, Daddy. Chouza *means* lucky."

Karp put his fork down and stared at his daughter as the light slowly dawned.

In order to prevent immediate divorce proceedings being initiated by his spouse, Karp sat still and finished his dinner, which, after he was made to eat it, he greatly enjoyed, having subsisted entirely on *chozerai* for nearly seventy-two hours. As soon as he could, however, he left the table and called Roland's office, fully expecting the man to be at his desk at seven-fifteen, and not being disappointed.

Roland didn't want to believe it. It could be a coincidence. Unsaid was his reluctance to accept as fact something that seemed so obvious when explained, especially from Karp, especially originating from Karp's linguistic genius of a kid, an unfair advantage to Karp, like a bad hop off a manhole cover in stickball. A do-over.

Karp had some notion of this element in the man's psychology and persisted. "Roland, focus on this! It explains everything—what we knew before and stuff I just got from Fulton. The Mexican boys roll into town. They know nothing, but they have a big load of brown heroin to sell. The Arabs are in the dope business already—"

"I thought they were terrorists. Now they're dope lords? You're getting your James Bond movies mixed up."

"Hey, terrorists need money too, especially a guy like this Ibn-Salemeh, a loner. He's also working with Khalid, who we know is a drug runner from way back. But that's *why* Morilla was investigating them in the first place. So they burn Morilla's cover, which I can believe, because these guys have been going up against the Israelis for years, and they're good, and then they shoot Morilla, rip off the Mexicans, and frame them for the cop killing. That explains the Arab gunman we got wrapped up."

"Bullshit, it does! Why in hell would Khalid kill his own guy to get the Obregons off the hook?"

"Ah, there's the ringer in this whole thing. Look—the Mexicans are in jail on the frame. They don't like it. So they bring in some muscle from out of town—"

"Some 'muscle from out of town'?" Roland spoke as to a child who had just done explaining that her dolls came alive at night.

"Yeah, Roland, just listen, would you? This guy moves in with Obregon's girlfriend in the apartment in Washington Heights. He goes after Khalid. There's a gunfight, and this Arab who shot Morilla is killed. Now Khalid's in a jam. He's sold the dope—we know that from Narcotics—so he's got the money. He could care less if the Mexicans are in jail or not, because he's not planning on spending a lot of time in the New York dope business. His main thing is to get this Obregon shooter off his ass because he doesn't want him to queer his real agenda, which is blowing stuff up for the cause. So he gives us his Arab gunman, who's conveniently dead. The brothers walk, but let's say they want their cash back too. Not so fast, thinks Khalid. He sets up a meet in the garage in Brooklyn, the Mexican gets there and finds out it's a trap. Bang! Rockets, machine guns . . . and a chase that ends up in Williamsburg and kills seven cops and a dozen or so other people. Our Mexican walks away, buys Hasidic clothes, and disappears. He surfaces uptown, gets jumped by a strong-arm crew, and kills two of them. Oh, I almost forgot—he also killed Ray Netski. That explains the Russian bullet, and I guarantee you the fingerprints in the Chrysler are going to match the prints of the unknown guy in the Netski murder scene."

Roland was chuckling. "I love it! I see Omar Sharif as the Arab, and Cheech and Chong as the Obregons. Liz could do a cameo as the girl—"

"Come on, Roland, think! You know it works."

"I don't, and you know why? Among a hundred other reasons, because when we picked up the Mexican brothers at the airport, they were carrying a couple of million bucks. They were never ripped off or they got their cash back somehow. So why would your supposed Mexican hit man go to that garage to meet your supposed Khalid?"

Karp had to admit not having an answer for that one. "But it doesn't matter, Roland—he was there. Check the prints, you'll see I'm right."

"Anything to put your little mind at rest," said Roland, still laughing. "Now, take some hot cocoa and go to bed."

To his shame and annoyance, it took Karp the better part of an hour for the answer to flutter into his mind. But when he called Roland back, the man had already left for home.

For Roland, this was the first two floors of a brownstone on East Seventy-fifth Street off Madison. It was quite dark when he arrived there some time after eight, and he was annoyed to see that the light over the doorway had gone out. He bid good night to Bert Hillyer, his police driver, and walked to the door. Hillyer did not drive away immediately, but wasted some time with a radio call he did not need to make, because he had been told by acting Captain Clay Fulton to make sure that his passenger was tucked in for the night, or at least arrived safely in the marble lobby of his building.

Roland occasionally discovered women waiting for him at his door; he tried to discourage the practice. He often came home with a woman, and he did not care for scenes played out on the street between two of them. This one was standing at the top of the short flight of steps, leaning against his door. She wore tight jeans and high-heeled boots and a dark sweater, with a dark raincoat over it. A large leather bag depended from her shoulder. Her raincoat hung open, and he could see the points of her breasts in the dim light from the street lamp. A blonde, or was that a wig? Roland did not care for wigs either. He came closer, his keys in his hand, and looked at her face. Nice cheekbones, dark skin, big eyes. She was heavily made up. Roland tried to place her and drew a blank—no, there *was* something familiar about her face.

"Can I help you?" he said stiffly, placing his key into the lock of the heavy wrought-iron and glass door.

"Yes," she said. "You can take me to where the Obregons are."

Roland looked at her, startled. His recent conversation with Karp came back to him at the same time as he recalled where he had seen that face, a pretty good sketch of which was in every precinct house and police car in the city. A thrill of fear started in his belly and he shouted, "Hillyer!"

Something shiny came out of the bag. Roland spun and started to run down the steps. He saw the door of Hillyer's car open, and then there was a flash from behind bright enough to cast his own shadow before him, and he felt a blow strike his back and heard a sharp, loud pop, not that much louder than the sound of a pulled champagne cork. He was no longer running, he found, but stretched out facedown on the pavement. There were several more pops and flashes, and the sound of rapid footsteps receding. He heard distant sirens before he fainted.

SEVENTEEN

Dressed in gray coveralls, his Arabic finery neatly folded into a plastic bag, Chouza Khalid watched the bomb come up out of its fiberglass casing. Big Mahmoud was pulling on the chain hoist, what the Americans delightfully called a come-along. The squat, rounded cylinder contained two hundred and fifty kilograms, over five hundred fifty pounds, of RDX high explosive. Although in its present unarmed state this was about as dangerous as so much sawdust, he was being extremely careful.

The thing cleared its former coffin and came down on a wheeled dolly. The transport plug was still in its nose. The detonator was still in its cardboard tube, which had been shipped in a separate crate. Mahmoud got busy with wrenches, removing the fins from the carcass of the bomb. Khalid was no stranger to explosives, and had set a bomb or two in his time, but he did not care for them, abhorring in his marrow the idea that a lump of what looked like clay could instantly convert itself into an inferno and make a person (perhaps even oneself!) utterly vanish from the earth.

He walked out into the main bay of the warehouse, passing the elevator shaft into which he had encrypted Bashar, and the place where he had dumped used oil and sawdust over the bloodstains, checking to see if anything showed (nothing did) and experiencing real satisfaction about how that business had all worked out.

Near that place, Rifaat was filling five-gallon plastic cans with diesel fuel from a fifty-five-gallon drum fitted with a hand pump. Out on the dock and a safe distance from the fuel, Abdel was busy with a cutting torch and a rusty sheet of one-inch steel plate. Khalid thought that the fuel and the steel plates represented overkill, given the power of the bomb they had, but Ibn-Salemeh was quite precise in the way he wanted things done.

And thinking now of Ibn-Salemeh, Khalid returned again to what the man had said the other night. Crown Heights. No one knew that Khalid had a house in Crown Heights. He had kept that place secret from everyone, especially from his employer. Perhaps it was just a way of speaking, mentioning neighborhoods—he could have said Park Slope or Cobble Hill. Or maybe not. Was he letting Khalid know in his typically elliptical way that he knew about the house? If he knew about that, what else did he know? Khalid felt a warm flush break out on his forehead and on the backs of his hands. If Ibn-Salemeh knew, then perhaps Bashar also knew. He looked down at the oil smear on the floor and recalled what had lain there. If Bashar knew, then the Mexican knew too. He looked at his watch, suddenly close to panic.

"Abdel," he said, "I must go on an errand. We have three hours until the boy arrives, and I'll be back before then. Hussein!"

The other man looked up from the white Cadillac, which he had been cleaning.

"I need the car for a while. Give me your cap and jacket."

"It's not your fault, Butch, stop it!" said Marlene for about the sixth time.

They were in a crowded waiting room off the surgical ward of Bellevue Hospital. Karp was slumped in a pink plastic chair not nearly big enough for him, emitting at short intervals sighs, groans, and muffled curses. The place was full of cops, in uniform and plain clothes, dropping by to check on Roland and on Hillyer. Roland had taken a nine through the small of his back; the kidney was involved. Hillyer had been shot twice through the chest and was in worse shape. Both were still in surgery. Their assailant had vanished as usual.

Karp glowered at her and stifled a curse. Of course it was his fault. He should have realized instantly that the only reason for the unknown Mexican shooter to show at Khalid's garage was that the Obregons had told him to. They had their money, and now they were using Khalid to dispose of an embarrassing and now unnecessary shooter. Khalid would be delighted to oblige in getting rid of someone who had caused so much trouble. As for the shooter, once he had escaped from the trap, it would be obvious to him what had gone down, and his first thought would have been to get the Obregons. And who knew where the Obregons were? Not in jail—that would be easy for him to check. No, they were being held as material witnesses, and naturally the prosecutor in charge of the case, whose face and name had been plastered over television for weeks, would know this location.

"I should have seen it," he muttered to himself.

"What?"

"Nothing," said Karp and studied the print of a sailboat hanging opposite, a form of art clearly aimed at keeping the mind away from thoughts of loved ones in surgery.

"Hi, Clay," said Marlene. Karp tore his eyes away from the sprightly sloop. Fulton was leaning against the door of the waiting room, looking gray and grim. They both looked at him expectantly, as if he were the surgeon. He shook his head.

"They're still in there, is what I heard." He sat on one of the pink seats, sighing.

"I have to go," said Marlene, glad that there was someone else to wait with Karp, and to his questioning look, she replied, "Church. It's Good Friday. I'm going with Lucy."

"That's probably a good place to be," Karp said. "Pray, huh?"

Marlene nodded, hugged both men, and left.

"Hell of a note," said Fulton after a silence. "Another cop, a prosecutor."

"Why can't we seem to nail this guy?" asked Karp.

"Why? It's a big town. It's only been a couple of days. We didn't even figure him for a Mexican until this morning. We'll get him. He's got no place to run and no place to hide."

"Who *is* he? Do we have any idea?"

"Well, the Obregons aren't talking, and we don't have any real leverage on them until we have this asshole in custody. By the way, we found the Erbes girl. In Santo Domingo, the D.R. The Feds have a team there trying to get her out, but she's fighting it. She does not want to see this Mexican or the Obregons ever again. So that could be a blank too on the big questions. Did they import a killer? Who is he? Why should they tell us?"

Why indeed? After a while Karp said, musingly, "You get used to there being rules, you know? I talked with Jack about this the other day. You don't shoot cops unless you're totally hyped up or into some wacky politics. You *never* shoot judges or prosecutors."

"Not never . . . you took a bullet a couple years back, I recall."

"Right, the exception that proves the rule. The guys who shot me were Cuban gangsters. This guy is a Mexican gangster. And the Arabs, the terrorists—it's a different culture, where the cops and the judges are just part of a different gang. The idea that there's a system, a rule that's somewhere up above street life, the scrabbling and fighting, just isn't there. It's just naked power, no limits . . ."

"Yeah, and you know, Stretch, a lot of the folks uptown think that's what we got already," said Fulton lightly, and then regretted it, for Karp rounded on him vehemently.

"And they're fucking *wrong!* You know they're wrong, Clay. Your whole life says that. There *is* a difference. Are there bad cops? Sure. Does the system creak and moan? It does. But there's *still* a difference, and the *guapos* and the hustlers know it; they fucking *depend* on it, which is why a couple of cops can go into a dope market and pull guys out and arrest them and nobody'll say boo, guys with guns, guys with knives. Anyplace in the city they can do it—there's no casbah in New York, there's no place where a cop can't walk, because the cops don't shoot kids when storekeepers pay them to like they do in Brazil, and they don't moonlight as death squads for the government like they do down in Central America. Okay, it's thin. God, if *anybody* knows how thin it is, it's me, but it's still there. But these new guys—it's not there to them at all. They're importing Mexican rules, Lebanon rules, into New York. And we're starting to respond in the same way—like another gang—and all the local shitheels who think that's just fine are coming out of the closet, they love it." He paused, suddenly aware that the other people in the waiting room were staring at him, apparently distracted from the soaps playing on the TV that hung from the ceiling.

"I want it to stop," he finished lamely, feeling ever more a jerk.

Fulton, however, was smiling at him benignly. "That was a pretty good one, Stretch. You need to save that for the closing when we get these bastards. Speaking of which, I think we caught us a little break last night."

"Ah, good news for a change!"

"It could be," said Fulton more cautiously. "Say what you want about the FBI, when they tackle something they're thorough. The phone in Khalid's office was used to make a dozen or so calls to a number in London. They asked the Brits to check it out. An empty office, no surprise there, but the Feds also asked for a phone record from *that* phone and it came in on Telex late last night. A couple of calls made to Abu Dhabi down there on the Persian Gulf, some big sheik, Rashid something or other. Meanwhile, they're running all the phone records against visas—did anybody these bastards called enter or leave the U.S. recently? And it turns out this Sheik Rashid's private jet landed at Kennedy the other day, seven passengers, the big kahuna and six buddies checked through INS."

"And . . . ?"

"And the Feds raid the airplane, and what do they find? Seven guys eating sandwiches and watching TV. The INS swears there were only seven people on that plane, and seven people in Arab costumes were seen leaving the airport in a stretch limo. What do you think of that?"

"It sounds like they're bringing in reinforcements. Do you have the seven guys yet?"

"No," replied Fulton with some heat, "but if the NYPD can't find seven guys in head rags and bed sheets, we'd better hang it the fuck up."

El Chivato had no objection to wearing women's clothing and had often done so in making an approach for an assassination. In Mexico he had known tough and experienced bodyguards to continue making lewd remarks and sucking noises right up to the moment he killed them. When he was a boy, his older sisters had delighted to dress him in girl's clothes and do his face and his hair. He did not mind this either, although he had shot several men who had suggested that he looked like a girl. Consistency in these matters was not something that much troubled El Chivato.

In the Midtown parking garage where he had spent Thursday night, he strolled back and forth as if coming from a car, smiling brightly at all he met until, after the morning rush was over, he spotted a slim blond woman locking a gold Nissan Maxima. He smiled at her too, and she smiled back, and when she had just gone past him, he whirled and cracked her over the head with his pistol. She fell and he hit her again.

It took less than three minutes to stuff her in the Nissan's trunk and get under way, with her purse and ID on the front seat and her big sunglasses on his face. He drove to Brooklyn at a sedate pace, to Park Slope, but when he passed Seventh Avenue and Ninth Street, he saw that the street ahead was filled with police vehicles and a cop was stationed at the corner to divert traffic. He allowed himself to be diverted.

As he drove to the other address he had tortured out of Bashar, he reflected on how foolish he had been to approach the prosecutor. If the Obregons went to jail again, that was no problem, for no place was easier to get into than a jail. He would come back at a later date, when the police no longer sought him quite as avidly. If the Obregons were released, they would eventually return to Mexico, and that was no problem either, as he could certainly find and kill anyone in Mexico. Naturally, if he had a good, easy chance he would do them, but it was something he could leave for later. No, it was this maddening pressure of time that had thrown off his instincts, that and the fever. His wound was not healing; the whole side of his body was now red and swollen, and it hurt, although he tried to push back the pain and the hot fog that clouded his vision and his judgment by eating Percodan and aspirin like gumdrops. He shook four more tablets, two of each, into his hand and swallowed them dry.

There was the house. El Chivato found a parking space opposite and watched it for a while. His forehead broke out in a sweat, and he was glad he had sunglasses. The day was overcast but bright, and the light bothered his eyes.

He left the car and went through the overgrown front yard and around the back of the house. The back door had grilles and a new lock on it, but underneath it was the old-fashioned glass-windowed kind, dating from the days when this had been a civilized street and the resident housewife might have looked through that window, pushing back a thin white curtain to smile at the delivery boy. El Chivato went back to the car, opened the trunk, wrestled a tire tool out from under the woman's flaccid body, and went back to the house, where he used the tire tool to pry up the grille. He broke a pane and let himself in.

The backdoor led via a short hallway to the kitchen, which was clean and in reasonable repair. Not so the rest of the house. The first floor was a ruin of fallen plaster, hanging wiring, and cracked wood, dimly lit by sunlight entering through gaps in the plywood covering the windows. It had clearly been used at some time in the past as a haunt of junkies. El Chivato wrinkled his nose and climbed to the second floor. There one bedroom and its adjoining bath had been renovated to a degree. They were clean at least and supplied with electricity and water. There were sheets and blankets on a simple cot that made up the bedroom's sole furniture. A cardboard carton held folded clothes—jeans and shirts, socks and underwear. On the sink in the bathroom he found toothpaste, a toothbrush (quite dry), and a bottle of aspirin. El Chivato took the bottle and descended the stairs, past the first floor, and through a door he found behind the main staircase.

A hanging lamp cord brushed his face. He yanked it and walked down the narrow, worn steps. A large, empty room, floored with concrete. Dim light entered through narrow, filthy windows near the ceiling. A door from this led to a smaller room with an oil furnace in it, a square brown box that stood next to the cylindrical gray coal-burning unit it had replaced. He pulled another hanging string and turned on the overhead bulb.

As he did so, he heard a faint noise coming from behind a new, steel-framed wooden door built into the brick wall next to the coal furnace. It was locked from the outside by a turn bolt. El Chivato flattened himself against the wall, turned the bolt, and flung back the door. Nothing. He peeked around the frame, pistol pointing, and saw a young girl crouched on a mattress. At first he thought she was a black girl, but closer inspection showed that she was merely filthy with coal dust. He asked her who she was, and she told him her story, how the man she had heard called Chouza had kidnapped her on behalf of her family, who wanted her dead because she was a whore, although she wasn't really. As the girl prattled on, El Chivato considered whether it would harm his enemy worse to kill the girl or let her go, and decided that it was the latter. He asked her when Chouza would return, to which she replied that she didn't know, but that she had not been fed that day, and so she expected him at any time. He always comes down here? Yes. He made a decision.

"Go," he said, "but before you leave, lock me in here."

"Why?" Fatyma was mildly surprised at being rescued by a transvestite. She had known several on the Deuce, and most of them had been eccentric in one way or another. Wanting to be locked into a coal cellar was, however, a new one.

"Just do it," he said, and gave her a look that made her swallow hard. He sat down on the cleanest part of the mattress and leaned against the brick. Fatyma shut the door and turned the bolt.

After that she went immediately to the coal furnace, knelt, rummaged in the ash grate, and pulled out a plastic-wrapped package the size of two bricks. Peeling back a corner of the plastic, she saw that it was composed of currency—twenties, fifties, and hundred-dollar bills. She ran upstairs to the kitchen and washed her face and her hands at the sink, and found a grocery bag into which she placed the package. She found a steak knife in a drawer and put that in the bag too. Then she went searching for clothes, because she was not about to walk through the streets in a T-shirt and panties. In the upstairs bedroom she found a pair of jeans, which when hoisted to breast height and tied with a strip of cloth torn from the bed sheet, and hacked off for length, would serve as a covering. She found some rubber zoris in the bathroom, slipped them on, put the money in a shopping bag she had found, and slipped out of the house. A few streets away, on Atlantic Avenue, she found a large, cheap variety store, where she bought herself several outfits, a straw handbag, some sneakers, big sunglasses, a large and unlikely platinum-blond wig, and a cloth suitcase to hold what she wasn't wearing. Then she hailed a cab and told the driver to take her to the airport.

Khalid entered his house by the front door and went immediately to the kitchen to prepare a meal for his prisoner. He began to fill a pot at the sink. When he saw the soot stains, he let out a cry of dismay and dropped the pot. It made a sound like a gong. He checked the back door, saw the broken glass, ran down the cellar stairs, knelt by the furnace door, his pulse thrumming in his ears. He reached deeply into the ash grate and let out another cry and a string of curses. One of his packages was gone. And the other one, all the way in the back . . . ? He grasped it with sweating hands and drew it out, holding it to his breast like an infant.

He stayed there a moment, willing his stricken brain to unfreeze. Someone had broken in and taken half his money and released the girl. Ibn-Salemeh or the Mexican? Certainly, the Mexican. Ibn-Salemeh had been playing sheik since the last time Khalid visited the girl, and if any of the others had explored the furnace, they would have taken all the money—and told Ibn-Salemeh that Khalid had been skimming money and Khalid would now be floating in the harbor. So where was the Mexican now? With the girl? Or . . .

At that moment Khalid noticed that the door to the coal cellar was closed. And locked. Why would the girl lock it behind her? He drew his pistol from his waistband and fired a half dozen shots through the wooden door. Then he turned and ran, as the door panel flew into splinters from the sleet of automatic fire that came from inside the coal cellar.

"I must go now," said Walid importantly, looking at his watch. He was tired and irritable, having been up all night repairing the damage that the dirty Jews had done to their bakery and baking too. His father had burned his hands extinguishing the fire in the shop, preventing the flames from reaching the kitchen. Although Hassan could not bake at present, there was nothing wrong with his mouth, and he found plenty of fault with Walid's technique. Toward dawn, having, of course, overexerted himself, he began to have trouble breathing, and was now under observation in Bellevue, which was why Walid was free with the truck on a Friday afternoon.

"Can I come with you?" asked Posie. They were lying on a bed of cardboard cartons in the back of the bread van. Posie felt pretty good, even though Walid didn't know shit about women; it had been necessary to show him where everything was and what it was for. She still hadn't let him do it yet—Marlene had reiterated her orders about that the other night—but she figured a quick blowjob wasn't really *doing* it, and the poor dude was popping out of his pants. It went like a trick a biker she once knew could do, cracking the top off a beer bottle with his teeth, and the foam gushing out, that fast. And it was nice to be with a guy who was *grateful* instead of like you were lighting their cigarette or something. She had her dress unbuttoned all the way down the front and her breasts out of her bra. His head was resting on these now. Another neat thing about Walid, he didn't get up right away after he shot his rocks, like some guys, like you were a Kleenex they'd just used.

"No, because it is a secret," said Walid. "I am not allowed to talk of it."

"Oh, come on, man! You could tell *me*. Who am I gonna tell?"

Walid sighed and nuzzled deeper into those unbelievably soft pillows. It was moving too fast for him. His life had not prepared him for these events: first nineteen years in which all he had to do was obey older people, first his uncles in Palestine, then his father, then Ali and the others, which hadn't worked out too well, he had to admit, and then his sister disappearing, kidnapped by the Zionists, and Chouza and his mission, which was something he might have imagined, at least, politics, the struggle, and now this girl, a gift, it seemed from heaven, well, not heaven perhaps, but not, in any case, something he was going to take any chance on losing.

"It is a secret," he repeated. "They are going to put special equipment in my truck. For operations."

"What do you mean, operations?" Posie knew that this was the kind of stuff Marlene wanted to know, although he hadn't mentioned his sister at all, which was supposed to be the point.

"Secret operations." He suddenly felt the urge to move and turned his head away from her and rose. "You must get dressed now and go," he said. But she rose too and followed him and put her arms around him from behind.

"Aw, Wally, couldn't I just come along a little way? I could get out when you do the secret stuff. Please?"

"Where is Hussein?" asked Ibn-Salemeh, frowning. He did not like it when plans were changed.

"He is helping Abdel with the steel. It was a bigger job than we thought."

Ibn-Salemeh grunted and swept out of the hotel room, followed by Little Mahmoud, both of them in robes. Khalid was wearing a chauffeur's black coat and cap, with a clip-on leather bow tie. He felt only slightly less foolish than he had in the robes.

It had not, in fact, taken the NYPD long to find out where a bunch of rich Arabs were staying, just, as it turned out, twenty minutes too long, which was about the interval between the white Caddie pulling away from the curb, and the arrival, at the same curb, of Detectives Raney and White. They showed their warrant and went upstairs with the assistant manager. Behind the desk, a young man, late of Amman, Kingdom of Jordan, waited until the elevator door closed and made a phone call to a number he had been given.

Holidays are time machines, was Marlene's thought as she knelt in Old St. Pat's and listened to the familiar Good Friday service: this is the Wood of the Cross on which was hung the Savior of the World, said the priest, and she responded with all the others, come, let us worship. It was all in English now, not Latin, and she had

Lucy there next to her, solemn and still, but it did take you back, she thought, to all the churches she'd been in, back to St. Joseph's in Ozone Park, Queens. She looked sideways at the small dark head beside her, saw the entranced expression, and felt a pang of envy, and a greater one of regret. Apprehension too: she recalled vividly what it had felt like, the Real Presence, as they say, at nine, ten, and eleven, and afterward the fading, the loss, so gradual and subtle that you didn't even know it was gone, and one day it was just words, and you had it not. Sex and modern rationalism: a hard combo for anything to go up against, and in her case it had been no contest, and yet here she was still going, still kneeling, still offering her child to the Church, and all of her liberal friends thinking she was dotty on the subject. As she was, although none of her liberal friends went armed all the time and shot people on a fairly regular basis, and tortured people, and sent their gormless nursemaids out to seduce terrorists, and so they were perhaps not entitled to an opinion about why Marlene chose to open herself, on Sundays and holidays, to the possibility of infinite mercy.

The priest was consuming the Host, facing the stripped altar ("Lord, I am not worthy to receive you"), and in fact Marlene did not feel worthy and declined. Lucy shot her a worried look, but moved out of the row toward the communion rail, her back stiff and pointing straight up to Heaven.

The service over, the congregation having filed silently out in the traditional way, they went to their car. On the drive home, Marlene noticed that Lucy was as still as one of the plaster saints in the place they had just left.

"Are you okay, Luce?"

"Sure. Why?"

"You're not moving. I thought you might be sick or something."

"No, Tran is teaching me how to be still. He says it'll improve my concentration, and also make me ready for, you know . . . like, an attack."

"Uh-huh. Is it working?"

"I think so. I do conjugations and vocabulary in my head. I think my memory is improving. And I'm more relaxed. I don't get so pissed—I mean, annoyed at things. The twins, school stuff. I still get a kind of annoyance when they mention the Jews in church. I think about Dad."

"Well, that was a long time ago," said Marlene carefully. "I think they've dropped the business about the guilt of modern Jews."

"I know that. Sister Teresa explained that part in Sunday school. But it's still in the words. They didn't change the Gospels. And like the news and stuff? The Arab terrorists and those black guys. Do you think they'll ever like *genocide* Jews again, like in the old days?"

"No, and in any case, it's unlikely they'd start in New York. Does it worry you?"

"No, not really," said Lucy. "We have guns. Do you think when Tran dies, he'll be a holy soul in purgatory?"

Marlene had to clear her throat. "Well, you know that's hard to say, Lucy. It's not something I'm comfortable speculating on." What a mealy-mouthed answer, thought Marlene. The kid's looking for spiritual guidance, and here I am . . .

"At least he'll have me to pray for him," said Lucy. "I'm probably the only one in the whole world he'll have praying. Do you ever think about that? What it's *really* like after you die?"

"As little as I can. When I do, it's me being carried up to Heaven by angels blowing trumpets." Meant as a light remark, but Lucy responded straight-faced.

"You know, Mom," she said, "honestly, the way you're going . . . I wouldn't count on it."

The radio detonator was manufactured in Czechoslovakia and was an excellent and reliable design. Ibn-Salemeh sat at a table made of pallets and plywood in his warehouse and tested its circuits with a Radio Shack galvanometer, one of the few articles of equipment he had purchased in New York. That too was part of the plan—everything had been shipped in through America's porous borders—no suspicious purchases of ingredients, no risky thefts to accomplish. What they needed was in the crates. He picked up the code transmitter and gave it to Khalid, who walked away with it to the end of the warehouse. At Ibn-Salemeh's shouted directions, he pushed buttons and Ibn-Salemeh noted with satisfaction that the detonator armed itself and sent the correct signal to the circuit that actually fired the detonating charge. He called Khalid back.

"Does it work?" Khalid asked.

"Perfectly. Are they almost ready?"

Khalid went to check. The Daoud bakery van had been backed up to the lip of the loading dock. The steel shelves that had lined both sides of the van had been removed, and the men had just finished bolting the last of the thick steel plates into place. The five-gallon cans, twenty of them, were filled and lined up on the dock. Khalid squatted down and looked inside the van. The driver's side, the floor, and the overhead had been reinforced with the plate steel. The passenger side remained the original thin sheet-metal. Khalid understood the principle. When a bomb explodes, a relatively small volume of solid turns almost instantly into a very, very large quantity of hot gas. The key word is *almost*. Left to themselves, explosives explode spherically, exerting equal pressure in all directions, but if early in the explosion the nascent event is directed, shown that there is less resistance to expansion in one direction than in another, then the explosion can be directed, shaped even, like an ephemeral sculpture. This was the point of the steel plates. When the 250-kilogram bomb detonated, it would first vaporize the plastic fuel cans and ignite the diesel fuel. The fetal inferno would probe its womb, seeking a way out. In the first few milliseconds of its existence, it would discover the weak passenger-side wall, and that is where the main force of the explosion would go. A great fiery bubble would erupt from the side of the van. Traveling at thousands of feet per second, it would knock down, pulverize, and roast anything in its path.

Walid was confined to the warehouse office while they worked on his truck. He looked at his watch every five minutes, and wondered if Posie would be waiting at the arranged place when they let him go. Previously, when alone and with nothing to do, he had thought about self-sacrifice, and about honor, which involved slaughtering his sister; and he had also thought, in a vague, incoherent way, about sex. Now he thought more concretely, about breasts, and about the slippery feel and scent of the woman's genitals, and about how she squirmed and cried out when, after much instruction, he was able to manipulate them in a satisfactory way. Dying for the cause had become less attractive to him.

They finished bolting in the plates and returned the shelf units to the interior of the van. They rolled the bomb out on its dolly. Ibn-Salemeh screwed the radio fuse into the detonator and placed it into the fuse socket in the nose of the bomb. He supervised the movement of the bomb—three men working slowly and in complete concentration—from the dolly to its place on the lowest shelf on the driver's side. It was secured to the shelf with strapping. A

290 / *Robert K. Tanenbaum*

plywood box, painted black, was fitted over it. Then the jerry cans of fuel were arranged around it, taking up the rest of the lower shelf and most of the one above it.

"Fine. Get the boy," said Ibn-Salemeh.

Walid came out, blinking. He was told to get into the truck. Khalid spoke to him through the window.

"Here are your orders: you must first of all behave normally. Go directly home. Go to the mosque. Bake your bread. Tomorrow morning and Sunday you will travel the route you have been traveling these past weeks, exactly. Exactly! Do you understand?"

"Yes. What have you done to the truck?" He shrank from the other man's glare. "If someone asks."

"We have installed communications equipment," said Khalid. "Very advanced, so the Zionists will not be able to spy on us. This is also the explanation of the steel plates. It is shielding, you understand?"

"Yes. What is that smell?"

"Diesel oil. It is for a secret generator we have. You will be informed where to take it through the communications device."

"Really? But I have no earphones."

"There is a loudspeaker. Believe me, Walid, you will have no trouble hearing it."

"Roland's back with us," said the D.A. when Karp came into his office. "The hospital just called. Hillyer's in intensive care; they doubt he'll make it. My God! I've lost count. What is that, eight cops? Why can't they catch this guy?"

Karp sat down in a side chair, massaged his brow, and said, "I asked Fulton that very question just now. It's not so crazy when you think about it. How do we catch any criminal once we have his face? The cops hit the usual hangouts, ask around. Snitches love dropping one on a cop killer. Yeah, that looks like Ernie. He hangs at the White Rose on Third. Guys have girlfriends, pals, relatives. This guy's from out of town. He's got no known connection in the City except the Erbes woman and the Obregons. The woman, we now find, ran to the Dominican Republic last week. The Obregons we have. He doesn't hang out. He changes his appearance. Hillyer said, just before he went out, that the guy showed at Roland's as a woman."

"Wonderful! And on the Arab front?"

"Some progress. They located the house in Park Slope the Arabs were using and raided it. Not much in it, and what there was led to stuff we already knew about. Packing material from the basement seems to match the stuff found in the Daoud van, but we knew that too. These guys are good, boss."

"Yeah, and I'm tired of hearing that. What about the airplane business, that sheik?"

"Same thing—the cops arrive at the Carlyle, where they were staying, and just missed them. They're at large in a white stretch limo, if you can believe it. The cops are stopping everything that even looks like a white Caddie limo. The beautiful people could be in for some lumps. Expect irate calls."

"I'll brace myself. Any other good news?"

"No. Beatings and scuffles all over town, mini-riots. The cops canceled leaves this afternoon, indefinitely, until these guys are in the can. Easter weekend. So we got fifteen thousand armed men wandering around the city, all of them with attitudes. To add to the civic peace, Rabbi Lowenstein has announced a rally and a march down Bedford Avenue on Sunday."

"I heard. The cops refused a permit."

"Right, but he claims he's going ahead with it anyway, according to my many contacts in the Jewish community."

"I thought he died," said the D.A.

"Thank you," said Karp sourly. "You forget, my brother is a fanatic too. I got one of my infrequent calls from him this afternoon, asking me to use my influence to get the permit issued. When I told him I thought it was a shitty idea, he vouchsafed to me, in so many words, that the rabbi didn't need no stinkin' permit."

"Christ!"

"Yeah, that too, Easter Sunday. I realize the big churches have toned down the anti-Semitic aspects, but there's a lot of little churches in town that haven't got the message. Then you've got a huge black community, maybe a fifth of them either Nation of Islam members or sympathizers. There's a Muslim leader in Bed-Stuy who's saying that if the Jews do a march, he's going to take his people out on the streets too. Okay, that's Brooklyn, but if Brooklyn goes up, we won't be far behind. The other thing is, we got a lot of itchy, scared cops looking for a thin Hispanic guy armed with a machine gun and grenades. There are at least fifty thousand people in the city who fit that general description, not counting girls, who he might be too. Okay, let's say a cop spots somebody he thinks might be our guy. What's he going to do? Excuse me, sir, or ma'am, could I see some identification? No, he is not. He's going to pull his piece and scream, 'Freeze, motherfucker!' This is going to cause tensions in the Hispanic community. The wrong people are going to get shot. It won't do, Jack."

"What's the alternative?" asked Keegan.

"We have to draw him to a place *we* choose, where there won't be any confusion, and where there's a reduced chance of bullets taking out innocent people. And we already know what'll draw him."

"Meaning . . . ?"

Karp took a breath. He had been thinking about this since the meeting at the FBI, and discussed it with Fulton, who said, when heavily pressed, that it was feasible, and now he laid it in front of Keegan, briefly, ignoring the growing frown on his boss's face.

"Absolutely not," said Keegan forcefully.

"I'll take that as a provisional yes," said Karp.

"We are not going back to the hotel," said Ibn-Salemeh.

The six other men looked at him in surprise.

"Why not?" Khalid asked.

"Because the desk man called on the car phone with the arranged signal. The police were there. They knew we were there."

A silence, then a chorus of confused expostulations. It was Khalid who first divined the implications. "Then they have the plane too," he exclaimed. "What has happened?" Khalid's tone was not what it usually was when he addressed Ibn-Salemeh. The others noticed this. Each man made a small nervous gesture or cast a glance, and a rippling movement passed through the little group, as if an animal were moving through high grass. Ibn-Salemeh did not seem to notice this.

"Obviously, they found it and discovered that the people who left the airport were not those who arrived from overseas. It does not matter."

"How does it not matter?" Khalid cried. "That plane was our escape. How are we going to get out of the city after the bomb explodes on Sunday?"

"The bomb will explode tomorrow," said Ibn-Salemeh abruptly. "On Saturday."

Another stunner. All their planning had been based on a Sunday target.

"The longer we stay in the city, the more risk we endure. We will stay here tonight. It is not as comfortable as in the hotel, but adequate. Tomorrow we will take the gray van, which is a perfectly clean vehicle that no one is looking for, drive to the target, wait for the bread truck, detonate the bomb, and drive slowly away. We will cross the river and drive to Detroit, where we have friends. We can then easily cross the border and fly out of Canada on Canadian passports." He paused to see what effect this was having. Nods. "Which I took care to provide for all of us in case something went wrong with our first plan. You should know that there is always a backup." Smiles now; the crisis was over. The remarkable Ibn-Salemeh had again outsmarted his enemies.

"Throw some tarpaulins and trash over that Cadillac," he ordered. "We don't want anyone seeing it from the street. Rifaat! Take the van and get us something to eat. Oh, and buy one of those portable television sets. We must continue to keep informed. What is it, Hussein?"

Hussein was looking confused. "Effendi, the Cadillac—does this mean we will not be returning it for the deposit?"

Ibn-Salemeh stared at him in amazement. Then he burst into uproarious laughter and clapped the man hard on the back, and after a moment the others joined in. Even Khalid.

EIGHTEEN

Marlene dropped Lucy off at the EVWS, where the twins were being made much of by the residents and staff, had a few words with the crippled, but by-God-back-on-the-job Mattie Duran, got laughed at by same because of the Hadassah operation, made some calls out of Mattie's office, and had a few words with Tran about the weekend's chores. (Easter was not normally a domestic-violence accelerator on the scale of Christmas or Thanksgiving, but families did get together then, and for some families this was not wise. Daddy might bring a fluffy ducky for the kiddies just to show he was still a good dad, and a couple of quarts of malt liquor for himself, and at the end of the afternoon the ducky might well be the only thing walking.) This accomplished, she drove up to Fifty-eighth and Fifth.

She found a growing mess. The organization had invited over two hundred of its hardworking youth leaders from around the country to come to New York, enjoy themselves, and hear uplifting speeches. Four charter buses had been engaged to ferry these people around the city, and bring them by headquarters for various events, one each day of the weekend. They had not, however, arranged with the police to suspend parking on Fifty-eighth Street, so that the buses had to disgorge while double-parked, thus completely blocking the traffic on Fifty-eighth Street, both of which are violations of the NYC traffic code, which fact was being pointed out to the bus drivers and the youth leaders by a cop (summons book in hand) when Marlene walked up, she having cleverly parked in a garage on Sixth.

Marlene dived in, spread charm, explained that in fact Osborne had arranged for the parking restriction, but the current emergency had prevented the police from tagging the block, and in general resolved the dispute to the satisfaction of everyone except the youth leader, a chubby person from Minneapolis, who did not like the idea that the buses would have to disgorge some unknown distance away, requiring several hundred out-of-towners to run the deadly gauntlet of a New York thoroughfare. Keeping her temper and a straight face with some difficulty, Marlene promised to provide security for these expeditionaries. The group dispersed; the buses stenched off to their barn.

The headquarters of the Women's Zionist Organization of America is a six-story brown brick building with peculiar bricked-in arches on its front that give it the air of a converted fire station. At the security desk inside the tiled lobby, Marlene spoke with the head of the square-badge detail, a large, overweight ex-cop named Bogle, who did not conceal his reluctance to take Marlene or her authority seriously. Once again she kept her temper in check and brought the man sullenly through his security arrangements. They toured the building and its entrances, checked the fixed and mobile posts and the communications arrangements (Marlene asked for and was given, not without complaint, a radio tuned to this net). Leaving instructions to call if anything unusual happened, which she knew would be ignored for anything under a major asteroid impact, she sought out Amy Weinstein, got a rushed minute, flashed the face, scattered assurances, and made her exit. She was somewhat surprised that she had not lost her temper, or quit this wretched job, for which she gave credit to St. Ignatius of Loyola, whose spiritual exercises—undertaken by order of Father Dugan—she had put to good use in guarding against the sin of Wrath. The saint advised his followers to focus during the first week on some particularly troublesome sin and, when finding oneself falling into it during the day, to touch one's breast in a particular way, to express sorrow. Marlene noted that the lapel of her raincoat already had a little dark spot where her thumb had ground against it. It was vastly harder than she had thought it would be, this continuous, rigorous inspection of conscience and motive, and she was astounded to learn that the absence of faith (as she thought) did not diminish in the least the power of the technique, which in the past had enabled Jesuits to smile as Hurons yanked out their fingernails.

When she arrived home with her brood, Posie was waiting. She swept the twins up in her arms and talked the most nauseating babytalk to them, which they ate up, and then there was supper to prepare and the boys to feed and get settled, so it was some time before Marlene could get her alone for a debriefing.

"I think I'm in love," Posie said. "He's *so* great!"

"Ah, well, that's terrific, Posie, but what about his sister?"

"Oh, he doesn't know anything about that," said Posie dismissively. "He thinks his friends got hold of her, though. The other Arabs." She grinned again, clearly besotted. "Marlene, he's so great—he, like, *talks* to me, and reads me poetry, except it's in Arab and I can't understand it, but it sounds great anyway, and God, he knows all kinds of stuff, about, you know, politics and how the Jews are doing bad stuff to them, the Arabs, and all."

"Oh?" With a frozen smile.

"Yeah, I didn't know *any* of this stuff—like the Jews are trying to take over the whole world and make everybody slaves?"

Marlene ground her thumb into her breastbone, and did not roll her eyes. "Posie, um, I don't think you should believe everything Walid tells you about that."

"No, but Marlene, it's *true*! He showed me, it was in a *book*. I mean, like, they *printed* it." She wrinkled her brow in unaccustomed thought. "I forget the name of it, though—something, something Zion . . ."

"The Protocols of the Elders of Zion?"

Posie's face lit up. "Yeah! Did you read it too?"

Marlene placed her hand on Posie's and said, as gently as she could, "Posie, no, I haven't because that book is a forgery. It's fake. Everybody knows that. Some Russians made it up a long time ago. It was one of the things the Nazis used."

Blankness, the smile fading.

"You know who the Nazis were, don't you?" Marlene asked carefully.

"Like skinheads?"

Marlene suppressed a sigh. She didn't have time for this. She already had three actual children to raise without having to be responsible for this one, and so she said, rather more sharply than she had intended, "Right. Meanwhile, besides being God's gift to women, Walid is something of a maniac on the subject of his sister, and if he gets to her, he's going to kill her, which is going to put a major crimp in your romance. So—you said his friends have her. Does he know where his friends are?"

Posie's face had now taken on the one other major expression in her repertoire besides beaming delight, which was mulish stubbornness. Marlene had observed this many times in the past, when Posie was attempting to protect men who habitually beat her senseless. There was probably no limit to how far she would go to protect someone who treated her well, and read her poetry and Nazi propaganda.

"No," she said. "He doesn't talk about that. Honestly, Marlene, I'd tell you if I knew where she was. I'm, like, I don't want her to *die*."

With that Marlene had to be content, for the present, although she was oppressed by the feeling that this was not one of her more brilliant plans.

Posie went off to tend her charges, while Marlene went to her office and looked at the city street map Tran had left on her desk. She examined it idly and folded it to the section that showed Hadassah headquarters. It was a large-scale map with public parking clearly marked. The buses would have a choice of places to park. She was wondering whether she should annoy Bogle with this, and make sure he coordinated with the bus company, when Lucy's shriek broke in: "Mom! Come here! Daddy's on TV."

El Chivato was not used to writing, but he struggled on, his ballpoint carving ruts in the cheap pad. Had he been in Mexico, he would have called, even though he knew his mother would cry, and drive him crazy with her crying, but here, who knew how to make the phones work? In Mexico you called the operator and told her what to do, and in a few moments there came the connection. Or more often not, in which case one waited and tried again. Here, there were only recordings and incomprehensible instructions. He expected that he would be dead when she got the letter, which was entirely his fault, and he was writing to say that she should not blame herself, that her prayers were as efficacious as ever, but that he, Fernando, had sinned by not staying where he belonged, and by coming to this insane place, and by not returning when he should have. His lust for revenge had been too great, which his

mother had warned him about; let God punish was what she always said, but did he listen? No, and therefore his luck had run out
completely. He still could not believe that he had missed killing the
Arab for a second time, he who had always succeeded on the first
try. God was clearly angry with him.

He stopped writing and stared at the television. It was a defec-
tive set, and the people on it were orange and distorted. Or maybe
it was him. Things were looking strange to him lately. He supposed it was that he was close to the world of the dead now, and
he could see a little way into it. Picking up his pen once more, he
commended himself to his sisters, gave an accounting of the money
he had hidden and all monies due him from Don Vincente, the
names of some reliable boys who would help her out should Don
Vincente prove reluctant to pay, begged her pardon, solicited her
prayers, and bade her farewell. He kissed the letter and placed it in
an envelope.

He went to the bathroom and scrubbed the remains of the
makeup off his face. He was staying in the Hotel Estes, a small pile
of box-like rooms on the western borders of Times Square, most of
whose tenants were working whores and transvestites. El Chivato
fit right in. He regarded himself in the mirror dispassionately. The
bloom was certainly off the rose. Deep circles had appeared beneath his eyes, and his cheekbones were staring from skin that
looked like old parchment. His lips were cracked and crusted. He
thought he looked ten to fifteen years older than he had when he
arrived, and he thought that the police would be hard pressed to
connect the sketched face they had with his present appearance.

He lay down on the lumpy bed and tried to focus on his next
move. He had run out of addresses for the Arab, except one, the location of the target of their bomb. That was on Sunday. Lucky
would be there to set it off by radio, the skinned man had been
clear about that. So he would be there too.

Meanwhile, aside from that, he was at liberty. He watched a quiz
show for a while, too exhausted to rise and switch channels. Then
from within a fevered half doze he heard a familiar name. Immediately, he sharpened and watched what was happening. There were
the Obregons, being escorted out of a building. There was a picture
of another building, a hotel where, the announcer said, they were
being kept. A sign hanging in front of it read TERMINAL HOTEL.
Then a tall man appeared before a battery of microphones and

said something about material witnesses and lawyers and investigations, which El Chivato ignored. But his plans had now changed, and so he paid attention to the name of the man when it appeared in white block letters along the bottom of the screen, and he wrote it down on his pad.

"Daddy, we saw you on television," piped Lucy when Karp arrived home, tired and late.

"Yeah? How was I?"

"You looked like a television guy. I'm going to a sleep-over at Mary Ma's house."

A bustle at the doorway then, as Karp hung up his raincoat and kissed his daughter good-bye and his wife hello, and shot his usual suspicious look at Tran, who was taking his girl away, and patted the hound.

"Did I look like a TV guy?" asked Karp when they were alone, sitting in the kitchen.

"No, you looked like one of those fluff features when they get a new animal at the zoo, and the camera gets trained on the endangered species of bear from Uzbekistan, which always looks like it wants to be somewhere else. What was the point of it anyway? Moving the Mexicans from one place to another doesn't seem like such a big deal."

"Yeah, well, I guess I should've discussed it with you beforehand," said Karp uncomfortably, "because it comes under the heading of maybe endangering the family. Jack didn't want to do it, and neither did Clay, but we have to get this bastard without another half dozen or so people getting killed. Or more. So they went for it."

"It's a setup," said Marlene.

"Yeah. The hotel we moved them to is city-owned, a tax-delinquent seizure, evacuated and full of cops. I'll be down there all day tomorrow, with Clay. There's supposed to be an unmarked outside here until we nail him."

Marlene was silent, staring into space after he said this, and he asked hesitantly, "Are you angry about it? I mean, I don't think there's really much—"

"Oh, no, it's not that. I was just thinking about role reversal. It's usually me who pulls stuff like this." She grinned at him. "As a matter of fact, I was thinking about how to tell you how *I* endangered the family, and this just makes it easier."

Karp clenched his fists, screwed up his face, and bent over, as if in the throes of an appendicitis attack. "Okay, tell me."

So she told him the heartwarming tale of Posie and Walid and their romance, and concluded with, "I was going to do my usual what-he-doesn't-know-won't-hurt-him deal on you, and I felt bad about it, but seeing as you beat me to it . . ."

"Yeah, we're a pair now," said Karp. "Somebody is going to rat us to Child Protection if we keep this up. So she didn't get anything out of the Arab kid?"

"Besides poetry and anti-Jewish politics, no, although there's still a chance that he'll spill his guts at some future date. Posie has certainly bought his line; he shouldn't be too suspicious of her. On the other hand, she might just join the enemy camp. I got the feeling she knew stuff she wasn't telling."

"A matched pair," said Karp, "forty watts between the two of them." He laughed ruefully. "My God, this is one for the books: it's like Bullwinkle and Natasha. By the way, the first time she dresses the twins in little S.S. uniforms, she's out of here."

"It was worth a shot," said Marlene weakly.

"Right, from a BB gun. Anyway, it might be best if you and the kids went to a hotel where the cops could keep an eye on you for a couple of days."

"I don't think so," said Marlene immediately and in a tone that did not invite argument. "I have to work this weekend, and the kids are safer here with Tran and the dog than they would be in a hotel being watched by a couple of bored detectives. No, don't give me that look. Cops are cops, not bodyguards. Tran and Sweetie would both take a bullet to protect the kids, which I don't think you can say for the average cop. And I can take care of myself."

Looking at the drugs in his hand, El Chivato tried to remember which was which. He had bought Percodan, D-amphetamine, and penicillin from the kid out on the Deuce last night: two kinds of tabs and a cap. He decided it did not much matter and took a pair of each. He was in the tiny bathroom at his hotel. The mirror still sent back only bad news; he looked like one of the sugar skulls that Mexican children eat on the Day of the Dead. On impulse he wet his hair and soaped it with the little cake provided. Then he took out his skinning knife and shaved his head. He grinned at himself.

The drugs would keep him going long enough to do what was necessary. Clearly, if he was going to die here, which he now fully expected, then it was essential that the Obregons and Lucky die before him. He believed that otherwise he would stay on earth after he died, haunting them, and not ascend to the place in Heaven secured for him by his mother's goodness. He knew where Lucky would be on Sunday. The key to the Obregons was this *fiscal* on television, Karp. He had already looked up his address in the phone book, and he had gone by Friday night to take a look at it, a quick walk by the corner, a glance down the street. There was a car with two men in it parked across the street, and when he cruised by an hour later, they were still there. So he had come back to his hotel.

The two detectives posted outside the Karps' loft were stiff and bored by seven-thirty, and so they did not pay much attention to the various people who passed in the early morning. None of them, in any case, matched the description of the man they were looking for: a young couple, black-clad, with spiked hair; an older white guy carrying a tool case; a woman carrying a large leather portfolio; a bald guy with a cane; a dark-skinned kid on a bicycle. This last alone was worth a second look, because they were ready for a young Latino male, but the kid zoomed by and around the corner of Howard Street. They decided he was not worth chasing. Later on the Saturday morning became busy, for in this section of the city industrial firms, galleries, and restaurants take advantage of the relative lull in traffic on that day to make deliveries of large items. Trucks began unloading and the foot traffic picked up. When their relief arrived at ten past eight, they mentioned the kid on the bike and nothing else.

Miller and Logan, the two detectives on the eight-to-four shift, settled down to what they both expected would be an uneventful eight hours. They were used to this; stake-out work is much like war—endless boredom punctuated at long intervals by moments of terror and violence. They thought the real action would take place down at the Terminal Hotel, if and when this Mexican scumbag showed up.

A Plymouth sedan arrived from the direction of Grand and stopped in front of the Karp loft. The two detectives tensed, and then relaxed when they saw a middle-aged black man emerge. They knew who he was. He spoke into the communication grille in the wall and then entered the elevator when it opened. Five minutes later, the same man emerged with Karp, and they drove away in the Plymouth.

Around half past eleven, the two detectives were discussing who should go for takeout and what the takeout should be when a motorcycle pulled up with a man and a child on it. The man pulled the bike up on the sidewalk, chained it to a standpipe, and waited in front of the elevator while the child—who revealed herself as a little girl when she took her helmet off—spoke into the grille. They too disappeared into the elevator. Two minutes later, the elevator door opened again and a young woman emerged. She had a nice, if hefty, body, which Miller commented upon as she walked rapidly up Crosby toward Grand.

"The baby-sitter," said Logan.

"She can sit on me any day," said Miller. "So . . . you want a meatball hero from Lucca's?"

An alarm siren sounded somewhere down the street. The policemen paid it the same attention as everyone else did, which was none.

In the loft, Marlene poured coffee for Tran in the kitchen. The babies were set up with pots and utensils on the floor. The dog was locked in a closet as a punishment for tearing up a garbage bag. He had taken it like a man, but now he was whining and scratching the door. Lucy was in her room falling into a doze after her all-nighter with her pals. Marlene turned on the exhaust fan and lit her first cigarette of the day (limit four), and Tran lit his eighth. They smoked and drank coffee companionably for a while, talking in French to each other and to the boys, smiling when one of the boys responded with a Gallic diphthong. Zak crawled into Tran's lap to try to eat his cigarettes or spill steaming coffee on both of them. Zik started to imitate his brother by climbing onto Marlene, and thus they were both encumbered and incapable of any dramatic action when El Chivato walked into the kitchen with Lucy, his arm around her neck, holding a pistol to her head.

They all stood around on the warehouse dock, looking natty in their suits, despite a night spent sleeping on pallets and tarps. They each had a turn in the bathroom and the use of the group's razor, and all had emerged clean-shaven and smelling of the same aftershave lotion. Ibn-Salemeh had insisted on this; the police would be reluctant to bother a group of men who looked like corporate trainees on their way to learn about personnel policies. He was now distributing identification documents and plane tickets. Khalid looked at his and frowned.

"Effendi, these documents, this passport—they are in my own name."

Ibn-Salemeh smiled at him and replied, "Yes, I know. It is a detail, but there is a small possibility that the documents will survive the blast."

"What blast?" Ibn-Salemeh chuckled and looked around the little group, inviting them to join in the fun. "Why, the *bomb*, of course, the event we have been working toward these many weeks, especially you, Chouza, and we all appreciate it, so much so that we have decided to send you along with Walid, another brave martyr to our cause."

Khalid felt Big Mahmoud's large hand enclose his arm and felt Mahmoud's large pistol press into the small of his back. He looked around and met only the sort of cold, somewhat disgusted glances that people direct toward dead animals.

"Did you imagine, Chouza Khalid, that I could not *count*," said Ibn-Salemeh in his usual schoolmasterly tone, "that I was some kind of fool? That somehow I would not discover that you had murdered Bashar and Ahmed and stolen well over half the proceeds from our transaction with the Mexicans? And also disposed of the girl, without doubt to your own profit. Last night I sent Rifaat there to your house you thought I didn't know about, and he finds no girl there. How much did you get for her?"

Khalid felt sweat break out on his face. "Nothing, effendi, I swear—she escaped. It was the Mexican who helped her, this boy the brothers hired. He also killed Bashar and Ahmed. And Jemil at the garage when we tried to trap him. He took rockets and Kalashnikovs from us. He is a devil, effendi. It was not my fault, I swear."

Ibn-Salemeh was shaking his head and holding high an admonishing finger. "No, no," he said, "now you insult me, Chouza, you insult me. You ask me to believe that some little Mexican bandit escaped from two experienced *fedayin* and then stole money from them. How was this done? And then he escaped from an ambush? Your problem is that you don't watch enough television. Didn't you understand that the discovery of Bashar's corpse and the arrest of the Mexican brothers with their money and the details of the events in Brooklyn last Tuesday would be reported over and over again? And that I would be able from this to figure out what is really going on? American television, Chouza—it is an education in itself."

Khalid had not understood. And there was nothing more to say. Even he could not untangle the net of truth and lies he had spun. He had skimmed money, true, but all the rest of it was actually due to the Mexican boy, yet even if he could have made Ibn-Salemeh believe it, he deserved death for incompetence alone; he would have done the same in Ibn-Salemeh's place. His luck had gone, and the little glimmers of escape he had seen in the past weeks had been merely the glint of her crown as she danced out of sight, the pathetic hallucination of a doomed man. He hung his head. Ibn-Salemeh gestured, and Mahmoud and Hussein seized Khalid roughly and took his gun and his fat money belt, and bound him with gaffer's tape, including a strip over his mouth, and wrapped him tightly in a tarpaulin lashed with more tape. They loaded him into the van, and they all set off.

The first thing Marlene said was, "Do nothing! Do you understand?" She said this in French, to Tran, who had already snaked his hand behind his back to get his gun. He relaxed and grunted assent. Marlene looked El Chivato in the eye and said, "You're sick. You look like you have a fever."

El Chivato was not expecting this. He was expecting fearful trembling, screams, pleading, not a concerned inquiry about his health. Also, where was the man?

"Where is Karp?" he demanded.

"He's at the Terminal Hotel with several hundred police officers, waiting for you to show up," said Marlene. "Why don't you let go of Lucy? No one here is going to hurt you. Would you like a glass of water?"

This had to be a trap of some kind, thought El Chivato. He snapped his head in all directions, turned from side to side, dragging the girl with him. She made no resistance; another peculiar thing—usually they struggled. This girl seemed to be boneless, almost sagging against him, as if they were in a dance. Yes, a trap. It had been too easy to get in here. Into a building down the street with a crew of loaders, up to the roof, ignoring the alarm at the door, across several roofs to this building, down one flight of the fire escape and in through a conveniently open window.

The woman spoke again. "It's not a trap, you know. We're just a family relaxing on a weekend. My name is Marlene. This is Tran. This baby is Zik and that's Zak. The girl you're holding is Lucy. Won't you let her go? There's no need to point a gun at her."

El Chivato felt the world move under him. This was wrong; she was trying to trick him, with that soft voice. He thought about his mother and his sisters, something he never did when he was working. His hand tightened on the pistol. He would shoot someone. That would stop the soft talking.

Marlene looked deep into her daughter's eyes. She composed a message and sent it out through her eye. Don't be afraid, the message said. If you die, you will go straight to Paradise and I will be right behind you. There is nothing to fear.

Lucy was, in fact, not afraid. She had experienced a moment of sharp terror when the man had grabbed her in the hallway on her way to the bathroom, but now she felt clear and tingly. It was a kind of dream, a different kind of reality than regular life. Her mother was doing something now, something important, and she knew that she should join in this. She said, "If you have a fever, you should drink plenty of liquids. Would you like me to get you a drink of water?"

She spoke Spanish in the accent of the border, an accent that El Chivato had heard all his life. He released her neck and looked down at her, astounded. She looked up at him, calmly and without fear, like Carmen, his smallest sister. He was thirsty, parched. He nodded and she went to the sink and filled a glass and brought it back. No one moved, not even the babies. He drank, draining the glass.

Marlene saw that he was not a pathological killer. She had known a substantial number of such killers in the past, and this boy was not like them. There was no smirking evil on his face. He got no twisted human pleasure from killing. He would, if asked, make no attempt to justify or rationalize himself, any more than a leopard does when it rends a gazelle. He was an animal. A wounded one. There was nothing in his eyes but animal blankness and a dull ferocity.

Marlene said, "If you shoot that gun here, the police outside will hear it and call more police and you will die here, whatever you do to us. What you should do is leave the children with Tran, and I will go with you and be your hostage and take you to where the Obregons are. You may not get in, you may be killed, we both may be killed, but there is closer than here."

El Chivato thought about this for a moment. He turned his gaze onto the *chino*. This was a hard man, a very hard man, and he would not remain forever there like a statue. He could not stay here, and the woman was correct about shooting. It would do him no good. The drugs were boiling in his body now, and he felt better than he had in some time, although not entirely in his right mind. He said, "And the girl goes too."

Down in the street, Miller had gone to get lunch. Logan saw the elevator door open, and saw Karp's wife and daughter emerge, accompanied by a thin bald man in a long canvas coat. Where the hell did he come from? he wondered, and then realized that this was the guy. The three walked toward a yellow VW square-back parked up the street. Logan felt sick and frightened. He knew he was not going to get out of the car and stand up to this crazy bastard alone. He picked up his handset and called it in.

In a van parked at the corner of Ninth and Fifteenth, across from the Terminal Hotel, Clay Fulton took the call from Central. "Tell him to follow them and not to do anything. Repeat. Do not attempt to stop the car or interfere with the guy in any way! Keep this channel open and pass on any changes. Right. Right. K."

"What's happening?" asked Karp. He and everyone else in the cramped command vehicle looked at Fulton.

"He's got Marlene and Lucy, and he seems to be heading north," said Fulton. "Christ, Butch, I'm sorry."

Karp felt his stomach vanish. "Your guys! How did he get by them?" he cried.

"I don't know, man—the roof maybe. But he's got to be coming here. Where else would he go?"

Walid's first regular stop on his cake route was a deli on Canal, near Centre Street. A small order, and then he would pick Posie up at Broadway and Grand. Saturday was an easy day, because the Midtown places were mostly closed. Still, he had been instructed to drive the whole route, just as he did every day. It had something to do with the new radio. He got out of his seat, picked up the marked carton, and let himself out the back.

When he returned, he was surprised to find two men leaning against the truck, with a long, tarpaulin-wrapped bundle at their feet. They explained that in the bundle was a Zionist spy they had captured. Walid was to take him aboard the truck. Later, he would be informed where to deliver him for interrogation.

"By the radio?"

"Yes, the radio," one of the men said, and they both smiled. He opened the door, and they loaded the roll into the truck.

Posie was waiting at the appointed place. She scampered in and gave Walid a long kiss and a giggle. He drove the truck away from the curb, none too steadily, she hanging about his neck and licking his ear. He made his next delivery, a restaurant in SoHo. As Walid parked, she wandered into the back of the truck, stole a sweet bun from a bag, saw the rolled tarp, felt a thrill of satisfaction. The honey! she thought. He's brought something for us to lie on. Her nesting instincts aroused, she knelt by the roll and began to strip the tape away with her short, strong nails.

The bundle moved and mewed. Posie let out a yelp and jumped away.

"What are you doing?" Walid was staring in from the driver's compartment, his face pale.

"Wally, there's a guy in this tarp."

"Yes, he is a Zionist spy. Now leave him alone and come up here."

"Don't you want to see what he looks like?" asked Posie. She pulled at a strip and a corner of the tarp fell away. The man's face was red with strain as he tried to make himself understood through the tape across his mouth.

"*Allah wa akbar!*" cried Walid. "It is Khalid!"

"He's a Zionist spy?" asked Posie, confused. "I thought he was in the good guys."

Khalid was flopping like a gaffed wahoo and making strangled sounds. Walid tore the tape from his mouth. After one huge breath Khalid said in Arabic, "Untie me! We must get out of here immediately."

Walid looked doubtful and wrung his hands. He looked at Posie, who said helpfully, "Ask him why they tied him up."

Without waiting for translation, Khalid said forcefully, "Because of *you*, Walid. I could not let them sacrifice you, even for our cause.

I am too soft-hearted for this work, and so they want to kill me, and—"

"What—what do you mean, 'sacrifice'?" asked the youth.

"The bomb! That thing right there"—he gestured with his eyes and chin—"is a 250-kilogram Russian bomb. The route they told you to take carries you past a nest of Zionists they wish to destroy. When your truck reached it, they planned to push a button and bang! No more Zionists. Also, of course, no more Walid. When I objected that you were too noble a youth to lose in this way, they decided to make me share your fate. Now, if you please, dear Walid, untie me!"

Walid stared at him, pop-eyed. In truth, some months ago, had someone asked him to blow himself to pieces to advance the cause of Palestine, he might well have agreed. Now, however, he had met Posie, who seemed unimpressed when he raised the possibility of self-sacrifice. Easy work, good dope, and getting laid a lot was what Posie believed in. Walid had not been laid yet, but it had been as much as promised, and he very much did not wish to go to paradise before experiencing this aspect of life on earth.

"I can't believe—" he began, but Posie broke in, saying, "Ah, come on, Wally—you been suckered. It happens to me all the time. Untie the dude and let's get small before that goddamn thing goes off."

Walid took out a knife and cut Khalid free. The first thing he did, still staggering from the strains of his confinement, was to look out the dim rear windows of the bread truck. As he expected, he spotted the gray van double-parked a half block down Broome Street.

"They are here," said Khalid. "Quickly! Go out the front on the street side!"

"What! I can't leave my truck," cried Walid, vibrating with distress.

Khalid grabbed the front of Walid's shirt and hissed, "Idiot! In two minutes someone back there will start wondering why you don't drive on. Do you think they will hesitate to cut your throat? And hers?"

This, it turned out, was the deciding consideration. The three left by the curb-side door and walked quickly around the corner onto Wooster Street. It was a fine, warm spring day, and Wooster was full of tourists and SoHo residents. They passed through the crowd and slipped into a coffee shop, choosing a table in the back, near the service door. After twenty minutes of nervous waiting, it was clear that there was going to be no pursuit. Khalid relaxed slightly and considered his options.

NINETEEN

As soon as Marlene and Lucy left with the Mexican, Tran snatched up the babies and their travel bag (diapers, toys, and nap bottles) and ran down one flight of stairs. The loft beneath the Karps' was occupied by a sculptor and his companion, Larry Boudreau, who was a pediatric nurse at St. Vincent's. Boudreau had worked the night shift on Friday, and was roused from bed by the importunate pounding on his door. He opened it bleary-eyed, but immediately snapped to when he saw the expression on Tran's face. It was not the first time he had been knocked out of bed by some medico-criminal crisis of the family upstairs.

"What's wrong?"

"Marlene, Lucy kidnapped," said Tran, reduced to his Charlie Chan–oid English. "Take babies. I must go follow."

He thrust the two squirming lumps into Boudreau's arms, dropped the travel bag, and raced down the steps.

Once on the street, he unchained his motorcycle, cranked it up, and headed north. He caught sight of the yellow car and its unmarked pursuer at Broadway and West Houston. The cop had not done anything stupid yet, and Tran expected that he was being controlled by whoever was in charge of the trap. They would go to the Terminal Hotel, then, at which time Tran would be able to make some move. He hoped that he would not die in this incident, for he wished very much to see Lucy grow up, but he was certainly prepared to do so in her interest.

Marlene drove the yellow car, glancing to the side every few moments to make eye contact with Lucy, who sat in her new still mode on the seat beside her. The Mexican was slumped in the back, his eyes half closed, his pistol held loosely on his lap. Marlene was under no illusions as to his state of alertness, and she had no dramatic plan to influence events. It was like one of Lucy's elementary school jokes: where do you take an eight-hundred-pound gorilla in a VW? Anywhere he wants to go.

El Chivato was staring at the girl, who occasionally looked back at him with curiosity rather than fear. He was not in pain, only aware that his body was broken in some irreparable way, and his thoughts raced over the surface of his life like a dragonfly over a pond, never penetrating the surface of the events, incapable of deriving some deeper meaning from the actions of his short existence. He hoped that it would not be necessary to kill this child. He asked her, "Where did you learn to speak Spanish like you do?"

"A friend of my mom's taught me. She's a Mexican from Texas."

"Ah, Texas!" It was uncanny how much she sounded like Carmen. "I am from Arizona, from Nogales. But I live in Hermosillo. My family is still in Nogales. Nogales, Mexico." Some family chat: he named himself and his siblings and their ages. Lucy asked polite questions. Then she asked, "Why are you killing people?"

El Chivato shrugged and answered. "They are my enemies or they are the enemies of my friends. So I kill them."

"Jesus said we should love our enemies," said Lucy primly.

"Jesus Christ?" asked El Chivato. Lucy nodded.

"That is ridiculous! Why would he say something so stupid? Jesus Christ was not stupid."

"It's in the Bible," offered Lucy.

"Then the Bible is wrong,' said El Chivato definitely, his jaw getting stiff. Lucy wisely turned the conversation to food preferences.

I can't believe this, thought Marlene, and then, but why not? How is it different from the rest of my life? My little girl is chatting in border Spanish with a heavily armed Mexican *chutero* whom I am chauffeuring to a police trap set up by my husband. We'll all be killed and they'll make a TV special about it. I should have, on second thought, gone to the hotel like Butch said, but maybe he could've gotten in there too, and maybe some cops would've gotten hurt. I hope that cop following me doesn't try anything. They're probably calling Osborne now, wondering why I haven't shown up at Hadassah. Maybe the *chutero* will let me stop by, check in, make sure nobody's blown anything up, and as she thought that, in the slightly manic way that thoughts drift across the surface of our minds when our deepest attention is focused on some vital transaction, the whole thing popped into her mind, like a strobe-lit photo.

"Jesus Christ, what an idiot!" she cried out, and the car swerved. "They're going to blow it up!"

The Arabs were going to blow up the Hadassah building. Not the U.N., not the bridges or tunnels. Walid's truck. They knew he had a truck, had used it, in fact. Tran's map. Why hadn't she seen it? The neat looping blue line Tran had drawn, with all the stops marked, and that inexplicable loop north and east down Fifty-eighth Street, when his last delivery was on Forty-sixth and Sixth. They wanted him to show his truck on the route so that if anyone was watching, they would become used to a white bakery van going down that particular street, twice a day. The street was right by the back of the Plaza Hotel; there were dozens of delivery vans going by on regular schedules. And, of course, they were going to do it today. Today or tomorrow, on both of which days the building would be full of over two hundred Zionist youth leaders from all over the country. And the wife of the president of Israel.

"Who, Mom? Who's going to blow what up?"

"The Arabs. And Fatyma's brother, Walid. And—oh, God! Posie's with him. They're going to blow up the Jewish organization I was working for. Probably today!"

To her immense surprise, El Chivato said, "Not today, Sunday."

"You *knew* this? How did you find out?" Marlene asked, searching his face in her rearview.

He shrugged. "I found out. It was not hard. Tomorrow I will go there and kill him too."

"Oh, for God's sake, you! Let me tell you something, whatever your name is—"

"His name's Paco, Mom."

"Paco—you're not going *anywhere* tomorrow if you go by that hotel today. You will be dead or in jail. Why can't you understand this? There must be a hundred cops down there, and they're all waiting for you to show up."

"They will not shoot me while you are with me."

"Yes, they will! They have guys that can take the nose off a fly at two hundred yards. They'll blow you up as soon as you stick your head out of the car. And what makes you think your Arabs are going to do it on Sunday? Why not today?"

"I was told. I believe him."

"Right, but maybe that was before you started using the police force for target practice. This is a whole different situation now; this is not normal sleepy New York. Every cop in the city who isn't after you is after those guys, and they're close, real close. They've stuffed up all the holes, they cut off the escape route they were going to use. They've got to get out of town or get caught, and the target they're aiming at is the same today as it would be tomorrow. So why should they wait? I'm telling you, man—they're going to be there today, this afternoon."

The car approached Fourteenth Street, and El Chivato said, "The next left."

Marlene slowed for the light, and when it went green, she shot through the intersection and headed north on Sixth. El Chivato straightened up and raised his pistol menacingly. "Stupid woman! Didn't you hear me? I said, turn left!"

Marlene pulled the car over to the curb, stopped, and turned to face the Mexican.

"Listen to me, Paco. You want to kill me and my little girl? Go ahead. It's just two more bodies, and why should you care? But I tell you as sure as the sun is in the sky, you can't get to the Obregon brothers. You *can* get to Chouza Khalid, a man who tried to kill you, the man whose crimes brought you away from your home to this city. And you can prevent hundreds of people from getting killed at the same time, not that you care about that, but I do. So— I'm going to drive to Fifty-eighth Street. You want to shoot, shoot!"

She turned to the wheel again. El Chivato felt rage building in him. He aimed his pistol at her head. Then the little girl said, in that clear and familiar voice, *"Más vale un toma que cien te daré."*

The words acted upon him like an electric current. It was a well-worn family expression, one of his mother's favorites. Better to grasp one than try for a hundred. This was true. Somehow his mother was speaking to him through this child. He had heard of such things, of course, but only with respect to the recently dead. His mother was not dead, but naturally, she being a saint, the rules did not necessarily apply to her. He sat back in the seat and let the hand holding the pistol fall to his lap. "All right. Go!" he said.

★ ★ ★

"Where are they now?" Karp asked. He felt unnaturally calm, and in some corner of his mind he recognized that this was due to a kind of habituation. The loved ones of cops and firemen and test pilots got to this point, he knew, and they either broke away, went batty, or resigned themselves to the possibility of loss, accepted this awful set of feelings as a concomitant of their love. Karp had over the years of being with Marlene clearly reached this point. But his throat still felt like it contained a large, angular, dry object, an empty box of Fig Newtons perhaps.

Fulton said, "What?" into his mike, then, "No, keep following, but keep your distance. K." To Karp he said, "They're not coming here, it looks like. She just drove past Sixteenth on Sixth. What the hell are they doing?"

Karp didn't know. He was an observer here, with nothing to contribute. He thought, Marlene is up to something. He took some deep breaths and watched his friend talk back and forth with the central police dispatcher as he vectored mobile units from all over Manhattan toward the vehicle that contained Marlene and Lucy and the unknown assassin.

"Something is wrong," said Ibn-Salemeh. "He should have moved by now. Hussein, go see what is going on."

Hussein left the driver's seat of the gray van and trotted up the street to the bread truck. He came back on a run. Breathless, eyes bulging, he said, "They're gone! The boy and Khalid are not there."

Ibn-Salemeh pursed his lips, maintaining his usual calm face while he considered what to do next. Clearly, it had been an error to place Khalid alive in the truck. The boy was undisciplined and, it seemed, could not resist a glance at a Zionist spy, and the results were now plain. Ibn-Salemeh knew it was a personal fault, but he could not resist the satisfaction of imagining Khalid lying helpless, waiting for the bomb to go off. In mitigation, it was acts of that sort that enhanced his legend, and the legend was what gave him power.

He felt their eyes on him as he came out of his contemplation. Fixing Hussein with his gaze, he ordered, "Hussein will drive the truck. I will drive this van. Now, go!"

Hussein did not move. Ibn-Salemeh heard a murmur behind him. He felt a great wave of anger, which he suppressed. The project was in danger. Someone was going to notice the bread truck parked for so long, and the streets were unusually thick with police.

"Then I will drive the truck," he said. "I will park it in front of the target and walk back to Sixth Avenue, where you will be parked, Hussein, at the southeast corner. We will set off the bomb and drive north."

He opened the door of the van and prepared to get out. A hand fell on his shoulder. Big Mahmoud said, "Effendi, the detonator?"

"The detonator?"

"Yes. You cannot take the detonator into the truck with you. It is too dangerous. We will keep it here."

"It is safe. The arming switch is set to off."

There were grumbling sounds from the dim rear of the van. Mahmoud said, "Still. These are rules we all agreed to follow." The huge hand was outstretched, like a salver. Gritting teeth behind his bland smile, Ibn-Salemeh handed over the squat plastic cylinder and walked up to the bread truck. He thought, When we are back in Tripoli, I will see every one of them dead.

"Do you mind if we sing?" asked Marlene. She had just spotted Tran in her side mirror as they passed Thirty-fourth Street. The traffic was unusually light for a sunny Saturday. The unmarked police car was keeping a car length behind. Tran had shot out between lanes and hung there for a good while so that Marlene would be sure to see him. The window was open, and she had her hand resting on the sill. She made an okay sign with her hand. Tran dropped back into his lane.

El Chivato did not mind, although it was a new wrinkle in his experience. His clients more often prayed than sang. It was another aspect of what was already an unreal situation. He hoped his mother would speak to him again through the girl.

Marlene began to sing a nursery song Lucy had known since forever. "*Sur le pont d'Avignon, on y danse, on y danse . . .*" She sang two choruses, Lucy joining in, and then she began a verse Lucy did not know because her mother was making it up as she went along:

"Ma fille, écoute bien, il te faut s'échapper
Nous nous arrêterons au feu rouge
Du feu vert, quand je diterai, 'Va!'

Ouverte la porte et sorte
Reste immobile sur le pavé
Tran nous suit en moto, dite lui tout, des Arabs, des Juifs, de la bombe
Si tu comprendes, faites une signe de tête."

Marlene sang this through twice. Lucy hummed along in harmony with it, and at the end nodded her head sharply several times, as if transported by the simple tune. The light ahead at Thirty-seventh Street turned yellow; Marlene shifted lanes so that she was at the head of traffic when the light went red. They waited. For the busiest shopping day of the week there seemed oddly few people crossing the street in front of them, and the city sounds seemed unusually rich in sirens.

The green light lit. Marlene, in a conversational voice, said "*Va!*"

Lucy flung open the door and rolled out of the seat. Marlene floored the pedal and popped the clutch in one coordinated motion. The little engine whined, and the VW leaped forward, not like a Corvette, of course, but hard enough to press the surprised Mexican back into his seat and fling the door closed with a bang. An instant later he had recovered, and Marlene felt his hand knotted painfully in her hair and the muzzle of his pistol grinding into the tender spot below her ear.

"Stop the car! Stop the car *now!*" he demanded. His mother.

"No," answered Marlene. "Go ahead and shoot. You'll last five seconds more than me, and your enemies will be laughing at you. The idiot shot a woman and the cops killed him. Look out the goddamn window!"

El Chivato looked. The street was full of blue and white police cars. One of them was level with the VW, and in its passenger seat was a grim-faced, flak-vested, helmeted cop pointing a twelve-gauge Mossberg shotgun out the window straight at him. He cursed and let go of Marlene. Then he kicked the front seat forward and slid himself into it. Marlene watched Tran and Lucy on the Jawa shoot ahead down the empty avenue. She kept driving north on Sixth Avenue, accompanied by twenty-two police cars.

"Lucy's out of the car," shouted Fulton. "A guy on a motorcycle just picked her up. Cars in pursuit."

"That would be Tran," said Karp. "He's a good guy. Call them off."

Fulton looked at him sharply. "What's going on?"

"I have no idea," said Karp, "but Marlene's got something going. Make sure nobody queers her act."

He had removed his tie and jacket, and he drove carefully, easing the clumsy truck through the traffic on Sixth. At Fourteenth, he saw a large number of flashing red lights ahead, so he turned left and proceeded north on Eighth. He turned right on Fifty-seventh, north on Sixth, and right again on Fifty-eighth. He noted in the long side mirror that the gray van was right behind him.

There were two black limousines parked in front of number 50, which told him that the distinguished guests had arrived and were in the building. He double-parked at the service drive of the hotel opposite, went into the back of the truck, grabbed a cardboard tray stacked with white pasteboard boxes, and went out through the double doors in the back.

"Hey, buddy!" shouted a large man in a gray uniform. "You gonna be long?"

"Three minutes only," replied Ibn-Salemeh and trotted quickly down the street, pausing occasionally so that it seemed like he was looking for an address.

Back in the gray van, Hussein studied the street through his side mirror. Some kind of parade? The street was full of police vehicles flashing their lights.

"I don't like this," he said.

El Chivato saw the van as soon as they passed Fifty-seventh Street. The last time he had seen it was just before they captured him, coming toward him, but he recognized it from the rear too, a gray Chevrolet with blacked-out windows and Jersey plates. He said to Marlene, "Pull over by that gray van. Now stop."

Marlene stopped the car. All the police cars stopped too. Hussein looked out his window and saw the head of death grinning at him. Death reached out a hand and tossed a ball into his lap.

El Chivato said, "Drive!" Marlene hit the gas, the VW lurched forward, there was an enormous thunderclap of sound behind them, the rear window of the VW shattered and fell inward in crystal rags, and Marlene saw through the rearview that the gray van was gone, replaced by a smoky bonfire.

"What was that?" asked Lucy in alarm.

"An explosion of some kind," said Tran, "but certainly not the one we are worried about. The truck is still there and intact."

He had scooped Lucy up off the pavement and placed her behind him on the motorcycle. He had intended to follow Marlene, but when Lucy, shouting, had told him where Marlene was going and about the Arab bomb, he had turned on the speed and preceded her to the building on Fifty-eighth Street. He had seen the bread truck park and the man get out. Now he was following the man. He saw him stop when the explosion went off around the corner.

Ibn-Salemeh paused at the corner of Sixth and Fifty-eighth and stared at the wreckage of the gray van and of his careful plans. He sighed and placed his cake boxes down by a wastebasket and headed north on Sixth. He had no pressing appointments, sufficient money, an excellent set of false papers, and a ravaging thirst. He entered a luncheonette and ordered an iced tea.

"Is that truck going to explode?" asked Lucy as they walked past it.

"Perhaps. For that reason we must hurry to get away."

"But we have to tell someone!" said Lucy, and she broke away from Tran's hand and went up to a man in a gray uniform standing near the door of a building opposite the truck.

"There's a bomb in that truck," she said, pointing.

The guard looked down at her without interest. "Yeah?' How do you know?"

"My mom told me. You should check it out and call the cops." She skipped away to where Tran was waiting impatiently.

"He just blew up a van," said Fulton. "On Sixth at Fifty-eighth. Tossed a grenade into the window. The guy's gone crazy. I'm going to stop him."

"I don't think that's a good idea," said Karp, "not until you find out who was in that van. Remember, this bastard's fighting a war with our other pals. Where's Marlene now?"

Fulton listened to the chatter on the radio for a moment. "They just hung a left on Central Park South." A long pause. "They're heading south on Ninth. They're coming here."

"That's what I thought she'd do eventually," said Karp.

"She? I hate to tell you, Butch, Marlene's not in charge in there."

"Oh, no?" said Karp.

Ibn-Salemeh, lost as he was in rueful thought, did not pay any attention to the oriental man and the little girl when they entered the luncheonette until he heard himself addressed in French.

"Excuse me, sir, but I believe we are acquainted."

The Arab looked up, scowling, and answered in Arabic, "I have no idea what you're talking about." To his immense surprise, the little American girl answered in Palestinian-accented Arabic, "We can speak in Arabic, if you prefer. I would be happy to translate."

Tran grinned as the Arab's jaw dropped, and he slid into the seat opposite. Lucy sat next to him. He continued, in French, "In fact, sir, I believe you do speak French, for I well recall many long conversations we had about our plans to overthrow the imperialist yoke. Moscow, 1965. You were using the name Feisal at the time. Feisal Anani, if I recall. I was using Pho Nguyen Binh. Do you remember now?"

Ibn-Salemeh felt his mind skidding like a Buick on glare ice. It could not be that a senior Viet Cong cadre in the company of an American child who spoke Palestinian Arabic was sitting with him in a restaurant in New York, chatting about a meeting in Moscow fifteen years ago. An insane coincidence? It had to be.

Ibn-Salemeh smiled and shrugged, and answered, again in Arabic, "Please, I cannot understand what you are saying."

Lucy translated this into French. Her eyes were shining, and she had to concentrate hard to maintain the correct posture and deportment.

Tran said, "You still don't remember me? Ah, how quickly we forget our idealistic youth! Once I too thought it was amusing to set bombs and murder innocent people. Now I prefer to kill only the guilty." Tran saw the man tense at the word "bomb" and thought, in another two seconds he will push the table over on me and run, and so he brought his Tokarev pistol out and pointed it at Ibn-Salemeh.

"Should I translate that, Uncle Tran?" asked Lucy.

"No, it will not be necessary. We have come to an understanding. There must be a phone here. Please go and call the police."

She went off to call, and Ibn-Salemeh said, in French, "Why are you doing this? After what they did to you? The bombs? The tortures? What kind of man are you?"

"I often wonder," answered Tran pleasantly. "Once I had attachments to my homeland, and in my dreams I still do. But my attachments in this life were all severed. The Americans killed my wife and child, and the rest of the people I cared about were destroyed after the war, by people who were not too unlike you, sir. Now I have formed attachments here in this remarkable city, that little girl among them, and I must object to bombs that might hurt them."

"Bourgeois sentimentality!" snarled Ibn-Salemeh.

"*Précisément!*" said Tran, beaming.

Marlene said, "You don't have to do this, you know. I could take you to a hospital."

El Chivato looked at her through the red tunnel that represented the dregs of his vision. "They would never let me out of jail."

"But you'd be *alive*. That's something. You could see your mother again, and your sisters."

He curled his lip, speaking slowly around quick, shallow breaths. "You are a fool if you think I would allow my family to see me in prison." He stared out through the windshield at the front of the Terminal Hotel. It was a five-story dirty brown brick building with a heavy vertical sign and double glass doors leading to a small lobby. There were no cars parked on the street in front of it and no sign of a police presence within. Outside, of course, a solid line of police cars blocked off both Ninth Avenue and Fifteenth Street in both directions.

He's going to shoot me now, Marlene thought. It's the end of the line for him, why shouldn't he take me along? She tried to compose her thoughts. What a terrific life I've had, she thought, and now no worries about cancer or Alzheimer's. She prayed briefly, waited. She opened her eye and stared into the red-rimmed blankness of El Chivato's gaze. This poor bastard, she thought. What a fucking life!

"Please," she said, "live."

He reached into his coat and brought out a crumpled envelope. "Send this to her. I didn't have no stamp." She took it. He said, "Get out of the car!" and she did.

El Chivato slid over to the driver's seat, gunned the engine, and drove directly toward the glass doors of the Terminal Hotel. He crashed through them into the lobby. There was an instant's hush. Marlene discovered her knees no longer worked. She sat down on the curb.

Then the automatic fire started, and it went on for a very long time, a continuous roaring clatter. Marlene bent over and put her hands over her ears. Later, she learned that he had managed to shoot five cops, but since they were all armored like Ivanhoe, no serious damage had been done, and also that the medical examiner had found 126 bullet holes in his body, a NYPD record.

Cops surrounded her. One of them was Raney, in a flak vest.

"We solved the case, Raney," she said inanely.

"Yeah, kid, we did," he said gently and led her off.

It took several hours to reunite the family Karp. The police insisted on taking Marlene to a hospital, which was standard procedure for hostages. At the luncheonette, a heavily armed assault team arrested Ibn-Salemeh without incident, but they also arrested Tran for possession of an unregistered weapon, as a result of which Lucy threw a fit so violent that she was taken to juvenile detention. Karp and Fulton raced around town with screaming sirens, gathering up first Marlene, then Lucy (Marlene had to be physically restrained from striking a social worker), and finally Tran. Karp dropped the charges against him so hard it made the walls shake.

At a little past six, then, the Karps, Tran, and Fulton arrived at Crosby Street in Fulton's car. As none of them had eaten since the morning, Marlene invited them all up for a feed. Posie greeted Marlene at the door.

"Marlene! God, what a day! You'll never guess what happened."

"Try me, Posie," said Marlene wearily. She had almost completely forgotten the girl during the day's interesting events.

"There was a bomb in Walid's truck."

"Really!"

"Yeah, no lie. We ran like crazy. Walid's afraid to go home, his old man's gonna kill him. Marlene, it was like the movies. We're just driving along, and these Arab guys put this, like, rolled-up tarp in the truck, and I go over and there's a *guy* in it. And we like open it up and it's this dude Chouza Khalid that Walid knows from before, and he tells us about the bomb, and we let him loose and then we booked out. God, I was scared!"

Fulton and Karp and Marlene exchanged looks. Marlene asked, "So what happened then, Posie?"

"Oh, we went into this place to sit down and, like, figure out what to do. Khalid was really on a downer because, like, these guys had ripped off all his bread and his ID and all. So I said, hey, the lady I work for like can help you out, because these women? They're running from guys beat them up and stuff, and she like gets them away and maybe she'd help you too. And he goes, I don't have any money, and I go, shit, she does it for free. And he goes, what about the cops, and I told him, hey, she doesn't mess with the cops and they don't mess with her. So they came back here and I, like, warmed up that Chinese stuff from the other night for us. I hope that's okay."

Marlene took a deep breath. "That's fine, Posie. Are you saying that Chouza Khalid and Walid Daoud are here? Right now?"

"Yeah," said Posie, her smile sagging slightly. "You said I could entertain my friends in my room sometimes, and the boys are fine. I figured they would be at Larry's, and I checked in there and . . ."

"It's fine, Posie. I tell you what: I think we'd all like to meet your friends. Clay? Why don't you lead the way?"

On Easter Sunday, Marlene took her kids out to Ozone Park to spend the holiday with her family. There was an egg hunt in the tiny backyard for the twenty-odd cousins in Lucy's generation, and it was a tradition important enough to Marlene that she was willing to stand the grilling from her folks about her recent exploits, and to bear the associated load of guilt. ("What're you, *crazy*! I almost had a heart attack! Your father couldn't eat!") Karp had to work. Chouza Khalid was spilling his guts out at the jail, and Karp had first dibs, and every agency from the Brooklyn D.A. to the CIA was lining up, hat in hand, for a taste. Rabbi Lowenstein held his march without either incident or publicity, the media being fully occupied with the capture and shoot-out stories. The Muslim march never developed.

On Monday, Marlene cold-cocked a TV reporter who was trying to interview her child. The reporter insisted to the policeman on duty in front of the Karps' loft that he arrest her for assault. He declined to do this, having seen not a thing, but he did confiscate the cameraman's tape as evidence, which tape later proved to be completely blank. The press got the hint, and after a day or so the Karps were left alone. On Tuesday, Rabbi Lowenstein was arrested along with several young Israelis, and accused of conspiring to firebomb the Daoud shop and two other Arab businesses. He gave an impassioned speech at his arraignment, comparing his arrest to Kristallnacht, but this was not much covered by the press.

On Tuesday, the United Jewish Philanthropies announced that their $25,000 reward would be given to Tran Vinh and Lucy Karp for the capture of the terrorist chief.

Marlene thought this hilarious. "What are you going to do with all that money, Tran?" she asked.

"I believe I will invest it in stocks," he replied after due consideration. "I will first determine which companies are best at grinding the faces of the poor and exploiting the oppressed masses of the Third World. These, I have heard, are the ones to choose."

"Sounds like a plan," said Marlene.

On Friday, Karp came home from a hard day (he was doing his regular job and helping out with the preparation of the case against Ibn-Salemeh, who still insisted he was a Lebanese businessman named Ali Ibrahim Mansoufi and knew nothing of any bombs, and keeping an eye on Homicide while Roland Hrcany was laid up), sat down to dinner, and looked down in amazement at the steaming bowl his wife placed before him.

"What is this?" he inquired.

"What does it look like?"

"It looks, smells, and"—using his spoon—"tastes like matzo-ball soup."

"It *is* matzo-ball soup. I went down to Rivington Street today and got an elderly kosher chicken for the purpose, and your daughter sculpted the balls with her own semi-Jewish hands. How is it?"

"It's incredibly good. Thank you, Lucy." He paused. "Is there some special reason for this that I'm missing?"

"Well, as it's the first day of Passover, I thought it'd be nice to recognize the other half of your children's heritage."

"It *is* nice," said Karp, abashed. "Are we going to have seders from now on?"

"Not unless you want to," said Marlene. "I just primed the pump."

Lucy trilled some Mandarin and translated: "Respect for ancestors is the basis of character."

"I'll think about it," said Karp, which seemed to satisfy the moment, because Marlene smiled and handed him a postcard. "This came today."

Karp took it. It was a picture of the famous Hollywood sign, white letters on a hillside. On the back it said: "Dir Luci: I am fine. Im having apratment in Hollywood hills and boyfriend in movie busnis. He thinks im eiteen ha ha. His gets me scrin test soon and I will be star soon too. On day I com see you. Bye bye. Yor freind, Fatyma."

"Well, well," said Karp. "I guess we should contact the authorities out there. Technically, she's a fleeing felon. Old Khalid claims she lifted around two hundred K off him, quite aside from the manslaughter charge we had pending."

"You wouldn't!" said Marlene.

"I'll think about that too. What's this Arabic stuff down at the bottom?"

Lucy got her dictionary and consulted it. She said, "It means, 'Everything has transpired according to the will of God.' "

· A NOTE ON THE TYPE ·

The typeface used in this book is a version of Plantin, designed in 1913 by Frank Hinman Pierpoint (1860–1937). Although he was an American, Pierpoint spent most of his life
working in England for the Monotype company, which he
helped found. The font was named after Christophe Plantin
(1514?–1589), a French bookbinder who turned to printing
and by midcentury had established himself in Antwerp as the
founder of a publishing dynasty—like Pierpoint, one who "made
good" away from home. Plantin was not, however, a designer
of type, nor was the modern font strictly speaking a revival
(Pierpoint was unenthusiastic about Stanley Morison's re-
vivals at Monotype in the 1920s). Plantin was based on what is
now known to be Robert Granjon's Gros Cicero font, created
for but never used by Plantin, which Pierpoint found in the
Plantin-Moretus Museum. Later, its full-bodied but compact
quality attracted Morison to Plantin as the model for Times
Roman.